**From the moment James T. Kirk steps** aboard the *Enterprise*—the youngest captain in Starfleet's history—things begin to go wrong. His Vulcan science officer, Mr. Spock, considers Kirk impetuous; the ship's chief engineer thinks him an inexperienced young hotshot; his chief medical officer hasn't bothered to show up yet; and the new helmsman would rather be someplace else entirely. To top it all off, Starfleet Command has assigned the *Enterprise* a disappointingly tame task: to ferry a troupe of vaudeville performers on a morale-raising mission to Federation starbases—in short, a USO tour.

Then the largest spacecraft anyone has ever seen suddenly appears in the ship's flight path . . . and on their first mission together, Kirk and the entire *Enterprise* crew are facing what could truly be mankind's *final* frontier. . . .

# Look for STAR TREK Fiction from Pocket Books

# STAR TREK®

# ENTERPRISE
## THE FIRST ADVENTURE

## VONDA N. McINTYRE

POCKET BOOKS

New York    London    Toronto    Sydney    Tokyo

An *Original* Publication of POCKET BOOKS

POCKET BOOKS, a division of Simon & Schuster Inc.
1230 Avenue of the Americas, New York, NY 10020

STAR TREK is a Registered Trademark of
Paramount Pictures Corporation.

ISBN: 0-671-65912-X

First Pocket Books printing September 1986

18  17  16  15  14  13  12  11  10  9

To Linda M., Katya, Rosie, Dottie, Mary, Liz, and Beth,
to Ann, Anne, and Vera,
to Susan & Danny, because of all those Thursdays;
and to Pat and Staarla.

# ENTERPRISE

# Prologue

BLOOD FLOWS IN strange patterns in zero gravity—

Jim Kirk cried out and flung himself forward, reaching—

"Gary, no—"

As Gary Mitchell collapsed, Jim struggled forward, fighting to see, fighting to stay conscious despite shock, fighting to move through the pain of his crushed knee and his broken ribs, fighting to breathe against the blood in his lungs. If he lost the fight, his closest friend would die.

A scarlet net drifted across the image before him, and he thought that he was blind.

Jim bolted awake, gasping. He had been dreaming. Dreaming again. "Carol . . . ?" He wanted to hold her, to reassure himself that he was right beside her, not back in the disaster of Ghioghe.

Then he remembered, almost as if he were waking from a second dream, that he no longer lived in Carol Marcus's house, he no longer slept in her bed. He was alone.

As his room's computer sensed that he was awake, it lightened the darkness around him. He wiped cold sweat from his face and touched the scar on his forehead. At Ghioghe, before the gravity went out, blood from the gash flowed down into his eyes and obscured his vision.

He wished he could go back to sleep; he wished he could sleep without dreaming. But he knew he could not. Besides, in fighting the recurrent nightmare Jim had left the bed-clothes twisted and sweat-damp and clammy. He threw them aside and rose.

Jim Kirk, the newest captain in Starfleet, the youngest

officer ever to reach the rank of captain, the hero of Axanar and, more recently, of Ghioghe, the next commander of the constellation-class starship *Enterprise,* had lived for the past two weeks in a rented traveler's cubicle, one of a hundred identical cubicles facing another block of a hundred identical cubicles, in a building similar to at least a hundred other sleeper buildings clustered near the spaceport.

In his current odd emotional state of excitement over his coming command, worry over Gary Mitchell, and pain and confusion over the way his affair with Carol Marcus ended, Jim had lived here without noticing the shabby surroundings. Not that his own furniture, which he had left in storage during this visit to earth, had much over the plastic built-ins of the sleeper. Jim had never got around to replacing much of the beat-up junk left over from student digs. But he did have a couple of pieces of heavy old oak from the farmhouse in Iowa, and a single Persian rug he had bought on a whim even before he realized how much he had liked it, and before he realized how much the liking would cost if he let it develop.

He could barely stand in the sleeper; he could just lie down in the bunk, if he restrained himself from stretching. He looked around. He would have claimed intimate familiarity with the place, but the claim would be a fraud. Had he been asked to describe it, he would have failed in every particular. His indifference to it turned suddenly to revulsion.

He dragged his small suitcase from the tiny storage shelf, pulled it open, and flung into it his few possessions: a couple of books, including one that had belonged to his father; a thin sheaf of family photos; a letter from Carol. He could not decide if throwing the letter away would start healing his wounds, or deepen them.

"Computer."

"Ready."

"Close out my account here."

"Done."

Jim slammed shut the suitcase and fled the sleeper without a backward glance.

Outside, in the darkness preceding dawn, Jim felt as if his nightmare still lurked at the edge of his waking perceptions. He always had the same dream, never about the breakdown of pattern, the miscommunication that led to the battle, not about the battle itself, not even about the actions he had taken that saved most of his crew but left his ship, the *Lydia Sutherland,* a battered, broken hulk drifting dead in space. Instead, the dream always repeated those interminable few minutes in the rescue pod, when Gary Mitchell almost died.

Jim climbed the stairs to the entrance of the Starfleet Teaching Hospital, being careful of his right knee. So far, this morning, it had given him no trouble. He headed for the regeneration ward. No one stopped him. He had asked, ordered, pulled rank and pulled strings to get official permission to be here outside of visiting hours. Finally he simply ignored the rules, and now everyone was used to seeing him.

As he had every day since getting out of regen himself, Jim entered Gary's hospital room. Gary Mitchell lay in a regeneration tank, drugged and sleeping and immersed up to his neck in translucent green regen gel.

Gary hated being sick. It hurt to see him like this. All the specialists kept congratulating themselves on his progress. But to Jim he looked wasted and frail, as if the gel were draining his youth instead of restoring his body. Gary's thirtieth birthday had passed right after he entered regen. Jim was a year and a half younger, just turned twenty-nine, impatient with the aftereffects of his own injuries, anxious for his friend to get well.

He sat down beside Gary and spoke to him as if he could hear him.

"They keep telling me you'll wake up soon," Jim said. "I hope it's true. You've been here too long, and it isn't fair. You would have come out of Ghioghe without a scratch if you hadn't come back for me." Jim stretched his right leg, testing his knee. He had begun to trust the new joint; physical therapy had built up its strength so it no longer collapsed at awkward moments. He still had exercises he was supposed to do every day.

"They also claim you can't hear me because of the drugs. But they're wrong. I don't much care if they think I'm nuts to talk to you." Jim remembered his last few days in regen, a twilight of half-sleep, confusion, and dreams. "I saw it all going wrong at Ghioghe. I still can't believe Sieren could make a mistake like that. I saw—this is going to sound weird, Gary, I know it, but I saw the pattern of what was happening. I *knew* that if everyone would calm down for thirty seconds, if all the commanders held their fire for another minute, the crisis would pass. But it didn't happen that way. Lord, I admired Sieren." Jim could not believe Sieren had made the mistake, could not believe Sieren and so many others had died. He took a deep breath. "I saw the pattern, I knew how to fix it, but I couldn't do anything, and it all went wrong. Is that how it was for Sieren? Is that how it would have been for me, if I'd been in command at Ghioghe? Axanar could have turned out just the same, but it didn't. We came out of that one covered with glory and holding a peace treaty. Was that just good luck?"

He thought Gary's eyelids flickered. But it had been a reflex, or Jim's own imagination.

"It's all right," he said. "Sleep, get well. I have to go up to the *Enterprise* soon, but if the ship has to do without a first officer for a few months, it will survive. I've nominated you to the position, my friend, as soon as you're ready for it."

"Good morning, captain."

Gary's heavy dark hair had slipped down across his forehead. Jim brushed it back.

"Captain?"

Jim looked up. Christine Chapel, a member of the staff of the intensive-care unit, stood near. Jim had heard her, but he had not realized she was talking to him. He was not yet used to his new rank. His promotion had come while he was still in regen. He went to sleep a commander whose space cruiser had been blasted around him; he woke up a captain with a new medal and a constellation-class starship soon to be under his command. "Sorry, Ms. Chapel. Good morning."

"The biotelemetry on Commander Mitchell is very encouraging. I thought you'd like to know." A striking young woman, she wore her blond hair feathered around her face.

"Then why doesn't he wake up?" Jim said.

"He will," Chapel said. "He will when he's ready."

She handed him a printout flimsy.

After spending so much time here, he had learned to make sense of it. He scanned the printout. It did look good. The troubling tangle of neurons in Gary's regenerating spinal cord had sorted itself out, and the vertebrae had solidified from their earlier ghostly shadow, when they were only cartilage. As far as Jim could tell, Gary's lacerated internal organs had completely healed. Jim handed the printout back.

"I see he has the heart of an eighteen-year-old," he said.

She smiled. The hoary old regen joke had a dozen punch lines. The standby was "Yes—in a jar on his closet shelf."

"Has Dr. McCoy called to ask about his progress?" Jim said.

"No."

"Strange. We're supposed to transport to Spacedock later. I hoped Gary would be with us . . ."

"Maybe Dr. McCoy decided to extend his vacation."

"It's possible." Jim chuckled ruefully. "I did a better job than I meant to when I bullied him into taking some time off. I don't even know where he went."

"Can I ask you something?"

"Sure."

"Why does Dr. McCoy call Commander Mitchell 'Mitch,' while you call him 'Gary'?"

"Everybody calls Gary 'Mitch' except me. He picked up the nickname during our first midshipman training cruise. But I'd already known him for a year, and somehow I just never got around to making the change."

"What does he call you?"

Jim felt himself blushing. He wondered if he could get away with telling her that Gary called him Jim, like everybody else. As soon as Gary woke up, though, he would blast that fiction out of space.

"He calls me 'kid,' " Jim said. "I'm a little younger than he is, and he never lets me forget it." He did not tell her he had been the youngest in his class by more than a year. He knew what she would say: "Precocious, weren't you?" Being called precocious at fifteen or at twenty was bad enough. At twenty-nine, it was ridiculous.

"You've known Commander Mitchell for a long time, haven't you?"

"Ten years. No, eleven." Jim had lost three months in the regen bed. He shipped out to Ghioghe in spring, when the hills east of the city were green from winter's rain; when he woke up, only two weeks later in subjective time, the hills were golden and tinder dry with summer. Now, autumn approached, and Gary was still here.

"He *will* be all right, captain. I promise you that."

"Thank you, Ms. Chapel. Ms. Chapel . . ."

"Yes, captain?"

"Would you do me a favor?"

"If I can."

He stopped, wondering if he should ask her to do something all the experts said was useless. "I know it isn't supposed to make any difference, but I keep remembering the time before I woke up. I could hear things—or I thought I could hear—but I couldn't open my eyes and I didn't know where I was or what had happened to me. While Gary's still asleep, would you . . . talk to him? Tell him what's going on, tell him he's going to be all right . . ."

"Of course I will," she said.

"Thank you." He stood up reluctantly. "I'm supposed to report to Spacedock soon. I'd like to leave a note—?"

"You can use the office in back."

The note was hard to write, but he finally got something down that he hoped would be reassuring.

In the doorway of the office, he stopped. Her back to Jim, Carol Marcus stood at Gary's bedside with Dr. Eng, one of the regen specialists. They inspected Gary's life-sign readings and compared the printout with Carol's projections. Unlike the specialist, Carol was not a medical doctor. She was a geneticist; she had developed the protocol for Gary's treatment and for Jim's.

Jim remembered the first time he saw her, the first thing she said to him. When he began physical therapy, he lasted about five minutes into the first session. Trembling with exhaustion, sweaty and aching, thinking himself ridiculous to be so weak, he noticed her watching him and wished no stranger had seen him like this. Bad enough to have McCoy hovering like an encouraging mother hen.

But Carol overlooked Jim's exhaustion, the scar on his forehead, his hair plastered down with sweat. She said, "I wanted to meet the person who belongs to this genome."

She was serious and elegant, funny and good-humored.

She was one of those rare scientists who make intellectual leaps that turn into breakthroughs. She was extraordinarily beautiful, with her smooth blond hair and deep blue eyes. Jim felt an immediate attraction to her, and though her job did not require her to visit intensive care, let alone therapy, she often stopped in to see him.

The first time he left the hospital they went walking together in a nearby park. By the time the hospital released him, Jim and Carol had fallen in love. She invited him to move into her house.

Three months later, he moved out. He had not seen her for the past two weeks. He had an irrational urge to step back into the office and stay there till she left.

Don't be ridiculous, he thought. You're both adults; you can be civilized about this. He started toward her.

Dr. Eng pushed her short dark hair back behind her ear, made a notation on the printout flimsy, and glanced at Carol with a concerned frown. "What are you going to do?"

"Do? I'm going to do all the things you're supposed to do under these circumstances," Carol replied. "You didn't think this was an accident, did you?"

"No, of course not, it's just—Why, Captain Kirk! How nice to see you looking so well."

Carol turned, uncharacteristically flustered. "Jim—!"

"Hello, Carol." He stopped. He wanted to say everything to her, or he wanted to say nothing. He wanted to make love with her, or he wanted never to see her again.

"Talk to you later," Dr. Eng said, and made a diplomatic exit.

"How are you feeling, Jim?"

He ignored the question. His heart beat hard. "It's wonderful to see you. I have to leave soon. Can we . . . I'd like to talk to you. Would you have a drink with me?"

"I don't feel like having a drink," she said. "But I will go for a walk with you."

Jim paused beside Gary, still hoping he might awaken. He did not. "Get well, my friend," Jim said, and left Ms. Chapel the note to give him when he regained consciousness.

They did not have to discuss where to go. Jim and Carol walked toward their park.

7

Without meaning to, exactly, Jim kept brushing against Carol. His shoulder touched her shoulder; his fingers touched the back of her hand. At first she moved aside.

"Oh—" Carol said impatiently the third time Jim touched her. She took his hand and held it. "We *are* still friends, I hope."

"I hope so, too," Jim said. He tried to pretend the electric tingle of physical attraction no longer existed between them, but he found it impossible to deceive himself that much. Being near Carol made Jim feel as if a powerful current cast a web over both of them, exchanging and intensifying every passion.

"Are you sleeping any better?" Carol said.

Jim hesitated between the truth and a lie. "I'm sleeping fine," he said.

Carol gave him a quizzical glance, and he knew he had hesitated too long. She had held him too many times, when the nightmare slapped him awake in the darkest hours of the morning.

"If you want to talk about it . . ." she said.

"No. I don't want to talk about it," he said in a clipped impatient tone. Talking about it would do nothing but give him an excuse to wallow in grief and regret. That was the last thing he needed, and the last thing Carol needed to hear. Besides, if he told Carol now that he still bolted out of sleep with a shout of pure fury, tangled in cold sweat-soaked bedding, surrounded by the shreds of dream, confusing darkness with being blind . . . If he told her about trying to go back to sleep in the shabby, cramped traveler's cubicle . . . If he told her about lying wide awake and exhausted in the night, wishing desperately she was still beside him, then he would seem to be asking her to take him back out of pity instead of love.

"No," he said again, more gently, "I don't want to talk about it."

Still holding hands, they reached the small park and set out along the path that circled the lake. Ducks swam alongside them, quacking for a handout.

"We always forget to bring them anything," Carol said. "How many times have we walked here—we always meant to bring them some bread, but we never did."

"We had . . . other things on our minds."

"Yes."

"Carol, there's got to be some way—!"

He cut off his words when he felt her tense.

"Such as what?" she said.

"We could—we could get married."

She looked at him; for a moment he thought she was going to burst out laughing.

"What?" she said.

"Let's get married. We could transport to Spacedock. Admiral Noguchi could perform the ceremony."

"But why marriage, for heaven's sake?"

"That's the way we do it in my family," Jim said stiffly.

"Not in mine," Carol said. "And anyway, it still wouldn't work."

"It's worked for quite a number of generations," Jim said, though in the case of his own parents the statement stretched the truth. "Carol, I love you. You love me. You're the person I'd most want to be with if I were stranded on a desert planet. We have fun together—remember when we went to the dock and snuck on board the *Enterprise* for our own private tour—" At her expression, he stopped. "It's true."

"Yes," she said. "It's true. And I've missed you. The house is awfully quiet without you."

"Then you'll do it?"

"No. We talked about this too many times. No matter what we do, it wouldn't make any difference. I can't be with you and you can't stay with me."

"But I could. I could transfer to headquarters—"

"Jim . . ." She turned to face him. She held both his hands and looked into his eyes. "I remember how you felt when you found out you're getting command of the *Enterprise*. Do you think anyone who loved you would want to take that away from you? Do you think you could love anyone who tried?"

"I love you," he said. "I don't want to lose you."

"I don't want to lose you, either. But I lost you before I ever met you. I can get used to the quiet. I can't get used to having you back for a few weeks at a time and losing you over and over and over again."

He kept seeking a different solution, but the pattern led him in circles and he could find no way out.

"I know you're right," he said, miserable. "I just . . ."

Tears silvered Carol's dark blue eyes.

They kissed each other, one last time. She held him. He laid his head on her shoulder with his face turned away, because he, too, was near tears.

"I love you, too, Jim," she said. "But we don't live on a desert planet."

On the marshy bay side of the island, where the shore and the shallow warm saltwater met and blended, mangrove trees reached out onto the black mud flats. The tide receded, leaving behind a rich rank odor. Night fell and earth's moon rose, full, silvering the dark water and the black mud.

Commander Spock of Starfleet, science officer of the starship *Enterprise*, citizen of the planet Vulcan, watched and smelled and listened to the marsh. The undeveloped side of the island showed no evidence of human or other sentient presences. The rich ecosystem fascinated him. The dopplered whine of mosquitoes, rising as the insects approached him, falling as they fled, formed a background to the low cries of owls and the sharp sonar of bats. He could trace their flight by the whisper of their wings. The owls flew with a feathery swoop, the bats in a series of abrupt direction changes. A snake slid from shore to water, the sound of its long, smooth slither barely changing as it made the transition. On the tide flats, small crabs danced. The claws of a fat raccoon scraped mangrove bark; its paws padded on the mud; its teeth crunched. In the morning, nothing would be left of the captured crab but a small pile of crumbled shell.

The local inhabitants of the island claimed cougars still lived here, but Spock suspected they made the claim for the benefit of tourists.

Toward dawn, a blue heron sailed out of the dark sky and plashed into the shallows. It stalked over the water, feet and beak poised. Spock wondered what it was hunting. He took off his boots and rolled up his pants and waded into the thick silty water. He could feel the vibrations of living creatures through the soles of his feet, like a constant low electrical current. His toe encountered a hard shape, which he picked up and swished through the water to wash off the worst of the mud.

The mollusc was about half the length of his thumb, a univalve, its shell patterned delicately in black and white. Its body tapered to a point and its apex spiraled to a peak in a series of small sharp points. The creature itself had retreated inside the shell, drawing its horny operculum tight into the opening. Spock stood motionless till the gastropod gradually thrust out its feelers, its head, its body, and crawled across his hand.

Spock returned the king's crown to the bay and started back to the conference center, taking the long way around the tip of the island. The marsh gave way to the ocean side: white sand, dune grass, palms. As the sun cleared the horizon, he reached a secluded beach. He went for a long, hard swim, testing himself against the currents.

As a child Spock had not learned to swim. His home planet, Vulcan, spun hot and sere around its ancient scarlet sun. Large bodies of open water were rare on Vulcan, for the world retained barely enough water to sustain its ecosystem. Early the first morning of the conference, before anyone else had risen, he took himself off alone and gingerly attempted to swim. His tall spare body was not naturally buoyant, but after a few floundering false starts he managed to stay afloat. Once he figured out how to make forward progress, his skill increased rapidly.

Several kilometers from shore he paused to tread water. The tip of the island was a thin white streak of beach and a thin green streak of vegetation. Eyes open, he let himself sink beneath the water. A meter beneath the surface, a barracuda gazed at him stonily, its powerful silver torpedo form motionless except for the occasional flick of a fin. Spock knew it to be a ferocious predator. He searched his mind for fear; he found none. Vulcans trained themselves to maintain an emotionless state of equanimity under all conditions: Spock continually tested himself against that ideal. He resisted fear and pain; with equal determination he resisted pride and despair, joy and grief, and love.

One moment the barracuda peered at Spock, the next it vanished. Its streamlined shape cut through the sea with barely a motion, and Spock was alone. Perhaps the barracuda had no interest in the copper-based green blood of an alien; or perhaps it simply was not hungry.

He swam to shore, toweled off the saltwater and smoothed down his short black hair, dressed, and crossed the beach. White sand gave way to dune grass; dune grass gave way to trees and shade. A few human people already lay on the sand, exposing themselves to the sun. Humans had evolved beneath this yellow star. Unlike Vulcans, they possessed some natural protection against ultraviolet radiation. Nevertheless, Spock thought they took an unnecessary risk. Some wore bathing costumes, which struck him as ridiculous: inadequate protection from the sun on the one hand, an obstruction to swimming on the other. He saw no point to the use of clothing as decoration.

Though it was broad daylight when he reached the conference center, the lobby was deserted. Most of the other participants had either left after the presentation of the final papers the day before, or they had partied late into the night and now still slept. Deltan people, particularly, showed a considerable tolerance for engaging in intellectual discussions all day and carousing most of the night. They did their celebrating in a private group, however, claiming they could not risk damage to other beings with frailer emotional capacities. The other beings, including human people, apparently took this as a challenge. The resultant commotion helped Spock decide to avoid the wild portions of the conference center and spend most nights exploring the wild portions of the island instead.

"Excuse me, Commander Spock? You have a package."

Spock went to the desk. Someone had gone to a great deal of trouble and expense to send it rather than to have it synthesized locally; messenger stamps covered the wrapping. Spock accepted the package. His mother's handwriting addressed it.

He took it to his cabin and regarded it curiously before breaking the seals. Though he had been on earth, and on Spacedock in high earth orbit, for some months, and though his parents currently resided on earth, he had neither visited nor called them. Sarek, his father, the Vulcan ambassador, disapproved of Spock's decision to join Starfleet. The breach in their relationship extended over some years, now;

as he saw no way to heal it, Spock accepted it. He seldom communicated with his mother, either. Unlike his father, she could accept his making decisions about his own life. She never tried to win him to Sarek's point of view. But the disagreement between her husband and her son put her in an awkward middle position. Though Spock did not admit to feeling any pain over their estrangement, he was not indifferent to the feelings of his mother.

People who looked at Spock saw a tall, slender man of completely controlled physical power; green-tinged complexion, upswept black eyebrows and deep-set dark eyes, smooth black hair cut in straight short bangs, ears tapering up to points: a Vulcan. Or so most people perceived him. But his blood was not completely alien to the seas of this world, for his mother, Amanda Grayson, was a human being. She possessed all the feelings and emotions of a human being. Though he wished his mother could escape her feelings, Spock knew that the tension between him and Sarek hurt her deeply. His only solution, unsatisfactory as it might be, was to stay away.

He opened the package. It contained a short note of greeting that wished him well, made no mention of his silence, and hardly hinted at the intense emotions behind it. Only the signature broke the cool tone: "Love, Amanda."

The package contained a shirt of brown silk velvet embroidered with gold at the neck and sleeves. Spock gazed at it, wondering what had possessed his mother to send it to him. It was the sort of garment one might wear to a party, and surely Amanda knew that he attended only the parties he could not avoid, parties to which he would be required to wear Starfleet formal dress. Being human, his mother was more subtle and less directly logical than a Vulcan. That did not necessarily make her actions less meaningful or less comprehensible. Spock understood, after a moment, that she hoped for him to find other rewards in his life than his work. She wished him happiness.

He tried the shirt on. Of course it fit. He had to admit that he found the texture of the fabric aesthetically pleasing. He folded the gift into its package and slipped it in with his other belongings, among the memory modules and a bound copy of the paper he had presented.

His vacation had ended; it was time to return to the *Enterprise*.

Cadet Hikaru Sulu danced back, sprang forward in a lunge, and retreated before his opponent's saber could score the winning touch. He lunged, lunged again—and the scoreboard flashed the final touch of the final match of the Inner Planets all-around fencing championship.

The referee awarded the point, the saber match, and the championship to Cadet Hikaru Sulu.

Almost oblivious to the reaction of the audience, gasping for breath, his heart pounding after the long and intense match, Hikaru raised his mask and saluted his opponent. He had competed against her in the intercontinental championships, when he became the first Starfleet Academy fencer in ten years to win a place on the pan-earth team. Her school took most of the other positions, and she was team captain. He had never beaten her before.

She stood with her head down and her saber hanging by her side. She had won this competition two years running. She *owned* it, by right and by tradition as well as by training. She belonged to one of the most powerful families in the Federation, an aristocracy of old money and old accomplishment. Fencing was their sport. How dare a Starfleet Academy fencer, a provincial, practically a colonist, come in and think he could destroy her sweep?

When she raised her mask, she looked so angry, so stunned, that he feared she would leave the floor without observing the conventions of politeness.

He extended his ungauntleted hand to his opponent. She always moved gracefully, athletically, but now she had to force herself to stiffly shake his hand.

On the sidelines, Hikaru tried to think of something to say to her, but she flung her mask and saber and gauntlet on the floor and shrugged off the coach's consolation.

She glared at Hikaru. "You illiterate peasant!" she snarled. Followed by her teammates, her admirers, and the coach, she stalked into the locker room.

" 'Illiterate peasant'—?" Hikaru was tempted to quote a few lines of poetry. If his opponent's parents, whose families had done nothing within living memory but protect their positions, had literary pretensions, then their library shelves probably held a copy of one of Hikaru's father's books. *Fire in Frost,* maybe, or *Nine Suns.*

Probably, Hikaru thought sullenly, an unread copy.

One team member lagged behind. "Proud of yourself?"

"Yes," Hikaru said. "I am." For all his opponent's lack of grace in losing, she was the best saber fighter he had ever seen. He had not expected to beat her.

"She would've been the first fencer to take the saber championship all three years."

"What do you expect me to do?" Hikaru asked angrily. "Fall on my sword in remorse?"

The team member scowled and strode away.

Hikaru had believed if he were good enough, they would accept him. They would forget his lack of position and his poverty and respect him for his accomplishments. He had been foolish to believe that. He had no chance of being accepted; he had never had a chance. Even if his parents' careers were lucrative, which they were not, only the old money and the old positions and the old connections counted.

Despite himself, Hikaru started to laugh. Finally, the snobbery had passed beyond the limits of pain. Finally, he could only find his teammates hilarious, and, in a strange way, pitiful.

Right after the medal ceremony, he put his weapons in their case and returned to the Academy dorm to study.

Because his mother worked as a consulting agronomist, his family had moved from world to world throughout his childhood. His education had been thorough in some subjects and nonexistent in others. Classes at the Academy were a constant struggle to catch up punctuated by an occasional subject that he could have taught better than the professor.

Starfleet had granted him the assignment he requested, but his being allowed to take it depended on his commission, and his commission depended on his final grades for the final term. He had to do better than just scraping through.

With the championship medal cold in one hand and his weapons case heavy in the other, with his teammates off somewhere mourning their champion's loss instead of celebrating his victory, he wondered again if he should have quit the team months ago. He would have had more time in which to study. But the truth was he loved to fence, and the training gave him the energy to keep on studying. And maybe it kept him sane. Even early on, when he first realized he was competing in the chosen sport of a completely different social group, he enjoyed fencing too much to quit.

Now, a week later, near dawn, Hikaru strolled along a beach, kicking away the memories of the championship match as he kicked the damp sand. At the edge of the sea, a glassy sheet of water swept across a scattering of smooth-worn and ageless pebbles. The sea and the sand and the wind and the small polished stones at the waterline all sparkled with a cold hint of autumn.

He had won the championship, and the grade; he had his commission and he had his assignment. He was done with the fencing, done with the finals, done with the Academy.

He returned to his beach camp, where smoke from the fire crosscut the brilliant salt tang. Sparks flew when he threw another piece of driftwood on the fire.

He sat down and leaned against a huge storm-burnished piece of driftwood, an uprooted cedar tree polished to silvery gray. The sun's edge cleared the horizon, rising into air too pure and sky too clear to explode into sunrise. In the east, the sky lightened. Overhead, it glowed an intense indigo. In the west, the stars still glittered in the night.

Only a few hours remained of his leave, only a few hours more of peace and solitude and learning about his home world. He had been born on earth, but raised on a dozen alien worlds. He had spent the last three years here, but study and practice had taken all his time till now.

He had chosen to spend his leave by the ocean not because he particularly wanted to, but because he could afford neither the time nor the money to go offworld. At the age of twenty, he had seen mountains higher than the Himalayas, deserts wider and dryer and crueler than the Sahara, all manner of wonders, planetary and stellar. Stories of earth's splendors never impressed him.

But after a few days alone beside the sea, he found himself

gripped and held by the quiet beauty of his unknown home world.

I used to believe I could make myself at home anywhere, he thought. But now I know I never felt at home at all. Not compared to the way I feel now, sitting beside earth's greatest ocean.

But soon he must leave; soon he would be on his way to the border to serve on *Aerfen* with Captain Hunter.

Basking in the warmth of the fire, he dozed off.

Koronin strode across the dark landing field, ignoring the shabby ships that hunkered in the dust. Ships that visited the Arcturan system had left their best years far behind them, whether they originated in the Federation, in the Klingon Empire, or as some unlikely hybrid of orphan parts and cobbled-together retrofitting.

But one ship on the field was different.

The cold keen night wind ruffled powdery dust against Koronin's boots and pressed her cloak around her. It caught her long copper hair and blew it back from her high fore-head, from her brow ridges. It fluttered her unfastened veil over her shoulder.

She paused some paces from the sleek new ship. Starlight gleamed from its smooth flank. No one—certainly no one in the Arcturan system—had seen its like before. The wide-winged body, the long slender midsection, and the spherical prow gave evidence of the ship's descent from the favored design of the Klingon military. But the design had evolved to produce a unique ship.

And now it belonged to Koronin, who was an outlaw and a fugitive.

She touched the key to the locked hatchway. The key and the ship exchanged complex electronic communication. Knowing that the key or the ship might be rigged to destroy her, Koronin tried to maintain her philosophy of fatalism. But the possibilities that this craft opened for her excited her beyond any chance of calm.

The hatch opened and she stepped inside.

The command balcony could wait. The secured hatch of the work pit opened at Koronin's approach.

"My lord—" The serjeant cut off his words when he saw Koronin. His brow ridges contracted and his bushy eyebrows bristled.

Koronin read his confusion. She did nothing to alleviate it, but let it increase as she stood before him in silence.

"My lady," he said quickly. "This is the work pit, no fit place for a citizen of . . . of your position. If you permit, I will show you the way to the command balcony, where you may wait in comfort for my lord."

Koronin smiled. It amused her to be taken for the mistress of the ship's previous owner. She approved of the speed with which the serjeant recovered from—or concealed—his surprise. She saw in him a valuable assistant, if he could be subverted to her interests.

She held up a thread-thin gold chain. At its end spun a life-disk, its colors already fading to the clarity of death.

"Your lord will not be returning," she said. "This ship belongs to me."

The other crew members had merely glanced at her with jaded curiosity when they thought she was their master's newest favorite. Now that she claimed instead to be their master, they stared at her: some astonished, some terrified. A bare few reacted with joy and relief before they realized what a small chance Koronin had of keeping the ship. They instantly put on expressions of neutrality.

Agape, stunned, the serjeant tried to make sense of her claim. "You killed my lord—you robbed him—?" He stopped. No one could simply steal the electronic key and use it to come on board. It contained safeguards against such an occurrence.

"Your lord transferred ownership to me. He lost to me in a game of chance. A fair game. But afterward, he thought better of his bargain."

She flicked the chain so the fading life-disk snapped upward. She caught it and folded her hand around it as if she were oblivious to its sharp edges. As she fastened the disk to the long fringe on her belt, she deliberately turned her back on the serjeant.

When the serjeant attacked, she spun and blocked his blow. His force staggered her, but her resistance threw him off balance. He snatched at the blaster on his belt. Koronin disdained to use a powered weapon against him. She drew her dueling blade and slashed the serjeant's arm. He shrieked in agony. The blaster flew from his hand. Koronin scooped it up and pocketed it.

The serjeant huddled on the floor, trying to staunch the flow of blood from his forearm. He bled heavily, but the bleeding was, ultimately, superficial. Koronin had carefully avoided the arm's major circulatory paths. She despised unnecessary killing.

"Stand up." She placed the point of her blade at the side of his throat.

He moaned, protesting, terrified. His brow ridges paled and shriveled, for he hovered on the edge of shock. He rose unsteadily. His gaze froze on her blade. As he watched, Koronin's glassy weapon absorbed the blood that glistened on its surface. The color of the blood-sword deepened.

"The ship belongs to me," Koronin repeated. "The crew is mine, and you are mine. I will permit you to determine your own fate. You may swear yourself to me, or you may die."

The serjeant's master had disgraced himself. The serjeant could accept the disgrace, or he could renounce it and accept Koronin.

He did the honorable thing.

"I swear myself, and the crew as I command it, to your service." He hesitated.

"My name is Koronin."

"I swear myself to your service, Koronin."

She drew back her blade and sheathed it. A single drop of blood welled from the serjeant's throat. "My belongings will arrive soon. When you have seen them safely delivered to the balcony and when you have prepared the ship for liftoff, you may doctor your wounds."

He acknowledged her right to demand that her tasks take precedence over his pain. "Thank you, my lady."

"My name is Koronin!" she said angrily. Her hand tightened on the grip of her sword.

He hesitated. He had offered her the title as an act of courtesy and she had refused it. He could not know why. In his pain and shock and fear, he cast about for the reason he had offended her.

"I use no title," Koronin said, her tone harsh but no longer angry. "Carry out your orders."

He slowly sank to his knees before her. "Yes, Koronin."

She turned her back on him and on the crew. No one moved against her. She secured the work pit, sealing the crew at their stations but leaving the serjeant free, and hurried to the command balcony to make herself familiar with the controls.

She wanted to be far from the Arcturan system when the rulers of the Klingon Empire learned of their loss.

She would take their newest ship and see what mischief she could make for the Federation of Planets.

# Chapter 1

COMMANDER SPOCK PAUSED before the cabin of the captain of the starship *Enterprise*. In eleven years he had never stepped inside this cabin, though he had worked with Christopher Pike more closely than he had worked with any other human being. Pike was a very private man. Mr. Spock approved of the captain's reserve.

The Vulcan knocked on the cabin door. He expected no answer.

"Come." The door slid aside.

Spock stood on the threshold. He had not planned what to say.

Pike rested his elbows on his desk and his chin in both fists as he gazed at the crystals that covered the desktop. Of various sizes, various colors, some held static images and some had captured moving scenes. Spock's keen vision picked out familiar vignettes and landscapes. He had not known that Captain Pike made memory crystals of the worlds his ship visited.

Pike glanced up. His pensive attitude vanished. He waved his hand over the crystals. The images faded. The crystals darkened, then cleared to complete transparency.

"Good afternoon, Mr. Spock."

"Commodore Pike."

"Not commodore! Not yet. I'm still a captain till this evening." Pike swept up the crystals and poured them into a drawstring bag. They clicked and rattled.

"Very well, Captain Pike," Spock said.

"Ship's business?"

"No, sir. The *Enterprise* is prepared for change of command."

"Good." He drew the strings tight, tied the bag shut, and tossed it into a nearly empty suitcase. "Not much to show for eleven years, is it?"

"Captain?"

"Never mind. I'm just feeling my age."

Spock considered. Captain Pike had not yet reached fifty earth years of age. On Vulcan, he would still be considered a youth. No doubt he looked forward to his approaching maturity.

"Yes, captain. Congratulations, sir."

"Congratulations?"

"Yes, sir. On your promotion. On your increased responsibilities."

"Oh. Right." He smiled a private smile that did not seem to contain much humor.

Spock did not understand it.

"Did you want to talk to me about something in particular, Mr. Spock?" Pike said.

"Change of command offers little opportunity for conversation, captain. I came to speak to you now . . . merely to wish you farewell."

"Merely?"

"Yes," Spock said. "Words of farewell are perhaps not logical, based as they are in superstition, in wishes for good fortune, but . . ." He did not know what else to say. "I have learned much from you, captain."

"That's high praise, Mr. Spock," Captain Pike said. "Thank you."

"Perhaps we will have the opportunity to work together again, sometime in the future."

"Does that bother you, Mr. Spock?"

"What, captain?"

"I never asked you if you wanted to be promoted off the *Enterprise* along with me. I could have recommended that. If I had, you'd be on your way to being my executive officer at a starbase."

"I am aware that this is often done," Spock said. "Captain Kirk has recommended two of his senior officers for positions on the *Enterprise*. That is his privilege, as it is your privilege to choose your own executive staff."

"I probably should have talked to you about it," Captain Pike said. He rearranged the articles in his suitcase and sealed the case shut. "But I made the choice for you, because I was afraid that if I made you the offer, you might feel compelled to accept it. Compelled to leave the *Enterprise*. Did I make a mistake?"

"Sir?" Spock said, feeling confused.

"You have a highly developed sense of responsibility, Mr. Spock. You don't necessarily choose the path that's best for you."

Spock perceived Pike's comment as criticism, but he did not understand its aim. " 'Best' is a highly subjective term, captain," he said. "Vulcans attempt to eliminate subjective terms from their decisions. The goal of a Vulcan with my background and training is to increase the store of knowledge available to sentient beings."

"Maybe I didn't make a mistake, after all." Captain Pike hesitated. "When people of my background and training say good-bye, they shake hands. But Vulcans . . ."

"I will shake your hand, Captain Pike, if you wish it," Spock said.

The captain and the science officer clasped hands for the first and last time.

Uhura beamed on board the *Enterprise,* happy and rested and glad to be back and at the same time wishing the festival had lasted for another week. She stowed her things in her cabin and set her comm unit to call her on the bridge if her package arrived while the *Enterprise* was still in port. That was not likely, but, well, anything could happen. Then she changed out of her festival costume, a long dark-red dress with Celtic embroidery at neck and wrists, and into her uniform; she changed from Uhura, musician, citizen of the Bantu Nation of United Africa, into Lieutenant Uhura, communications officer of the starship *Enterprise*.

The activity on the bridge would have looked like uncontrolled chaos to a stranger. Uhura had seen the chaos many times before. She understood its workings and its ebb and flow. It changed, it evolved; it would evolve more during this trip than it ever had since the first time Uhura came on board.

Captain Pike had been promoted. This evening he would be replaced. Throughout the ship, anticipation and curiosity and apprehension about the new captain mixed with regret for the departure of their respected and loved commanding officer.

The sound level on the bridge dropped precipitously.

Commander Spock had arrived. Everyone fell silent, not through fear, not through dislike or reluctance to be over-heard, but because Mr. Spock's very presence inspired a more serious attitude.

He glanced around the bridge, then took his place at the science station as if unaware of his effect. Uhura doubted, though, that Mr. Spock missed anything having to do with the *Enterprise*.

"Good morning, Mr. Spock," Uhura said.

"Lieutenant Uhura."

"Did you enjoy your vacation?"

"The time was intellectually stimulating," he said. She had not seen him for a month or so; he seemed even more intense and self-controlled than usual.

"I bought an Irish harp," Uhura said.

"I beg your pardon?"

"I went to the Irish Harp Festival in Mandela City. And I ordered a harp. Siobhan might finish it before we ship out, but I'll probably have to wait till our next stopover."

"Why was an Irish harp festival in Mandela City? Mandela City is not in Ireland."

"They have harp festivals all over the world, Mr. Spock. They're thinking of having one off earth soon. There are more harp players outside Ireland than in it. You don't even have to have red hair." She smiled. "Siobhan does have red hair . . . but her skin is darker than mine. She makes the most beautiful harps I've ever seen."

"I will be interested to observe how it is played."

"So will I—I hope it comes before we leave. Any word on where we're going, and for how long?"

"Our orders will of course be given first to the new captain," Mr. Spock said. "But . . ."

Uhura had never known Mr. Spock to engage in idle gossip; yet somehow he always knew the most recent changes in Starfleet plans and policy.

"What, Mr. Spock?"

"The ship is neither prepared nor fueled for a long voyage, and the full scientific staff has not been assigned. One may deduce a trip of limited duration."

"I see." Uhura felt disappointed. Rumors had been flying about the Federation's exploration plans, and everyone on the *Enterprise* had been hoping, expecting, to take part in that mission.

The lift doors opened and Chief Engineer Montgomery Scott burst onto the bridge.

"I'm an uncle!" he exclaimed. "Will ye have a cigar, Lieutenant Uhura? Mr. Spock, a cigar to celebrate!"

As Scott rounded the bridge handing out cigars to all and sundry, Uhura wondered what to do with the cylinder of rolled tobacco.

"Congratulations, Mr. Scott," she said when he completed his circuit and beamed with pride at her and Spock. "And thank you. I probably shouldn't smoke it on the bridge, though."

"What is the function of this object?" Spock asked.

" 'Tis a cigar, Mr. Spock. 'Tis a tradition to hand out cigars at the birth of a baby. My little niece is two days old. Dannan Stuart, her name is. A heroic name! 'Tis my first time to be an uncle. Though," he said, as if telling a secret, "the baby is verra . . . verra *small.*"

Uhura smiled. "She'll get over that, Mr. Scott."

"I still do not understand this object. This cigar." Spock rolled the cigar between his elegant, powerful fingers. The tobacco rustled.

"Be careful, Mr. Spock! Ye should light it, not mash it. Ye'll bruise the tobacco!"

"But this appears to be made of dried leaves," Spock said. "How can one bruise—" He raised it, sniffed it, drew it quickly from his nose. "This is tobacco, Mr. Scott. It contains noxious chemicals."

"Aye, 'tis true," Scott admitted. "But 'tis the *tradition,* d'ye see?"

Spock regarded the cigar a moment longer. "I believe I

understand," he said. "During a time of critical overpopulation, the birth of a child would have required an adult to die. The adults resorted to a sort of lottery to decide who must make way. Your customs . . . fascinating. Not efficient, but fascinating."

"It wasna quite like that, Mr. Spock—"

Spock handed him the cigar. "I am sure you meant to compliment me, but I should prefer not to participate in your lottery."

Jim transported up to Spacedock. Why did I say that to Carol? he thought. I knew what she'd say. She's said it before. *I've* said it before. I know what it's like to be part of the family of a Starfleet officer. What happened to all my unbreakable resolutions not to do that to anyone?

"Jaime? Jaime Kirk!"

Jim turned toward the familiar voice. "Agovanli!"

The large person before him grasped his ankles with his knee-pincers and spun about on his central foot. Jim grabbed his mane. Agovanli set him down, whuffling and blowing his hot, fragrant breath in his version of a hug.

"Congratualaations," Vanli said. His voice could rattle wall hangings. "Congraatuaalations on receiving the *Enterprise!* I aam poised with anticipaation of what you will do with it now thaat you haave it."

"I'll take that as a compliment," Jim said. "I think."

"I will buy you a lunch and a drink, to celebraate."

Just then that sounded like a good idea to Jim.

Vanli took Jim to his favorite restaurant, an environment three-quarters tropical island at night, one-quarter space station. They sat in an area that passed for *al fresco* on Spacedock: a view-bubble protruding from the side of the station, with a 180-degree horizontal and 90-degree vertical star view. An enormous fluorescent-orange rhododendron loomed over Jim's left shoulder.

"Jaime, I discovered something quite wonderful at my last duty station. Some humans—Do you know this? Your cultures are so diverse—Some humans mix different alcoholic entities together to create new sensations."

"I have heard of that," Jim said.

"Oh, excellent, we will try some." He studied the menu

set into the tabletop, blinking his great orange eyes. "Aah, thaat sounds interesting." He twined together several of the tentacles of his hands and pushed the order button. The lid of the table slid aside for a tray-sized platform bearing two tall drinks.

Jim looked at Vanli's choice with disbelief. Layers of liquor of different shades of amber and gold filled the glasses. A straw and some fruit protruded from the top.

"Aa 'tropical zaambie.' Is my pronunciation correct?"

"Close enough. 'Zombie.' "

"A beautiful word. Mellifluous. Are you familiar with the language? Do you know what it might mean?"

"I don't know what language it comes from. But I know what it means. It's a dead person who still walks around and thinks it's alive."

"How quaint. Your customs never fail to delight me. But what is the 'tropical'?"

"Must mean the fruit."

"Of course—even a zaambie must eat."

Jim gingerly lifted his glass.

"No, no, no!" Vanli rumbled. "Use the straw! You insult the builder if you disturb the laayers."

"Vanli, nobody built these drinks. The table synthesized them for us."

"The principle remains. It arrives in layers, it must be drunk in layers."

"All right, if that will make you happy."

Jim took a careful sip of the darkest layer of the drink. The deep amber liquor exploded against his tongue and blazed trail down his throat. The stuff was at least 180 proof. He gasped and smothered a cough, which caused the fumes from the liquor he had drunk to roar into his nasal passages and flame against the fumes from the zombie's top layer, which rushed into his nostrils.

"How pleasant," Vanli said, oblivious to Jim's reaction. "I have only a taster's tolerance for aalcohol, aas you know, but this is enjoyable. What do you think of it?"

" 'Enjoyable' doesn't even begin to describe it."

Vanli took another gulp. " 'Enjoyable' *is* too mild a term."

"Excuse me," Jim said, dropping his fruit on the floor.

"I've dropped my fruit." He bent down and poured nine-tenths of the zombie into the potted rhododendron. The rhododendron leaned closer, as if anxious for another drink.

Vanli slurped at the bottom of his glass.

"That was excellent," he said. "But it was such aan enjoyaable experiment—I believe I shaall experiment again. Do you wish to choose something, Jaime?"

"How about a 'Virgin Mary'?" It might be cocktail hour on Spacedock, but for Jim it was still morning.

Vanli looked up Jim's suggestion. "You're teasing me."

"Zombies are pretty powerful," Jim said. "It doesn't hurt to alternate them with seltzer water. Or tomato juice." He could feel the rum in his stomach, like a small hot coal. He had skipped breakfast, and though Vanli had invited him to lunch they had yet to eat anything. Intoxicating beverages nowadays contained enzymes that eliminated the danger of long-term damage. But the short-term effects had not been tampered with, and Jim was beginning to experience them.

"Jaime, Jaime, you know I never do more than taste my drinks. This one sounds delightful. Aa 'blaack saamurai.' "

"No," Jim said. "I draw the line at sake and soy sauce. You have to keep the stuff in the same bottles they use for positrons."

Vanli pouted. "Here is one called the 'fruit punch.' What could be more innocuous?"

He pushed the button before Jim could object. This time two pineapples appeared, or two things that bore a certain plasticized resemblance to pineapples. Straws stuck out of their sides. The synthesizer created the drink with the pineapple shell around it rather than synthesizing a knife cut around the outside and marks inside where the pulp had supposedly been removed.

Jim wondered how to pour this drink into the rhododendron, then realized that Vanli would not be able to tell if the level of the liquor had decreased unless he shook the pineapple, juggled it, or made a forward pass with it. Unfortunately, he might do any of those things.

Vanli's pineapple emitted muffled slurping noises. "Do you like it?"

In the spirit of experimentation, Jim tasted the drink. He tried to reply, but though his mouth moved, fire had paralyzed his tongue and his vocal cords. He ordered the first thing that looked cold and relatively innocuous. It popped through the center of the table. He grabbed it and drank it. Overwhelmed by a powerful peppermint taste, the burning eased.

Vanli consulted the menu. "What are you drinking? A 'flowing spring'? I believe I'll have one, too. Such imaginative names!" Vanli made appreciative humming sounds.

Jim looked more closely at the menu. A 'flowing spring' consisted of vodka infused with peppermint. The 'fruit punch' contained several fermented and distilled fruit juices, none pineapple and none from earth, plus a high proportion of ginger. When the peppermint began to wear off, his tongue still felt like a cinder. No wonder.

And his head was full of fuzz.

Jim fumbled with a piece of the table setting, dropped it for real, and used the opportunity of picking it up to pour the rest of his flowing spring into the rhododendron. Jim hoped the plant had a high tolerance for alcohol. One branch drooped over his shoulder, as if in need of support, or perhaps of someone to drive it home.

Better a rhododendron than me, he thought. Besides, I can't be the first person to ever give the vegetation in here some high octane fertilizer. I wonder if there's a society for the prevention of cruelty to rhododendrons? If so, I could be in big trouble.

Thinking over what he had just thought, he thought, I could be in big trouble anyway.

The cold woke Hikaru from a sound sleep. His fire had died. His breath steamed in the chill of dawn. The rising sun cast purple rays across the eastern horizon. Hikaru brushed wet sand over the gray ashes and climbed the grassy bank above the beach.

He could hear his communicator beeping even before he opened the door of the tiny cabin. He hurried inside and dug through his pack, finding it at the very bottom.

"Sulu here."

"Spacedock. We've been trying to reach you for hours."

"I'm on leave."

"You have new orders. Prepare to beam up."

"I need a few minutes—I'm not dressed and I'm not packed."

"No more than five minutes, lieutenant."

He scrambled into his uniform, stuffed his other clothes in his pack, and slung the strap of the scabbard of his antique saber over his shoulder. Excited, he thought, Starfleet must have found a transport heading for the frontier. They're sending me to report to Captain Hunter on *Aerfen* already!

"Are you ready, lieutenant?"

"I'm ready." If I'm not, he thought, I never will be.

"You're on your way to your new ship, lieutenant. Transferring control to *Enterprise*."

*"Enterprise?* Wait, there's been a mistake—"

The cold prickle of the transporter beam enveloped him, sparkled him out of existence—

—and re-formed him on the transporter platform of a starship.

"Welcome aboard the *Enterprise*. So you're the new helm officer. I'm Kyle." The transporter technician shook his hand. He was tall and wore his light brown hair brushed back. Friendly smile lines crinkled from the corners of his eyes.

"Who's in charge?" Sulu's good mood had vanished.

Kyle considered. "Since Commodore Pike isn't on board, and Captain Kirk hasn't arrived, and change of command isn't till this evening," he said thoughtfully, "that leaves Mr. Spock."

"Where is he?"

"Anywhere and everywhere," Kyle said, with deliberate ambiguity. "But you might try the bridge."

Hikaru dropped his dufflebag and stalked out.

"Wait a minute," Kyle said. "You forgot your stuff!"

"No, I didn't," Hikaru said. As soon as he got things straightened out he would leave and take it with him.

Hikaru had never been on a constellation-class starship. For training cruises, he had always managed to finesse his way onto the smaller, more agile craft he expected to be flying. Having stormed out without asking Kyle for directions, he walked obstinately down the corridor with no idea where he was going. He fetched up in a dead end. He had turned himself around without ever having made a turn. This did not improve his humor. He retraced his steps, puzzling out the codes at each intersection, till he made his way to a turbo-lift.

"Destination?" it said.

"Bridge."

A moment later the doors slid open again and he stepped out. The bridge was crowded with techs and ensigns and other assorted crew members. Everyone appeared to be doing at least two things at once. A crew member nearly bumped into him on her way to the lift, for she was reading one list on her electronic clipboard and marking off items scrolling past in a window on the screen.

"Excuse me—" She tried to pass him.

He moved in front of her. She looked up, blinking.

"Who is Mr. Spock?" he asked.

She gestured toward the science station, where a tall figure in blue sat at a computer console, so intent that his back seemed to form a barrier to the outside world.

"Mr. Spock?" Hikaru waited. "Mr. Spock!"

Spock turned and rose, as if uncoiling. He gazed down. If the interruption annoyed him, he did not show it. He was a Vulcan.

"What is it?"

"My name is Sulu—"

"The new helm officer. There is your station." Commander Spock turned away.

Hikaru touched his sleeve. Spock stiffened. Without making any overt sign of displeasure, he moved so he faced Hikaru again, and so Hikaru no longer touched him.

"There is more?"

"There is a mistake. I'm not supposed to be on the *Enterprise*."

"You are assigned to the *Enterprise*."

"How do you know? You haven't even looked at the postings! You didn't even check!"

With resigned patience, Spock played his fingers across the controls of his computer. Hikaru's name glowed in gold letters on the screen. Hikaru Sulu. Helm officer. Starship *Enterprise*.

"I don't understand," Hikaru said. "I had my orders. I'm

supposed to be on my way to the frontier. To join Captain Hunter's squadron."

"Then you are most fortunate to have had your orders changed," Spock said.

"I don't want my orders changed! I liked the orders I had! I requested those orders!"

"Indeed?" Spock said. "Fascinating."

"Starfleet promised me—"

Spock raised one eyebrow. "Starfleet makes no promises in matters such as this."

"But—"

"Starfleet assigns its personnel where they will be most useful. A senior officer's request takes precedence over mere personal preference. Captain James Kirk requested that you be assigned to the *Enterprise*."

"Why?" Hikaru asked, mystified.

"I am sure," Spock said, "that I do not know."

"I don't have any experience piloting a starship. He's got me mixed up with somebody else, or he just made a mistake—this is ridiculous!"

"If you wish to inform your commanding officer that you believe him to be a fool, that is your own business," Spock said. "However, my observations of human nature suggest to me that the statement would not be favorably received."

"I've got to get reassigned to *Aerfen*."

"You would choose to serve on the border patrol rather than on the *Enterprise*, which has the ability to expand the limits of exploration?"

"Yes," Hikaru said. "I would."

"I fail to understand why."

"Then you never lived on Ganjitsu." Hikaru wished he had not said the last. He was angry and upset; he did not want to talk about Ganjitsu or *Aerfen* or Captain Hunter. Now the science officer would fix him with his intense gaze and insist on an explanation.

To Sulu's surprise, Spock did nothing of the sort.

"Ganjitsu," he said thoughtfully. "This explains much. However, nothing can be done at the moment. The *Enterprise* departs tomorrow. Finding another helm officer by then would be impossible. You must request a transfer."

"And then what?"

"And then wait."

Hikaru blew out his breath in frustration.

"In the meantime," Spock said, "computer has routed to your station a list of the tasks you must complete."

Hikaru took the defeat as a temporary setback.

"You are aware," Spock said, "that the captain must approve your request before you file it."

"No," Hikaru said. "I wasn't." But I probably should have guessed, he thought. He passed the empty captain's seat and stopped at the helm officer's station.

His list of duties included his share of preparing the ship for departure, his cabin assignment, information on the change-of-command ceremony, and an order to make an appointment with the ship's surgeon for a complete physical. He grimaced. He hated physicals. He wondered if he might arrange to fail it, but abandoned the thought. If he were too unhealthy to remain on board the *Enterprise,* which had state-of-the-art medical technology, he would certainly not get sent off to the frontier, where they made do with medics and patchwork surgery.

The scabbard of his saber bumped against his chair as he sat down at the helm officer's place. He slipped out of the strap and stowed the saber under his console.

He had never, in real life, handled a constellation-class starship. But he had trained on enough simulators to know what they felt like: clunky, unresponsive, and slow.

It occurred to him that he could claim complete incompetence—and demonstrate it—in order to get himself posted off the ship. But that would do him no more good than failing his medical exam. Feigning incompetence would damage his reputation, not to mention endanger the starship. On the other hand, he might win his transfer if he made it possible for his successor to replace him without any fuss or trauma.

That meant doing the best job he could. Time vanished as he melded himself with the workings of the ship.

Koronin stretched in smuggled silks. She enjoyed the slide of layers of satin, the softness of layers of thick fur pelts. She had come upon an oligarchy transport, and she took it unawares. Now the command balcony of the fighting ship contained the pick of the prize's cargo, never mind what she might have sold it for deeper inside the boundaries of the Klingon Empire. Koronin liked profit, but preferred luxury.

The ship's command balcony overhung the whole length of the work pit. Floor ports, canted panels of one-way glass, and armored sensors spied out upon the stations. The shipmaster could oversee each subordinate without vulnerability. Koronin disdained the safeguards. The serjeant of the pit had sworn himself to her, and none of the crew much regretted losing the government officer from whom she had taken the ship.

No doubt he had treated his crew with as little consideration as he offered his relatives. He had as much as sold the future of his family when he lost to Koronin, for the government would ruin him—and all the members of his lineage, if necessary—to recover his losses. He should have known better than to gamble stakes he could not afford to lose. He was, of course, beyond caring.

*Quundar,* as she had renamed her ship, possessed speed and firepower to waste; and Koronin was an excellent pilot. Before the government could take back the ship and the crew, they would have to catch her.

If she could remain free long enough to succeed at two or three audacious raids against the Federation of Planets, the oligarchy would add her name to the select list of independents whom they overlooked. Fragile agreements and tacit neutralities prevented official oligarchy forces from harrying the instruments of the Federation. Independents had more freedom.

Koronin laughed with contempt. She could amuse herself, increase her worth, fill her command balcony with luxuries approaching decadence, live outside the law, and reap gratitude for it. The oligarchs could not stop her. What could they do to her? Kill her? Before she ever set out on this course she accepted that someone might kill her one day. The prospect held no fear for her. As for their weapons of confiscation and ruin: Koronin had no assets outside the ship for the government to seize, and no family for them to torment. No, no family: the Federation took care of that, and her own government let the outrage pass unanswered.

Only Koronin had survived, barely past childhood, without friends or patrons to plead her cause. Now she was grown, and she had scores to settle with the oligarchy and with the Federation.

The star map formed at her command. Space controlled by the Federation glowed red, a great spreading mass, a gigantic corruption. One long, narrow, vulnerable projection thrust into Klingon territory: the Federation Phalanx. Its existence offended her; its very name insulted her. And in the Arcturan system, where outcasts of both societies met on terms of indifferent neutrality, those from the Federation found great amusement in repeating their repellent jokes loudly enough for everyone to hear. The Kumburanya lacked the morals to find such gibes offensive, but Koronin, a Rumaiy, found them nearly intolerable.

She expected nothing better of the Kumburanya. They were the majority group in the Klingon Empire; Kumburan nobles formed the oligarchy, controlled resources and expansion, and indulged in discrimination against the Rumaiy minority to which Koronin belonged.

Koronin let the silks fall away. This ship would run forever without her attention; the denizens of the work pit had no way of knowing when she watched and when she rested, or when she might detect and punish a moment's preoccupation. She had complete power over them, for the oligarchy, in conscripting them, made them legal possessions of the ship and whoever controlled it. She could even program the computer to curb their errors for her, at whatever level of cruelty she chose. That way, though, lay true decadence: not the simple enjoyment of physical luxuries, but the laxness of body and mind that could bring her down as surely as it brought down the officer from whom she won *Quundar*.

She combed her long copper hair, ruffled her heavy eyebrows, and clothed herself in layers of silk and leather. She fastened her belt around her hips, taking pleasure in the length of her trophy fringe, which draped to her knee. She tied a soft length of gold ribbon across her forehead to hold the corner of her veil. The veil itself she let fall loose from headband to shoulder. As an outcast she declined to cover her face. Her family had possessed sufficient rank for all its members to veil themselves in public, but the family no longer existed, and would not again unless she reestablished it.

"This is Commander Spock. May I have the attention of the officers of the *Enterprise*."

Sulu started when the announcement broke through his concentration.

"The change-of-command ceremony will take place on the recreation deck in thirty minutes precisely. Dress is formal. Your presence is expected."

Sulu wondered where "Your presence is expected" fell in the spectrum between "Your presence would be welcome" and "You are ordered to attend." Since everyone on the bridge immediately began shutting down their stations, he had to assume it was more nearly a direct order than a friendly suggestion. But a great deal of work remained to be done at the helm. Besides, he had not been a member of the crew under the previous captain, and he had not yet reported to his soon-to-be-ex-commander. A change-of-command ceremony between two officers he had never met had nothing to do with him and his nebulous position. He called up the next-to-last set of specs and started going through them.

"Mr. Sulu."

He glanced up. Spock stood just behind him.

"Yes, sir?"

"Your concentration is admirable. You apparently did not hear the announcement."

"I didn't think the announcement applied to me, commander."

"Indeed. You have an . . . interesting . . . view on the subject of orders. Perhaps we should discuss this topic—at some future date when the pressure of time is not so strong."

"I didn't serve under Commodore Pike, and I . . ." Sulu let his voice trail off. His explanation was getting him nowhere with Mr. Spock.

"If you leave the bridge immediately, you will be able to prepare yourself and report to the ceremony on time," Spock said, as if Sulu had said nothing in his own defense.

"Yes, sir." He slung the saber scabbard over his shoulder.

"Mr. Sulu."

"*Yes*, sir."

"Starfleet formal attire does not include a dress saber."

Sulu blushed. "I know that, sir."

He left his station, aware till the lift doors closed of Mr. Spock's enigmatic gaze fixed on a vulnerable point between his shoulder blades.

The ship's operating system had already taken his measure. By the time he found his cabin, the door recognized him and opened at his approach. He stepped inside and slipped the saber belt off his shoulder.

First he noticed that someone had delivered his belongings to his cabin. Second he noticed that compared to an Academy dorm room, his cabin was enormous. It contained a bunk, a desk and chair, a comm terminal, a synthesizer outlet, a decadently large storage closet. On the frontier, one arrived with a minimum of possessions and left the same way. The fighter ships had no room for anything more than necessities, no extra fuel for pushing around excess mass.

A set of hooks hung on the wall above the desk. They would be the perfect place for his saber—

Wait a minute, he thought. I'm not going to *be* here long enough to make myself at home.

He hurried to the synthesizer outlet and touched the control plate. Before he gave it any commands, it slid a formal uniform into his hands.

"Commander Spock's instructions," the computer said.

Everything was just a little too efficient around here for Hikaru's taste.

He jumped into the shower for a minute, jumped out, and put on the uniform and his boots. He had not quite had time to get all the sea spray out of his hair. Feeling aggravated, he left his cabin and went in search of the recreation deck.

Though Jim stopped even tasting the drinks Vanli ordered, he did not get much more sober. Vanli grew more cheerful, more insistent, and more intoxicated.

"A toast to Captain Kirk! I always said you'd make admiral, or prison, before you reached thirty."

"I'm twenty-nine, Vanli. I'd have to work at it to accomplish either within your time limit."

"Ah, but you're a captain, and I'm only a lowly lieutenant commander. You've traveled fast and far."

As the incipient depression of too little food and too much alcohol slid and sneaked through his system, Jim concluded that most of his achievements had occurred through a combination of good luck, good intuition, and good timing, not through deliberate efforts of intellectual, physical, or ethical strength. The exhilaration of success could briefly make him believe he could do anything, but the arrogance soon wore off and left him with only the truth.

"Is that why you're trying to get me drunk, Vanli?"

"What? No! You deserve your prizes, and I deserve what I've won. Which isn't half bad, come to think of it, except perhaps compared to you. No, oh, no . . . I just thought, when I saw you, how funny Robbie was on the day he got his commission . . ." Vanli collapsed across the table, his tentacles twining and twisting over his eyes, his breath blowing hot and cold with laughter.

Jim blushed. At the time, getting Robbie drunk had seemed like a good joke. He looked decidedly green during the ceremony at which he was commissioned. As green was not his natural color, his commanding officer noticed his distress. Fortunately, he put it down to nerves. In retrospect, the joke seemed juvenile and cruel.

"Vanli?" His friend's breath had evened out; he was asleep. "Come on, Vanli, time to go."

When Vanli slept, his whole body attained the consistency of his tentacles.

Jim looked at the time. Shocked, he jumped up. Unless he hurried, he was going to be late for change of command.

"Vanli!" He shook Vanli's arm. Vanli gave a muffled grunt. He jammed his shoulder under one of Vanli's arms and heaved him up. Since his friend weighed several metric tons, Jim could only guide him in a direction he was willing to go. Vanli stood, happily sluggish, unsteady.

"Are we going to another paarty?"

"We're going back to your ship," Jim said.

Vanli tried to sit down again. Jim staggered. His right knee twinged a warning.

"Maybe there's another party." Just because Jim did not know about it did not make it untrue.

"Oh, well, aall right." The weight on Jim's shoulder eased, from crushing to merely painful. "Another paarty?"

Jim fumbled for the credit recorder and winced when he saw the bill. He paid for the drinks with one hand and guided Vanli away from the floor with the other.

"Let's go."

"O-kaay, Jaime." Vanli began to make a buzzing, purring noise, his equivalent of a contented hum. Though he could move faster than any human being when he chose, he ambled with frustrating sloth.

"Come *on,* Vanli. If *you* don't hurry, *I'm* going to be late. Damn your so-called sense of humor, anyway."

Vanli chuckled. "You'll thank me, Jaime."

"Thank you? For trying to get me drunk before change of command?"

"Some ceremonies are better endured with the use of a crutch," Vanli said.

"A crutch is what I'm going to need, after I get you back to your ship. Can't you walk by yourself?"

He extricated himself from the confusion of Vanli's arm and tentacles and rubbed his own shoulder.

"Waaalk by myself? Of couuaaarse."

Like a great tree cut off at the roots, Vanli toppled slowly, gracefully, and with enormous dignity. Jim grabbed him and pushed with all his force to keep his friend upright.

"You see?" Vanli said. "I'm quite caapable of naavigaating on my own. You maay proceed aalone."

"I couldn't possibly," Jim said. "What would I do without you?"

They reached the bay where Vanli's ship and the *Enterprise* lay docked.

On one of Vanli's digressions, Jim guided him out of the main passageway, through deserted conference rooms and storage lockers. If he took Vanli through the kitchen, which ought to be deserted, they would be nearly as far down the mooring bay as Vanli's ship. From there, Jim could take him to his cabin with a minimum of fuss.

Sounds emanated from the kitchen. A crew must be cleaning it after some gathering of VIPs deemed too important or too particular to be served a meal from the synthesizer. Jim wondered what celebration had taken place, and when, and if he had been invited but missed the invitation in the midst of his preoccupation with Carol and with Gary, and, if he had not been invited, why.

Jim pushed open the kitchen door.

Steam and the scent of several worlds' delicacies wafted past. He stopped, astonished.

What's going on? he thought. What VIPs are on Space-dock that I didn't even hear about? I usually keep up on Starfleet matters—or at least on the grapevine, at least when I'm near home port.

Deciding that it would be easier to lead Vanli through the kitchen than to renegotiate the back route, Jim guided him through the door.

"Mmm, dinner," Vanli said, looking around and blinking his huge amber eyes. He snagged a pastry from a carefully arranged tray.

"Hands off, Vanli!"

"It waas too symmetrical." Vanli munched contentedly. "Not baad."

A tall being with silvery skin, wearing a traditional white chef's hat and carrying a long wire whisk dripping with batter in one seven-fingered hand, confronted them.

"You cannot come in here."

"Got turned around," Jim said. "We'll just go out that way, all right?" He gestured toward the far door and tried to guide Vanli past the chef.

Vanli flicked one tentacle toward the whisk and scooped off a drop of the batter. Momentarily speechless with outrage, the chef glared from Vanli to his whisk and back again.

Jim tried to hurry Vanli along, but Vanli paused to lick the batter off his tentacle.

"Mmm," he said. "Compliments to the chef. Chocolate. My favorite. Earth's only major contribution to the galaxy."

"Get *out* of here!" The chef waved the whisk at them, scattering blobs of chocolate cake batter around the kitchen and on Vanli and Jim. The chef herded them toward the nearest exit. Jim tried to help Vanli along and wipe the chocolate off his shirt at the same time.

The chef hurried them out of the kitchen and into the corridor. The door slid shut behind them and whined as it locked.

Jim stopped short. They were immediately across from the *Enterprise*'s docking bay. People had already begun to gather. Most stood gazing through the viewports, their backs to Jim, watching the moored *Enterprise* and the activity inside Spacedock. No one yet had noticed Jim and Vanli. Jim could hear another group of people approaching from beyond the curve of the corridor, and he could swear he recognized the voice of Admiral Noguchi, congratulating Christopher Pike on his promotion to commodore.

Far from preparing for a ceremony of which he was not aware, the chefs and subchefs and staff worked to create a celebration for the officer he was replacing. Given Chris Pike's reputation, Jim should have realized that the change-of-command ceremony would be much more than a small, matter-of-fact transfer.

"Vanli, we've got to get out of here," he whispered, keeping himself between Vanli and the wall.

"I'm coming, I'm coming." Vanli's voice rumbled through the corridor.

Jim ducked his head, hoping the Starfleet people would only notice Vanli, who strolled leisurely around the next bend in the corridor despite Jim's attempts to hurry him along.

Jim breathed a sigh of relief. The hatch leading to Vanli's ship lay just ahead.

The officer of the day pretended not to notice Vanli's state of inebriation, and she did not even raise an eyebrow at the chocolate cake batter.

"Permission to come aboard, lieutenant."

"Permission granted."

Jim hurried Vanli into the nearest turbo-lift. As the doors closed, he thought he heard the officer of the day giggling, but he could not be sure.

The lift carried them to officers' quarters. Jim found Vanli's cabin and gratefully let him curl up on his bunk.

"There's aa bottle of saaurian brandy in my cupboard," Vanli said. "Let's have aa toast to your new mission."

"Neither of us needs any brandy, saurian or otherwise," Jim said. He jabbed at the keys of the synthesizer. Flinging off his civvies, he ran through Vanli's shower. By the time the sonics had finished vibrating the cake batter out of his

41

hair, the synthesizer had delivered his uniform and Vanli had fallen asleep once more. Jim struggled into the uniform—drat the fancy belt!—and pulled on his boots and hurriedly combed his hair with his fingers.

At the door, he glanced back at Vanli.

"Sleep well, Vanli."

Jim bolted for the turbo-lift.

He raced toward the docking bay, passing the officer of the day again.

"Clear sailing, captain," she said as he went by.

42

# Chapter 2

JIM POUNDED THROUGH the Spacedock corridor toward the *Enterprise*. He slid to a halt. He could hear the low murmur of a crowd of people. Gasping, he straightened his formal tunic.

Lightheaded, still panting, Jim made himself breathe regularly. He forced himself into a semblance of composure.

He strode around a bend. VIPs packed the access tunnel. Starfleet officers, civilian dignitaries, and reporters from every news medium in the Federation all focused their attention on the other end of the corridor.

"Excuse me," Jim said to someone at the back of the crowd. "I'm supposed to be up front." As he moved through the crush, he became acutely aware of the eyes—pairs of eyes, circles of eyes, compound eyes—swiveling toward him. Everyone had come to congratulate Christopher Pike on his promotion to commodore, but at the moment most of them were staring at Jim.

Captain James T. Kirk, outwardly calm, pretending he barely noticed the gathering of half the brass in the Federation, strode toward Admiral Noguchi and Commodore Pike.

As he passed among the blue or red or gold of Starfleet uniforms, the black wool or brilliant silks of civilian formal clothing, two people more plainly dressed caught his attention. He stopped short. His composure evaporated.

"Mom! Sam—!" He hurried to them, hugged his mother, and clasped his elder brother's hand. "What are you doing here? When did you get here? How long can you stay?"

His mother smiled. "We came to see you take command of the *Enterprise*, of course," she said.

"But if you don't hurry up," Sam said, "they're going to auction it off to the highest bidder."

Jim glanced at Noguchi and Pike. Far from being ready to find someone else to take over Jim's command, Noguchi looked patient and amused. Anyone who spent time in space understood that the joy of seeing one's friends or relatives after long separation overwhelmed mere protocol.

Why, then, did Chris Pike stare at him with such grim disapproval?

Jim hugged his mother again, clapped Sam on the shoulder, and joined Noguchi and Pike, taking his place at Pike's left hand. The three walked together through the access tunnel to the *Enterprise*. The onlookers followed.

For the first time—officially—Jim approached the *Enterprise*. He had to behave as if he had never seen it before, as if he had not spent early-morning hours walking through its deserted corridors, its bridge and engine room and sick bay, its labs and computer section, even its arboretum and its recreation deck.

A tall, ascetically spare Vulcan stood at the main entrance hatch of the *Enterprise*. He wore a formal uniform in the blue of the science section.

This must be Commander Spock, the science officer of the *Enterprise*. Jim knew his reputation, but almost nothing of the Vulcan himself.

Jim had little use for science officers. They always wanted to impart far more unsolicited information than he needed at any given moment about any given problem. And every time he had made the mistake of actually asking a science officer a question, he had ended up feeling that he might as well be back in an Academy lecture hall.

Jim probably would not have much interaction with Commander Spock. With any luck, the Vulcan would be one of those withdrawn intellectual types who preferred to remain secluded with experiments somewhere in the depths of the ship's laboratories.

"Permission to come aboard, Commander Spock."

"Permission granted." The Vulcan spoke in a completely

44

emotionless tone. He stepped aside for Commodore Pike. "The ship, sir, is yours."

Without responding, Pike boarded the *Enterprise*.

As Jim passed Commander Spock, the Vulcan regarded him briefly, coolly, hardly appearing to notice him at all.

Mr. Spock took James Kirk's measure as the young captain followed Commodore Pike onto the *Enterprise*. The science officer had made it his business to learn about Captain Kirk. Starfleet was handing the ship over to a hero.

Commander Spock had little use for heroes. Whatever the self-sacrifice required for heroism, however commendable or admirable the actions might be, a person could only become a hero within an environment of chaos and destruction. In Commander Spock's view, foresight and rationality should prevent the evolution of any such environment. He wondered if James Kirk, facing a crisis, would choose rationality, or succumb to the lure of heroism.

The recreation deck had been turned into a reception hall. All the starship's officers had gathered there. A podium and lectern stood on the stage at one end; tables along one wall held trays of delicacies, ranks of champagne bottles, rows of sparkling glasses.

Commodore Pike led Admiral Noguchi and James Kirk to the stage. Noguchi invited the audience to be seated, paused for them to settle, and launched into a speech.

Though he was far from intoxicated, Jim had drunk enough to feel slightly disconnected from himself and his surroundings. His attention kept drifting. He sought out his family, wondering how long they could stay and how much time he would be able to spend with them. Astonished and delighted by their presence, he nevertheless wished they had come for some other occasion, or no occasion at all, when he could go on leave and give them his full attention.

Mom looks well, he thought. Much better than when she decided to go to Deneva to visit Aurelan and Sam. Dad's death hit us all, but it hit her hardest.

His vision blurred. Applause began. Jim jerked his attention to the present. Admiral Noguchi had finished his speech. Blinking furiously, Jim clapped politely and hoped no one noticed he was fighting tears. He had no idea what

Noguchi had said. For all he knew, Jim was applauding a compliment directed toward Starfleet's youngest captain.

Noguchi surrendered the lectern. Pike stepped forward, paused, and spoke with great deliberation.

Jim did not know Pike well. He had not even crossed his path for several years. But the commodore's appearance shocked him. Pike was only fifteen years older than Jim. Yet he looked so old—! Gray flecked his dark hair, and two vertical lines furrowed his cheeks. Pain or grief or exhaustion deepened his eyes.

". . . And I know," Pike said, "that Captain Kirk will find the *Enterprise* and its crew as faithful as I did."

Pike's eyes, too, filled with tears. Jim imagined himself in Pike's place: an honored officer; a commodore who would soon command far more than a single ship.

Far more, and far less. Without his own ship, he was planetbound and deskbound, responsible to a bureaucracy rather than to a quest for exploration and knowledge. For all Pike's honors and rank, Jim Kirk would not have traded places with him for anything in the universe.

"Captain," Pike said. "The starship *Enterprise* is yours." He shook Jim's hand.

After more polite applause, the audience fell silent. They looked at Jim. His mother and his brother looked at him. Pike looked at him. Noguchi looked at him. Jim had worried for days about what he should say, but he had somehow never got around to writing anything down. His hands grew cold and damp.

He hoped his hesitation would be taken for dignity or for a becoming modesty rather than for the utter terror it was. He hated public speaking. Jim Kirk's father had been a champion debater; Jim had sought out the extracurricular activity that conflicted most efficiently with debate, then joined it: the Academy judo team. He could get slammed onto a tatami mat several hundred times each evening, or he could get up to speak in front of several hundred people several times each month. He preferred the former then; he preferred it now. But he would not get out of this obligation with an exhibition of martial arts.

He clenched his hands around the edges of the lectern. The hard wood corners cut into his palms. Jim imagined that the whole *Enterprise* crew watched him with skepticism, compared him to Chris Pike, and found him lacking; he imagined that the Starfleet brass already wondered what in the universe could explain the hotshot reputation of this sweaty, speechless starship proto-commander. He wondered the same thing himself, not for the first time.

At the most important point of his career, he could think of no words at all. Living up to the expectation of his superiors, his peers, his family, living up to his own expectations, would take effort and discipline, every bit he possessed . . . and perhaps more. That was what scared him.

And it was the last thing he could say out loud.

"I . . ." He stopped, wishing desperately for inspiration. He caught Sam's eye. Sam put on an expression of rapt attention. Jim looked away. "I'll do my best to follow the tradition Commodore Pike has begun, for the starship *Enterprise* and for its officers and crew." He blurted out the words. If he looked at Sam, he would dissolve into laughter. He wanted to groan with embarrassment. What had he said? What did it *mean*? He should have been able to come up with something better than a line an ingenuous Cub Scout would disdain to use.

Yet the audience applauded him as politely as they had Noguchi, if not with the respect and admiration they had offered Pike. Jim remembered the one rule of public speaking that he did know: Shorter is better.

He surreptitiously rubbed his clammy palms down the sides of his pants just as Admiral Noguchi reached out to shake his hand.

Jim hoped Noguchi would return to the lectern and announce the next mission of the *Enterprise*. And he hoped he knew what it would be. The Federation was poised on the edge of an unprecedented expansion of the boundaries of explored space. Jim wanted to be in the vanguard of the discovery of new worlds, the contact with new peoples, the search for knowledge. He knew that the Federation planned an expedition toward the heart of the galaxy, to a region high in type G stars. Around such suns, carbon-based life, "life as we know it," had the best chance to appear and to evolve.

Jim wanted that mission. He wanted it so badly he could reach out and feel its shape with his empty hands. He had some hope of getting it, some hint that it might be given him. And Starfleet owed him this one.

They could hold only a single factor against him. He had never left Federation space. He had never participated in a first contact.

But Christopher Pike had the most first-contact experience of any officer in Starfleet. They were not giving the mission to him.

So obviously, Jim thought, they ought to give it to me.

But Noguchi said nothing of what he planned for his newest captain. A chime called attention to refreshments. Stewards popped corks from bottles. In a moment, the ceremonial atmosphere changed to the ambience of a party.

"Congratulations, captain." Noguchi smiled mischievously. "I have a surprise for you. No, don't quiz me. It's nearly ready, just be patient."

Jim felt that Noguchi had as good as told him his next assignment: the exploration voyage. His excitement and anticipation and joy felt like the bubbles in champagne.

"Hey, Jim—"

Sam's arm fell across his shoulders. Jim turned toward his brother. Sam grinned. Jim no longer tried to hold back his laughter.

"Great speech," Sam said.

"I agree completely," their mother said, smiling.

"Thank you, thank you." Jim gave mock bows to the points of the compass.

"Winona," Admiral Noguchi said to Jim's mother. "It's a pleasure to see you again. Especially now."

"It's been a long time, Kimitake, hasn't it?"

"Yes. A long time. Since before . . ." Noguchi stopped. "Well. George would have been very proud, I think."

"Yes. He would."

Noguchi offered Jim's mother his arm. "We mustn't offend the chefs by ignoring their day's work," he said. "I understand they've created quite a spread for us."

"Absolutely true," Jim said, then, quickly, "I mean . . . I heard the same thing."

Noguchi looked straight at him. "I'm told that the chocolate cake is particularly delectable. Winona?"

"Thank you, Kimi."

They walked away arm in arm, leaving Jim speechless.

"Jim, seriously, congratulations."

Jim grabbed his brother by both shoulders. "My lord, I'm glad to see you. When did you get in? Where's Aurelan? How's my nephew? Why didn't you tell me you were coming?"

"We just arrived. There's a xenobiology conference, so we got our ways paid. We weren't certain we'd arrive in time for the ceremony. We figured if we did, we'd surprise you. Peter's fine—he's learning geometry. Aurelan—" He smiled fondly. "She sends her love. But she's in the middle of an experiment and she couldn't leave it."

"You look great, Sam. Everything's going well?"

"Never better."

His elder brother was a handsbreadth taller than Jim, a handsbreadth wider across the shoulders. Living on a frontier world had tanned his skin and put lines around his eyes and mouth, good lines, of laughter and of squinting into the distance of a new planet. His eyes were the same hazel as Jim's, the same as their father's. Deneva's sun had bleached Sam's dark blond hair to streaky gold.

At the buffet, Sam handed him a glass of champagne, took one himself, and raised it in a toast.

"To my little brother and his ship." He drank.

Jim accepted the toast, but the last thing he wanted was a glass of wine. He exchanged it for a glass of sparkling cider.

"How's Mitch doing?" Sam asked. "And where's Len McCoy?"

"Gary's recovering. They claim. As for McCoy, damned if I know. I expected him to be here. Listen, Sam, Starfleet hasn't given me the orders for the *Enterprise* yet. If it's what I think—what I hope it is, it's going to take us a while to get ready. I'll have a little free time to spend with you and Mom."

"That would be great. But Jim—you've been waiting for this ship since you were fourteen. We didn't come here to hold you back from it. Don't worry. If we don't have time to catch up now, we will later."

"Yes . . . but it's been so long since I saw you."

"Mom's coming back to earth," Sam said. "Deneva's done her good. And she loves being a grandmother. I never saw her enjoy anything as much as she enjoys spoiling Peter. Jim, you ought to—" He stopped, heeding Jim's expression.

What I ought to do, Jim thought, is tell Sam what a fool I made of myself in front of Carol this afternoon.

"You ought to visit us and see how you like being an uncle," Sam said. "Anyway, Mom and Aurelan and I wrote a paper—it's coming out in *Jox*. She wants to follow up on it on earth. In Iowa, back on the homestead."

"That's good news," Jim said. If their mother was able to work again in the field she loved so much, then she had escaped the depression into which their father's death had plunged her. And despite the offhand way in which Sam tossed it off, placing a paper in the *Journal of Xenobiology* carried a great deal of prestige.

Sam nibbled on the corner of a slice of cake. "Jim, aren't you going to enjoy your own party? Kimitake was right—the chocolate cake is terrific."

"Captain Kirk."

Jim turned. "Commodore Pike," he said. "Congratulations. Sir, this is my brother, Sam Kirk."

"Dr. Kirk." Pike barely nodded. "You'll excuse us."

"Certainly," Sam said pleasantly, as if Pike had not as much as told him to get lost. "Talk to you later, Jim."

Pike stalked off. Jim had little choice but to follow.

"This is a good ship," Pike said. "A good crew." Pike could have eased the tension by putting them on a first-name basis, but he chose more formal terms. "They'll take care of you, captain. Do them the same courtesy."

"I'll do my best, commodore."

"Well. You'll want to meet your other officers. The *Enterprise*'s previous first officer received her own command. Your science officer will fill the position."

Jim was too startled to be diplomatic. "Commodore, I'm sorry if this conflicts with the plans of Commander Spock, but I've nominated Gary Mitchell to the position of first officer—" As he spoke, the party suddenly fell into one of those odd random silences. Jim shut up. At the same time, a vehement Scottish burr cut into the quiet.

"I canna understand why Starfleet *will* persist in handin'

over its best ships to inexperienced tyros—" He heard his own voice. He stopped.

Pike had brought Jim to a group of three officers. They turned, wondering if he had overheard them, just as he wondered if they had overheard his tactless remark.

"Captain Kirk," Pike said, "Commander Spock."

"Commander Spock," Jim said. He refrained from offering to shake the Vulcan's hand, not through resentment but because he knew Vulcans preferred not to be touched.

"Captain Kirk." Commander Spock acknowledged him with an inclination of his head. He showed no sign of having overheard Jim's conversation with Pike.

"Chief Engineer Montgomery Scott."

"Mr. Scott."

"How d'ye do, sir," the engineer said stiffly. The compact, stocky engineer had to fumble his champagne glass from right to left before he could shake hands with Kirk. He wore his uniform jacket with a kilt and sporran. "Ye have the finest ship in Starfleet to live up to, captain."

"I'm sure I do, Mr. Scott." Jim tried to give no more sign than any Vulcan that he knew what Scott thought of him, and he chose not to notice Scott's implied challenge.

"And Lieutenant Uhura, your communications officer."

"Captain Kirk," she said, her voice low and musical.

Her long, fine hand curved gently around his. He expected fragility. Instead he sensed the strength of intensity, the firmness of intelligence. He forgot his uneasiness, Scott's belligerence, Spock's unreadable expression.

Beginning with his first command, Jim had trained himself not to get involved with anyone to whom he might have to give an order. Interactions between commander and subordinates must be kept at an impersonal level. Anything more than strict civility could wreck morale faster and more thoroughly than any outside force. So Jim schooled himself not to react to beauty, at least not under shipboard conditions. He made himself nearly impervious to charm, and he resisted becoming too friendly with anyone, man or woman, whom he commanded.

Meeting Lieutenant Uhura made him wish he was still a second lieutenant, free of all the responsibilities a captain carried, so he could sit at her feet and gaze into her deep brown eyes and listen to a voice like song.

She drew her hand away. Jim realized he had been gaping at her like a witless schoolboy.

"Er, yes, Lieutenant Uhura. Glad to make your acquaintance."

The three officers had spent years working out the formula by which they interacted. James Kirk introduced a new unknown into the equation. They sized him up, measured him, and wondered if he could center himself within their orbits, or if, like a rogue star, he would enter their system on a hyperbolic course, perturb their paths, and leave chaos behind him.

Pike started to say something, then apparently thought better of it.

"I have an appointment," he said. "I'll have to take my leave of you now. Uhura, Scotty—"

"Good-bye, sir."

"Fare ye well, sir."

"And Mr. Spock . . ."

"Live long and prosper, Commodore Pike."

"Thank you."

He turned and walked away, straight and tense.

On the other side of the rec deck, Hikaru Sulu stood alone, holding a glass of champagne he had snagged from a steward so he would have something in his hand. Drinking anything would put him straight to sleep. Other than a few hours' nap on the beach, he had not slept in two days.

Compared to parties at the Academy dorm, this party remained horribly staid. He supposed the same would be true of most formal Starfleet affairs. Hikaru knew no one; all the other guests stood in tight clusters, offering little opportunity for him to introduce himself.

He compared this experience to the time five years ago, back on Ganjitsu, when he had sneaked on board *Aerfen* to have a look around. Of course he got caught, but instead of tossing the fifteen-year-old colonist out, Hunter's second in command showed him around. He had felt welcomed. On the *Enterprise*, he felt alien.

Never mind; with any luck he would be gone before he got acquainted with anyone.

He could not help overhearing conversations. They helped him understand the somber mood. The officers of the *Enterprise* regretted the departure of Christopher Pike. They were not sure what to expect of the new captain. They had heard the confused official reports from Ghioghe: James Kirk had lost his ship in that disaster, but in doing so he had saved the lives of many people and nearly lost his own. He had come out of it with a medal, a promotion . . . and the *Enterprise*. They knew his reputation: youngest midshipman ever to enter the Academy, youngest captain in Starfleet. But no one knew if Kirk was a hotshot space jockey who worked his crew like machines and kept all the glory, or if he included his people in a partnership of sentient beings worthy of a share in the honors as well as the risks.

"Hikaru?"

Surprised to hear his given name, Sulu turned.

"Dr. Kirk!" he said.

"I thought it was you," Sam Kirk said. "How are you? My gods, you were just a kid when I saw you last." He grinned and shook his head ruefully. "Why do people always say that to their friends' children?"

"I don't know, doctor," Sulu said.

"My name's Sam. When you were twelve, okay, I was 'Dr. Kirk.' But here you are, in Starfleet—in the Academy?"

"I just graduated."

"Congratulations. How are your folks?"

"They're fine. I think. Sometimes it's hard to tell from letters. I call them when I can."

"When did you see them last?"

"I haven't been home since I entered the Academy. It's too far, too expensive. I was hoping to get out there pretty soon, but . . ." He stopped. It was all too easy to remember the homesickness he had felt his whole first year at the Academy, too easy to let in the pain of expectations disappointed. "But that isn't going to work out." He changed the subject. "Are you related to Captain Kirk?"

"Jim's my kid brother. He's following the family tradition." Sam gestured, indicating the ship, meaning Starfleet in general. "I was sorry to see that your mother isn't attending the xeno conference."

"She couldn't. She's way out by the Orion frontier. It's a

ten-week trip by passenger liner. She couldn't afford to leave for the whole growing season."

"And your father? I just bought his new collection. He really does catch the feel of living and working on a new world." Sam chuckled. "The first time I read one of his poems, I thought, well, that looks easy, anybody can be a poet. So I tried it. It *isn't* easy. In fact, I can't do it at all."

"Not many can," Hikaru said. When he was much younger he used to wonder exactly what his father *did*. Sometimes it seemed like he did nothing. A few years later, when Hikaru tried his own hand at poetry, he learned how much work went into its creation. Even the "nothing" time was hard work.

"Is he writing something new?"

"He only just finished *Nine Suns*," he said mildly. "He gets a bit of a rest now." People asked him that question all the time.

"Oh, of course, I see," Sam Kirk said, offhand. "How do you like the *Enterprise?*"

"I don't know."

"Come on—I'm not going to go carrying tales of disaffection back to my little brother."

"Honestly—I don't know. I've only been here since this afternoon. I never met Commodore Pike. I haven't met Captain Kirk. I've hardly met anybody. I was supposed to be posted to the frontier."

"I expect you'll like it here. It's true, Jim does have the capacity to be a stubborn—" He stopped and smiled sheepishly. "But he's basically a decent sort."

"That's good to know," Hikaru said, keeping his voice carefully neutral.

Sam glanced across the room. "Looks like Pike is finished with him—come on. I'll introduce you."

Hikaru followed, nervous, trying to think of the best way to bring up his transfer with the captain.

Jim sipped his fruit juice, wondering how to break the awkward silence Christopher Pike had left behind him.

"Finished the official business?" Sam slung his arm over Jim's shoulders.

Jim started. He had not heard Sam approach.

54

Sam glanced after Pike, who left through the main entrance without speaking to anyone, without looking back.

"What did Pike want?" Sam asked dryly. "To give you officer-and-gentleman lessons?"

Jim elbowed his brother in the ribs. Too much had already been said directly or overheard for one evening. Perhaps Pike had good reason for his abrupt attitude, and perhaps he did not, but they could discuss him somewhere well out of the hearing of his former colleagues.

At Sam's comment, Commander Spock grew cool.

"Like Commodore Pike," he said evenly, "I, too, have . . . responsibilities to attend to. If you will excuse me."

"I'll come wi' ye," Scott said hastily. "The . . . the engines need checkin'."

"Very well," Jim said.

They left the room.

Uhura had overheard Captain Kirk's remark to Commodore Pike; she knew that if she had heard it, Mr. Spock could not have missed it. And she knew perfectly well that James Kirk had overheard Scott's comment. She weighed pretending neither remark had ever been uttered.

"Captain," she said, choosing her words carefully, "we've all been with Captain Pike for a long time. People take time to get used to change."

"I see that," he said. "And some take more time than others."

Unaware of the incidents or the tension, Sam broke in. "Jim, I want you to meet Hikaru Sulu. His folks are old friends of mine and Aurelan's. His mother's a colleague."

"Sir," Hikaru said.

"Mr. Sulu, of course." James Kirk extended his hand in a firm grip. "Have you met Lieutenant Uhura?"

"Very briefly, sir."

"I appreciate your cutting your leave short in order to join us," Kirk said.

"Yes, captain, I'd like to discuss—"

"How did your fencing tournament go?"

"Uh . . . I won, sir," Hikaru said, surprised that Kirk even knew about it.

"Which division? Epée? Saber?"

"Saber and the all-around, sir."

"The all-around! Congratulations. I did a bit of fencing in school—we should set up a match sometime."

"Yes, sir," Hikaru said. Maybe he could get the transfer before he was forced to defeat his C.O. in a fencing match. "But, sir—"

"Sam, let's get Mom and I'll take you on a tour."

"Captain—" Hikaru said again.

"Sure," Sam said. "In a minute. Hikaru, I was in the lab the other day. I needed a normal human blood sample—"

"What?" Hikaru said, distracted. His hands felt damp and cold and his heart pounded from the adrenaline: he was trying to tell a captain of Starfleet that the captain had made a mistake, and it was not an easy job.

"To use as a control," Sam said. "So I volunteered one of my graduate students. All I wanted was a couple of cc's of blood. But he backed off from my perfectly harmless hypo at half the speed of light, and he said, 'No, no, you can't take blood from me—I'm a facultative hemophiliac!' "

Sam waited expectantly.

Hikaru stared at him, then suddenly burst out laughing.

James Kirk stared at them both as if they had lost their minds.

"That's a good one," Hikaru said. "But I'll bet you don't find too many people to tell it to."

"I thought I might get some use out of it at the conference, but I wanted to try it on somebody first."

"Have you thought of handing out universal translators when you tell it?" Jim asked dryly.

Sam laughed. "Excuse us, Hikaru, Lieutenant Uhura. Come on, Jim, let's go see your ship, and I'll explain everything to you."

They drifted to the edge of the crowd. They joined their mother and Admiral Noguchi, who were talking over old times and recalling George Samuel Kirk, Senior. Noguchi and Jim's father had served together, but now, as the admiral reminisced, describing events Jim had never even heard about, the young captain felt a sudden pang of resentment. Noguchi had probably spent more time with George Kirk than Winona, Sam, and Jim put together. It was the chosen life of a Starfleet officer, the life Winona knew about when she chose him.

But their lives, the lives they chose for their children, precluded the possibility that George would have much effect on Jim or Sam. They had barely known their father. Perhaps, if he had lived, they would eventually have learned to know him better. For himself, Jim doubted that a parent and a child could become friends as adults, if they had been strangers when the child was young.

Their father was never reconciled to Sam's rejecting the place in the Starfleet Academy that had been reserved for him, for George Samuel Kirk, Jr., at his birth. It was Jim who followed George into Starfleet. But, Jim reflected, he would change the pattern of his father's life as profoundly as Sam. He was glad that Carol had refused him. Jim would never leave someone behind who would wait for his visits, a stranger.

Jim felt recovered from his afternoon with Vanli. He moved away long enough to get a glass of champagne. When he turned back, Winona and Sam were greeting an old Starfleet acquaintance and Jim was alone with Noguchi.

The older man smiled mischievously. "I'll be making an announcement shortly, Jim," he said. "I think you'll find it interesting."

"Admiral, Commodore Pike has informed me that Commander Spock has been given the position of first officer."

"That's right. I approved his promotion myself."

"I was under the impression that I'd have some say in my senior staff."

"You were out of commission when the choice had to be made. Why? Surely you can't object to Mr. Spock."

"It has nothing to do with Spock, admiral. I've nominated Gary Mitchell to the post. I wasn't aware of any objection to him, either."

Noguchi shook his head. "No, Jim. It's impossible."

"Admiral, I was hoping you'd back me up on this."

"I could, but I won't. One of Starfleet's strengths is its diversity. You and Mitch are simply too much alike. A first officer should compensate for your weaknesses and temper your strengths. I want you to work with someone who will create some synergy."

"I wasn't aware," Jim said stiffly, "that you feel I have weaknesses that need compensation."

"Don't get your torus pinched, Jim," Noguchi said. "This is supposed to be a party."

"Then I'd like to discuss the subject in a more appropriate setting."

"But it isn't open to discussion," the admiral said. To underline his meaning, he went in search of another conversation and left Jim fuming.

I have a couple of months, at least, before Gary's ready, Jim thought. Maybe by then I can convince the admiral . . . He put aside his aggravation, confident that eventually he would change Noguchi's mind.

"Ready to give us that tour?" Sam said cheerfully.

"Sure." Even the meddling of Starfleet brass could not damage Jim's joy at seeing his mother and his brother again. "Come on, let's get out of here."

They went into the ship's quiet corridors and left the noisy party behind.

"Jim," Winona said, "are you really all right?"

"Of course I am, Mom. Good as new, they say. I wish you wouldn't worry about me."

"Worrying comes with the job."

"You never tell us anything, dammit," Sam said. "How do you think we felt when we found out you'd been in the hospital and hadn't even told us?"

"What could you have done? Come back to earth? By the time you arrived, I'd be all right or it'd be too late."

"Under what circumstances *does* your family get notified?" Winona asked. "When you're dead?"

"That's close, Mom. I know how you feel, but nothing else makes sense. I'm sure Dad left the same instructions."

"Yes," Winona said. "He did. But I hoped yours might be different."

Jim refrained from saying something he would later regret. He did not want to argue with his mother, even though he felt she had delivered him a low blow.

"Say, Jim." Sam's cheerfulness sounded forced. "The biologists' grapevine has been working overtime lately."

"Oh? What about?"

"Don't you know?"

"Why should I know?"

"The grapevine carries rumors about other subjects than theoretical biology."

"In other words, Carol Marcus and I are hot gossip."

"You've got it, brother. What's the story?"

"There isn't any story," Jim said. "And as far as hot gossip goes . . . the temperature registers absolute zero."

"Oh," Sam said. "Damn. I hoped . . . Carol Marcus is good people, Jim."

"We're getting into dangerous territory." Jim changed the subject abruptly. "Do you want that tour? There's a lot to see. The bridge is incredible." As he described the ship, his concern about Gary and his disappointment about Carol slipped briefly away. He could not have pushed aside his enthusiasm if he had tried. "Mom, Sam, why don't you write a grant proposal for some deep-space research? You won't believe the labs on this ship. First I want to show you the observation deck—"

He led them deeper into the *Enterprise* and into an ordinary-looking lounge at the back of the saucer section.

"Watch this!" he said. "Open!"

The shield drew back from the crystal wall, revealing a 180-degree view of the cavernous volume of Spacedock. A mechanic in a pressure suit sailed past.

"You've *got* to come out with us sometime and see interstellar space from here!"

"I'd like that," Winona said. "Jim . . ."

"Yes, Mom?"

"I'm going home. The house hasn't been opened in five years, and . . ." She stopped. "Jim, if you can—if you want to—come for a visit . . . if you want to come home . . ."

"I . . ." He could hardly conceive of returning to the Iowa farm. He had not visited it since the service for his father. The farm held memories, good and bad, that he would no longer be able to keep locked away if he returned. Just to consider going back made him imagine that he smelled hay drying in the sun. He shook his head, trying to be amused at the strength of the memories, but disturbed nonetheless.

"Wonder if the tree house made it through the last five winters," Sam said.

"I'll try to visit, Mom." Jim hoped he was telling her the truth. "I don't know when. It depends on my orders."

He closed the shield, hiding the crystal wall and the lights and activity of Spacedock. He wished the *Enterprise* were sailing among the stars with no barriers and no limits. Out there difficult decisions seemed much easier to make, and the complications of life never doubled and redoubled.

"Come on," he said. "You've got to see the labs."

Sam glanced at him quizzically. "I thought you'd never been on board this ship before today."

Jim blushed. "I mean—Oh, hell. I sneaked on board . . . Carol and I sneaked on board a few weeks back. Just for a look around. I couldn't resist. But keep it quiet—it's bad form." He left the observation deck and led them to the turbo-lift.

"Someday, Jim," Winona said, more concerned than chiding, "you're going to step out of bounds and somebody is going to notice."

"I'd have to run into a real hard-liner to have any trouble over my visit."

"Starfleet is well supplied with hard-liners."

"You can't get anywhere in Starfleet unless you push the limits. If you don't, you end up mummified at a desk."

"And if you push them too far," Sam said, "you end up mummified at a desk. Like Chris Pike."

"What are you talking about?"

"That's the gossip—Pike spent too little time playing Starfleet politics, too much time annoying the wrong people, and struck out on his own a few times too often."

"So, as punishment, he gets promoted to commodore?"

"Yes. And you pity him because of it." The turbo-lift slowed and stopped.

"That's ridiculous."

"Don't discount your brother's advice so cavalierly, Jim," Winona said. "It isn't nearly as ridiculous as—" The lift doors opened. She interrupted herself. "I don't remember that Starfleet vessels smell like horse barns."

The evocative scent of drying hay wafted through the lower deck. Jim frowned. "They don't." Unsettled, he led the way from the turbo-lift. In a starship, anything strange or unknown could mean danger.

The horse-barn odor grew more intense. Unless the ventilation system had broken down, the only possible source was the shuttlecraft deck at the far end of the corridor.

The double doors slid aside. Squinting in the dim light, Jim strode onto the catwalk above the deck.

The shuttlecraft had been moved to one side, crammed close together and walled off with portable partitions, leaving most of the deck space open.

A makeshift pen stood in the center of the deck. Straw littered its floor. A dark shape hunkered inside it.

"What in the world—!" Winona joined him on the catwalk.

"Lights." The deck lights faded on.

The iridescent creature snorted and bolted to its feet, spraddle-legged and challenging, its small head up, ears pricked, nostrils flared. Its coat shone in shades of black and purple and green.

"What *off* the world is more like it," Sam said.

It saw them. It snorted again and stamped the deck, its hooves ringing on the metal plates. More like an eagle than a horse, it screamed.

And then it arched its neck, reared, and pawed the air.

With a sound like storm-wind against ancient trees, it spread its great black wings.

# Chapter 3

JIM, WINONA, AND Sam stared in amazement.

"Is it just me who's dreaming this, or are both of you dreaming it too?"

"That's fantastic," Sam said. "I had no idea anyone had gone so far with restructured recombinants! It is Terran, isn't it? Not an offworld species?"

"How should I know?" Jim said, irritated. All he wanted to know was how it got onto his ship, and why.

"I'm afraid it's going to hurt itself," Winona said. "I'll try to calm it down."

The creature beat its wings and screamed again.

"Mom—that thing is dangerous!"

"What do you people think you're doing?"

Jim hardly had time to turn toward the new voice. A small black-clad figure ran past Winona and plunged headlong down the companionway, barely touching the treads. Her iridescent black hair streamed behind her. She ran across the deck toward the terrified horse—horse? She dropped the boots she carried and slid under the corral rail. Afraid she would be trampled, afraid the creature might even take off and attack her with its hooves, Jim rushed after her.

The horse snorted and quieted. Its wings still fluttered, outstretched, as if it were an eagle keeping its balance on the gloved hand of a falconer. Its shoulders gleamed with nervous sweat. It put its head down and buried its nose beneath the arm of the stranger.

She whispered to the creature, scratched its ears and

cradled its head and blew in its nostrils. It sighed back, a soft and quiet sound. She stroked its neck and tangled her fingers in its mane. The straw crackled as the creature shifted its weight to sidle closer to her. It placed its hooves only a handsbreadth from her bare feet.

"For gods' sakes, be careful," Jim said.

"Be quiet," she said in a low and soothing voice, without turning to face him.

"You're going to get stepped on!"

"No, I'm not, don't worry. Besides, she's not even shod—and she's very light on her feet." She smiled at her own joke, then sobered again when she saw Jim's expression. "What did you do? You scared her to death."

"I turned on the lights," Jim said, his irritation increasing. "I wanted to know who rearranged my shuttlecraft deck."

"Are you the deck officer? Admiral Noguchi said you were on leave till this evening, and then you'd be busy—he said she'd be safe here, and nobody would bother her."

"Admiral Noguchi—?"

"This is the only place she can stay for a long trip."

"What long trip?!" Jim said.

She fed the creature a piece of carrot, though Jim would have sworn her hands had been empty. "She won't hurt your deck, especially if you don't scare her again."

"I'm not the deck officer."

"Oh. What's the big deal, then?"

"I'm the captain," he said. He took the steps of the companionway three at a time and headed toward the turbolift. As he reached it, the doors slid open. Admiral Noguchi hurried out, so intent on the transmission flimsy in his hand that Jim had to step back quickly to keep the older officer from running into him.

"Sir! Admiral Noguchi!"

"Jim!" He sounded disappointed. "What are you doing here? You've discovered my surprise, I suppose—did you meet Ms. Lukarian? We can make the announcement together."

"But I thought—Who is Ms. Lukarian? You mean that— that Amazon down on my landing deck trying to keep her flying horse from destroying the place?"

"Jim, get hold of yourself! You're practically hysterical.

What's the matter with you? Have you had too much to drink?"

"No, sir. At least, I didn't think so. Admiral, there is a creature obstructing my shuttlecraft deck."

"Calm down, Jim. You're not going where you'll need a shuttlecraft. Not this mission."

"What exactly," Jim said, suspecting that he no longer wanted to hear the answer, "is the mission?"

Noguchi handed him the transmission flimsy. "An elegant solution to the traveling salesman problem, wouldn't you say?"

Jim looked at it. What traveling salesman? Noguchi had cut orders for the *Enterprise* for the next three months, during which the ship would spend a day at each of thirty different starbases, starting with Starbase 13.

"The Phalanx?" Jim said. "Starbase 13? Starbase 13 is a waste of time and resources. It ought to be shut down!"

"Starbase 13 is of tremendous strategic importance. I'm afraid I gave the mathematicians some problems when I insisted your route begin there." Noguchi chuckled. He explained the difficulty of determining the most efficient route among several different points. Mathematicians had solved the traveling salesman problem in two dimensions, but three dimensions added several levels of complexity.

"I . . . I don't understand," Jim said. "What's the *mission?*"

"I had three major factors to consider," Noguchi said. "First, to give you a chance to regain your strength—"

"There's nothing wrong with me!" Jim snapped. "I'm perfectly healthy."

"Second," Noguchi said, ignoring Jim's protest, "to give you time to acquaint yourself with ship and crew."

"That's why I've been looking forward to a challenging mission, sir—"

"And third, to deal with the results of the starbase survey. You did see them, didn't you?"

"No, sir, I didn't. I was out of touch—I'm completely recovered now!—but I *was* out of touch for a few months."

"The results were a shock, Jim. On every starbase we surveyed, morale is terrible. Especially," he said, "at Starbase 13. We take people and send them off to the corners of the universe, away from their homes and families, and we completely ignore their needs. I'm going to change that. I've chosen you to help me."

They reached the catwalk and Noguchi climbed down the companionway. Jim followed. Sam and Winona remained at the corral, where Ms. Lukarian toweled her creature's sweaty shoulders. Winona rubbed the creature behind the ears, while Sam inspected the complex joint of wing to body.

"Ms. Lukarian," Admiral Noguchi said.

She turned, smiling. When she saw Jim her expression clouded. "Admiral," she said, and, warily, "captain."

"Jim, I want you to meet Amelinda Lukarian, general manager of the Warp-Speed Classic Vaudeville Company. Ms. Lukarian, Captain James T. Kirk."

"How do you do, captain."

His fingers closed over hers, nearly obscuring them, but her hand was hard and strong, with traces of callus.

"Vaudeville? What's vaudeville?" Jim tried, and failed, to place the word in the realm of high-energy physics, as "warp-speed" seemed to indicate, or in the realm of commercial applications of faster-than-light travel, as the "company" hinted. And where did the flying horse fit in? A trademark? An advertising gimmick? If it were either of those, how had Starfleet become involved?

"Vaudeville is entertainment," Lukarian said.

"You'll be at the company's disposal during its tour."

Speechless with shock, Jim stared at Noguchi.

"This animal is incredible, Jim," Sam said. "The anatomical problem of the wings—"

"Admiral, you can't mean Starfleet has assigned the *Enterprise*—"

"Shh, Athene, easy," Winona said, trying to calm the creature, which started at Jim's raised voice. "Jim—"

"—that Starfleet has assigned a constellation-class starship with a crew of four hundred thirty to ferry around a—a mutant horse and its trainer?" Jim felt as if even his mother had taken sides against him.

"Don't shout," Lukarian said. "She's mostly Arabian—she's very high-strung. You'll frighten her again."

"I mean to tell you," the admiral said calmly, "that *I* have given you the task of getting the vaudeville company to the starbases to perform for Starfleet personnel, safely, on schedule—and without argument. I also have given you command of this ship. Neither order is carved in stone. Is that understood?"

His last three words brought a sharp tone to his voice. Jim met his gaze. Staring into the older officer's hard brown eyes, he began to believe the legends of the admiral's temper, glacially slow to break, but volcanic in intensity.

"Any further questions, *Captain* Kirk?"

Jim hesitated for perhaps a second, almost a second too long. "No, sir," he said before Admiral Noguchi spoke again.

The admiral turned his back on Jim. "Ms. Lukarian, are your people comfortable? Do you have everything you need?"

"Some of them are a little shaken up," she said. "Most of us have never been in a transporter before. Athene and I came up in a courier ship, so she's a little nervous. We're used to traveling by train."

"I'm sure, once you get your space legs, you'll find it quite tolerable. It's extraordinarily beautiful in space." He chuckled. "And you'll find that you have more room to move around in than you would on a train." Noguchi clasped Lukarian's small hand. "I'm grateful for your willingness to assist Starfleet on such short notice. And I'm looking forward to making the announcement. Are you ready?"

"As soon as one of the riggers gets here to stay with Athene. Are you sure you don't want us to perform?"

"That is a very generous offer," Admiral Noguchi said. "But I planned for you to be guests tonight. I don't think guests should have to sing for their supper."

"Okay. I'll bring the company upstairs in a minute."

"Good. Please don't hesitate to call on me at any time. My office will always know how to reach me."

Admiral Noguchi climbed the companionway to the catwalk and disappeared, leaving Jim and Lukarian facing each other.

"This is impossible," Jim said. "Simply impossible."

"I can't afford to lose this commission," Lukarian said. "We're not leaving—there's no way you can make us."

"Would you like to bet on that?"

"Ease up, Jim," Sam said.

"Name the amount," Lukarian said. "Losing couldn't make things any worse."

"Don't challenge me on my own ship, Ms. Lukarian," Jim said. "It's a very foolish thing to do."

"Rather like opposing an admiral's pet project," Winona said, not to Lukarian but to Jim.

"I *will not* give up this commission." Lukarian's voice hardened. Behind her, the winged horse sensed the anger between the humans. She snorted and stamped nervously, prancing from one side of the small corral to the other.

"You're scaring her," Lukarian said. "Will you leave?"

"Jim," Winona said as Jim was about to retort. Her tone was both angry and disappointed.

"*What*, Mother?"

"Surrender gracefully."

Jim felt that he had a right to be furious—in fact he thought he had kept his temper remarkably well under the circumstances. Still, his complaint was more with Admiral Noguchi than with Amelinda Lukarian.

Athene nudged Lukarian. Lukarian put her arms around the creature's neck, whispered to it, and laid her cheek against its dark forehead. "Go away," she said.

Winona touched Jim's arm and gestured toward the exit.

"Try to keep that beast under control, Ms. Lukarian," Jim said.

On the way back to the recreation deck, Jim and his mother and brother maintained an awkward silence. When they heard the clatter and hum of the party, Winona stopped.

"I have to get some sleep," she said. "It's been a long day."

"Do you want company back to the hotel?" Sam said.

"Don't be silly. Enjoy the party, Sam. Jim, I want to talk to you."

"I ought to—"

"This won't take long." She walked down the corridor toward the Spacedock gangway.

Sam gave him a sympathetic shrug. They both knew better than to argue with her when she used that tone.

Her arms folded and her head down, Winona gazed thoughtfully at the deck.

"What's the matter, Mom?" Jim asked.

"You have an interesting way of handling Starfleet politics, Jim. Not very effective. But interesting."

"But I thought . . . the admiral led me to believe . . ."

"Kimi never does anything without a good reason. That's beside the point. We aren't discussing his behavior, we're discussing yours. He gave you an order and you argued with it—because it didn't suit your fancy!"

"He could have—"

*"We aren't talking about him!"* she said angrily. "Don't you remember anything your father told you? Don't you even remember the mistakes he made? You can't navigate through Starfleet politics by the seat of your arrogance! Someday you're going to need—to be forced—to disobey the command of a superior officer. You're going to have to defend your actions. If you've built a reputation as a headstrong twit, you'll get your legs kicked out from under you. Not to mention your career."

"I think my actions speak for themselves."

"Do they? What, exactly, do they say? Let's take an example. You were incredibly rude to that little child—"

"Little child? She's an adult sentient being—who has a screaming monster on my shuttlecraft deck!"

"She's no more than twenty and she's responsible for a whole company, not to mention the 'screaming monster.' Can't you see she's hanging on to this job for her life?"

"No, and I don't see how you could, either."

"It was obvious. It sounded to me like this is her company's last chance to survive!"

"Maybe if they're living that close to the edge, they *ought* to go out of business."

She looked at him for a moment, uncomprehending, then shook her head. "It's too bad, Captain Kirk, that everybody can't be as perfect and successful as you are."

She turned without another word and walked away from him, out of the *Enterprise* and into Spacedock. He took one step after her, then stopped. He had no idea what to say to her, and she was so angry—he was so angry—that if he followed her they would get into another argument. Yet Winona had made an irrefutable point. He had been inexcusably rude to Amelinda Lukarian.

He headed toward the recreation deck, wishing he could go anywhere else besides back to the party.

Sam waited where Jim had left him, leaning casually against the bulkhead with one knee drawn up and the sole of his boot pressed against the wall.

"All clear?"

Jim shrugged.

"Reading the riot act time, huh?" Sam said.

"She's not real happy with me," Jim said. "But, dammit, Sam—I wanted . . . I *expected* . . . a decent assignment from Noguchi. I earned it—I deserve something—!"

"Something where you could cover yourself with more glory?"

"Glory?" He turned on his brother, furious. "Do you think that's why I'm in Starfleet? Do you think getting blasted into the middle of next week qualifies as glory?"

"No. But I'm beginning to wonder if you do."

"I don't. Believe me, I don't. The last six months were no fun."

"Then why don't you cut yourself a little slack? If you can't, let Kimi do it for you."

"I don't want any slack—especially from my C.O.!"

"He didn't mean it as an insult. Look, he's known our family for a long time . . ."

"That's just fine," Jim said. "That's just what I need, an admiral who treats me like I'm still fifteen."

Sam grinned. "No, he treats *me* like I'm fifteen. That's when he met me. He treats *you* like you're eight."

"Did anybody ever tell you how effective your reassurance is?" Jim said with sarcasm.

"People tell me that all the time. People come to me especially to get reassurance. And I'm assuring you that Kimitake Noguchi is giving you a gift. Try to accept it in the spirit in which it's offered."

"When he makes that announcement, I'm going to be a laughingstock! You'd give this job to somebody who can't do anything else, somebody you don't trust anymore, somebody washed up, used up—" He caught his breath, suddenly afraid the pain would return, the pain and the nothingness.

"Jim!" Sam grabbed him around the shoulders.

Jim pulled away, embarrassed.

"Is that what you're afraid of?" Sam said.

"I'm not afraid—"

"Stop it! Don't hide from me! Maybe you can hide from everybody else, but you can't hide from me!"

"How can I know," Jim whispered, "when I get a mission like the last one, how can I know how I'll react until I face it? I have to be sure, Sam. I have to know if I . . ."

"If you still have your nerve?"

Jim could not reply.

"You're not broken, Jim. Dammit, don't you think I'd feel it, don't you think I'd know if you were?"

"*I* don't know!"

"I think Kimi's right to give you this time," Sam said. "I think you need it."

"I don't—and I don't think I need any more lectures from my own family, either!"

He fled into the party and hid himself in the crowd.

Soon the vaudeville company arrived. Jim tried to listen while Admiral Noguchi introduced them, but he had to put most of his attention into pretending he liked the idea of spending the next three months with a bunch of entertainers, traipsing around the Phalanx.

Koronin looked for her pet. "Come, Starfleet!"

The little pink primate whispered at her from the nest it made at her feet each night. It climbed from the fur blanket it had adopted as its own, bounded across the bed, and leaped to her shoulder.

"There," she said, "are you hungry? Be a good pet. Put on your costume and perhaps I'll give you breakfast."

Starfleet comprehended perhaps one word in a hundred, but "hungry," "costume," and "breakfast" formed a major portion of its vocabulary. Her pet climbed down her leg and scampered around the bed, looking for its clothes: little black trousers and a gold velour shirt.

It amused Koronin that the creature looked so much like a type of human being, for among the species of the Federation, humans most earned her ire. It amused her to dress her pet in the uniform and insignia of a Starfleet officer. It did not amuse her that the creature rebelled against its cunning boots. Koronin could force Starfleet to wear them, but the primate staggered when it tried to walk, slipped and fell when it tried to climb, crouched on the floor and chewed at the leather around its toes when it grew frustrated, then huddled in a miserable heap and whimpered until Koronin freed it of the footgear. The staggering and slipping and toe chewing afforded Koronin hours of laughter, but the huddling and whimpering bored her. Even a good swat would not move the creature when it got to that state. So for the moment she let it go unshod. But she was determined eventually to break it to the boots.

While Starfleet rooted for its clothes like an idiot child, Koronin checked the control surfaces of the ship. Gold inlay traced filigree patterns on panels of translucent pink jade. The government officer had spent great sums on the visual decoration of his command balcony. Koronin supposed the officer assuaged the guilt he felt for such expenditures with the cold sparseness of his personal area. That suited her; the officer had lavished money or credit on things with which Koronin would not have bothered, leaving her the pleasure of ripping out his hard bunk and suiting her own fancy in replacing it.

She wondered how many loyal subjects of the empire knew the uses to which the oligarchy put their tithes. She wondered how many loyal subjects knew about the oligarchy in the first place. Koronin had been raised to revere the empress, but among the highest class it was an open secret that the oligarchs controlled a powerless, toothless, heirless sovereign. The outcasts knew the secret and held an invidious rumor in great credence: Koronin had heard, from numerous sources, that the oligarchy deliberately allowed the empress's brain to deteriorate to the vegetative state, then kept the body alive with machines and replacement therapy. When Koronin was younger she might not have believed it; but she believed it now.

"Starfleet!"

The pet yelped in fear, scampered to her, and cringed at her feet.

"So," she said. "You got your shirt on correctly today. You may have some breakfast, then."

The animal moaned and wiggled with pleasure. She held a bit of fruit just out of its reach and laughed as it leaped at her hand.

"Be still!"

Starfleet crouched, quivering, following the food with its intent and mournful gaze.

"Good," she said, and gave it the fruit.

It gobbled the fruit and looked around for more.

Koronin forgot about the animal. She studied the free-floating star map to decide the best way to harry Phalanx shipping. Too near the main body of Federation space would bring a patrol after her; too near the far tip of the intrusion and *Quundar* would meet the defenses of a Federation starbase. But the center, now: the center seemed quite vulnerable.

"Serjeant."

"Yes, Koronin."

He answered with commendable deference and he used the proper form, no longer addressing her as "my lady." Spoken by a member of a bandit work crew, the title was an insult.

She took the title most seriously; she would not use it again until she regained it in the eyes of the highest stratum of her society. But she would regain it.

"Prepare a course to the Federation Phalanx."

Starfleet stewards never let the detritus of a party collect; half-empty glasses and dirty plates, littered trays and open bottles vanished as soon as they appeared. When all but a few guests had strolled off to their beds, a single table held a few bottles of cooling champagne, a fan-shaped array of champagne flutes, and a tray of hors d'oeuvres, as if in preparation for another, much smaller party.

Jim sat by an observation port, occasionally glancing into the Spacedock bay. He was too tired and keyed up even to feel sleepy. He wanted to try to explain to his mother why he had been so angry; he wanted to talk to Sam and apologize for blowing up at his concern. But Winona would be sound asleep, and Sam, still going strong, had liberated a guitar when the musicians were dismissed. He played it softly, accompanying Lieutenant Uhura, who strummed a small harp and sang a lilting Irish song. A couple of the members of the vaudeville company remained, but Amelinda Lukarian had vanished.

In a better mood, Jim would have joined the singers and happily listened to Lieutenant Uhura all night long. Instead, he rose and left the hall, pausing at the serving table to pick up two glasses and a full bottle of champagne.

"Jim, wait!"

Sam joined him at the turbo-lift. He carried a third glass and a small storage container.

"I wondered how long it would take you to get around to this," Sam said.

"Maybe I'm just going off to get drunk. In private." The turbo-lift arrived. Jim got inside.

Sam glanced at the glasses. "My brother, the two-fisted drinker."

Jim grinned sheepishly and let Sam into the lift. "I certainly appreciate this show of moral support."

Sam tossed the container in the air and caught it. Carved vegetables rattled against the translucent plastic. "I'm just coming along to make friends with the horse."

They paused at the top of the catwalk. Lukarian had pulled a cot close to the corral so she could sleep with one hand stretched through the rails. The winged horse stood near her, dozing, its nose brushing Lukarian's fingers. The lustrous black of the creature's coat shaded to deep purple and peacock blue at the tips of its ears, on its legs, in large dapples across its back and flanks. Its mane and tail cascaded in random locks of black and intense blue and purple and iridescent green. It had folded its great wings to its sides, and the color of their feathers blended with the shades of its coat.

"We'd better come back later," Jim said.

At his voice, Athene raised her head, snorting. Lukarian sat up, blinking away the sleep.

"What do you want?" She kicked aside the blanket. She had changed out of her black suit into drawstring pants and a baggy slouch shirt.

Jim climbed down the companionway, holding the bottle and glasses in one hand.

"I came to apologize," he said.

"We brought a peace offering." Sam opened the container and brought out a handful of carved vegetables. "Does Athene like carrot roses?"

"Yes. Carrots, anyway. She's never had anything quite so elegant as a carrot rose."

As Jim opened the champagne, Sam offered Athene a carrot. She approached him warily, her wings fluttering. For all her apparent ferocity, she had calm, soft, gray eyes. She stretched her neck toward him, like a crafty old pony suspecting a bridle hidden somewhere, such as behind Sam's back. She lipped the morsel from his palm.

"Did the admiral order you to come down here?" Lukarian said. "It doesn't matter whether you apologize—I'm not pulling out, no matter what. I'd prefer to be booked where we're welcome, but the company can't afford luxuries like being picky."

"He didn't make me apologize," Jim said. "And there's no need to back out of the commission." He laughed, without humor but with the understanding of irony. "Besides, it wouldn't change things if you did. The admiral has made up his mind. If you quit, he'll just find somebody else."

"And if you quit?" Lukarian said.

"I'm not allowed to quit," Jim said. He thumbed the cork out of the neck of the bottle, being careful not to pop it and spook the winged horse again.

Lukarian chewed her thumbnail thoughtfully. "This isn't quite what you expected, is it?" she said.

"That's . . . an understatement."

"Pax?" Lukarian asked.

"Pax."

They shook hands, more civilly this time.

The winged horse finished chewing Sam's carrot rose, put her head over the bars of the corral, and nudged Lukarian, who stretched out her hand and let the creature nip up something from her palm. The horse's teeth crunched on a bite of carrot while Jim tried to recall when Sam had given Lukarian any of what he had brought, or when she had put her hand in her pocket. Her hand had been empty a moment before. He shrugged to himself and poured champagne for her, for Sam, for himself.

"To . . . to peace," he said.

Their glasses touched with a high, light ring.

"How did you get to be a captain?" Lukarian absently scratched behind her creature's ears.

Jim's fair skin colored. "Just lucky, I guess."

Lukarian blushed too. "I didn't mean it like that. I meant, aren't you kind of young to be a captain?"

"I'm twenty-nine," he said. "Well out of short pants. Aren't *you* kind of young to run a . . . a vaudeville company?"

"That's different," she said. "I sort of inherited my job from my daddy."

"So did Jim," Sam said with a grin.

"I didn't know Starfleet worked like that," she said.

"It doesn't," Jim said. "Once you get to know my brother, you'll find he has an unusual sense of humor."

"Oh." She gave them both a quizzical glance.

"What's the use of this corral?" Jim said. "Can't it just fly out?"

"Jim, look at the wing ratio," Sam said. "There's no way it could get off the ground at one gravity."

"She can't fly out," Lukarian said. "But she can jump out if she's scared enough."

"I'd rather not have her running loose on the shuttlecraft deck," Jim said.

"Someone's always with her. Last night I was only gone for a minute. I was trying to change and get everybody organized and—It was bad luck that you came in right then."

"Why do you have a flying horse, if it can't fly?"

"My daddy got her when she was just a filly. I didn't think we should buy her. Vaudeville is supposed to have animal acts, but Athene—I knew, I just *knew,* that if we exhibited a winged horse without flying her, the audience would get cranky. I was right, too. Besides, equiraptors all go crazy. But of course as soon as we got her, I fell madly in love with her. I was just the right age."

"Equiraptor?" Jim said. "Not pegasus?"

"No. Pegasus was mythical. Athene is real. Besides, 'equiraptor' is more accurate. She has some bird-of-prey genes—she can eat meat. I don't suppose you brought any shrimp, did you? She loves shrimp."

"I'll bring shrimp next time."

"How many of her are there?" Sam asked. "Who did the recombinant work? Why haven't I heard about it?"

"There's a guy up—down—in the northwest. He has a whole herd—a flock?—of them. He never publishes, he gets too much flak from the pure-genists." She grimaced with disgust. "They're perfectly willing to buy steak-flavored soy protein. It makes their food bills lower, and never mind that you mix forms a lot farther apart than birds and mammals. But if you say, Hey, boys and girls, let's make a chimera, let's make a flying horse, they start screaming 'pagan witch-craft!' "

Sam chuckled, recognizing the type. "You said winged horses—equiraptors?—go crazy. Because they can't fly?"

"It isn't that they can't fly, but that they believe they ought to be able to fly. If you see the difference."

"What gravity can they fly in?" Sam asked.

"The theory is, around a tenth of a g. Nobody's tried it. It costs too much to counteract the gravity field over as big an area as you need."

"It shouldn't cost that much," Jim said, glancing around the shuttle deck and feeling disappointed, despite himself, that the fifteen-meter ceiling could hardly give the winged horse much room in which to fly.

"It costs too much if you have to do it on the budget of a vaudeville company," Lukarian said. "But it would be quite a sight, wouldn't it?"

"It would indeed," Jim said.

"My friends call me Lindy," she said.

"His friends call him Jim," Sam said.

She glanced quizzically from brother to brother.

"That's right," Jim said. "My friends call me Jim."

# Chapter 4

ON THE BRIDGE of the starship *Enterprise,* Jim Kirk prevented himself by force of will from tapping his fingers on the armrest of the captain's seat. The last thing he wanted was to let everyone know just how nervous, aggravated, and upset he felt.

This morning he had bid farewell to his mother and brother at such great length that when they finally did depart, they departed with relief. He hardly blamed them. He felt too worried to make intelligent conversation or even to exchange family gossip, and, after all, only a finite number of ways exist to say good-bye.

He had given the ship a complete inspection, he had conferred with Lieutenant Uhura about the communications network and with Commander Spock over data analysis systems. Mr. Spock answered all Jim's questions emotionlessly, in detail, and in terms Jim had mostly never heard, much less understood. Despite his stoic exterior, Mr. Spock seemed to suspect that Jim was testing his competence, that Jim was seeking an excuse to displace him from the position of first officer.

Jim even asked Amelinda Lukarian if her company needed extra equipment or supplies. "Jim, all I need is a good juggler," she said. "I don't suppose you can juggle, can you?"

As it happened, he could, in a manner of speaking, but he hardly intended to admit it and find himself on stage at the next starbase, clutching two beanbags and trying to keep the third in the air. The only time he could get all three bags simultaneously airborne was when he dropped them.

Amelinda was too keyed up by the Starfleet commission, too excited over going into interstellar space for the first time to pick up on his hint that he wanted an excuse to stay in port another day.

On reflection, he could hardly blame her. She might be persuaded to conspire to delay the *Enterprise,* but she would do it reluctantly, trying to balance the assumption—unjustified, he hoped—that to refuse to help Jim would damage their fragile truce, against the assumption—entirely justified, Jim felt—that insisting on a delay would win the company no points with Admiral Noguchi. The admiral had already called Jim once, wondering in an elaborately casual fashion just when Jim intended to set out.

In short, Jim had kept the *Enterprise* in the docking bay as long as he could, and far longer than he wished to. He could not delay much longer.

He did not want to leave without Dr. Leonard McCoy, though, and Dr. McCoy was nowhere to be found.

The last few months had been hard on McCoy. Though he had kept Jim and Gary and the other survivors of Ghioghe alive, the doctor had been all but excluded from their treatment once they got back to earth. It took specialists, the specialists told him.

So, when Jim recovered from the regen drugs enough to notice McCoy's aggravation, he encouraged him to take some time off. *I bullied him,* Jim thought. *I might as well admit it. But where did he* go?

McCoy had left no itinerary; if he had his communicator, he was ignoring it.

The *Enterprise* could not function without a chief medical officer. Leaving Spacedock without a doctor would be unfair to ship and crew; it would be dangerous. If McCoy did not appear soon, Jim would have to request another doctor. Maybe he ought to request a search party at the same time.

"Captain Kirk," Lieutenant Uhura said, "Spacedock Control sends its compliments and asks if you would like to make a reservation for a time of departure."

Jim detected Admiral Noguchi at work.

"Send my compliments to Control—correction, address

my compliments to Admiral Noguchi at Spacedock Control, and request a departure clearance for . . . sixteen hundred."

"Aye, captain."

Uhura relayed the message. Jim willed the departure time to be too crowded. Sixteen hundred was the closest thing to a rush hour that Spacedock possessed. Being bumped from his requested time would give him the excuse to stall for a while longer.

Jim rehearsed possible retorts: "Very well, if Spacedock can't handle its traffic well enough for us to depart at a civilized hour, *Enterprise* will leave at oh two hundred." He wondered if he could pull off the cool contempt that line required.

"Control reports that they have logged sixteen hundred as departure time for *Enterprise*," Uhura said.

Damn! Jim thought.

"Very good, Lieutenant Uhura," he said. "Thank you." He rose. "I'll be in my quarters."

He left the bridge, fuming at himself for being caught in his own cleverness. He could have requested eighteen hundred, even twenty, and got away with it, but he gambled and he lost. Now, unless he tracked McCoy down within an hour, he would have to report him missing and he would have to request another doctor; and he would have to explain himself to Admiral Noguchi.

In his cabin, he opened a private communications line. Jim received no answer when he called McCoy's Macon, Georgia, apartment. Not even a concierge replied, for the doctor disdained to use any robot or computer controls in his living space. He even washed his own dishes, on the rare occasions that he ate at home instead of going out. His club had no idea where he might be.

Jim thought for a moment, then called an old friend of McCoy's, an adviser from medical school.

Dr. Chhay, though thirty years McCoy's senior, had none of his old-fashioned objections to robot servants. The distinctive electronic voice of a brand-name concierge answered Jim's call.

"One moment, please. I will see if Dr. Chhay is free."

The doctor's image appeared. Jim had met McCoy's mentor only once, but he could hardly forget the unique blend of

79

types that made up her features: gold Asian eyes, golden-brown hair with eastern European curl, a café-au-lait complexion, emphasis on the café. She must have been heartbreakingly beautiful even as a young woman, and maturity had given her an elegance and presence that at first had knocked Jim flat and later made him feel, in a strange and tongue-tied way, that he was in the company of royalty, the real thing, not the commercial figureheads that had passed for royalty for the last couple of hundred years.

"Hello," she said. "It's—Commander Kirk, is it not? Leonard's friend."

"Yes, ma'am," Jim said. "It's captain now."

"Congratulations."

"Thank you." He blushed furiously. Why did I brag about making captain? he wondered. He cleared his throat in embarrassment. "I'm sorry to bother you. I just wondered if you'd seen him recently."

"No, I haven't. The last time I saw him was when we all had dinner together. Can it have been over a year ago?"

Jim's only pleasant memories of that dinner were of Dr. Chhay. Leonard and his wife's brittle civility had been worse than outright conflict. A few weeks later they finally decided on a permanent separation.

"Yes, ma'am, almost two years now."

"Is he all right?"

"Yes, ma'am, I'm sure he is. He's just . . . momentarily misplaced."

Her glance combined doubt with mild amusement. "Surely Jocelyn knows where he is."

"I don't think so—I mean," he said quickly, "I haven't reached her yet." McCoy must never have told Dr. Chhay of his and Jocelyn's divorce. Maybe I should tell her, Jim thought; and then, It really isn't my place to tell McCoy's friends the details of his personal life; and finally, It's too late now, anyway.

"Give him my regards when you see him, captain," Dr. Chhay said. "We must all get together again sometime."

"Yes," Jim said. "I will. Good idea. Thanks."

"Good-bye, captain," she said.

"Good-bye, Dr.—" He let his voice trail off, for her image had faded from the screen.

Why did I make such a fool of myself? he wondered. He sighed, and tried to console himself with the thought that he might not be the first man to turn into a babbling moron while trying to talk to Dr. Chhay.

Jim thought for a moment. Dr. Boyce, chief medical officer of the *Enterprise* during most of Chris Pike's command, now headed medical services at Starbase 32. He was too far away to be of any help. But his replacement, Mark Piper, had retired to earth. Jim put through a call. Maybe Piper could be persuaded to return to active duty until McCoy turned up.

Dr. Piper's image appeared on the screen. Thank you, Dr. Piper, Jim thought, grateful to reach someone who answered calls in person.

"This is Mark Piper," the image said. Jim started to reply, but the image kept talking. "If you leave your name, I may call you back. Then again, I may not."

Jim swore softly as the recording informed him that Dr. Piper looked forward to getting in some serious staying at home.

Jim's plan sank.

It probably wouldn't have worked anyway, Jim thought. Piper doesn't sound anywhere near ready to come back out of reserve.

Jim left his name anyway. McCoy had planned to get together with Piper to discuss the ship and its crew. Perhaps somewhere in the conversation he had mentioned where he planned to go on his vacation. But unless Piper called him back almost immediately, the information would arrive too late.

Jim began to admit to himself just how worried he was. Reluctantly, he placed one last call.

The screen presented him with audio-visual patterns meant to be soothing. Electronic interference hinted at a transfer through several numbers. From New York to—? Jocelyn might be anywhere in the world, or off it.

The screen cleared and renewed itself.

"Oh," Jocelyn said. "Jim. Hello."

She looked very much the same as the last time he had seen her: an intense, spare woman, black hair caught in a fashionable chignon. She resembled McCoy in her disdain for some modern conveniences. She did not trouble to conceal the gray in her hair.

"Hello, Jocelyn. Long time, and all that."

"Are you calling for Leonard?" She sat at a desk in one of her offices; behind her lay the Singapore skyline. She had never spent much time in Macon even when she and McCoy were together. When Jim thought of her, he thought of her in New York, or in London.

"Yes," he said. If she knew where McCoy was, if he was with her, then they must have changed their minds. They must be getting back together. This surprised him, but, then, McCoy had been surprising Jim for a number of years now.

"Tell him it's no use," Jocelyn said. "Jim, please, I don't want to hurt him anymore, and I don't want to be hurt anymore either."

"Er . . ." He had misunderstood her; she had asked him not if he wished to speak to McCoy, but if he was calling on behalf of him. "I know, Jocelyn, and I'm sure he doesn't want that either." He wondered how to end the phone call without hurting her, without making her worry about someone she could no longer love.

"What *does* he want?"

"What? Oh—nothing. I just called . . . I was on earth, but I'm leaving soon, I just wanted to say hello and good-bye for old times' sake."

"Then why did you say you were calling for Leonard?"

"I didn't—I mean, I'm sorry, I misheard you when you asked me that. Static on the frequency."

"I see," she said. She waited, but Jim could think of nothing more to say.

"Well, good to talk to you," he said with forced cheerfulness. "Take care of yourself."

"Good-bye, Jim," Jocelyn said. Her image faded.

Jim sagged in his chair, defeated. He could think of noplace else to call, no one else to ask about McCoy, nothing else to try. Besides, his hour had expired ten minutes ago.

The white-water raft crunched against the shore. Leonard McCoy dismounted from the boat's inflated rubber side, shouting with surprise and blowing out his breath as he landed up to his knees in the frigid water of the Colorado. His feet had been immersed in it for so long that they had gone numb, making him forget just how cold it was. It crept through the interstices of the legs of his wet suit. The cold was a shock, but soon his body heat warmed the water.

McCoy and the others grabbed the lines, dragged the raft onto the beach, and shed their life jackets.

Then they fell into each other's arms, laughing and crying, energetic and exhausted, elated to have made it, sad to have reached the end of the trip.

They started to take off their wet suits. The hot gravelly sand drove the cold from their feet. They dug through the boat bag, looking for canvas shoes worn ragged in only two weeks' time.

The archaic fastenings of McCoy's wet suit had seemed odd at the beginning of the trip. After a day or two, they were as familiar as the sealer on his everyday clothes.

But now he fumbled at the snaps because tears blurred his vision. He had enjoyed the last few days more than he had enjoyed anything for years. Even when he knew for sure he would be late, he still enjoyed it. He had regained his ability to stop worrying about things he could not control.

He shed the wet suit like a reluctantly discarded skin, smiling at the metaphorical aspects of his actions. Under it he wore a thin shirt and a pair of rumpled, ragged Bermuda shorts. Both had been new when he set out. Neither was fit to be seen in anymore, anywhere but here.

"Jean-Paul," he said.

The guide gave him a warm hug. "It's okay," he said. "Go join your ship. But don't think you can get off so easy next time! Next time you stay and learn to pack the boat." He grinned. "I'll make a guide of you yet."

McCoy hesitated, then raised his hand in farewell to them all, turned, and sprinted toward the office.

The manager glanced up as he entered. "Ah," he said. "You're a bit late. Everyone make it?"

"Made it just fine." If the manager could act so blasé about the possibility of losing a boat full of people, so could McCoy. "Use your comm?"

The manager nodded at the battered unit on his desk.

McCoy called the *Enterprise*. He fumed at the delay of getting a ground-to-space frequency. Why hadn't he brought along his communicator?

Then he thought, You didn't bring your communicator on purpose. For one thing, it's against the rules. For another, you can't hear it beep and not answer it. Don't let the universe drag you back into its modern state of hyperactivity.

He smiled to himself and waited.

*"Enterprise,* Lieutenant Uhura here."

"This is Leonard McCoy, chief medical officer. What's the plan?"

"Dr. McCoy! What are your transporter coordinates?"

"I have absolutely no idea," he said.

The manager recited a set of numbers.

"Stand by to beam on board," Lieutenant Uhura said.

The cool tingle of dislocation caught him and sucked him away.

The turbo-lift carried Jim Kirk toward the bridge. Perhaps the lift would break down, stranding him in the guts of his ship. He could imagine sitting here for the rest of the afternoon, closed off from the unwanted duty of reporting a friend AWOL, from the unwanted mission, from the civilians roaming his ship, from the admiral watching for any sign of weakness or broken nerve.

The lift stopped. Jim squared his shoulders and paced onto the bridge, too tense for pleasantries. "Lieutenant Uhura, open a channel to Starfleet Command."

"Aye, captain," she said. "Sir, Dr. McCoy has reported. He should be in the transporter room by now."

Before Jim had a chance to enjoy his relief, anger and outrage overwhelmed him. Since, apparently, no one had bonked McCoy on the head and left him wandering amnesiac in a dark alley, then why had he neglected to check in? Had his easy southern style so overwhelmed his courtly southern manners that even common courtesy became too much trouble?

Jim leaned back and rested his hands on the arms of the captain's seat. "Cancel that last order," he said offhand, keeping his voice calm. "I'll see Dr. McCoy on the bridge."

"Yes, captain." She relayed the message. "He says he'll be up as soon as he's stopped in his cabin, sir."

"Tell Dr. McCoy," Jim said, "that I'll see him on the bridge *right now*."

Uhura's side of the conversation indicated that McCoy objected to the order, but Jim could not take it back even if he wanted to. That was all he needed, for the members of his new crew to believe he ran his ship on favoritism. He gazed stonily ahead at the blank viewscreen.

When the turbo-lift doors slid open, Jim heard Uhura's soft exclamation of surprise. Sulu glanced back, tried to suppress a grin, and returned to his position.

Jim turned.

Dressed in damp rags and an unlaced pair of antique shoes, sunburned on face and neck and arms, his bare legs pale except on his left thigh, where the skin had turned black, purple, and green around a nasty scrape, his hair uncombed and uncut, wearing two days' growth of beard, Leonard McCoy, all innocence, said, "You wanted to see me, captain?"

Jim leaped up. "Good lord, Bones!"

Jim stopped, aware of the startled silence that had fallen over the bridge. He detected an amused glint in McCoy's eye.

"Please come with me, Dr. McCoy. We have ship's business to conduct. Mr. Spock, take the conn. Prepare for departure at sixteen hundred."

Jim strode past McCoy. He expected everyone on the bridge to burst out laughing any second. Perhaps they would, as soon as the lift doors closed behind him. But somehow he thought that while they might laugh at him to his face, they would not laugh at him with Commander Spock in charge.

Commander Spock watched with detached interest as the new captain hustled the disheveled officer from the bridge.

"That was Dr. McCoy?" Lieutenant Uhura said as the lift doors closed.

"That was Dr. McCoy," Spock said. "The new chief medical officer." All morning, Spock had been aware of Captain Kirk's surreptitious efforts to locate the doctor. He had thought to offer his assistance, which he believed would

85

be considerable, but refrained from doing so precisely because of Kirk's apparent wish that no one notice what he was doing. Perhaps the captain desired privacy because he expected to find Dr. McCoy in just such a disreputable state. But if that were true, why insist on his presence on the bridge? Spock wondered if he would ever begin to understand the motives of human beings.

"I hope he's all right," Uhura said. "He looked like he'd been in an accident."

An accident that occurred some time ago, by the appearance of his injury, Spock thought.

"One may also hope," the Vulcan said, "that he takes better care of his patients than he does of himself."

In the turbo-lift, Jim glared at McCoy with a mixture of relief and anger.

"Bones, what happened to you?"

"Nothing." McCoy glanced at himself as if noting for the first time how he was dressed. "Why? Don't you like the newest fashion?"

"It's—" Jim looked McCoy up and down. "Not *quite*—how shall I put it—the thing on a starship."

"You didn't give me a chance to change. I did try, you know." He reached down and took off one ragged shoe. A handful of sand slid from it and scattered onto the deck. He took off his other shoe and brushed the rest of the sand from his bare feet. "How's Mitch?"

"He's . . . still in regen. They say he's getting better."

"And Carol?"

"I guess she's fine."

"You *guess?*"

"Things didn't work out!" Jim said angrily. "Let's forget it."

"But—"

"I don't want to talk about Carol Marcus!"

McCoy frowned. "Are you all right?"

"*Yes*, I'm all right! Why do people keep asking me if I'm all right? Bones, where the hell were you? What did you do to your leg? I was about to send out the hounds. You were supposed to report two days ago!"

"I know. And I missed your party." He ran his fingers through his tangled hair, pushing it back. The sun had burned his hair to coppery streaks and drawn a network of fine white lines in the deep tan around his eyes.

"Where were you? I nearly had to report you missing!"

"Relax, Jim, I'm here, aren't I? I was on vacation. At your insistence, as I recall."

"I know that."

"I went on a river trip. Once we reached the border, I got here so fast I didn't even help fold the boat."

*"Fold* the *boat?"*

"Sure. It's rubber; you need to rinse it off and deflate it and fold it up when you're done with it."

"You rode down a river in a rubber boat?"

"That's the idea."

"The sun must have gotten to you."

"I went to the Grand Canyon," McCoy said. His enthusiasm spilled over and obliterated the sparring. "White-water rafting. Have you ever tried it?"

"No."

"It's unbelievable. It's magnificent. We're traipsing off to the far corners of the universe, while there are incredible places on our own planet that we haven't even seen. Jim, it's something you've got to experience!"

"That's what you said about mint juleps," Jim said. "What did you do to your leg? And none of this explains why you didn't let me know you were going to be late. You could have saved me having to give a lot of evasive answers."

"The canyon's a historical preservation area. Comm units are forbidden, even primitives like radios and wrist phones."

"That's barbaric," Jim said. "You *paid* for this?"

"I paid extra for it!" McCoy said. "You can't just go on a trip like this. You have to buy extra insurance and swear on your grandma's motorcycle that you won't sue the rafting company if you fall in and drown."

"I don't see the attraction," Jim said.

"It was just about the most fun I ever had in my life. Jim, you're too dependent on all this high-tech stuff."

"We'd be in big trouble without all this high-tech stuff. If you'd had high-tech stuff your leg wouldn't look like that." Just looking at the bruise made Jim's knee ache.

McCoy shrugged cheerfully. "We flipped the boat. I got in

the way of a rock. We lost some of the equipment—thought we'd lost a couple of people, but we found them again. That's why I was late." He smiled fondly at the memory. "And some of the food got ruined, so we've been on short rations the last couple of days."

"Why didn't you have something beamed—" Jim stopped. McCoy had told him the canyon was a historical preservation area and he knew parks of that designation forbade transporter beams. Yet the transporter was so much a part of the background in his life that he could hardly imagine not being able to call one out of the sky. The transporter was less likely to fail when he needed it than, say, the air supply.

The lift stopped in officers' territory. McCoy got out. "It was a great vacation, Jim."

"It doesn't sound great to me. It sounds like you need a vacation to recover from your vacation. I wish you'd left word—" The lift doors tried to close. Jim put his hand in the way of the sensor.

"I didn't want to be tracked down!" McCoy said, an edge in his voice. His dark tan made his kindly eyes deep and intense. The fine white squint lines disappeared when he narrowed his gaze. "I didn't want to be able to call for help and get it. I wanted to see if I could do something for myself for a while, without a safety net. Can you understand that, Jim?"

Taken aback, Jim hesitated. "Yes," he said. "Yes, I do understand that. I'm sorry I jumped down your throat. I was worried. It made me mad."

"Apology accepted. Do I have time to bathe and change before I have to get to work?"

"No, but I think you'd better bathe and change anyway. And do something about that stubble."

"I was thinking of growing a beard."

McCoy was pulling his leg. Jim grinned. "There's no rule against silliness, even in Starfleet."

"Please use the turbo-lift in a courteous fashion," the computer said. "Please free the lift doors."

"I wish they'd make a rule against talking elevators."

"See you later."

Already walking down the corridor, McCoy raised his hand in acknowledgment, then abruptly turned back.

"Jim—"

Jim shoved his hand between the lift doors again. They sighed open. A warning signal made a couple of abortive buzzes. Its next noise would be an ear-splitting shriek.

"Just how far did you go in trying to track me down?"

Jim took his hand away from the sensor just as the alarm began in earnest.

"You don't want to know," he said, and let the doors close between them.

Sulu flexed his hands nervously. He imagined all the things that could go wrong during his first try at piloting a constellation-class starship. Running the *Enterprise* into Spacedock's doors would no doubt get him a transfer, but he doubted it would get him the transfer he desired. More likely it would give him a transfer to a scow hauling ore to be made into alloys to repair the damage he had done to the dock and the ship.

He could make a mistake of a much lower magnitude and still make a fool of himself. On the other hand, considering some of the things he had already seen on this ship, Sulu decided he would have to foul up fairly seriously for anyone even to notice. He smiled, remembering the captain's reaction to the appearance of the chief medical officer.

*I almost wish James Kirk had been on board when I arrived with my saber,* Sulu thought. *I probably could have gotten my transfer without even asking.*

The ambient noise of information from computer and crewmates flowed around him like a gentle tide. The captain ordered the moorings cleared. Sulu felt a change in the lie of the ship. By no sense he could name, he knew the *Enterprise* floated free. It surprised him that one could feel the freedom in a ship this size, for it would certainly handle like an antimatter-powered barrel, a huge wallowing mass with enormous engines to wrestle it from place to place.

Time to take it in hand. He touched the controls.

The ship shuddered to starboard and dipped like a wounded bird.

"Mr. Sulu!" the captain shouted.

Sulu wrenched the *Enterprise* to port, overcompensated, and had to drag the ship out of the threat of spin and tumble. The ship quivered in his hands, as delicate as a solar-powered sailboat. He gulped.

The intercom burst into activity as every department in the ship demanded to know what had happened.

"Mr. Spock! Take the helm."

"My attention is fully occupied, sir," Spock said.

"I can get us out of Spacedock, captain!" Sulu said. His face turned scarlet with humiliation.

"I'm sure you can, Mr. Sulu. What I'm not sure of is that there'll be anything left of Spacedock after you do."

Sulu protested, but Engineering, demanding most insistently of all to know what had happened, distracted Captain Kirk. Mr. Scott objected to the abuse of his steering engines at least as adamantly as if he himself had been injured. Kirk had his hands full trying to put in a question or a word of reassurance.

Sulu still had control of the ship, which at the moment was drifting more or less in the direction of the Spacedock observation windows. Gently—very gently—he eased the *Enterprise* to a safer path.

"Mr. Scott!" Kirk said for the third time.

Scott paused. "Aye, captain?"

"Damage report, Mr. Scott."

"The engines, the housings—they're no' designed for such use—"

Sulu called on the impulse engines. They delivered the faintest thrust to the ship, just enough acceleration to press it toward the Spacedock doors.

"What's the damage, Mr. Scott?" Kirk said again.

"Well, sir, there isna any *damage,* if ye put it—"

"Then why are you calling the bridge? Don't you have anything constructive to do?"

After a moment's silence, Scott replied, "I will certainly do my verra best to find something, captain."

"Very good, Mr. Scott. Carry on."

The *Enterprise* cleared the dock. Space opened out before it.

A twinge of dizziness swirled before Sulu's eyes. He

released his breath, wondering when he had begun holding it.

"Mr. Sulu," Captain Kirk said.

Sulu pretended to be too busy to turn around. The last thing he wanted to see was the look on Kirk's face.

"Yes, captain."

"Spacedock appears still to be there."

"Yes, sir."

"No damage done."

"No, sir."

"And no harm, I'm relieved to say."

"Me too, captain," Sulu said. Relief was hardly an adequate word.

"Navigator, plot a course to Starbase 13—"

Sulu applied reverse thrust to the *Enterprise* and brought it almost to a standstill, relative to Spacedock.

Kirk cut off his words. His silence descended.

Collision warnings sounded. Sulu acknowledged them and shut them off. "Sailboat, captain." Sulu increased the magnification on the viewscreen. Off their port bow, a solar-powered boat sped across their path. Hundreds of times the size of its capsule, the sail showed its nearly invisible black surface to the *Enterprise*. It tacked. The gilded side of the sail reflected a bright crescent across the *Enterprise's* sensors.

The viewscreen damped the intensity of the light.

"I see it, Mr. Sulu," Captain Kirk said. "Good work. That skipper has more nerve than sense."

"And in human-controlled regions, such as this one," Mr. Spock said, "that skipper has the right of way as well."

"It's tradition, Commander Spock," Kirk said. "I thought Vulcans respected traditions."

"We do, sir. However, Vulcan traditions make sense."

Kirk looked skeptical, but the tension faded from the bridge. The sailboat passed very close before them. After it cleared their path, Sulu set the *Enterprise* under way.

"Course to Starbase 13 entered, captain," the navigator said.

"The *Enterprise* is clear of traffic and cleared for warp speed, captain," Sulu said.

"Warp factor one, Mr. Sulu."

"Warp factor one, sir."

The *Enterprise* sped majestically toward the stars.

It's too bad I'm going to request a transfer, Sulu thought. I could get to like this ship.

When the director of the oversight committee of the Klingon Empire—that is, the head of the oligarchy's secret police—tried to contact the commander of the newest fighter ship in the fleet, a prototype and test vehicle for which everyone had great hopes, he received no reply. He increased the intensity of his contact attempts, but the ship was nowhere to be found.

This caused the director considerable consternation. If the commanding officer of the new ship had lost it—to mutiny, or accident, or sporting too close to the Federation—he could not be excused. And if he had been so foolish as to lose it to capture rather than to destruction, if he had actually given it into the hands of Starfleet—for the first time, the director felt glad that the Federation took such scruples to return prisoners alive and undamaged. In the unlikely event that the officer were a prisoner, that he were still alive, the director would himself take the responsibility for disciplining him.

The director felt too much anger to experience grief. When another emotion did cut through his anger, still it was not grief, but fear. If the government determined fault, if it decided the officer had acted out of incompetence or malfeasance, the officer's family would be responsible for the tremendous value of the ship.

The director of the oversight committee had worked long and hard to get that particular ship for that particular officer. And he had worked long and hard to amass great power and resources during his own tenure. Now it looked as if all his power, his work, and his resources would vanish between the requirements of the oligarchy and the mistakes of the officer.

He diverted all his operatives to the search for the new ship, the ship commanded by his son.

Jim invited Lindy's company to dine at the captain's table that evening; he looked at the paperwork already piling up for him and decided to leave it till later; he continued his exploration of the *Enterprise*.

Most of the science section was deserted. It would be staffed after this tour, but Starfleet saw no point in keeping a hundred scientists on a starship that was going nowhere worth exploring. Jim wondered how he was going to get through the next three months.

He paused outside Engineering.

Go on in, he told himself. Your chief engineer may think you're green behind the ears and wet as grass, but he's hardly going to say it to your face.

He went on in.

"Good afternoon, Mr. Scott."

"Er . . . Captain Kirk."

"I thought I'd get acquainted with the ship."

"Verra well, captain." He remained where he was, neither offering to show Jim around nor going back to his own business.

Jim walked around him.

The place gleamed with care. No wonder the *Enterprise* and Commander Scott enjoyed such a high reputation in Starfleet. Jim had begun to wonder about the curmudgeonly engineer, but he could see that the respect had been earned.

"I'm very impressed, Mr. Scott."

"Then—ye'll want to be making some speed trials, will ye, captain?" Scott said hopefully.

Jim started to jump at the chance—but stopped long enough to consider. If the ship traveled full-speed to Starbase 13, not only would it have to remain there for several extra days—and no telling how the Klingon oligarchs would react, never mind that the stop would be boring—but the ship would have to push its fuel reserves to get all the way to the end of the Phalanx and out again. He did not want to refuel at 13, because all 13's supplies had to be imported.

"Not just now, Mr. Scott. Maybe later in the trip."

"But, captain—"

Jim knew that if he let Scott persuade him, the temptation would be too much. "Later, Mr. Scott," he said shortly.

Scott retreated into silence. Jim left Engineering, aggravated with himself for coming so close to letting his own preferences override the best interests of his ship and crew.

He decided to go back to his cabin and do some paperwork after all.

During the slight, barely noticeable checking of his stride, Spock progressed from a quickly repressed sense of surprise at the scene in the mess hall, through a brief impulse to retire to his cabin, to a determination not to let the changes alter his routine.

The *Enterprise* seldom carried civilians, at least not this many civilians. Their costumes—and some of their dress seemed to be costume, rather than current fashion or ethnic style—glared among the Starfleet uniforms. The civilians talked and laughed in an uninhibited fashion, no doubt because they had no superior officer to answer to, only a general manager. The manager sat at the central table with her company and with a Starfleet officer—the ship's new surgeon, Spock realized. Barbered, cleanshaven, and dressed in decent clothes, Dr. McCoy had made himself presentable. Earlier this afternoon, Spock would not have been willing to swear that such a feat was possible.

The chair at the head of the table remained empty.

The manager hugged one of her performers. Spock doubted such behavior to be conducive to discipline.

Two human beings in baggy black and white checked suits rose. First one, then the other, performed odd foot motions loudly accompanied by a sound which Spock identified as metal on the soles of their shoes rapping against the deck. Their compatriots egged them on with shouts and cries. Spock wondered if he were witnessing an altercation that he would have to stop. No, they were engaged in an informal competition, each trying to complicate a basic series of steps till the other failed to duplicate it. By the third variation the pair had attracted the attention of every being in the mess hall. The cheers and exclamations approached cacophony.

At the synthesizer, Spock obtained his usual salad. He proceeded toward his usual table.

Several of the new officers—Sulu, the navigator Commander Cheung, and Hazarstennaj, a lieutenant from Engineering—sat there, watching the performance, talking animatedly, laughing, joking with each other. Spock hesitated, but several chairs remained at his table and he could think of no logical reason to avoid using one.

The two performers finished their demonstration with overstated bows to their impromptu audience and to each other. The hall erupted with a final round of applause. Spock placed his tray on his table.

The three younger officers stopped applauding, stopped cheering, and fell silent. Spock nodded to them. They stared at him. He sat down.

"Uh, Mr. Spock," said the navigator.

"Yes, commander?"

"Nothing. I mean, hello, sir."

As Spock raised a bite of his salad, its odor assailed him. He lowered his fork and gazed at his meal. Though Spock preferred his greens to possess a distinct bite of chlorophyll, without any admixture of hemoglobin or myoglobin or whatever animal protein preceded the greens in the synthesizer, he could subsist on poorly designed food. However, he had noticed long since that a starship crew's morale depended heavily on the quality of the food. He was—for the moment—first officer; he must pay attention to factors about which he was personally indifferent.

The greens smelled as if the meat analogue were incorporated into their substance, rather than being an incidental admixture. In fact, they smelled like a dish of which Captain Pike had been extraordinarily fond: boeuf bourguignon, a loathsome concoction of animal protein and fermented fruit pulp. Spock respected Pike as he respected few human beings, but Pike did have human flaws. Eating boeuf bourguignon was one of them.

He glanced at the meals of his table partners. Sulu had chosen broiled fish, the navigator an offworld variation of glazed fowl, and the Engineering lieutenant a steak. As the lieutenant belonged to a carnivorous felinoid species, the steak was raw. When he noticed that, Spock rather wished he had chosen another table. Odd that the smell of raw meat had escaped him.

None of them had eaten much.

"Are your meals satisfactorily synthesized?" he asked.

They looked at each other. The navigator giggled.

"Erroneous synthesis is a serious problem," Spock said. "I did not intend levity."

"I know, Mr. Spock," Cheung said. "But we were just talking about the food. It's been getting worse all day."

"Does starship food always taste this bad?" Sulu asked.

"The synthesizer must be reprogrammed. I suspect that the repair crews adjusted it at Spacedock."

"Anything's a disappointment after fresh salmon," Sulu said. "But this tastes like . . . chicken."

"I knew I was challenging the synthesizer," Cheung said, "so I suppose I was asking for it."

Spock tried to sort out her syntax, but failed. "I beg your pardon, commander, but do you mean you got the meal you asked for, or you did not get the meal you asked for?"

Cheung grinned. "Neither. Both. What I asked for was duck lu-se-te. It's a variation of duck à l'orange, but lu-se is from my home world, and it's green. I didn't expect the synthesizer to know what I was asking for. It didn't reject the request . . . but it didn't exactly fill it, either. This tastes like . . . wood pulp waste with sugar syrup."

The food sounded abhorrent, but many of the foods humans ate sounded abhorrent to Spock. "Am I correct in assuming this is not what you wished it to taste like?"

"You are correct," she said.

"Wood pulp and sugar syrup would be an improvement on this!" Hazarstennaj growled and thrust a shred of bloody meat before Spock's nose. "Taste it!"

Spock barely prevented himself from recoiling. "Your assurance that it is unacceptable is quite sufficient."

"No, you must taste it to get the full effect," Hazarstennaj exclaimed. "It tastes like—" She sneered. Her long ruby fangs glistened against black and silver striped fur. "It tastes like *vegetables*."

Spock raised an eyebrow. He took the morsel from Hazarstennaj's long, slender fingers, smelled it, then gingerly put it in his mouth and chewed.

If one ignored the visual stimuli, it was quite acceptable. It looked like meat but tasted like avocado, an earth fruit for which, in the spirit of self-control, Spock curbed his inclination.

Spock speared a bit of his salad and offered it to Hazarstennaj. "Perhaps you will find this to your taste."

Hazarstennaj growled. "You wish me to eat—leaves?"

"Hazard will never live it down if she eats a salad, Mr. Spock," Commander Cheung said.

"The salad may be her only choice, if she wishes animal protein in her dinner."

Growling softly, Hazard plucked the leaf from Spock's fork. With trepidation she placed the bite of salad in her mouth, ready to spit it out at the least excuse. She closed her eyes and gulped it down. "It is *cooked*," she said.

"That is true," Spock replied.

She blinked, looked at her steak and at his salad, and exchanged the positions of the plates. "Better than nothing," she said. "I will trade you."

"Very well." Spock dissected the steak-disguised avocado. "Commander Cheung, Lieutenant Sulu, will you have some? It tastes—I assume—more acceptable than wood pulp waste or sugar syrup." In addition, there was a good kilogram of it on the plate before him, and it would be a lapse in dignity—not to mention restraint—to eat it all.

"Thanks."

Spock and Cheung and Sulu shared Hazard's meal; Hazarstennaj, who ate only once each day, gulped down the salad and ordered another one. She ate most of it with enthusiasm, then curled her tail around her hind feet and picked delicately at the leftovers while her companions finished their dinner.

Another member of Hazarstennaj's species approached the table. Spock and Hazarstennaj noticed him at the same time. This was not the other felinoid, a security officer, who worked on board the *Enterprise*, but an unfamiliar individual. His sleek black silver-tipped fur rippled over taut muscles when he moved.

"They need not even disguise their vegetables to make you eat them," he said to Hazarstennaj, a snarl of contempt in his tone. "Have they declawed you as well?"

Hazarstennaj moved in a languorous curve and faced the other being. Her ears flattened against her skull; her shoulder blades hunched. Her ease changed to threat.

"Ignorance does not become us," she said.

"Nor do vegetables!"

With a violent scream, Hazarstennaj launched herself at the other being. Sulu leaped to his feet, about to try to separate the pair as they rolled over each other and snarled and shrieked.

"Sit down, Mr. Sulu," Spock said.

The young officer did not hear him. Overcoming his reluctance, Spock grabbed his arm.

"Mr. Sulu, sit down."

"But, sir—they'll hurt each other!"

"Sit down," Spock said a third time. He lowered his hand, trying not to bruise Sulu's arm; Sulu had no choice but to accede to his command.

"They'll kill each other!"

"Do as I say."

Spock thought Sulu might try to resist him, an even more foolish idea than trying to separate Hazarstennaj and her new acquaintance. But the shrieking diminished to low snarls, to a purr. The two beings rose, unhurt, rubbing each other beneath the chin in greeting. Sulu subsided, astonished.

"What is your name? You smell familiar."

"I am Hazarstennaj."

"I am Tzesnashstennaj!"

They lapsed into their own speech, of which Spock could make out a few words. The similarities in their names indicated that in the past, a past so distant their species knew almost nothing of it, their ancestors had come from the same band. Or so they believed; so the myths of their people claimed.

Sulu watched, mystified.

"They were greeting each other," Spock said, explaining the ritual insults and the mock battle.

"Oh."

Hazarstennaj plucked a leaf of the salad from her plate and offered it to Tzesnashstennaj. Tzesnashstennaj pulled back his whiskers in disgust, but since it would have been inexcusably rude to refuse the offer, he accepted it and ate it. His whiskers bristled forward.

"Unusual meat animals you keep on this ship," he said.

Hazarstennaj blinked slowly in satisfaction. "Sit," she said. "Join me."

Tzesnashstennaj glided onto the sitting platform beside her. They helped themselves to the remains of the salad.

"Do you perform?" Tzesnashstennaj said.

"Not for many years. It is too difficult to gather enough people."

"Perform with us," Tzesnashstennaj said.

"I will. And another of us lives on board."

"Excellent. Our troupe is small, more people will be welcome. Come and meet the others."

Chief Engineer Scott paused beside their table. "Lieutenant Hazarstennaj!"

" 'Hazarstennaj,' " the lieutenant said. Spock detected the difference, but he wondered if human hearing could.

"Lieutenant, I need ye in the engine room. Our captain has no stomach for speed, so we must keep close watch that the new drive plates stay polished—" He stopped. He looked at the salad. "Have ye begun eating greens?"

Tzesnashstennaj's ears swiveled in irritation.

"I do not take well to insults from . . . outsiders," Hazarstennaj said. "Even from superior officer outsiders."

Spock knew that the word "outsiders" in Hazarstennaj's language translated more accurately as "nonpeople" in Standard. In the spirit of interspecies cooperation, her species softened the meaning.

Then Scott saw the demolished remains of Spock's steak. His expression changed from surprise to shock.

"Are *you* all right, Mr. Scott?" Cheung asked.

"Aye, fine, but—" He shook his head. "Mr. Spock, what's wrong?"

"Nothing at all, Commander Scott."

"Aye, but—" He stopped again; he shook his head again. He started to say something more, then spied Sulu, who had been hoping to escape his notice. "Sulu! Ye are Sulu, are ye not?"

"Yes, sir."

"I'll have no more performances like this morning's!" Scott snapped. "Why, 'tis a disgrace, the caliber of graduates they let loose from the Academy!"

Sulu's cheeks burned with humiliation and anger. He said

nothing, for Scott would discount explanations as feeble excuses. Worse, he would be right.

"Mr. Scott," Spock said.

" 'Twas not so easy in my day."

"The captain considers the incident forgotten. I think it only courteous that you and I do the same."

Scott grumbled something about the caliber of Starfleet's new officers, but he said it nearly under his breath, so Spock chose to ignore it.

"Lieutenant," Scott said again to Hazard, "I need ye in the engine room." He gave Sulu a significant glance. "We may get more stress on the engines than we planned."

"Thank you for the excellent lunch, Mr. Spock," Hazarstennaj said.

Under Scott's disbelieving eye, Hazarstennaj finished the final leaf of salad. Accompanied by Tzesnashstennaj, she rose and took her tray to the disposal chute. Scott left the mess hall. Hazarstennaj and Tzesnashstennaj loped after him, shoulder to shoulder.

Unsuccessfully fighting an attack of giggles, Commander Cheung gathered up her plate and tray.

"I've got to run—I'll be late for a meeting."

Cheung hurried from the mess hall. Spock collected his plate and tray. He stood up, but Sulu remained.

"Commander Spock—" Sulu said.

"Yes, Mr. Sulu?"

"Why did you do that?"

"Because my body needs fuel to function, Mr. Sulu. Sometimes one cannot take excessive note of the form."

"That isn't what I meant."

"Please explain what you did mean."

"Why did you stick up for me to Mr. Scott? Why did you give me a second chance on the bridge?"

"As I told Captain Kirk: other matters occupied my attention."

"You could have piloted the *Enterprise* out of Spacedock with both eyes closed and one hand behind your back. I've heard enough about you to know that."

"The *Enterprise* is unique. It is common for new pilots— even for pilots accustomed to this class of vessel, not simply to its simulator version—"

Sulu blushed again. Spock had looked at his records and divined the meaning of their anomalies.

"—to require some time to accustom themselves to its handling. I should have discussed the matter with you, but as my attention *has* been occupied elsewhere, the opportunity did not present itself."

"Thank you," Sulu said.

Spock gazed at him with complete composure. "I find it odd in the extreme to be thanked for neglecting a part of my duty."

"Nevertheless, I'm in your debt," Sulu said.

"Vulcans do not collect debts," Spock said.

Spock picked up his tray and departed, leaving Sulu puzzled over someone who refused gratitude, who refused even thanks, for rescuing the career of a virtual stranger.

Vulcans must be even harder to deal with than rumors hinted.

At the captain's table, Leonard McCoy got tired of making up excuses for Jim's absence. After all, it was Jim's idea to invite the company to sit with him tonight.

"Pardon me just a moment," he said. "I'll be right back."

A minute later, the lift let him out in officers' territory. He headed toward Jim's cabin. He felt in better physical condition than he had enjoyed for years. Even the ache of his deeply bruised thigh muscle reminded him of a moment of sheer, terrified exhilaration.

He knocked on the door of Jim's cabin.

"Come." The voice hardly sounded like Jim's: tired, aggravated, impatient. In the past, Jim's mood always skyrocketed when he returned to space.

"Your guests are waiting," McCoy said.

Jim looked up bleary-eyed from the comm screen. Transmission flimsies and a yeoman's tablet and several crumpled coffee-stained plastic cups littered his desk.

"My guests?"

"Your guests. The company. Dinner."

"Oh, lord!" He jumped up. "I lost track. I don't believe it—I'm already behind in my paperwork."

"What is all this?"

"It's, you know—" He waved his hands. "Paperwork."

"Why are you doing it?"

ENTERPRISE

"It has to be done," he said, then, defensively, "I always do it. But I never had quite so much of it before."

"Where's your yeoman?"

"I don't have one."

"You don't *have* one?" McCoy said with disbelief.

"I've never had a yeoman."

"You were never captain of the *Enterprise* before."

"I don't want a yeoman. I don't need somebody fussing over me and sticking things under my nose to sign and being sure the synthesizer put the right stripes on my shirt."

McCoy drew up a chair and straddled it. "Jim, permit your old Uncle Bones to give you some friendly advice. You're commanding twice as many people as you ever have before. Starfleet paperwork increases in geometric—maybe even logarithmic—proportion to the size of the crew."

"It'll be all right as soon as I get caught up."

"You'll *never* get caught up. What's more, you *know* you'll never get caught up. This isn't your job anymore."

"I suppose you have a magical solution."

"You could send out a press gang—" At the change in Jim's expression, McCoy stopped. If he wanted Jim to follow his advice he had better stop teasing him. Otherwise Jim would never do it, no matter how sensible his suggestion. "Jim, go down to quartermaster's office, pick out a likely clerk, and promote them."

"It'll take me more time to train somebody to do this than it would to do it myself."

"Not in the long run. Not if you pick somebody with more than half a brain."

"Ever since I came on board this ship, people have been telling me to surrender gracefully."

"What?" McCoy said.

Jim sighed. "I said—I'll try it. On a *temporary* basis."

"Good. Now come on. If you think a feeble excuse like work will save you from what the synthesizer has laughingly billed 'dinner,' you've got another think coming."

Jim accompanied McCoy to the mess hall.

"Lindy, I'm terribly sorry," he said. "Ship's business—I hope you and your company will forgive my inexcusable tardiness—"

An older man, spare and dark-haired, wearing an immaculate and severely tailored suit, broke in before Lindy could reply. "If your tardiness is inexcusable, then how do you expect us to forgive it?" His black mustache curled up into double points at each end.

"Of course I forgive you, Jim, don't be silly." Lindy glared at the older man. "Mr. Cockspur was just joking."

"You youngsters are far too cavalier with the language," Mr. Cockspur said. "We should all endeavor to speak precisely."

"Let me introduce you, Jim," Lindy said. "A few people had to leave. You've already met Mr. Cockspur, our neo-Shakespearean actor."

The coldness between Lindy and Mr. Cockspur went beyond ill-mannered jokes. Jim hoped the performers could keep peace with each other during the tour.

Lindy introduced Philomela Thetis, a tall, elegant, heavyset woman, the company's singer; the tap-dancing team of Greg and Maris, who had come to dinner in his-and-her suits of black and white houndstooth check; Marcellin, the mime, a lithe, slender, dark man who moved with self-possessed certainty.

It seemed to Jim like a pitifully small and quiet group to set out to conquer thirty starbases. Everyone greeted him in a friendly fashion. Jim went to get some dinner, but found the synthesizer closed and blinking, "Down for repair."

"Count your blessings," McCoy said. "You wouldn't have liked it, whatever you got. If you could tell what you got."

Jim sat down to keep the others company—Lindy in particular. "By the way, Lindy," he said, "we got a greeting from—" He stopped, becoming aware of Mr. Cockspur's expression of indignation.

"I *was* telling of my sojourn in Lisbon," Mr. Cockspur said.

"Do go on," Jim said, trying to be polite.

"As I said, the performance was a triumph . . ."

And he did go on. Jim did not get a chance to talk to Lindy that evening at all.

# Chapter 5

HIS SHIP SHUDDERED around him and blood covered his hands—

Jim sat up with a start. Darkness dissolved as his cabin illuminated itself. His cabin on the *Enterprise*.

Someone was knocking on his door.

"What—? Just a minute."

Bleary-eyed, Jim Kirk struggled out of his bunk and grabbed his robe. He found it and fumbled his way into it, somehow getting the heavy silk twisted till he had one arm in an inside-out sleeve.

"Come."

The door slid open. A young crew member stood on his doorstep. Her eyes widened.

"Hello," he said.

"Hello." She looked everywhere but at him.

"What's the matter?"

"Uh, nothing, sir. I . . . I'm sorry, sir, quartermaster said be here this morning, but I must have misunderstood—"

Jim rubbed his eyes and yawned. Then he saw the chronometer.

"Good lord, do you know what time it is?"

"Yes, sir. It's morning, sir."

"This isn't morning, this is the crack of dawn!"

"I'll come back later, sir—"

"No, no, it's all right, come in. I just need a cup of coffee." This morning the synthesizer seemed to be working. "Stuff would shock anybody awake."

"I'm here to help with your files?" Her voice rose in an uncertain question.

"Right over there." He gestured toward the comm unit. His coffee arrived. He sipped it and made a disgusted noise. "This is bad even when the synthesizer works. Whoever designed the template got their idea of how it ought to taste from a third-generation reproduction of whatever they found in a wardroom coffeepot."

She moved around the periphery of the room, staying as far from him as possible and casting her gaze down.

First day on the job, Jim thought. It gets to everybody.

"Oh!" she said at her first view of the comm unit. "That's not right!"

He had spent half of yesterday trying to get the damned thing to make sense. His reward was a comm screen with sixteen overlapping message blocks connected by lines and arrows whose significance he had already forgotten; and now he got criticism from a wet-behind-the-ears crew member.

"All right, you make sense of it."

She stared at him, her eyes wide. "I—" she whispered. "I—"

It's too early for this, he thought, and fled into the bathroom.

The sonic shower and the coffee, which, though it tasted terrible, also was too strong, began to wake him up.

Did I snap at her? he wondered. He tried to convince himself he had not, but failed. Embarrassed, he dressed and returned to his cabin.

She sat at the comm unit with her back to him, her shoulders hunched as if she were trying to make herself even smaller than she already was. He tried to remember what she looked like, but recalled only huge blue eyes and close-shorn blond hair.

He cleared his throat.

She leaped to her feet and faced him, staring.

"As you were," he said. "I didn't mean to startle you." He gestured at the comm. "Looks better already. Yeoman, did I snap at you a minute ago?"

"Oh, no, sir," she whispered.

"I think I did." He smiled. "I apologize. I'm not at my best before I'm awake. Let's start over. Good morning. I'm Jim Kirk."

"Rand, sir," she whispered.

"Can you get me out of the hole I've dug, or will you have to start all over?"

She fumbled the commands. He wondered what was wrong, for she appeared to be doing what needed to be done. She stopped, put her hands in her lap, and clenched her fingers.

"Is it that bad, yeoman?" Every time he spoke to her, she flinched. He wished she would stop.

"I'm sorry, sir, it will take a little time to . . ." She stopped and began again. "I'm sorry, sir, I—I'm not too experienced . . ." Her voice trailed off.

He realized she was trying to figure out how not to tell her superior officer that he had made a horrible mess. He wanted to tell her it was all right, but considering his reaction to almost the first thing she had said, she would hardly have any reason to believe he took criticism well. As, in fact, he often did not. Probably the best solution was to go away, let her calm down, and come back later.

"I'm sure you'll do fine, yeoman," he said. "Lieutenant Uhura on the bridge will know how to reach me, if you have any questions."

"Yes, sir," she said, relieved. "Thank you, sir."

When ship's computer called him into sick bay and mangled his given name, it gave Hikaru Sulu some comfort. He still felt embarrassed over having botched the *Enterprise*'s departure from Spacedock, and he felt glad to know he was not the only entity on board who could make a mistake.

"Mr. Sulu, how do you do. I'm Dr. McCoy." They shook hands and McCoy glanced at Sulu's files. "Hikaru," Dr. McCoy said, mangling the name the same way the computer had. "Hmm. Don't believe I've encountered anyone named Hikaru before."

"Neither have I," Sulu said. "But, doctor—it's pronounced with the accent on the second syllable, not the first. The r is very soft." He pronounced his name for McCoy.

Dr. McCoy repeated it, getting it better. Hardly anyone ever got it exactly right.

"What does it mean?" Dr. McCoy asked.

"Why do people always think a name from an unfamiliar

language has to mean something?" Sulu said. He felt himself blushing. He knew perfectly well what it meant. It meant "the shining one," and he had encountered as much teasing about it as he ever needed. Hoping to sidestep Dr. McCoy's query, he said pleasantly, "After all—do you know what your given name means?"

"It means 'heart of a lion,' or something on that order," the doctor said. "But I see your point." He smiled. "Back to business. You're extremely fit, lieutenant, even for someone your age."

"Thank you, sir."

"Don't let this sedentary starship life seduce you away from that."

"I'll try not to. I don't think I will—I get too twitchy unless I get some exercise."

Dr. McCoy glanced at the sensors that blinked and bleated above Sulu's couch. "You have a phenomenally low pulse—did you spend time in a high-gravity environment?"

"Yes, sir, nearly a year."

Dr. McCoy nodded. "I thought that might be the explanation. The sensors show scars on your back and legs, too. Mind if I take a look?"

"You can hardly see them anymore." Sulu peeled off the upper half of the exam coverall. He was impressed that McCoy had made the connection. Few earth-normal populations of human beings lived on high-grav planets. No other earth-based doctor, even the ones at the Academy, had asked about the scars or his low pulse.

Dr. McCoy touched the old, faint scars beneath Sulu's shoulder blades.

"My mother had a consulting job on Hafjian," Sulu said. "We had an antigrav generator just big enough for our living quarters, but when we went out we used Leiber exoskeletons." Just the name brought back memories of how it felt to wear the harness for hours and sometimes days on end. The alloy frame helped support and propel the unadapted human body in high gravity. The exoskeleton served its purpose, but at the points of highest stress it always caused abrasion. And of course it did not prevent gravity from affecting the circulatory system.

"How old were you? Thirteen? Fourteen?"

107

"Exactly that," Sulu said. "We left just before my fourteenth birthday. How did you know?"

"You wore the exoskeleton during your major growth spurt," the doctor said offhandedly. "There's a characteristic shape to the scars." He unfastened the cuffs of the coverall and looked at the scars on Sulu's legs, just above and behind his knees. "They did heal well," he said. "Do they ever bother you?"

"No, sir. I hardly ever think about them."

"Should have been treated with fibroblasts in the first place," Dr. McCoy said. "New skin instead of scars."

"The technology wasn't available. Not on Hafjian. Not for something this trivial."

"Hmmph. We have the technology and to spare, here. Do you want to get rid of them?"

"No, sir, I don't think it's necessary," Sulu said, surprised at the reluctance he felt toward effacing the old scars. They were, he supposed, a part of his history.

"Very well. Just one other thing." Dr. McCoy glanced at the sensors again. "You appear to have sustained no damage at all from the gravity stress. But once in a while the effects are latent. In a few years they could catch up with you. It isn't anything to worry about, and it isn't even very likely. But it is something to be aware of."

"What kind of effects?" Sulu said, startled. This was something else no other doctor had ever mentioned. "And how long is a few years?"

"Heart problems, mostly. So you should be sure not to let more than three years pass between physicals after age seventy or so."

"I'll try to remember that, Dr. McCoy," Sulu said, thinking, A *few* years?

Half a century seemed an immeasurably long time.

For Commander Spock, a few minutes began to seem like an immeasurably long time. He had reached sick bay at precisely the time designated for his medical examination. The ship's new chief medical officer showed a fine disregard for punctuality. He had not yet finished with Mr. Sulu, though Sulu had been due back on the bridge five minutes ago.

"If you would reschedule my appointment, Dr. McCoy," Spock said without preliminaries, "I will return at some more convenient time."

"What? Oh, Commander Spock—no, don't be silly." He tossed Spock a medical examination coverall, a jumpsuit opaque to the eye but transparent to diagnostic sensors. He gestured to one of the cubicles. "I'll be with you in a minute." He closed the privacy curtain.

Spock changed into the coverall. If the cubicle had contained a comm unit, Spock could have worked while he waited. However, it did not.

Giving a physical exam to someone with the control of biological processes, the awareness of the body, that Vulcans possessed was a mere exercise. But Starfleet insisted that ships' doctors perform a baseline exam on all personnel. The exam had little to do with Spock and much to do with giving the doctor some familiarity with the beings he might be called upon to treat. However much practice the doctor might need, the entire process wasted Spock's time. The doctor's tardiness added to the waste.

Finally, Dr. McCoy strolled into Spock's cubicle. "Commander Spock, welcome to sick bay. I do believe you're the first person to take their physical on time."

"It is not on time," Spock said. "It is now eleven minutes beyond 'on time.' "

"I meant—never mind, let's get started."

Spock lay on the diagnostic table. The sensors blended into a harmony of sound and light, creating the precise pattern the Vulcan expected.

"As you can see, doctor, my health—"

"Stay right there," McCoy said sharply. "Why, Mr. Spock, I don't believe I've ever encountered a set of readings quite like yours."

"They are all within the range of Vulcan norm."

"Just barely, some of them." He regarded the sensors. "I would have thought a few of your human characteristics might come out in the mix."

"The Vulcan genome is dominant," Spock said.

"Superior genes, hmm? Do I detect a touch of Vulcan chauvinism?" McCoy said. He smiled when he said it. Spock knew that humans sometimes smiled when they insulted other people, and sometimes smiled when they said insulting things that they did not mean to be perceived as insults. Unfortunately, distinguishing between the two possible meanings could be difficult in the extreme.

"Not at all," Spock said. "It is a matter of experimental fact. Were we speaking Vulcan, the words 'dominant' and 'recessive' would imply neither superiority nor inferiority. One might perceive human chauvinism in your attitude that the traits of your species should prevail, despite laboratory evidence that they do not. Are you quite finished, doctor?"

"No, not by a long shot, don't move. I haven't had much chance to practice on Vulcans." He grinned. "Aren't you interested in contributing to my education?"

"I have fulfilled my obligation to regulations by submitting to this examination. I see no use in remaining while you satisfy trivial inquisitiveness."

"You haven't fulfilled your obligations till I say the exam is over. You'll be happy to know your physical health is excellent."

"I was already aware of that fact."

"What about your psychological health? Your emotional state? Are you having any difficulties you want to discuss?"

"Vulcans have no emotional state."

"Even equanimity is an emotional state!" McCoy said. "Besides, your physical characteristics may be mostly determined by your genes, but your psychological ones sure aren't. Your background has exposed you to complex cultural interactions, conflicting philosophies—"

"We are all products of our environments," Spock said. "Otherwise we would not be sentient beings, capable of growth. However, we are not unconscious products: we may choose and control our influences. I am not in conflict with my background. Vulcan philosophy permits me to conduct my life without emotionalism."

"There's a lot to be said for emotionalism."

"Indeed? In my observation, it brings only unhappiness."

"Oh, really? For example?"

"For example, Captain Kirk."

"What makes you think Jim Kirk is unhappy?"

"He made his feelings known when his choice of first officer was overruled."

"In your favor."

"That fact has nothing to do with our discussion."

"No? You have no feelings of pride in being promoted?"

"Pride? Pride is unknown to me."

"And I suppose you're going to claim you wouldn't have minded if Mitch *had* been promoted over you."

"Not in the least. Commander Mitchell has a reputation as a competent officer. It is not my emotional state that should concern you. It is Captain Kirk's."

"Meanwhile, you have no feelings, no desires—"

"Vulcans do not possess desires, Dr. McCoy. However, if I had human feelings, they would be . . . none of your business."

"Everything affecting the ship is my business. For instance, you served under Christopher Pike for a long time. You have no reaction to seeing him replaced?"

If Spock had felt regret at Pike's departure, he had suppressed the reaction. He saw no reason to confess his lapse to a stranger.

"You feel no disappointment?" McCoy asked. "No hint of human reaction amidst the Vulcan equanimity?"

Spock tired of the sparring. "Do you believe, Dr. McCoy, that no one before you has noted the inherent contradictions in the circumstances of my existence?"

"What are you talking about, commander?"

"Though I had no obligation to explain my choice of a philosophy to you, I have done so. Yet you refuse to accept this choice; indeed, you dispute my right to make it. I have not intruded upon you with suggestions as to how you could become more rational—though I could make such suggestions."

"Why, Mr. Spock, I do believe you're angry."

"No, doctor, I am not angry. But I see no point to wasting my time with fruitless discussions."

"All right, Mr. Spock, if that's the way you feel about it."

"That is what I *think* about it," Spock said. "There is a difference, though you choose not to perceive it."

McCoy picked up a hypo. "I'll let you take your thoughts right out of here—as soon as I get a blood sample."

"A blood sample is superfluous. The sensors have recorded all the factors of a baseline exam."

"I know, but I want to do a few extra tests—"

Spock rose. Once in a long while the emotions he worked so hard to repress struggled to expose his less than absolute control, but he crushed them mercilessly. McCoy would never know the depths to which his offhand comment wounded the Vulcan.

"Human or Vulcan, I am not your experimental animal."

"Wait, Spock, for heaven's sake! I didn't mean—"

Spock strode from sick bay, still in the coverall. He preferred returning to his cabin to dress. He could think of no logical reason why he should be forced to endure the doctor's needling, literal or figurative, and all too human.

But then, outside sick bay, Spock paused. He forced his emotions back under control, crushing the anger Dr. McCoy had made him feel. The humiliation he experienced in response to succumbing to the anger in the first place he dismissed as self-indulgence.

He considered the doctor's demand, then turned and strode back into sick bay without hesitation.

Dr. McCoy had busied himself with some files. He looked up.

"Yes, Mr. Spock?" he said stiffly. "What is it now?"

"If you believe it is your duty to take a blood sample, it is my duty to comply with your request," Spock said.

Dr. McCoy's expression remained hard. "It is, is it? Thank you for your condescension, Commander Spock. I'll make an appointment for you, for some other time. As you can see, I'm busy."

Spock regarded him, one eyebrow upswept, any question left unasked.

"Very well, doctor," Spock said, his tone even. "At your convenience." He departed.

McCoy watched the science officer leaving sick bay. The Vulcan showed no evidence of his previous brief loss of temper, no physical indication that McCoy's dismissal had irritated him. He walked as he always walked, with a controlled stride, his boot heels silent on the deck.

McCoy scowled at the unread file.

Damn your Irish temper, he said to himself. That wasn't an acknowledgment of your authority, it was a peace overture. Which you threw back in his face.

For a moment, McCoy thought to go after Spock. But he decided he had better let himself cool down for a while instead. Commander Spock's accusations of unnecessary medical testing had stung McCoy, perhaps because they were not entirely untrue. Mostly, but not entirely. Unique individuals need unique medical care, and preparing himself for emergencies was McCoy's primary motivation. Even if he did not expect emergencies on this trip.

But he could not deny that the researcher in him itched to take a close look at the cellular structure of a being half-human and half-Vulcan.

McCoy grinned. Commander Spock, he thought, you're just lucky I didn't demand a tissue biopsy. Wonder how you'd've reacted to that?

McCoy prepared for his next appointment. When the opportunity presented itself, he would make peace with Commander Spock. The doctor had no doubt that he could jolly the Vulcan into a better mood as readily as he had provoked the uncharacteristic offended outburst.

Appeal to his human side, McCoy thought. That will do it.

Lindy rested her elbows on the railings of the companionway and slid from the catwalk to the shuttle deck.

"Lindy, you're going to break an ankle doing that." Marcellin, the mime, rose from the deck chair near Athene's corral. Even when he wore no makeup and allowed himself to speak, he moved as if he were on stage. Lindy loved to watch him.

"No, I'm not, but you're sweet to worry. How is she?"

"Restless, of course. I don't suppose they've got a racetrack on this bucket, do they?"

"No, I'm afraid they don't."

"They ought to. It's big enough."

"Thanks for watching her. I'll see you at rehearsal."

"Right."

She watched him stroll away, admiring his graceful walk and his slender dark body.

Athene snorted and stretched her head over the top rail of the corral, looking for a treat. Lindy gave her a protein pellet and rubbed behind her ears, beneath her jaw, across her wide forehead.

"You think those goodies will always be there, don't you? What would you do if I lost my touch, huh?" She magicked another tidbit. Athene ruffled her wings and pranced in place. She needed to stretch her legs and her wings. The shuttle deck was big enough, but Athene could not run on the metal decking. She might slip or damage her hooves or her legs.

"I know it's hard to stand still for so long, but be patient and maybe something will work out, all right?" Athene tried to stick her nose in one of her pockets. "No, you don't need anything else to eat."

While she mucked out Athene's corral, she daydreamed about the future of the company. She had ambitions. She envisioned buying a star cruiser and performing all over the Federation. She imagined a cultural exchange with the Klingon Empire that would create goodwill not only between the people but between the governments.

First she would have to pull off this commission. She worried that a cultural relic from earth might not play before offworld audiences. But the acts were entertaining. Some people looked upon them as being three hundred years out of date. She preferred to think of them as having, some of them, a thousand years of history.

She wished she had more information on vaudeville. Scraps and dreams formed the basis of the company. Laser and tape records of real vaudeville did not exist, film was rare, stored information sparse, books few and far between. She visited the library of every town they stopped in, looking for information never committed to computer memory. She had found moldy old books, pamphlets, playbills, scarred microfilm of newspaper announcements that no one had looked at for centuries. After she took over from her daddy, she made some changes. He had not always got it right.

Lindy sometimes added anachronistic acts, like the hunt performance, but she knew when she was doing it. She would even admit it, if pressed.

Sometimes, she thought, you have to sacrifice a little authenticity to entertainment. If real vaudeville had been able to get a hunt performance, they'd've presented it, too.

114

When she had finished, she gave the equiraptor a good currying. The brush slid easily over Athene's glossy coat. Lindy used her bare hands to groom her wings. Like many genetically engineered creatures, even those developed by selective breeding before the invention of gene splicing, Athene needed human help for some abilities that an evolved creature would have developed. Corn plants had not been able to propagate independently for millennia; Athene could do a certain amount of rough grooming with her sharp front teeth, but she had no beak or talons. Lindy's hands did a better job of ruffling the feathers, working in the natural oil, and smoothing them again.

Last she cleaned Athene's hooves. She could smell the faint musty odor of an incipient case of a fungal hoof infection. She swore under her breath.

She stood up and patted Athene's shoulder. "Don't worry, sweetie. I'll do something about the deck. I don't know what. But something."

Athene nuzzled her side, trying to discover which secret pocket she carried the carrots in this time.

Lindy gave up putting off the work she was supposed to be doing. She spent the next hour roughing out a design for the tour's poster.

The doors of the turbo-lift made a fluttery noise as they tried to close against an obstruction.

Uhura glanced up. A young crew member—Uhura had seen her once or twice—stepped forward timorously, as if all that forced her onto the bridge was the knowledge that computer would chastise her if she stayed where she was.

Uhura thought, as she had before, that the young woman would be awfully pretty if she did not always look so terrified—and if she did not cut her hair so short and ragged. It would look quite nice if she let it grow or shaved it completely, but this unkempt in-betweenness did nothing for her.

Suddenly, as if starlight dispersed her fears, the crew member stared in wonder at the viewscreen. The small ports and screens in crew quarters gave only a hint of the powerful beauty of space at warp speed. Seeing it on the viewscreen astonished and transfixed the young crew member. Her gaze made Uhura see anew the steady glow of stars in all the colors of the universe.

Uhura crossed the bridge. "Are you lost?"

The crew member jumped. The pretty little moonstruck girl vanished and the terrified young woman reappeared.

"I don't bite." Uhura smiled at her. "Are you lost?"

"I'm . . . I'm the yeoman. I'm supposed to meet the captain . . .?"

"Welcome to the bridge. I'm Lieutenant Uhura." She waited for the yeoman to introduce herself.

The yeoman looked down. The mug's lid rattled—the child's hand was shaking!

"I mean—I'm not really a yeoman yet, but they said . . ." Her voice trailed off.

"What's your name?" Uhura asked gently.

"Janice Rand."

"Come with me, Janice, I'll introduce you."

"I don't want to bother anybody—"

"It's no bother. They'll be glad of the chance to stop having to look busy." Uhura gestured to the mug. "Would you like to put that down?"

"It's . . . it's the captain's."

"He'll be back in a minute. His place is down here."

Uhura put the mug on the arm of the captain's seat and took Janice's hand. The hard calluses on the child's palms startled her. She led the yeoman first to Mr. Spock.

"Mr. Spock, this is Captain Kirk's yeoman, Janice Rand. Janice, this is Commander Spock. He's the science officer and second in command of the *Enterprise*."

Janice held back as if Spock terrified her even more than everything else did.

"How do you do, yeoman." He returned to his work.

Uhura led Janice to the lower level of the bridge. "Mr. Spock is very private," Uhura whispered. "Don't take it personally."

"Is it true . . . is it true he can read minds?"

"Yes, in a way," Uhura said softly, then, at Janice's reaction, hurriedly added, "but he has to be touching you, and it's hard, and I don't think he likes to do it. He surely wouldn't without your permission. He only did it that one time because it was a matter of life and death." Captain Pike had omitted the incident from the official report and from the captain's log because of Mr. Spock's reticence. But everyone who had been on board at the time knew what had happened and what he could do.

Uhura did not think she had eased Janice's fear.

Hikaru Sulu, the helm officer, and Marietta Cheung, the navigator, made Janice more comfortable. They showed her the displays on their complicated consoles, and they were nearer her age—but how old was she? Uhura wondered. She did not look even eighteen.

"Of course, nothing interesting is going on now," Commander Cheung said. "It's pretty boring, going from one starbase to another."

Janice glanced at the viewscreen. "But it's so beautiful," she said. "And you see it all the time." The expanse of stars held her.

As Uhura had earlier, Sulu and Cheung followed her gaze.

Suddenly becoming aware of her own rudeness, Janice tore her attention from the viewscreen. "I—I'm sorry, I—" Her fair complexion colored.

"But you're right, Janice," Uhura said. "It *is* beautiful. Somehow we get used to it and we forget to look at it the way you do. It's good to be reminded." She squeezed Janice's hand.

"Ah, Yeoman Rand, you're here."

Startled, Janice jerked her hand from Uhura's. Captain Kirk strode onto the bridge.

"Lieutenant Uhura's introduced you around? Thank you, lieutenant. Yeoman, let me show you what I need you to do."

Janice gave Uhura the look of someone about to be eaten by lions.

"Don't worry—you'll do fine."

Uhura returned to her place. She did not envy Janice Rand the job of keeping the executive paperwork, arranging the captain's schedule, reminding him of appointments and changes, and handling problems or referring them to the proper department unless they would only get worse without Captain Kirk's authority. A list of the duties made the job look trivial. But Uhura had served on a ship with a disorganized yeoman. The captain had lived a life of chaos and everyone considered the subordinate incompetent. A yeoman who coped with the responsibility received little: no notice, few compliments.

Jim showed Yeoman Rand to the open console on the port side of the bridge. "It's traditional for you to use the environmental systems station," he said.

She inspected the daunting display panels.

"Don't be concerned about the complexity," Jim said quickly, hoping to ease the doubt and fear in her expression. "Computer runs all the environmental systems. But you can use this console as your work station on the bridge."

"Yes, sir."

"As soon as you can, put together an appointments schedule for me. I want at least half an hour with each person on board. Spread the meetings out during the transit time between starbases. Don't bunch them up into one or two weeks. Try to arrange it so no one will have to visit me in the middle of their sleep cycle—or mine. Be sure not to conflict with staff meetings or inspections. Make it clear that it's informal, that it's just a chat. But don't take no for an answer. Understood?"

"Yes, captain."

He nodded. "Make yourself familiar with your station. I'll need you in a moment—one of your duties is to register the log and bring me the seal to sign. But," he said, feeling bored, wishing he had anything to do but record log entries for a trip on which nothing would happen, "the entry won't take long to record."

"Yes, sir."

Instead of going to his seat, Jim gazed at the viewscreen. He tried to think of something to put in the log. "One o'clock, and all's well"? Accurate—but he doubted Starfleet would appreciate it.

He thought he smelled coffee—good coffee, too. He wondered where the smell was coming from.

The turbo-lift doors slid open to admit Lindy. She carried a roll of paper in one hand and a folder under her arm. She wore a suit of soft white leather. Her iridescent black hair streamed behind her, long and loose, unstyled.

"Jim, have you got a minute?"

Jim realized he was grinning foolishly at her. He composed himself. "I'm at your disposal."

"I could use some help with this poster." She showed him what she was working on.

He had neither graphics experience nor drawing ability; he failed to cobble up a believable excuse for helping her himself. He decided to give the job to Rand to see if she could handle independent work.

"Yeoman Rand," he said.

She flinched at the sound of her name. "Yes, captain?"

Impatient with Rand's terror, Jim let Lindy's poster roll itself up against his hands. "Lindy, Yeoman Rand will help you with whatever you need. Yeoman, you have my authorization to call on the ship's resources within reason in order to carry out Ms. Lukarian's wishes. For starters you'll need to find a graphics-oriented comm unit. Understood?"

"Yes, sir," she whispered.

"Thanks, Jim," Lindy said.

Lindy and Rand left to find the graphics terminal. Jim watched them go, wondering what he had done to frighten Rand so badly. He did not understand her terror. He wished he knew how to alleviate it. He wished he could think of a good reason to spend time with Lindy. He wished he could figure out where the smell of coffee was coming from.

When he took his place, he noticed the mug. Fragrant steam escaped from the vent-hole in its lid.

"What's this?"

"Yeoman Rand said it was yours," Uhura said.

Jim lifted the lid and was rewarded by the smell of coffee. He tried a sip. The covered mug had kept it hot, and, to his amazement, it tasted the way good coffee was supposed to taste. More than that, it tasted the way good coffee smelled.

Jim glanced after Janice Rand, bemused.

Janice Rand found the design room. Its enormous graphics screen glowed to life.

"Please show me what you have in mind, Ms. Lukarian."

"What I want, ma'am, is something attention-getting."

"You mustn't call me 'ma'am,' " the yeoman said. "I'm just a petty officer, and that isn't even registered yet."

"What should I call you?"

"Um . . . yeoman, if you want. Or Rand."

"How about Janice, and you call me just Lindy?"

"If that's what you'd like."

"It'd be easier, don't you think?"

"All right . . . just-Lindy."

Lindy giggled.

"We'd better do your poster," Janice said, serious again.

Lindy opened her folder. She enjoyed showing off the flamboyant designs. Whoever had painted them enjoyed their work.

"These are playbills—reproductions, I mean—from classic vaudeville companies." She unrolled her new poster and flattened out the curling corners of the paper. "I'm not happy with the design . . ." She had been designing posters for nearly two years, and she had never liked any of them. "It'll have to do, it's the best I can come up with. My daddy used to design a new one for every city. They were all different, but you could tell a hundred meters away that they came from our company. Unfortunately," she said, "that's one talent I didn't inherit." She scowled at the paper again. "Maybe the computer could fix it up a little?"

Janice flashed the scanner at Lindy's design.

Lindy groaned when it appeared on the screen, larger than life-size. "I wanted it to look classic but modern at the same time, but all it is, is awful."

"It isn't that bad," Janice said. She stroked the touch-sensitive screen. The letters straightened and fancied to a sort of neo-deco style.

"It never looks the way I imagine it."

"We could adapt something. One of your father's posters, maybe?"

"No!" Lindy was embarrassed by her own vehemence. "I mean it has to be different. We have different acts."

Janice glanced again at one of Lindy's reproductions. "I'm sure it's fine the way it is," she said. "But if you move this from here to here, and slide this over to this corner . . ." She rearranged it. "And make the background look like brush strokes, and clean up this line a little . . ."

Lindy gazed at the new design in silence.

"I'm sorry." Janice sounded scared. "I'll put it back the way it was." She reached to delete the changes.

"No, wait!" Lindy said. "Janice, that's beautiful. How did you do that?"

"You had all the elements already. There is one other thing—I don't mean to keep butting in."

"No, go ahead."

"Different beings see different kinds of light. So if you widen out the color range—" She made the changes.

"It looks awfully dark," Lindy said, doubtful.

"It wouldn't if you saw ultraviolet or infrared. But I can brighten the middle colors." She did so. "Before, if you were a Corellian, say, it would look like this." The computer performed the transposition. The poster darkened almost to black. "Now it would look like this." It brightened in a different way from the original.

"I wouldn't even have thought of that," Lindy said. "How do you find it all out?"

"I've lived a lot of different places. It wasn't anything I did anything special to learn."

"Want a job?" Lindy said.

"What?"

"I need a designer. You could join the company. I don't suppose you can juggle, can you?"

Janice hesitated so long that Lindy thought she might actually accept.

"I thought you were the designer." Janice's voice trembled.

"No, I'm the manager, among other things. What do you say? Do you want the job?"

Janice looked down. "I can't juggle."

"That's okay! I mean, that part was a joke. *Will* you join the company?"

"No." Her whole tone had changed; she acted withdrawn and fearful. "I signed on with Starfleet for two years."

"Oh," Lindy said, disappointed. "The offer holds, if you change your mind." She admired Janice's poster. "Hey, have you had lunch? Do you want to go get something?"

"No—I mean, I'm sorry, I can't, I left papers all over Captain Kirk's desk, I'm sorry, I have to leave."

"Okay," Lindy said as Janice hurried away. I guess I

don't know Jim well enough, Lindy thought. I wouldn't have guessed he'd get mad if she took a lunch break.

Janice Rand returned to the captain's cabin. She sighed. Helping Ms. Lukarian with the poster had put her awfully far behind. She had to admit she enjoyed the work, until she realized she had been talking to the manager almost as if they were equals. Lukarian had not seemed offended, but sometimes people covered up their anger for a while and then let it boil out all over you.

Janice envied Lukarian her freedom—freedom to choose how she would act and how she would dress and how she would look, unhampered by regulations and laws and proscriptions and rules. Janice allowed herself a moment to wonder if, now that she was in Starfleet, far from the world she had escaped, she might let her own hair grow a little. Then she shook her head at her own frivolity.

She set back to work on the executive files. Captain Kirk really had made a botch of them—she wondered why he had tried to do all the work himself—but with computer's help she got them straightened out and in a form that made them comprehensible and compatible, rather than awkward and unique.

She had access to far more computer power at the captain's comm unit than she ever had with quartermaster. She had the freedom to design her own work; she could speak directly to computer. Quartermaster only allowed his subordinates to work within a narrow frame that he designed. He disliked it if someone tried to suggest a quicker or more efficient method.

She did not explore the system too aggressively, afraid that she might somehow stumble onto something she was not supposed to see or know about, and set off an alarm.

She paused to stretch and rub her eyes.

"Yeoman, are you all right?"

Janice leaped up, alarmed by the unexpected voice.

"Yeoman! It's just me." Captain Kirk gazed at her with a bemused expression.

"I'm sorry, you frightened me, I didn't hear you—!" She clutched the edge of the desk. "I'm sorry, sir, I—" She had been daydreaming; she had no excuse. "I'm sorry."

"You're working late—the files must have been a mess."

"Oh, no, sir." She could hardly tell him the truth. She was glad she already knew how much this one disliked criticism. The ones who were most dangerous encouraged you to say what was wrong, then punished you for being honest.

"You've done enough for today. You run along. Come back tomorrow."

"I'm—I'm sorry I'm not finished, sir, but really, it will only take me another few minutes. Sir." She set back to work, wishing he would not watch over her shoulder. Soon he wandered away. A leather chair squeaked and sighed when he sat down; the pages of his book rustled as he found his place.

"Yeoman, I don't remember calling the steward—did you straighten up around here?"

She looked up, feeling her face pale with apprehension, then turn red with embarrassment. Her fair complexion shouted her emotions to the world, and she hated it.

I was afraid of this, she thought. He doesn't like people touching his things . . . or suppose he can't find something and thinks I stole it. I knew I should have put everything back where it was.

But she had not memorized where everything had been. If he had noticed the difference, he would have thought she had been snooping. "I'm sorry, sir, I didn't think—"

"Yeoman, stop apologizing for everything!"

"I'm sorry, sir, I mean, yes, sir."

He scowled. "I didn't intend to criticize. It wasn't necessary for you to clean my cabin, that's the steward's job, but thank you anyway."

"Yes, sir. You're welcome, sir."

She tried to work, but he shifted in his chair, cleared his throat, rustled pages. His impatience frayed her nerves. If he would only let her alone—

"Yeoman—"

"I'm almost finished, sir, honestly!"

"This isn't emergency duty—it isn't necessary for you to finish it tonight."

"It . . . it isn't?" she said, amazed. "Sir?"

"No, it isn't. I thought I said that already. Shut things down and go get yourself an early dinner. Rest your eyes.

123

Relax. Have a swim or a game of jai alai or whatever you like to do in the evening. Finish this tomorrow."

"Oh. All right, sir, if that's what you want." He probably wanted to check her work so he could get someone else if she was putting things in a muddle. She hoped he did not notice that she had barely started on his schedule.

She shut down the system. She would prefer to work. She could not swim. Her roommate played jai alai in the intramural league, but the dangerous game terrified Janice. People always started classes on the ship, but if she joined one everybody would wish she would go away. As for an early dinner—she preferred eating late, with no one else around. She hoped she knew table manners now, but she might make another mistake. Then everyone would laugh at her again.

An early dinner meant a long lonely evening in her cabin. If her roommate was there with friends, they would not talk to her. She evaded questions, so they thought she was stuck-up and creepy. Too late, she understood that the way to divert attention from her background was to ask other people to talk about theirs.

"Yeoman, how old are you?" Captain Kirk said.

"What? Sir—?" Her knees trembled. She collapsed at the comm unit, pretending to have one final task with the papers. She wondered frantically if it were he, not the science officer, who could read minds. If he could, he knew her secrets. She ought to break down and confess. But if she did, they might be lenient with her and send her back. She would prefer a reformation camp or even prison. They let you earn money in refo, didn't they? A little? She would have to pretend to be tough and mean and unrepentant so they would think she was unfit to be returned.

"How old are you?"

"I—I'm almost twenty, sir, I forget exactly, I always have to convert to earth-standard years."

"You don't look twenty," he said.

She distrusted his smile. She tried to laugh. It came out faint and false. "People always say that, sir."

"Decided young to go to space, eh? So did I. A family tradition? Or did you choose it on your own?"

Her carefully invented details vanished in her fear. "I

124

decided on my own, sir," she said, hoping she had never told anyone the opposite. Before he could ask her another question, she plunged ahead. "What about you, sir?"

He spoke about his background and his past, about his parents and his brother, about his best friend very ill in the hospital. At first her fear deafened her. But her ruse had worked, so she calmed a little and heard what he was saying. He had done fascinating things and visited fascinating places, and he told of them with wit and charm.

The charming ones were even more dangerous than the thoughtless ones or the cruel ones.

He stopped. "I didn't mean to go on like that, yeoman. You run along. I'll see you tomorrow."

Janice fled.

As soon as the door closed behind his strange skittish yeoman, Jim requested a private subspace channel back to earth.

The ease of communication would diminish soon. The Phalanx was an immensely long tentacle of Federation space stretching to Starbase 13 at its far end. It lacked subspace relay stations. Any Klingon patrol that happened to come by would try to jam the signals that did get through. This might be Jim's last chance of getting a comprehensible answer from earth till his ship reached the starbase and its powerful amplifiers.

The Phalanx made Jim uncomfortable, both the existence of it and the idea of taking his ship and crew into it. Starbase 13 guarded Federation territory of little worth and low population, a planetary system attached to the Federation by ill chance. He suspected that moving the people to a more hospitable planet and closing down 13 would cost less than keeping the starbase staffed, supplied, and protected for one year.

He waited impatiently for his call to go through.

Worst of all, the Phalanx made the oligarchy of the Klingon Empire particularly paranoid. And Jim could hardly blame them for their reaction. He would not like it if they extruded a narrow finger of territory several hundred light years long into the Federation.

He must be scrupulous about remaining within the Phalanx. Violating the borders of the Klingon Empire would be

ENTERPRISE

worth a court-martial and his career. If his ship survived the Guardians of the Empire.

The comm screen flickered. The geometric design of a commercial concierge appeared.

"Starfleet Teaching Hospital. Is this an emergency?"

"No, but this is Captain—"

"Please hold."

The image dissolved into pastel shapes, pastel music.

Jim knew the argument against abandoning Starbase 13 and relocating the people in its system. It would be perceived as a retreat. But Jim believed consolidation would prove far less provocative than continuing to rub the empire's nose in the existence of the Phalanx, especially if the Klingons knew the jokes the name brought on, or if their customs suggested similar crude humor.

"Thank you for holding," the hospital's concierge said. "What is your name, please?"

"Captain James T. Kirk, starship *Enterprise*."

"How may I help you?"

"Let me speak to Lieutenant Commander Gary Mitchell."

"What is your relationship to Commander Mitchell?"

"I'm his C.O." Jim doubted "best friend" would get very far with the hospital bureaucracy.

The image of a hospital room formed on the screen.

"Gary?"

Gary Mitchell still lay immersed in the regen gel. His eyes were closed; his dark hair fell across his forehead. If he were awake, aware, he would flip it back with a toss of his head; he would say that he really had to get a haircut; and then he would laugh and his hair would slide across his forehead again.

Gary looked frail and ill. His face was thin, his eyes deep and dark-circled. Jim blinked—and Ghioghe returned, the pain of his crushed ribs and shattered knee, the scarlet haze enveloping the universe when a deep cut across his forehead bled into his eyes. Other sentient beings bled that day: Jim remembered the blood. It slicked the deck, it beaded up and floated like drifts of a child's blown bubbles wherever the gravity failed. Red blood and yellow mixed into an intense burnt-orange; blue blood, dense and immiscible, flowed in

126

separate rivulets beneath patches of human blood, breaking out at the edge of a scarlet pool, expanding and glistening.

Jim caught his breath and shook off the flashback. He had thought he was done with all that.

Gary's eyelids flickered.

"Gary—?"

Gary moved restlessly. He came awake all at once, with a gasp and a start. Jim remembered how he had felt, engulfed in the regen bed, restrained gently but irrevocably. Those last few days as the drugs began to fade, he would try to move, try to turn or shift in his sleep, try to fight the restraint. It exhausted and infuriated him and held his freedom out of reach.

"Jim . . .?" Gary's voice was as frail as his body. "Hey, kid . . . did we make it through this one?"

"We sure did, Gary. Thanks to you."

"Let's not let them solve things that way again," Gary said. "Let's make them find some other way."

"That suits me," Jim said. "Gary, I just wanted to see how you were doing." He did not have the heart to tell Gary he had been overruled in his choice of first officer. Gary wanted the promotion as much as Jim wanted someone he knew and trusted as his second in command. The bad news could wait till Gary regained his strength. "It's good to have you back, my friend," Jim said. "Go to sleep, now. I know how it is. Go back to sleep."

"Who can sleep," Gary said, "who's covered with green slime?" He tried to laugh.

"You can." Jim grabbed at the anguish and relief he felt and clutched them tight.

Gary's eyelids drooped, but he jerked awake again. "Don't you leave without me, kid. Leave Federation space without me, and you're in lots and lots of trouble." He struggled against it, but sleep took him.

"Don't worry, my friend," Jim said. "We'll be ready for you when you're ready for us."

He broke the connection.

Jim flung himself into a chair in Dr. McCoy's office and put his feet on the desk, taking considerable pleasure in the solid thud of boot heels on wood.

"Do come in," McCoy said. "Sit down. Make yourself comfortable."

"The good news is, Gary's awake."

"He is! That *is* good news, Jim."

"I just got off the comm with him. He's still pretty groggy—but he's going to be all right, Bones."

"I never doubted it for a minute," McCoy said. "What's the bad news?"

"The bad news is, I took your advice—"

"And you've come for your medical appointment without my having to send out the hounds! Hallelujah, brothers!" He rose. "Into the coverall with you."

"No, no—I don't have time for an exam. I mean I took your advice about a yeoman."

"And—?"

"And every time I speak to her, I scare her. She's a real case. She apologizes continuously."

"Continually," McCoy said.

"No, dammit, *continuously*. Every time she says anything, she starts out with 'I'm sorry.' "

"Sounds pretty neurotic to me, all right."

"If that's true, how'd she get into Starfleet?"

McCoy laughed. "Jim, are you kidding? If Starfleet turned people down because of a major neurosis here or there, it'd have enough personnel for . . . oh, maybe one space cruiser. A *small* space cruiser."

"But—"

"We've all got our neuroses. I do, you do. Everybody."

"With the exception, I'm sure, of our Mr. Spock."

"Spock! Spock worst of all! He represses all of half his heritage and most of the rest of it. Vulcans' worst neurosis is they really believe they're sane!"

"What do you mean, half his heritage?"

"His human half, of course. On his mother's side, I believe."

"I thought he was a Vulcan."

"So does he," McCoy said dryly.

"What else do you know about him?"

"He isn't much for idle chatter. I've heard of him, of course. Then there's the usual stuff in the medical record. Incredible education the man's got, and he's taken advantage of his opportunities—he's worked with people most of the rest of us would be lucky ever to meet.''

"What do you mean, Bones? That he's well connected or that he's bright?"

"Bright? Bright hardly begins to describe him. He's brilliant, Jim. As for the other . . . he's only well connected if you count the relatives who are top-ranked diplomats or senior research scientists.'' McCoy grinned. "To tell you the truth, I never heard of a Vulcan whose family wasn't well connected.''

Jim felt in no mood to be amused. "Is that why he got promoted over Gary?"

"Because he has family connections and Mitch doesn't? I don't know. Why don't you ask him?"

"I can see that: 'Say, Commander Spock, is your success due to nepotism?' " Jim shook his head. "I'm not being fair. I know it. I haven't given him a chance. It's only . . .'' He changed the subject. "What am I going to do about Yeoman Rand?"

"Is her work poor?"

"Not at all. She made noise about her lack of experience, then pushed two buttons and the files made sense.''

"You aren't looking for a graceful way to demote her and send her back to quartermaster?"

"No, I just want her to stop flinching when I talk to her! I hope she doesn't turn up all bright-eyed at my cabin two hours before breakfast anymore, either. That much enthusiasm is hard to take at dawn.''

"Hmm,'' McCoy said.

"She has to use the comm unit,'' Jim said defensively.

"Why does she have to use your comm?"

"She has to work someplace—she can't spread my papers out all over the bridge.''

"Is the yeoman's comm broken?"

"What yeoman's comm?"

McCoy sighed and gazed in supplication at the ceiling. "Jim, you're still thinking in space-cruiser terms—and you need a grand tour of your own ship. Including the yeoman's cabin, which is down the corridor from yours.'' His voice trailed off. "Jim, you didn't promote her out of seniority, then leave her in crew's quarters?"

"She's who quartermaster sent, so she's who I promoted. As for the other—I never thought about it."

"That's hard on morale. Have her move. Then one of your problems is solved. Maybe two—maybe she flinches because the promotion's gotten her some heavy hazing."

"I doubt it. She flinched from the beginning."

"Then the flinching may take longer. I'll talk to her during her exam and see if I can find out what's wrong."

"Look, if she's seriously disturbed—"

"Jim! Half the time our neuroses are what allow us to function as well as we do in the circumstances we pick. I could give examples, present company included, but I don't have time to psychoanalyze you today. Though I *would* have had time to give you your physical, if I'd started when you got here."

Jim grinned. "So you would."

"But I don't now. So buzz off, I've got another appointment in ten minutes."

"Buzz off? Is that any way to speak to your C.O.?"

"Buzz off, *sir.*"


In a secluded alcove of the officers' lounge, Mr. Spock took up the challenge of a three-dimensional chess problem.

Ordinarily, Spock could concentrate with such intensity that he ceased to perceive voices and sounds. But this evening a strange, monotonous drone reverberated into his peaceful solitude.

At a table nearby sat several of the younger officers, Dr. McCoy, and Chief Engineer Scott. Mr. Scott seemed to have found a kindred spirit in Dr. McCoy. Spock respected Scott's ability, but thought his fondness for fermented and distilled beverages to be unfortunate at best. Spock added Scott's apparent rapport with McCoy to his short list of the engineer's less sterling qualities.

Scott often spent his free time in the lounge, spinning unlikely stories for junior officers who invariably listened without hint of incredulity. Spock had heard or overheard each story a dozen times. Whether Spock believed them, he seldom experienced any difficulty in letting them flow past him unheeded, like a river around an immovable boulder.

But a new individual had joined Scott's circle. Mr. Cockspur, a member of the vaudeville company, was an older man who wore his unnaturally thick and dark hair at a moderate length, meticulously styled. His mustache twisted to double points on each side.

Mr. Cockspur had taken Scott's place as storyteller. While Spock naturally found no amusement value whatsoever in Scott's tales—"yarns" might be a better term, as it implied a certain element of the fantastic—he was capable of appreciating the aesthetic of his performance. Mr. Cockspur's voice had none of Scott's cadences. It had no cadences at all. The sonorous monotone filled the hall; Spock found few elements of interest in the story. Everyone else listened with every evidence of utter captivation.

Spock had no illusions about his understanding of human beings. He had spent most of his childhood on Vulcan. What time he had spent on earth he had devoted to the study of science, not of humans and their perplexing nature. Despite his heritage, he found humans quite inexplicable at the most unexpected times.

This was one of those times.

The incomprehensible human entertainment consisted of a recital of every theater in which Mr. Cockspur had appeared, and every play in which Mr. Cockspur had performed. Spock thought of an analogy. Modern readers of the ancient earth poet Homer found the roster of ships in the *Iliad* excruciatingly tedious, but the ancient Greeks were said to have paid the rhapsodes, the reciters, enormous sums to repeat the roster of ships at celebrations. A citizen of a Greek city-state gained status by tracing ancestry to a certain captain of a certain ship of the strong-greaved Achaians. Perhaps Mr. Cockspur's listeners had heard of plays in which he had performed or theaters in which he had appeared; perhaps they experienced a thrill of recognition when he recited a name they recognized. It seemed an odd way to pass an evening, but, then, humans often passed time in ways that Spock thought odd.

By force of will, Spock concentrated on his chess problem and placed his attention among the pieces.

"Need an opponent?"

"No, captain," Spock said, without looking up. He had heard the approach and recognized the step, despite short acquaintance. Captain Kirk looked over his shoulder at the graceful sweep of the 3-D chessboard.

"Why are you playing alone?"

"Because, captain, no one on board plays at my level."

"You're modest, aren't you?" the captain said.

"I am neither modest nor immodest; both are character traits beyond which Vulcans have evolved. I state a fact." He regretted the loss of his peace and privacy, then reminded himself severely that regret had no place in the psychological makeup of a Vulcan.

"Are you playing black or white?"

"Both, of course, captain," Spock said.

"But black's move?" the captain said. "Of course?"

Was the captain's voice sarcastic or sardonic? Or did "belligerent" more accurately describe it?

Spock made a noncommittal sound. If Captain Kirk could determine from the unusual arrangement that black moved next, then he might be an adequate opponent . . . But he had a fifty percent chance of guessing the correct color, and that was the more likely of the two possibilities.

Spock concentrated on the chessboard. Queen to queen's pawn D-4 to threaten the white king? He moved the piece and thoughtfully drew back his hand.

"White to checkmate in three," the captain said.

Spock looked up in disbelief. Captain Kirk turned, leisurely surveyed the room, and strolled away.

Jim saw McCoy at a nearby table and started toward him. Then, too late, he noticed Mr. Cockspur holding court.

"And a year later when I returned, well, you can be sure they did not try to put me in less than the star's—"

"Hello, Jim." McCoy broke in over Mr. Cockspur's recitation before Jim could pretend he had been planning to go elsewhere all along. The officers rose.

"As you were."

McCoy dragged another chair into the circle. "Why don't you join us?" He quickly suppressed his grin.

Everyone at the table except Cockspur looked at Jim with expressions of supplication.

"Jim," McCoy said again, *"do* sit down."

"Yes," Cockspur said. "Sit down, whilst I continue—"

"Thank you." Jim tried to sound sincere. "But coming in on your story in the middle wouldn't do it justice—"

"No, you sure wouldn't get the full effect," McCoy said. "But don't deprive yourself in the meantime."

McCoy did his best to conceal a fit of laughter. Jim remembered what Winona had said to him—was it only two days before?—that applied right now: surrender gracefully. He gave McCoy a dirty look and joined the group.

Cockspur resumed his story. "I was just telling your crew of my appearance in Campbell City." His voice hit like a wall, as if he never moderated it from full performance strength. He proceeded to describe, in great detail, the play he had performed on the moon. He claimed to have written it. It sounded vaguely familiar to Jim, but he was certain he would have remembered Cockspur had he ever seen him perform. Unless he fell asleep, as he nearly did now. Jim jerked himself awake.

"My little play ran for six weeks on the dark side of the moon. An enormous success. As you see, I'm not completely inexperienced at traveling in your spaceships."

Jim wondered how Mr. Cockspur could spend more than two weeks—the length of the lunar night—on the far side of earth's moon and still refer to it as dark; he wondered how his officers liked being referred to as crew. Jim did not much appreciate having the *Enterprise* called a spaceship.

"The *Enterprise* is a starship, Mr. Cockspur," Jim said mildly.

"Precisely," Mr. Cockspur said.

"What I mean is—"

Cockspur interrupted him. "And rather a large and expensive spaceship, at that, to use for the transportation of," he cleared his throat, "vaudeville—or even some legitimate art—to the ends of the universe."

Though Jim had thought the same thing, he found himself in the awkward position of preferring to disagree.

"We aren't going quite as far as the end of the universe," he said.

"Nevertheless, your time and your ship would be put to better use fighting the enemies of the Federation."

Jim tried to hold his temper in the face of an earthbound

nincompoop who thought all Starfleet ships ever did was to blow people and planets out of the sky.

"We aren't at war with anyone, Mr. Cockspur."

"Ah, but there are worlds to conquer—"

"Have you ever been in a war?"

"I have not had that honor."

"Honor—! I'd have thought," Jim said, "in this day and age, that civilized beings would have progressed beyond violent colonization—beyond supporting genocide."

"Captain, you take this rather personally."

"Yes. I do. Both because of what I've seen myself and because my mother is part Sioux. Her family history—"

"Captain, captain! You're speaking of events hundreds of years in the past! What possible bearing could they have on us, here, now?"

"Every bearing." How had he got into this argument? Jim wondered if he could plead the press of duty and escape without appearing to be as rude as he felt like acting. He had made everyone uncomfortable except Mr. Cockspur.

Mr. Cockspur started to lecture Jim on colonization.

A shadow fell across the table. Jim looked up. Commander Spock stood nearby, silent, hands behind his back.

Even Cockspur noticed the Vulcan's presence. He stopped and stared at him as if Spock were an urchin who had interrupted history's finest performance.

"Would the captain oblige me," Spock said, "with the answer to a question?"

"Certainly, Mr. Spock. Pardon me," he said to Cockspur, concealing his relief. "Starship business."

"Pardon me, captain," Spock said. "Perhaps I misspoke—"

"No, no, not at all," Jim said. "I mustn't put leisure above a consultation with my first officer."

He nearly grabbed Commander Spock by the elbow to hurry him off and to keep him from wiping out Jim's excuse to escape. But he restrained himself from putting hands on a Vulcan. He and Spock walked away from Cockspur's captive audience.

"I needed only a moment," Spock said. "It was not my intention to take you from your . . . pleasure."

"My pleasure, Mr. Spock?" He laughed. "I heard Vulcans have an odd concept of pleasure."

"Regarding white to checkmate in three . . ."

"I apologize for barging in on your problem."

Spock raised one eyebrow. "Then . . . white cannot checkmate in three moves?"

"Yes, it can. Did you think I was making a joke?"

"One can never be certain," Spock said, "when a human being is making a joke."

"Usually we laugh," Jim said.

"Not invariably."

"No. Not invariably. Still, I wasn't making a joke."

"If the captain will indulge me . . . your comment has piqued my curiosity."

"In that case, of course I'll play out the problem with you." In the alcove, the chess pieces stood in the same positions. "Commander Spock, I thought Vulcans experienced no emotions. Yet you confess to curiosity."

"Curiosity is not an emotion, captain," Spock said as they sat down, "but the impetus in the search for knowledge that distinguishes sentient creatures. Your move, captain."

Jim moved his queen's knight.

Spock regarded the chessboard. One black eyebrow tilted to a steeper slant. He stared at the positions as if he had shifted into computer mode, as if he were calculating the effects of every possible move of every piece on the board. Jim had seen the opening in a flash of insight. Now, abruptly doubtful, he searched the board for some overlooked move, some schoolchild error.

Spock reached out. Jim forced himself to stay as collected as any Vulcan while he waited for Mr. Spock to make a move that Jim's intuition had not taken into account.

Spock tipped his king and let it settle back onto its squat base.

"I resign," Spock said.

Jim wondered if he saw the barest hint of a frown, the barest suggestion of confusion, in the Vulcan's expression.

"Your move," Spock said, "risked your queen and your knights. It was . . . illogical."

"But effective," Jim said.

"Indeed," Spock said softly. "What mode of calculation do you use? Sinhawk, perhaps? Or a method of your own devising?"

"One of my own devising, you might say. I didn't calculate it, Spock. I *saw* it. Call it intuition, if you like. Or good luck."

"I do not believe in luck," Spock said. "And I have no experience of . . . intuition."

"Nevertheless, that's my method of calculation."

Spock cleared the board.

"Would you care," Spock asked, "for a complete game?"

# Chapter 6

WHEN JIM KIRK arrived on the bridge the next morning, he felt great. He had slept the night through without a recurrence of his persistent dreams of Ghioghe. Gary Mitchell was on his way to recovery, the *Enterprise* was purring along without a hitch, and Jim had won last night's game of chess, nearly managing to crack Commander Spock's taciturnity in the process.

Jim felt pleased with himself. He was also sleepy. He wondered where Rand had gotten the incredible coffee she gave him yesterday. He wondered if there might be more of it somewhere.

Today it was not Yeoman Rand's fault that he got too little sleep. McCoy's advice appeared to have worked. Jim had seen nothing of her this morning.

No, his sleepiness was his own fault, and he did not care. He had traded half the night's sleep for the hard-played chess game with Commander Spock. He had won with a flamboyant, one might even say reckless, series of moves. Mr. Spock had been winning until Jim's final, exhilarating rally.

Mr. Spock, already at the science officer's station, showed no evidence of having been up till all hours.

"Good morning, Commander Spock."

"Good morning, captain."

"I enjoyed our game last night."

"It was . . ." Spock hesitated. "Most instructive."

Jim supposed that was as close as a Vulcan was likely to come to admitting he had enjoyed himself.

137

Jim thought back, trying to recall a moment when he had been on the bridge and Commander Spock had not. The science officer came early and stayed late. Maybe he wanted to demonstrate his devotion to his position as both science officer and second in command, to prove Admiral Noguchi had made the right decision.

Or maybe, Jim thought, the two jobs are too much for any single person. Maybe Noguchi should have let me make my own choice. And maybe Commander Spock shouldn't rub in the fact that I wasn't allowed to.

Jim received the reports of the bridge stations, which all boiled down to "nothing to report." Engines and systems functioning normally. On course and on schedule. No urgent communications from Starfleet. No emergencies.

At times like this, space travel could get boring. He wished something would happen.

He wondered if Rand had begun setting up his meetings schedule. And where was she? She should report here first every morning, but he had neglected to mention that to her.

He tried to reach her at the yeoman's cabin. Though he had left orders for her to move into it immediately, computer registered no occupant.

He checked his schedule. Computer showed one appointment today and nothing thereafter. He sighed, wondering if he had gotten himself stuck with a yeoman who did everything in a hysterical flurry at the last minute.

Then he noticed whom his first appointment was with: Leonard McCoy.

The turbo-lift opened. Yeoman Rand sidled to the environmental systems station and started to work.

"Yeoman Rand," Jim said stiffly.

"Yes, captain?" she whispered.

"About my schedule."

"Yes, sir, it's right here, sir."

"But you made an appointment for me with Leonard McCoy," he said. "Dr. McCoy and I have served together for years. Didn't you notice that we both came to the *Enterprise* from the same ship?"

"No, sir. He didn't say—I'm sorry, sir."

Dammit, she was flinching and apologizing again. He

started to say something soothing. He suddenly became aware of her appearance.

Her uniform easily two sizes too big, her hair rumpled—though how hair that short could contrive to rumple, he did not know—and her eyes watery, she huddled in the seat as if she could make herself disappear.

"Yeoman Rand, are you all right?"

"Yes, captain," she said in a small voice.

"What's your excuse for your disheveled appearance?"

"None, sir."

"Did you get my message about the yeoman's cabin?"

"Yes, sir, a few hours ago."

"Why haven't you moved in?"

"I'm sorry, sir, I . . . I just haven't." Her voice grew even smaller.

"Do it now. And don't ever—I repeat, ever—show up on my bridge in anything even hinting at your current state of disrepair."

She looked at him, stricken, fighting back tears. She leaped to her feet and bolted into the lift.

Uhura looked down at Captain Kirk. She found it hard to believe that anyone, under any circumstances, could speak to a child like Janice Rand in such a harsh tone. She put her station on standby.

"Excuse me," she said coldly. "I have a break coming." She left without waiting for Kirk's dismissal. The turbo-lift closed. "Take me wherever you took your last passenger," Uhura said.

The lift let her out into a deserted corridor, nowhere near crew quarters or officers' territory. Uhura wondered what Janice was planning to do. In her current emotional state, maybe she was not planning anything. Maybe she just wanted to go somewhere, anywhere, away from the bridge.

In the second briefing room she checked, Uhura found Janice crying uncontrollably with her head pillowed on her arms.

"Janice, don't cry. There, there, it's all right." Uhura sat beside her and put her arm around Janice's shoulders.

Janice flinched away, huddling in on herself, trying to stop crying and only making it worse.

"Everything's all right. It's going to be all right." Uhura patted her shoulder and stroked the irregular fuzz of her hair.

"I couldn't help it!" Janice whispered, her voice shaky and broken. "I understand why Roswind hates me now, but she hated me before when she didn't have any reason to, and it isn't my fault."

"Of course it isn't," Uhura said. She had no idea what Janice was talking about, but she kept on offering reassurance until the child calmed down.

After ten minutes or so, Janice cried herself out. Her face was red and her eyes swollen with tears and she sniffed occasionally. With her rough-chopped hair and her baggy uniform, she looked a mess. Uhura got a towel from the steward's station in the corner and gave it to her.

"Better now?" Uhura said. "Wipe your eyes. Blow your nose. There. Take a deep breath. Good. Now. Tell me what happened."

The words came out in a tumble. Janice had no conception of hazing. Sometime in her life she had decided, or had it demonstrated to her, that sticking up for herself was more dangerous than submitting to humiliation. This troubled Uhura; she wondered if Janice's spirit had been crushed beyond recovery.

"And then this morning," Janice said, "I went back to the cabin to get my things and move, and I just lay down for a second, only I was so tired I fell asleep and when I woke up I was late, and I put my uniform on only it was the wrong uniform, I know I ordered the right one but it isn't the one that was there when I lay down, and I didn't know whether to order another one and wait, or put it on and go to work, and Roswind laughed till I could hardly think." Her lips quivered. She hovered on the brink of tears. "She's so beautiful and I admired her so much at first, but all she ever did was make fun of me and laugh."

"Why didn't you just laugh, too?"

Janice stared at her, uncomprehending. "I had to go to work."

"She was teasing you, Janice. Maybe she let it go farther than she meant—I hope that's all it was—or maybe she's the sort of person who likes to see how far she can push you. Usually all you have to do is push back."

Janice said nothing. She sat very still, neither agreeing nor disagreeing, giving every indication of listening to what Uhura said to her. But the expression in her eyes was lost, distant, hopeless.

"Where are you from, Janice?"

"What? I'm sorry, I mean . . ."

"Where's your home world?"

"Oh," she said, her voice rising into a brittle false cheer, "I'm from all over, we moved around a lot."

"Who's we? Your family, your community? Where did you go?"

"Why are you asking me all these questions?" Janice cried. "Why should you care, what do you need to know for?"

"I care because it hurts me to see anyone as frightened as you are. I care because we have to work together, and we can't if you act like a scared sixteen-year-old."

Janice gasped and her fair skin paled. Uhura feared she would faint. The child flung herself on her knees at Uhura's feet.

"How did you find out? Oh, please, please, don't tell, don't tell anyone—"

"Janice—!"

"Please, I'll do anything! Just don't tell!"

"Janice, get up!" Embarrassed, horrified, Uhura practically dragged Janice up. "Stop it, now, stop it!"

Janice jerked herself away from Uhura. *"How did you find out?"* she cried.

Uhura realized what Janice believed. "Like a scared sixteen-year-old," Uhura had said. Without meaning to, Uhura had discovered Janice's secret.

"That doesn't matter," Uhura said.

"If you tell, I'll kill myself! I'll kill you! I'll—"

Uhura could not help but smile. She drew the terrified child into a hug. "Nobody's killing anybody. Don't be silly."

After a while, Janice's sobs subsided. She huddled against Uhura as if she were starved for comfort.

"However did you get into Starfleet at sixteen? They're

pretty strict about that." Starfleet would send younger ca-
dets, officer candidates, on heavily supervised training
cruises, but regulations permitted no human under seventeen to join the crew. Safeguards and double-checks prevented children of any sentient species from running away to
join Starfleet on a lark.

Whatever Janice Rand's motives, she had not run away on
a lark.

"When I was little, my family moved," Janice whispered.
"The warp engines blew, and we had to travel through
normal space. We accelerated almost to light-speed, so it
only took us a few weeks of subjective time. But objective
time, it was three years."

"Nobody ever corrected the records?"

Janice shook her head.

"I don't see how you got away with it." To Uhura, Janice
did not look anywhere near twenty. She looked like a
sixteen-year-old. But no one ever thought about her, no one
ever asked.

"I lied," Janice said. "I'm scared to, because when people
find out you've done it, they—they don't like it. But I had to.
People believe a big enough lie. They figure you'd never dare
say it if it wasn't true."

Uhura laughed, then sobered. "What are we going to do
with you?"

Janice's eyes widened. "You *are* going to tell!"

Appalled by the prospect of Janice's falling on her knees
again, Uhura tried to reassure her. But she was unwilling to
promise not to send her home. "Don't be so frightened. We
need to talk. Would going home be so bad? You're just a kid,
Janice. You ought to be going to school, back with your
family—"

"No! I'll never go back! You can't make me!"

"Don't you think they're worried about you? Wouldn't
they want to know you're safe, no matter what happened, no
matter what you did?"

"*I* didn't do anything!" Janice said. "But I will—I'll *make*
you put me in prison before I go back to Saweoure!"

"I'm not putting anybody in prison, Janice, and I never
heard of Saweoure."

"It's where we ended up after the ship lost its warp drive.

142

We didn't have enough money to get it fixed. We had to sell it and stay there. But you can't just stay there if you don't have any money. You have to be under somebody's 'protection.' " Quite calmly, Janice told her the rest of it.

When she finished, Uhura felt near tears.

"Janice . . ." She took a deep breath. "What you're describing is nothing but slavery! How is this allowed to go on? Hasn't anyone tried to stop it?"

Janice's voice turned bitter. "How should I know? Maybe it's easier for the Federation to think everything's all right. Maybe everybody likes it that way so they keep it secret."

Uhura welcomed Janice's bitterness and her anger, for it proved her spirit still existed. "How did you get away?"

"I sneaked me and my brothers on board a cargo shuttle. We were too ignorant to know it was impossible. Once the shuttle got back to its mother ship, we stayed hidden. It wasn't too hard. Then we hid in a crate of relief supplies, and when we landed we snuck into the Faience refugee camp—"

"You snuck *into* Faience?" The camp was a horror story of mismanagement and malice in the middle of a systemwide disaster, and many people had died needlessly.

Janice shrugged. Uhura felt a certain awe at the coolness with which Janice faced her past, if not her present.

"It was better than where we'd been," Janice said. "Then Starfleet came to relocate us, and that's when I found out I was legally three years older than I really am. I don't have any records except my birth certificate."

"What about your brothers?"

"They didn't even have birth certificates. The officials at Faience patted us on the head and said, 'Oh you poor children,' and registered Ben and Sirri. Since I was of age, I got their guardianship. I found them a good school, and I joined Starfleet so I could pay for it."

Amazed that anyone could go through what Janice had endured and survive, Uhura tried to think of some words of encouragement.

In the few seconds of silence, the young yeoman's steadiness evaporated as she waited for still another person with complete power over her to determine her fate.

"I'm almost seventeen," Janice whispered. "I mean I'm almost really seventeen, I think, as near as I can figure. I do my job, Uhura." She hesitated. "I guess you wouldn't know that from today, though."

"I think you should tell," Uhura said.

"No!"

"I think you should testify before the Federation of Planets Rights Commission. I think you should try to stop what's going on."

"I *can't*."

"Janice—"

"Uhura, you don't understand! I committed a crime by sneaking on board that cargo ship."

"It's illegal to prevent citizens from moving freely—"

"But it isn't illegal to charge a lot of money to get from one place to another, and I didn't pay for a ticket. Stowing away is the same as hijacking, on Saweoure. If I testified, the officials would call me a criminal and a liar and a thief. And they'd be able to prove what they charged me with. I did all those things. Please don't tell. Please."

"*You* should tell—you should tell the authorities what you told me."

"The authorities?" Janice said angrily. "Like who, for instance? Like Captain Kirk? He wouldn't listen to me. He'd think I was just making something up."

Uhura hesitated. If she had found all this out while Captain Pike still commanded the *Enterprise,* she would not have hesitated to urge Janice to confide in him. But she did not know Kirk well enough to have any idea how he might react to Janice's story. Janice certainly had little reason to have any confidence in his sympathy. Not after what had just happened.

"Please, Uhura," Janice said again. "Please don't tell."

Uhura replied with great reluctance. "All right. I promise. My word means something to me. I don't break it."

"Thank you, Uhura."

"I still think—at least consider talking to the Rights Commission," Uhura said. Before Janice could react with fear again, Uhura changed the subject. "Now let's get you fixed up and back to the bridge. The sooner you forget about this morning, the better."

"I have to . . . to go back to my cabin. I left my things on my bunk. Roswind will be there, I guess."

"Forget about your roommate. You move into the yeoman's cabin. Wash your face. Put on a fresh uniform. I'll get your things for you."

"Oh, Uhura, would you?"

"Leave it to me," Uhura said.


On the bridge, Jim sat stiff and angry, his arms folded across his chest. Blast Rand anyway, she had wrecked his good mood. Everyone pretended they had noticed neither Rand's embarrassment nor Uhura's anger. No doubt they all thought he had been too hard on Rand.

They could think what they liked. He could be as easygoing as anyone, but if people took advantage, things would have to change. He loathed having anyone play on his sympathy, especially with tears.

The lift returned. Lindy bounded out. Jim wondered why Janice Rand could not take her or Uhura as a model; and how had Rand managed to persuade the synthesizer to give her a uniform in the wrong size, anyway? That took real talent.

"Hi, Jim, I brought—"

An unbelievable noise drowned out Lindy's voice. A horde of tiny animals rushed past her, yapping and whining and barking, tumbling over and around each other as they invaded the bridge and nosed into every nook and cranny. At first Jim thought they were alien creatures, then he had a moment's awful fantasy that the *Enterprise* had become infested with rats, and finally he recognized dogs. Twenty or thirty miniature pastel-colored, frizzy-furred, sweater-clad, ribbon-bedecked dogs.

But dogs. If he stretched the definition to include poodles.

"Fifi! Toto! Cece! Come! Sit! Stay!"

An enormous person stood just outside the lift, calling orders in a great deep voice.

Completely ignoring him, a tide of poodles rose around Jim's feet. The tiny creatures snarled and yipped at each other and snapped at Jim's boots. One buried its teeth in his bloused right pants leg, then shook its head and growled and jerked at the fabric.

"Let go—go on now—ow! Damn!" He snatched his hand away. The little monster had tried to bite him! His finger smarted all around the red teeth marks.

"Pay no attention, he means nothing by it." Lindy's companion picked up the offending animal. "Fifi, evil puppy! You know you mustn't bite!"

Jim stood up.

"Get . . . these . . . animals—" Jim refused to dignify them with the word "dogs"—"off my bridge!"

"Don't worry, captain, they won't hurt anything. They've never been on a starship before. They're just excited." Fifi, a pink miniature poodle wearing a spangled blue sweater, nearly vanished in the massive hand.

"Jim," Lindy said, "this is my friend Newland Yanagi-machi Rift. You missed meeting him at dinner last night."

The poodles clustered around Jim, Lindy, and Rift, barking and whining and jumping and getting poodle hair and glitter on Jim's uniform pants. He was surrounded by a whirlpool of pastel fur, spangles, sharp little white teeth, beady brown eyes. He could stomp them into homogeneity, but they would make a lousy rug. His alternative was to pretend they did not exist.

"How do you do, captain," Rift said.

Jim looked at Lindy, who was trying not to laugh.

"And what do you do with the vaudeville company, Mr. Rift?" Jim asked. It was hard to talk through clenched teeth. "Do you sing?"

"Why, no, captain. Philomela is the singer in the family. I work with my puppies. They never cease to amaze me—I hope you have a chance to see us perform." He put Fifi on the deck. "Fifi, sit! Stay!"

Fifi scampered between Sulu and Cheung and vanished beneath the navigation console.

Sulu dived under the console. "Hey, come out of there."

"They're overexcited by the change in environment," Rift said fondly. "On stage, they're hardly the same dogs."

"Are those things housebroken?" Jim said.

"Of course, captain."

Rift was an amazing specimen of humanity. Aside from being two meters tall and about half that wide, he had bright blue eyes with an epicanthic fold over the eyelid, skin a few shades more golden than Sulu's, and curly flaming-scarlet hair. Why did the hairstyle, a complex topknot arrangement, look so strange, yet seem so familiar? Jim finally identified it as the traditional way of binding the hair of Sumo wrestlers, a fashion that had never been designed to restrain hair the texture of Rift's.

The traditional sport flourished in Japan now as it had for a millennium. Jim wondered what Rift's connection with it might be. Perhaps he actually was a Sumo wrestler. Just because Jim had never heard of a redhaired Sumo wrestler did not mean none existed.

"Pardon me a moment, captain."

Rift went to help Sulu and Cheung extricate Fifi from the underpinnings of the console.

"There's some question, though," Lindy said so only Jim could hear, "about whether the puppies are starship-broken." At Jim's expression, she barely managed to keep herself from laughing.

Newland Rift returned with the errant Fifi cradled in his enormous hand.

"Bad puppy," he said. "Say you're sorry." He held the pink poodle up to Jim's face. It growled, baring teeth easily the size of wheat grains. "Fifi!"

"Mr. Rift," Jim said, "get these animals off my bridge."

Rift looked both hurt and offended. "All right, captain, if that's the way you feel about it." He whistled and called to the poodles, who responded with another paroxysm of scampering and barking. But as Rift left the bridge, they formed a bouncing, furry swarm and followed him, the last little puffed tail vanishing just as the lift doors closed.

Lindy gave up trying to keep a straight face.

Jim heard muffled giggles all around him. "Doesn't anybody have any work to do?" he snapped.

Spock glanced up. "Yes, captain. But if something requires attention—?"

"Never mind, Commander Spock! Did you have *business* on the bridge, Ms. Lukarian?" Jim said coldly as she laughed.

"I came to introduce you to Newland."

"You've accomplished that."

"And I came to give Janice the first-off-the-press poster."

She stifled giggles and unrolled her paper. "She did a terrific job. You've got a treasure, Jim. Even if she can't juggle. Think Starfleet would come after me if I shanghaied one of its people?"

Jim restrained himself from telling her that she could have Yeoman Janice Rand right now. He looked at the poster. "It is eye-catching," he admitted.

"Janice designed it practically from scratch," Lindy said. "I brought one for you, too, but the first one is for her. Where is she?"

"She . . . er . . . she had some work on another deck. She'll be back." He felt a good deal less certain than he sounded.

"Okay, I'll wait. And I have one more small favor to ask. It's Athene, Jim. The deck's too hard—"

What am I, Jim thought, captain of an interstellar ark? If I have to worry about one more animal . . .

Yeoman Rand returned. She had changed her uniform and combed her hair; she looked fragile and unhappy, but she had retreated from the brink of tears. Without a word she took her station.

"Speak to my yeoman about any problems you have with your company, Ms. Lukarian," Jim said. "Or your pets. Now, I *do* have work to do—even if nobody else does."

Lindy smiled at him and jumped up all the stairs at once to join Yeoman Rand. Jim wondered if she ever just walked anywhere. And he wondered what he could do to get her to smile at him again.

"Captain, excuse me." Yeoman Rand spoke almost too softly for him to hear her.

"Whatever Ms. Lukarian needs, within reason, please take care of it."

"I will, sir. But you asked me to arrange your schedule, too. Computer has it now, if you want to review it to give me any changes." She hesitated. "I'm sorry for the misunderstanding about Dr. McCoy. He expects you in ten minutes. Shall I call him and cancel for you?"

"No, yeoman, never mind."

Pretending to be busy, he brought the schedule up on his notepad and glanced through it.

148

At least Rand had done as he asked this time. The appointments stretched over the next three months. He thought it important at least to meet everyone on board.

He stood up. "I'll be in sick bay for the next half-hour," he said to no one in particular.

No one answered.

The chaos on the bridge appeared to have passed for the moment, but Mr. Spock sensed that the experience he had just endured was not unique. When Captain Pike commanded the *Enterprise*, such chaos never occurred.

He opened a file in computer and began to compose his request for transfer to some other ship. Any other ship.

When Uhura arrived at Janice Rand's old cabin, the crew member who had admitted her glanced up with disinterest, then noticed Uhura's officer's stripes and jumped to her feet.

"Lieutenant!" she said. "Um—" She was very tall and extremely beautiful, and Uhura could understand why Janice felt overwhelmed by her.

"You are—?" Uhura said, deciding to let her stand and sweat.

"Uh, Roswind, ma'am."

"Roswind, I believe Yeoman Rand left some of her belongings behind when she moved."

"Uh, yes, ma'am. They're right over there."

"Thank you." She collected the possessions, thinking, Well, Roswind, you're not such a bully when you're outranked, are you?

"How is Janice doing, ma'am?"

"Captain Kirk is obviously impressed with her," Uhura said, reflecting that, from one point of view, the claim was no stretch of the truth. "Oh, by the way, Roswind, do you have any allergies? Hay fever, particularly?"

"No, ma'am, not that I know of. Not hay fever."

"Excellent." Taking her own good time, she rearranged Janice's belongings and tied them up in a scarf. She regarded the parcel critically, picked it up, and started for the door.

"Uh, ma'am?"

"Yes, Roswind?"

"Why, ma'am?"

"Why what?"

"Why did you want to know if I had any allergies, ma'am?"

"Because of your new roommate."

"I don't understand, ma'am."

"Some human beings react adversely to her species, but the reaction correlates almost a hundred percent with hay fever. So you mustn't worry."

"What species is she, ma'am?"

"Why? You aren't—" Uhura lowered her voice. "You aren't xenophobic, are you?"

Since xenophobia could get one dishonorably discharged from Starfleet, Roswind reacted most satisfactorily.

"No, ma'am, of course not! I get along with everybody! I was just—curious."

"I see. I'm sure you'll get along with her, too. Her people are intelligent and soft-spoken. Just one thing."

"What's that, ma'am?"

"Their planet rotates about every sixty hours, so their circadian rhythm is different from ours. She'll stay awake longer than you do, and sleep longer, too. Her people are known to react badly if they're awakened, so you'll want to be cautious."

"What do you mean, 'badly,' ma'am? You mean she'll jump up and hit you?"

"No, no, she'd never hurt you. Her people are quite timid. But shock might put her into hibernation. If that happens, she'll sleep for weeks. That wouldn't do her career any good."

"Oh," Roswind said. "I see. I'm sure we won't have any trouble, ma'am."

"Good. Well, Roswind, thank you for your help." She started for the door again.

"Lieutenant?"

"What is it, Roswind?"

"What does my new roommate look like, ma'am? Just so I'll recognize her, I mean."

"You won't have any trouble recognizing her," Uhura said. "She's green."

*   *   *

Jim strode into McCoy's office.

"How do you do, Dr. McCoy. I'm James T. Kirk, your captain. How nice to meet you, and what a surprise. Are you having any difficulties? All your supplies in order? What do you think of the ship?"

"How do you do, captain," McCoy said. "Everything's fine, just fine." McCoy tossed him a coverall.

"What's this?"

"Examination coverall."

"I *know* that—"

"Transparent to diagnostic signals—"

"I know that, too—"

"And you've got a free half-hour—"

Jim frowned. "This is a setup, isn't it? Between you and Yeoman Rand."

"It's a setup, but she didn't have anything to do with it. She said you wanted to chat with everyone on board the *Enterprise*—"

"And you conveniently forgot to mention that you've known me since I was a lieutenant."

"If you didn't want a get-acquainted appointment with me, you should have told her."

"She might have noticed we've shipped out together before."

"Oh, I see." McCoy nodded gravely. "Aside from learning a new job, and making sense of that mess on your desk, and spending the next week setting up your appointments, she's supposed to memorize all the *Enterprise* personnel service records. Overnight."

"No, of course not. It would have been convenient if she'd made the connection, though." Then something McCoy had said made a connection in Jim's mind. He swung McCoy's comm unit around.

"Make yourself at home," McCoy said dryly.

Jim started when he read the screen, for McCoy had been filling out a requisition form for a package of regen starter culture.

Jim tried to pretend he had not noticed the subject of the requisition. He called his own schedule from the files. He paged through it, noting its regular progression, day after day. In the last twenty-four hours or so, Rand had set up several hundred appointments for him; she had put them in clusters of a few each day, and though many members of the crew worked middle or low watch and slept odd hours, and some people worked on a schedule that had nothing to do with the twenty-four-hour circadian rhythm of the human majority on the *Enterprise,* Rand had somehow managed to keep his early mornings clear.

"It didn't take her a week," he said.

"What are you talking about?"

"I didn't think how long it would take to arrange that complicated a schedule till you mentioned it. Somehow, she's nearly done. She must have gone back to the bridge and worked all evening. Maybe all night."

McCoy looked over his shoulder. "You know, Jim, you're not supposed to work yeomen so hard they don't have time to sleep. I think it's against regs or something."

"I was really rough on her this morning." Jim tossed the exam coverall on McCoy's desk. "I'll see you later." He headed for the door.

"Jim, wait. You've got to have your exam." McCoy followed Jim into the corridor. "If you get it over with, you won't have to worry about it anymore."

"Who's worried?" Jim said without slowing down, determined to put off giving McCoy a look at his knee just as long as he could.

"Why do people hate physicals?" McCoy said plaintively as the turbo-lift doors closed between them.

Shaking his head, Dr. McCoy folded up the exam coverall and stowed it on a shelf. Jim Kirk could be exasperating, but he sure was never boring. McCoy remembered back a few years when Jim was just a lieutenant. He was brash and arrogant and impatient with anyone less able than he. That included most of his superiors. McCoy had known from the day he met James Kirk that the young officer would either mature into an outstanding commander or end up in the brig for insubordination. More than once it was a close call as to which it would be.

As a lieutenant, James Kirk had been like a colt held under too tight a rein. His promotion to commander of the *Lydia Sutherland* both gentled and strengthened him. The responsibility of leadership tempered his arrogance and his impatience.

McCoy could not help feeling an avuncular pride in Jim Kirk's achievements.

Now, if he could just get him to take his physical . . .

Uhura managed to keep from laughing in Roswind's face, but as soon as the turbo-lift doors closed safely behind her, she dissolved into giggles.

Halfway to officers' territory, the lift paused.

Captain Kirk joined her.

"I could use a good laugh, lieutenant," he said. "You wouldn't want to tell me the joke, would you?"

"No, sir," she said, coldly, still angry at him for the way he had treated Janice. "Captain, people are sometimes under pressure that you don't know about."

He raised his arms as if to protect his head from a blow. For one awful moment Uhura feared he, too, would fall to his knees at her feet.

"I confess! Mea culpa!" Captain Kirk's voice and actions seemed part mocking, yet part serious. He lowered his hands. "Dr. McCoy read me one riot act about Yeoman Rand, and I can't say I'd blame you if you read me another. If I promise to apologize, will you spare me?"

"I think you should apologize in public," Uhura said.

That brought him up short. He paused, considered, and nodded. "You're right," he said. "I bawled her out in public, so it's only fair. Now will you forgive me?"

"Yes, sir," she said. "Gladly."

"And will you tell me the joke?" He looked like a little boy who realized for the first time that his mischief had caused grief and pain. He looked like someone who needed reassurance. If he had been anyone but the captain of the ship, she would have let him in on her plans for Roswind.

"No, sir," she said. "I can't. It's personal."

Lieutenant Uhura got out of the lift in officers' territory. Jim returned to the bridge alone. Yeoman Rand glanced up from her conversation with Lindy, then looked away, afraid to meet his gaze.

"Lindy, would you excuse us?" Jim said. He spoke loudly

enough for everyone on the bridge to hear him. "Yeoman Rand, I spoke to you in an unpardonable manner this morning. I criticized you when I should have been complimenting your dedication. I apologize."

She stared at him in silence.

"Would you come with me, please?" He had no particular destination in mind; he simply found a corridor in which they could walk. "Yeoman, when's the last time you had any sleep?"

"I . . . I . . ." She took a deep breath. "I'm sorry, sir, I overslept. That's why I was late."

"Maybe the question I need to ask is how long did you work." She remained silent. "All night?"

"I'm sorry, sir. I tried to finish . . ."

"Yeoman, I appreciate your enthusiasm, but you aren't very useful if you're too tired to—to get the right size uniform out of the synthesizer—"

"I didn't—!"

He heard protest and anger in her voice, but she cut herself off quickly.

"You didn't what, yeoman?"

"Nothing, sir."

He sighed. She was still flinching. "There's such a thing as being too conscientious. There's such a thing as wearing yourself out before you've even gotten started."

"I'm sorry . . ." she said.

He felt like cringing himself. He could not figure out how to talk to her. "You don't need to apologize for being conscientious. I don't think I'm a tyrant—I don't try to be. But sometimes you'll have to work two watches straight. Maybe even work around the clock. I won't apologize when I ask that of you. I'll hand you trouble-shooting jobs that I expect you never to mention again, and like as not I'll forget to give you credit because I'll forget I gave them to you. Is that understood?"

"Yes, sir," she said, her voice feathery.

"There are times when you'll have to work harder than you've ever worked before." He noticed her ironic smile, which she repressed almost instantly. "But outside those times, you're going to have to use your judgment."

"I did use my judgment!" she said, flustered.

"Your judgment told you to stay up all night working on a job that didn't have to be finished for three months?"

"You said, 'As soon as you can, put together an appointments schedule for me.' My judgment told me that I have to answer to your judgment. Whether it's poor or—I mean, I'm not familiar with your judgment."

"I see." They reached the observation deck. Jim idly opened the shield to reveal the stars.

Janice gasped.

"It is quite a sight, isn't it?" Jim said. "Sit down, we'll talk for a few minutes." He gestured toward a chair where she would be able to see outside.

"But your schedule—"

"I still have a good fifteen minutes left of my appointment with Dr. McCoy. I shouldn't have snapped at you about that, either." He grinned. "He thought he'd found a clever way to get me in his clutches long enough to make me take my physical. Sit down."

She obeyed.

"I was thoughtless yesterday," Jim said, "and I was . . . unnecessarily harsh with you this morning. I apologize, and I hope you'll forgive me."

"There's nothing to forgive, captain."

"I think there is—and I think you ought to convince yourself that you have the right to be treated as a sentient being. Your feelings matter, too."

"I'll try, sir." She answered quickly, firmly: he suspected she was saying what she thought he wanted to hear.

"Did *you* make an appointment to talk to me?"

Her pale face burned. "No, sir. I . . . forgot."

"Tell me a little about yourself."

She gazed at him, straightforward, deliberate. Then she looked away and said quickly, "There's nothing to tell, sir. I got out of school, I joined Starfleet."

"Your family?"

"They're just ordinary people, with ordinary jobs."

"Sisters? Brothers?"

She said nothing.

"Pet goldfish?"

She nearly smiled.

"That's better. Well, yeoman, you're an enigma. Too bad the Foreign Legion was disbanded."

"I don't understand what that means," she whispered.

"It was a military organization, several centuries ago. People joined it who . . . didn't want to be asked questions."

She looked away, partly to avoid his gaze, partly to see the stars. The orientation of the *Enterprise* turned the galaxy into a great diagonal slash, eerie against the blackness.

"Never mind, yeoman," he said. "You're an adult; you have a right to your privacy. But if you ever feel you need someone to talk to . . ." She did not reply. Jim rose. "We'd better get back to the bridge."

She followed him out, pausing to glance back one last time. The shield closed over the viewport.

"By the way," Jim said, "Lindy complimented your work in the strongest terms. Where did you learn design?"

"Here and there. About Ms. Lukarian, sir—"

"What did she want this time?"

"Dirt, captain."

"Dirt—?"

"Bridge calling Captain Kirk."

Jim hurried to the nearest intercom. "Kirk here."

"Sir, there's a subspace communication—"

"Starfleet—?" His adrenaline level rose. An emergency . . . ? What would he do with the civilians? Or perhaps it was a message about Gary.

"Not Starfleet, sir. It's a private craft. He says . . . he's a juggler, sir."

Jim stared at the intercom. "A juggler?" He laughed. "Is Ms. Lukarian still on the bridge?"

"Yes, sir."

"I think it's safe to assume the communication's for her. Let her take it. I'll be up in a minute." Still chuckling, he entered the nearest turbo-lift; Rand followed. "You were saying, yeoman. *Dirt?*"

"Yes, sir. The deck is too hard for her horse's hooves, and the corral doesn't give Athene enough room to move around. She'd like to put a layer of dirt on the shuttlecraft deck—"

"We don't have any dirt!" Jim exclaimed. "What does she want me to do, deplete molecular storage to synthesize—dirt? No, it's out of the question. A layer of dirt—on the shuttlecraft deck? It's ridiculous!"

"I've spoken to Mr. Sulu and Mr. Spock and Lieutenant Uhura. We could do it." She outlined the proposal as they rose toward the bridge.

"No," Jim said. "I want to stay in warp drive."

"But Athene—"

"Athene will have to wait. A starship is no place for a bunch of animals in the first place!" The turbo-lift doors stood open. His voice had carried all the way across the bridge.

Lindy, sitting in his seat, glanced back at him.

"Oh, hi, Lindy," he said. "Er . . ."

"Jim, I've found us a juggler."

On the viewscreen, five blazing torches circled furiously, obscuring the juggler behind them.

He caught one, two, three, four, spun the last torch high out of range of the screen, and caught it as it tumbled into view. He extinguished the flames. He turned his head and pulled loose the length of blue ribbon at the nape of his neck. He shook his golden hair free as he bowed.

"You're in!" Lindy said.

The long, ascetic lines of his face broke into a brilliant smile. He put down the torches. His hair curled below his collar. He wore a single ruby earring. The blue of his eyes was so pale it was almost gray.

"Can you meet us on Starbase 13?" Lindy asked.

He frowned. "That's a good long shot for my ship. Why don't you stop and let me piggyback?"

Lindy glanced back. "Jim—?"

"I know these drifters," Jim said, annoyed. "He just doesn't want to pay for his own fuel."

The juggler smiled without offense. "I don't want to pay ransom to the Klingons, either, if they stray into the Phalanx when I pass by. I might get out of it, but I'd never get my ship back." He raised one pale eyebrow. It slanted upward, very like a Vulcan's. "Isn't that part of your job—protecting us civilians?"

Jim still did not want to stop, but the juggler had a good point. Venturing into the Phalanx unarmed and without a convoy could be risky.

"Very well," Jim said. "Give my navigator your coordinates."

"Thanks," he said. "You are—?"

"James Kirk. Captain."

"You can call me Stephen." As he shook back his hair, light glinted from the ruby earring and Jim got a good look at his ears.

Stephen was a Vulcan.

On impulse, Jim glanced at Commander Spock.

The science officer stared at the screen. His expression was hard, not with imperturbability, but with shock and violently repressed anger.

# Chapter 7

SPOCK COMPOSED HIMSELF after his untoward show of emotion. James Kirk averted his gaze, but Spock knew the captain had seen his reaction.

The workings of the bridge flowed over and around Spock. Lukarian and Rand conferred with Captain Kirk about dirt. Despite his intellectual interest in the project, Spock remained intent on his argument with himself.

The captain already had a perfectly appropriate, perhaps even adequate, suspicion of the vaudeville company's new recruit. Perhaps Spock need say nothing. Few human beings could comprehend the workings of his home world's politics and society; attempts at explanation merely confused them.

Spock tried to convince himself of the accuracy of his analysis, but could not dispel the suspicion that he was letting his preference for privacy interfere with his responsibility.

He shut down his station, rose, and left the bridge.

When he entered his cabin, the door shut out the cold yellow-lit dampness that most humans preferred. In a hot, dry, scarlet environment, reminiscent of Vulcan, Spock lay on his meditation stone. He relaxed his muscles in a prescribed sequence and let himself drift into deep thought.

When Mr. Spock left the bridge without a word of explanation, Jim said nothing. But he began to be annoyed when the science officer failed to return after a few minutes.

First Lieutenant Uhura, now Commander Spock, Jim thought. Was it standing operating procedure under Chris

Pike to stomp off the bridge whenever you didn't approve of something? If so, it's going to stop.

Yeoman Rand finished outlining the plan. It would work—nothing about it exceeded conventional techniques. But he was not happy about the project. It simply did not seem like a good idea to him to fill the shuttlecraft deck with dirt. He would have found some satisfaction in sinking the whole project. Petty satisfaction. He knew it, and he knew he felt like this because everything else had gone wrong all day.

"Mr. Sulu, lay in a course change for the rendezvous. Use a minimum of fuel. When we reenter normal space, I'll decide if it's feasible to proceed with this harebrained scheme."

He left the bridge.

He reached Commander Spock's cabin, knocked, and waited impatiently.

The door slid aside. Jim blinked, trying to focus on the tall, thin figure in the dim red light.

"May I come in, Commander Spock?"

"Most human beings find my quarters uncomfortable," Spock said.

"I think I can stand it," Jim said.

"The gravity—"

Jim stepped inside before he realized what Spock meant. He tripped on the level floor that felt like an upward step. The gravity gradient changed from earth-normal to something considerably higher. He came down hard, twisting his knee. He managed to keep his feet. He scowled at the offending deck before facing Spock again.

A long slab of polished gray granite lay against one wall of the stark, spare, dimly lit cabin. Jim wondered if the Vulcan aesthetic required sleeping on stone.

Spock gazed at him, impassive.

"Do you want to explain your behavior on the bridge just now?"

"No, captain."

Taken aback, Jim realized Spock was retreating into evasion by the route of literal-mindedness. Jim chose a more straightforward attack.

"Lindy's new juggler—do you know him?"

At that question, Spock hesitated.

"Yes, captain."

"Tell me about him."

"There is little to tell, beyond the obvious. He is a Vulcan."

"Not so obvious in the way he behaves. A Vulcan juggler?"

"Juggling is an excellent method of improving hand-eye coordination, Captain Kirk," Spock said.

Jim would almost have sworn that he detected a note of pique in Spock's voice.

"It takes intense concentration, patience, and practice."

"You sound like an expert," Jim said.

"I am hardly unique among Vulcans in developing the ability," Spock said.

"Maybe we don't need this fellow after all. Why don't you help Lindy out instead?"

"She did not ask me, captain."

Jim had been sidetracked, deliberately or inadvertently, but quite effectively. He wished the cabin were not so hot. "Tell me about your Vulcan friend."

"He is not," Spock said, "my friend." He gazed past Jim for a moment, his eyes focused on something invisible in the dim light, something no one else could see. "He comes from an unobjectionable family. He had an excellent education and many advantages. He has used these advantages to little purpose. His accomplishments are negligible. He has few inhibitions and less discipline. He . . . does as he pleases."

Jim frowned. "I don't understand the problem here, commander. You reacted to him as if he were a hardened criminal. But he sounds . . . 'unobjectionable.' " He shifted his weight to his left leg. The high gravity and the heat did nothing for his mood.

"He has been known to follow trouble, and one must also suspect the reverse. He . . . takes advantage. However, you determined that on meeting him; I saw no reason to repeat what you already knew."

"Now tell me what it is about him that you aren't telling me." A drop of sweat tickled Jim's face; he blotted his forehead on his sleeve.

"He . . ." Spock hesitated. "He seeks out emotional experiences."

Jim would have sworn Commander Spock was embarrassed, if he had not been told so often that Vulcans had no such reaction. He waited for Spock to continue. Spock said nothing.

"Is that *all?*"

"Yes, captain."

"Good lord! You acted like you'd seen an ax murderer."

Spock considered. "The analogy is not unreasonable. He is . . . a pervert."

Jim could not help it. He laughed. "Thank you for the warning, Commander Spock. I'll certainly keep it in mind when I'm dealing with Lindy's new recruit." Jim's right knee had begun to ache—so much for "as good as new"—and the dim light had given him the beginnings of a headache. "Will you grant us the honor of your presence on the bridge? Soon?"

"Very well, captain."

On his way out, Jim forced himself to walk without limping.

The *Enterprise* slowed from warp-speed and continued through normal space on impulse engines. Sulu scanned for Stephen's vessel; Uhura projected its image on the viewscreen.

Inspecting *Dionysus,* Jim understood why Stephen preferred piggybacking on the *Enterprise* to taking his ship on the long haul through the Phalanx. The decommissioned admiral's yacht had seen better days.

"*Enterprise* to *Dionysus.*"

"I hear you."

"We're extending the docking module at the port side of the shuttle deck," Jim said. "We can put out a tractor—"

"Don't bother."

"I'm going to go meet him," Lindy said.

"I'll go with you." Jim was looking forward to meeting this atypical Vulcan. Commander Spock's disapproval added to Jim's interest. At the door of the turbo-lift, Jim glanced back and said, "Commander Spock—would you care to be on hand to greet this old acquaintance?"

"I should prefer," Mr. Spock replied, "to decline that privilege."

Jim joined Lindy and they headed aft.

"Jim, I appreciate all your help," Lindy said.

"*My* help?" he said. "I didn't arrange the rather incredible coincidence that these coordinates just happen to fall within the system's Oort cloud."

Lindy grinned. "We had to pick Stephen up someplace, and he offered to come to the edge of the star system."

The lift stopped. Jim stepped out. His knee streaked pain down to his ankle and up to his hip, and collapsed under him.

"Jim! Jim, what—"

He lay on the deck with both hands clamped to his knee. He clenched his teeth, vaguely aware of the sweat on his forehead, the cold rough metal beneath him, Lindy beside him. Mostly, though, he was aware of the pain.

"I'll get help."

He grabbed her sleeve before she could stand. "No, I'm all right." He rubbed his knee. The pain receded.

"You don't look all right."

"I just twisted it." He struggled to his feet. "Mr. Spock keeps a Vulcan environment in his cabin—I walked into a gravity shelf I didn't know was there." That was the truth. It was incomplete, but it was true. He gingerly tested his weight on his right leg. The knee held; the ache threatened more than hurt.

"Okay," she said. "You're a big boy, your health's your own business."

Jim did his best not to limp as he crossed the catwalk and climbed down the companionway. In her corral, Athene weaved nervously, swaying back and forth. Two felinoids, one a member of the company and the other an *Enterprise* engineer, sat on the deck nearby.

"Hi, Gnash. Hi, Hazard," Lindy said. The equiraptor stood still when Lindy petted her.

"Athene will be glad of the dirt," Tzesnashstennaj said. "This is not a good place for her." He ducked his head beneath Hazarstennaj's chin. Their fur stroked together with a static crackle, and Hazarstennaj purred.

"I know," Lindy said. "Soon."

Jim crossed the deck to the docking module and opened the observation ports.

Lindy joined him. "What's a gravity shelf?" she asked.

"It's the discontinuity between two gravity fields that aren't connected through a gradient," Jim said. "When you go from, say, one g to two g's, it feels like you're walking up a step. Only the floor's still flat."

Stephen's ship had not yet come into sight. It would probably take half the day for the old ship to dock. I should have put a tractor on *Dionysus* in the first place, Jim thought, and dragged it in by main force.

"Can you change the gravity any way you want?"

"We create it—otherwise we'd be in freefall, or crushed by acceleration. We can change it. It's a lot of trouble, getting everything balanced." Jim opened a channel to the bridge. "Lieutenant Uhura, where's our guest?"

"He says he's on his way, sir."

Jim looked around again, but the port gave a field of view too limited to show him *Dionysus*.

"Anyway," Jim said, continuing his explanation, "the *Enterprise* has several different independent fields that interact. Almost every starship has a couple of zero-g nodes. I suppose that's true of the *Enterprise*." Back in the Academy, he thought, when we went into space, the null-grav points were the first things we looked for.

"Hmm."

His thoughts brushing past the null-grav points that might exist within the *Enterprise*, Jim glanced at Lindy.

She stared into space, her eyes focused on something more distant than any ship or star, some fantasy. Her iridescent hair swung forward, shadowing her face.

Jim felt himself caught in a sudden trap of envy: he envied the shadow, touching Lindy's cheek, he envied the flying horse, who could nuzzle the curve of her neck and shoulder, he envied the members of her company, who could unselfconsciously hug her. He wondered if any of them were special to her, or if she had decided, as he had when he accepted his first command, that she must never think of anyone under her authority as special.

"Captain!"

Uhura's exclamation startled Lindy. She raised her head. For a split second, her gaze and Jim's locked.

Then the urgent tone of Uhura's voice got through to Jim. Motion outside the ship drew Lindy's attention.

"Look!" She pressed close to the port and cupped her hands around her face to shield the glass from reflections.

Eerily silent in the vacuum of space, *Dionysus* drove directly at the *Enterprise*.

Jim shouted a curse. He clenched his fists against cold glass, infuriated. The shields had already begun to form, but too late—it had been like this at Ghioghe: a sudden plunge, a crash—

*Dionysus* blasted its forward rockets and decelerated hard. Though the viewport darkened to protect the interior of the ship from the light and energy, the dazzling flame half-blinded Jim.

But the port cleared, the shields faded, and *Dionysus* hovered beside the *Enterprise*. Starlight shone off jets of steering plasma before they dispersed into space. *Dionysus* docked with the barest hint of vibration, the barest whisper of sound.

"Wow," Lindy said. "I thought you said he didn't want to use any of his own fuel."

His fury barely attenuated by a grudging admiration for the pilot's flash and style, Jim flung open the hatch as soon as the sensors approved the seal between *Enterprise* and *Dionysus*. The pilot of *Dionysus* boarded the *Enterprise*.

"What do you mean by hotshotting at my ship like that?" Jim yelled.

"I thought you were in a hurry." Stephen smiled at him. A large tabby cat perched on his shoulder. "Glad to meet you, Captain Kirk." Stephen extended his hand.

Jim automatically reached to shake hands, the social convention so ingrained that it overcame his real wish, which was to sock Stephen in the jaw.

The cat launched itself at him and clawed its way up his arm. Jim yelped in surprise.

"How do you do, Ms. Lukarian," Stephen said.

"Call me Lindy, please."

As they greeted each other, oblivious to Jim, Jim found himself in his second face-off of the day. The vicious animal hissed, snarled, buried its talons in his arm and shoulder, and poised to rip out his eyes. Jim grabbed the monster with his free hand and tried to shake it off.

"Ilya!" Stephen said. "Quit it, come here."

The creature dug its claws into Jim's arm and launched itself at Stephen, rending the sleeve of Jim's velour shirt. The cat landed on Stephen's shoulder and twined its lithe body behind his neck. Its unnaturally long tail wrapped around Stephen's arm.

Jim clenched his fist, half in angry reaction and half to see if it still worked. His forearm and the back of his hand stung with deep scratches.

"He likes you, captain," Stephen said. "I don't think I ever saw him take to anybody so quickly."

"Likes me! What does it do to people it doesn't like?"

Stephen shook his head. "There are some things human beings aren't meant to know."

"Is he what I think he is?" Lindy asked.

As far as Jim was concerned, it was nothing but a cat. He felt embarrassed to have come off second in the altercation. He looked at it more closely. It was half again as large as the largest cat he had ever seen. It had puffed out its cinnamon-striped black fur till it looked even bigger, and it glared at him with bright green eyes. Its fur-tufted ears flicked forward, then flattened back against its head. Its paws, enormous relative to its size, had a fringe of fur between the toes. Its tail was probably half again the length of the cat's body, and it was prehensile.

"Just an ordinary little tabby cat." Stephen grinned. "No, you're right. He's a Siberian forest cat."

"I've never seen one. Can he do anything?" She offered her hand gingerly to the big cat, and it sniffed her fingertips and rubbed its forehead against her palm.

"Such as juggle?"

Lindy laughed. "Are you guys a team?"

Stephen shook his head. "He *can* do lots of things. But only when he wants to. He really is an ordinary tabby cat in that respect."

"That's too bad." Lindy gazed thoughtfully at the cat, as if considering ways to get him into the performance even if he would not perform.

Immediately noticeable differences separated Ilya from average cats. Far more subtle differences separated Stephen from average Vulcans. Perhaps four or five centimeters taller

166

than Spock, he was built along the same slender lines. Blond and blue-eyed Vulcans, while uncommon, came within the normal range of types.

But Vulcans always kept their bodies as tautly under control as they kept their emotions. Stephen moved with freedom and ease. His expression revealed him in a way quite foreign to other Vulcans.

And no Vulcan Jim had ever seen permitted his hair to grow as long and shaggy as Stephen's.

"Thanks for your hospitality, captain," Stephen said. "I'm not sure old *Dionysus* could have made it out to the Phalanx and back under its own steam."

"It had plenty of steam just now," Jim said angrily. "Your docking was dangerous and foolhardy—don't ever fly like that around the *Enterprise* again."

"Jim, come on," Lindy said. "It was a beautiful landing!"

"He didn't land, he docked," Jim growled, aggravated at Lindy for telling him something he already knew but which his responsibility to his own ship prevented his acknowledging or appreciating; irritated even more to be told it by a grounder who got the terms wrong.

"You did say you were in a hurry," Stephen said rather plaintively.

"Not in such a hurry I want my ship rammed."

"I didn't intend to scare you," Stephen said. "But don't worry, I won't do it again."

Jim's temper flared; he kept it in check only with difficulty. "See that you don't," he said.

Stephen watched the young captain stalk away. Human beings knew how to take offense. They did it with style.

"Welcome to the company," Amelinda Lukarian said. "I was impressed with your act—I hope you decide to join us permanently."

"I do, too." The moment's exhilaration of the dangerous docking maneuver faded and slipped away, leaving Stephen empty of feeling.

"I want to introduce you to everybody."

Stephen followed Lindy to the corral. He had already taken note of Athene, his well-trained mind judging the complexities of her design, the difficulties inherent in her creation. He would have done several things differently. It was only when Lindy stroked her neck and called her "pretty thing" that Stephen noticed that she was, indeed, beautiful. And so was Lindy.

"Tzesnashstennaj, Hazarstennaj," Lindy said, "this is Stephen. He's a juggler."

The two felinoids rose and circled Stephen suspiciously. Ilya began to bristle; he sat on Stephen's shoulder and watched them like an owl.

"And who is that?" Tzesnashstennaj said.

"That is Ilya."

"What is his relationship to you?"

"He's my pet," Stephen said.

"You keep a fellow creature in servitude?"

"I'd hardly call it servitude," Stephen said. "Though I will admit he's got me pretty well trained."

The two felinoids looked at each other. "Anthropoid humor," Hazarstennaj said.

"Carnivores require freedom," said Tzesnashstennaj.

"He has the same freedom I do. Without the responsibility."

"Typical. All anthropoids think other species exist for their amusement. Come here, little brother."

Ilya hissed and spat.

Tzesnashstennaj growled softly. "He no longer understands his need for liberty."

"Wait a minute," Stephen said. "Ilya's pretty intelligent for an animal, but he's not a sentient being. What are you so upset about?"

"Tzesnashstennaj," Lindy said, "you're still angry about that ignorant rube in Boise who called the hunt performance an animal act, aren't you? Outrage is bad for the system. Why don't you give it up?"

"That 'rube' gave me a lesson in the fragility of interspecies contact," Tzesnashstennaj said. "The keeping of pets is . . . provocative."

"You're welcome to try to talk Ilya around to your point of view," Stephen said. "But I don't think he'll be very interested."

"Please don't get into an argument over this," Lindy said. "You know what that would mean."

Tzesnashstennaj sneezed in disgust.

"No," Stephen said. "What would it mean?"

"A company meeting," Lindy said, her tone implying dire threats.

"Hours of tedium," Tzesnashstennaj said grimly. "Lectures by Mr. Cockspur."

"Maybe you'd better declare a truce," Stephen said.

Tzesnashstennaj growled.

Jim returned to the bridge. At the threshold of the lift, he took note almost unconsciously of the status of the bridge: Commander Spock in intense communication with his computer, Uhura and Rand completing the registrations and agreements, Sulu planning the weapons strategy, Cheung plotting a course. McCoy leaned nonchalantly against the captain's chair.

"I hear we're expecting some excitement," McCoy said.

"That's what I hear, too," Jim said. He slid into his place.

A few minutes later, Lindy and Stephen arrived, chatting and laughing. They sure took to each other fast, Jim thought.

Spock raised his head.

This time he permitted himself no reaction beyond looking Stephen over coldly. He would have turned his back, but Stephen strode toward him.

"How are you—"

Spock rose. His expression hardened. Stephen thought better of whatever he had been going to say.

"How are you . . . Spock?"

"I am well."

Everyone on the bridge pretended not to notice the interchange, except for McCoy. The doctor watched curiously.

"I cannot speak with you," Spock said. "I have duties to attend to." This time he did turn his back.

"Let's see what we're working on," Jim said.

Uhura tracked and magnified an irregular chunk of dirty ice. It tumbled across the screen.

"It will pass us eighty-nine seconds from . . . now," Commander Spock said. "If Mr. Sulu's touch on the photon torpedo is sufficiently delicate, he should be able to reduce a corner of it into water vapor and rock particles."

"Understood, Mr. Spock." Sulu grinned. "Two hundred metric tons of dirt, coming up."

Sulu tracked the only bit of matter on the short-range scope. The *Enterprise* lay within the system's Oort cloud, the band of debris left over from the formation of the star and its planets. The debris orbited far beyond the outermost world; at intervals some random chunk of primordial detritus would follow a long, elliptical path near enough to the star to blaze into a comet.

The concentration of matter was measurably greater here than in space between the system's planets, but "measurably greater" and "visually perceptible" were two very different things. The cloud contained a large amount of debris, but it contained more nothingness by high orders of magnitude.

The scope caught the chunk of rock and ice. Sulu waited. It tumbled. He studied its motion. He sought out a place that would shatter properly. He waited for a usable orientation.

He fired.

Photons lased against an irregular projection, blasting it away. Ice vaporized into a great cloud of steam, then froze instantly into a storm of ice crystals that glittered, expanded, dispersed. The proto-comet tumbled on in its orbit. Bits and fragments streamed from the crater, spiraling in a pinwheel pattern.

A cloud of rocky remains roiled and slowly expanded.

Lindy whooped in excitement, bounded down between Sulu and Cheung, and kissed each on the cheek.

"Hikaru, Marietta, thank you!" She hugged Jim. "Jim, Athene will be so happy!" She ran up the stairs, her hair flying, and grasped one of Uhura's hands, one of Janice's. "Janice, that was such a good idea! You'll have to come watch her when she's running—you all will. She's so pretty!" She stopped before Spock. "Mr. Spock, thank you."

"Thanks are unnecessary," Spock said. "You posed an intellectual problem, I helped to solve it."

"You'd better get Athene into the repair bay," Jim said. "We'll have to evacuate the dock before we can get the dirt inside, and it'll be noisy. The deck will transmit vibrations—shouldn't you tranquilize her so she won't panic?"

"No," Lindy said. "But I'll stay with her while the work's going on." She spread her arms, taking in the whole bridge. "Everybody—thanks!"

She vanished into the lift. Stephen, Jim noticed, left with her.

Jim felt as if he had been in the midst of a small but powerful whirlwind. The bridge, despite ambient sounds returning to normal, seemed terribly quiet.

"Put out a tractor beam, Mr. Sulu," Jim said. "You did a good job."

"Thanks, captain."

Jim felt strange, complimenting one of his officers for completing a task that Jim would have preferred not to do at all. Back in the Academy, he and Gary used to daydream about what they would be doing in ten years, what ships they would fly on, what missions they would command. The worst, the most boring assignment they could imagine was running an ore carrier, dragging rough-smelted slag from mine to refinery.

And the stuff I'm pulling on board isn't even ore, Jim thought. I hope this all turns out to be funny sometime in the future, because it isn't very funny now.

He absently rubbed his arm, which stung and itched from Ilya's claws.

"What happened to you?" McCoy said.

"What?"

McCoy indicated the scratches on Jim's hand. Jim realized that Ilya had completely shredded the sleeve of his shirt, Fifi had torn the hem of his right pants leg, and he was sprinkled all over with pink glitter.

"It's a long story."

"Want to tell it to me here? Or in sick bay, while I fix up those cuts?"

After what had just happened with his knee, Jim was not about to let McCoy get him into sick bay.

"Bones, to tell the truth, I don't want to tell it to you at all."

He left the bridge.

Jim paced through the ship, restless and irritable.

When did I lose control? he thought. When Stephen came on board? When Newland Rift's "puppies" jumped all over me? The first time that flightless horse reared and screamed, and Amelinda Lukarian ran past me with her hair flying? Or was it before I ever came on board, when Admiral Noguchi decided to honor me with his pet assignment?

To his surprise he found himself heading for the shuttle-craft deck. The routine operation of moving the comet debris into the ship made even more noise than he had expected. The tractor beams set up a nearly subsonic hum, the heavily filtered ventilators moaned, the mashed rock crashed onto the deck, and the rattling carried through the deck plates.

By the time Jim reached the observation window, the tractors had drawn in a layer of dirt half a meter deep. Of course it was not really "dirt." It contained no humus, no organic matter except perhaps a few random micrograms of amino acids. It was sterile and dead. Jim wondered how long it took to turn vacuum- and photon-sterilized detritus into fertile living topsoil.

He found himself wondering if the bio lab of the *Enterprise* had any earthworms.

Shaking off the fantasies, he descended a companionway that led to the repair bays.

"Lindy?"

"We're down here—number six." Eerie sounds reverberated along the walls and deck plates.

Lindy patted Athene and whispered to calm her. Sweat slicked the creature's shoulders and flanks as she shifted nervously.

Jim leaned on the rail that fenced off the number six repair bay from the access tunnel. He wondered where Stephen had gone, but he decided not to ask.

"Is everything all right?"

"The trouble is," Lindy said, "that when a horse gets scared, her instinct is to run. Here, she can't. So she gets more scared."

"The floor's covered already," Jim said. "The noise should stop soon."

As if he had ordered the noise to cease, as if he had waved

his hand in a magic gesture, the thrumming of tractor beams faded and died. Athene snorted and fluttered her wings at the change, but after that she acted calmer.

"Thanks," Lindy said to Jim.

"It was easy," he said, and smiled.

"Say, Jim . . ." Lindy said hesitantly. "About earlier. Stephen is, um, kind of flamboyant. A lot of performers are. We like to show off. I'm sorry that he scared you."

"It isn't a matter of being scared!" Jim said, stung. "But this—" He gestured around at the ship. "It's a big responsibility."

He felt as if her gaze could seek out every element in his body, all the way down to his memories and his fears.

"Yes," she said. "I know." Athene nuzzled Lindy's side. She gave the equiraptor a protein pellet.

"Where did that come from?" Jim asked, grateful for the interruption. "I always think your hand is empty—then you pull carrots and sugar out of thin air."

Lindy raised her hand, showed him the empty palm, reached up, and plucked a whole apple out of nothing.

"That's exactly what I do," she said. She fed the apple to Athene. It crunched loudly, solid and real. "I pulled it out of thin air. It's magic."

"That's a good trick," Jim said. "Can you do any others?"

"Of course I can. I'd be pretty lousy if all I could do was produce an apple." She glanced at him quizzically. "You know all the other players, but you never asked about me. I'm the magician."

"Based on the demonstration," Jim said, "if I can get a ticket to the Starbase 13 performance, I'll be in the front row."

"The company would perform for the *Enterprise,* if anybody asked," Lindy said.

Jim came to attention. "James T. Kirk, captain of the starship *Enterprise,* invites Amelinda Lukarian and the Warp-Speed Classic Vaudeville Company to entertain his crew." He dropped the formal pose. "If you're sure it wouldn't be an imposition?"

"We've all been waiting for you to ask!" She laughed.

"Jim, we're used to doing two shows a day. We're used to giving an evening performance, tearing down, traveling all night on the train, and setting up the next day in time for the matinee. This is more time off than we've had in years—it was beginning to make everybody nervous."

"Just let me know what you need."

She finished rubbing the equiraptor down and patted her on the flank. Athene's hooves rustled in the straw; she retreated to a corner and her rope net of protein pellets.

Lindy hitched herself up on the rail.

"We'll need a theater with a backstage . . ." Within a few minutes she had outlined the necessities of putting on a vaudeville show.

"It takes a lot of organization, doesn't it?" Jim said. "You do it well."

"I've done it for a long time."

"Did you help your father?"

"You could say that . . ." She sat side-saddle on the rail. "My daddy was one of the founders. He put himself into it at first—he even campaigned for the manager's job. But once he got it started, he wasn't really interested anymore. He was like that. And the company never caught on the way he thought it would. That didn't help his enthusiasm any. Somebody had to get things done."

"And that was you."

She shrugged.

"He campaigned?"

"Uh-huh. The company's a co-op. I'm a member, not the owner."

"What happened to your father?"

"Oh . . . greener pastures." She spoke in an offhand tone; she almost pulled off the casual dismissal.

"It must have been hard to take on all the responsibility—"

"No, to tell you the truth, it's easier now. At least I have the authority to go along with the responsibility. And his leaving wasn't that big a surprise. Besides, he waited till I was eighteen before he disappeared. It must have been hard on him, all those years, to be so tied down."

She did a good job of hiding her pain. Or perhaps she honestly did not feel hurt and abandoned by her father.

Perhaps Jim let his own feelings color his perception of hers.

"Things didn't change much," Lindy said. "And everybody finally got over thinking of me as a kid."

"He should have said something before he left."

"Maybe he was afraid to make me choose between him and the company. Maybe he knew what I'd choose." She leaned against the edge of the repair bay wall and drew up her knees, resting both feet on the rail, oblivious to the precariousness of her position. "I love the company, Jim. I love everybody in it. Performers are different from anyone else in the world. They can do things nobody else can do. When we do the show, we make people happy. And I think—I know!—that if we can keep going long enough to become known, we can make a real success of it."

"I wouldn't want to switch places with you," Jim said. "It'd be awkward to give an order and have the membership convene on the bridge to see if they approved."

Lindy smiled. "That could happen. But it usually doesn't. Artists are happy to have somebody else do the organizing. They don't like to be told what to do, but they do like to feel like somebody's taking care of them."

"How did you decide to become a magician?"

"Same way I got to be manager—because of my daddy. Jim, he's so good! I wish you could see him. He can do illusions you can't believe." She laughed. "I mean, people watching them do believe them, but people who know anything about stage magic don't believe they're possible. Even after they see them. Half his illusions I'm still not good enough to do."

"He sounds like an extraordinary person," Jim said.

"He is. I wish you could meet him—" She stopped and rested her chin on her knees. "I take that back. I'm not sure I do wish you could meet him. I don't know if the two of you would get along."

"Why do you say that?"

"He could be, well, difficult."

"And me?"

She smiled. "You can be difficult, too."

"I suppose that's true," Jim said. "But it comes with the job."

Athene, bored with protein pellets, returned to Lindy to nose around for carrots. Lindy produced one.

"How did the company get started?" Jim said. "Reviving a three-hundred-year-old form of entertainment isn't an idea that would occur to just anybody."

"The funny thing is, there are lots of people who perform in that style. Some of us began as a hobby. Some of the acts have adapted to modern times—Marcellin used to teach mime in the drama department of Monash University in Australia. Then there are magicians' clubs and tap dancing clubs. And lots of people juggle."

"So I've discovered," Jim said.

"No one in a long time had thought of getting a bunch of devotees together and starting a company. When Daddy and Marcellin and Newland got the idea—"

"Newland? You mean Mr. Rift of the 'puppies'?"

"Yes."

"I wouldn't have thought he had much . . ." Jim hesitated. He had spoken without thinking. "He didn't strike me as an entrepreneur," Jim said lamely.

"There's not a real entrepreneur in the bunch of us," Lindy said. "Even my daddy. That's one of our troubles. But Newland . . . he's the steadiest and solidest and most sensible member of the company. He's only silly over his puppies—he admits that himself. He's awfully easy to mis-judge—"

"So I see," Jim said.

"—but we never would have made it this far without him. He encouraged me to run for manager. He could have had the position if he'd wanted it. He said that between his and Philomela's kids, and the puppies, he couldn't spare the time. But I think he didn't want to oppose me, because he knew he'd win."

"Philomela," Jim said. "I met her at dinner the other evening, didn't I?"

"Yes. Our singer, remember? Newland's her husband."

"I know better than to judge other sentient beings on appearance," Jim said. "Maybe when it comes to my own species, I've got some lessons to learn."

"He is striking, isn't he? I think he enjoys the impression he makes. And it's great for publicity."

"Is he what he looks like?"

"Uh-huh. His family's Canadian-Japanese. The traditionalists didn't quite know how to react to a redhaired Sumo wrestler, but after he'd competed for a few years, he won even them over. He doesn't compete anymore, but he still meditates. He's a very spiritual person."

Jim shook his head. "You do have quite a group."

"It takes a certain kind of wonderful person to choose a profession that nobody around them understands. They're dedicated—sometimes they're single-minded. And unique. That's why I stayed with the company, Jim, even when I realized my daddy was about to leave. I love it, and I love all the people in it. Well, almost all."

"Almost all?"

She blushed. "I shouldn't have said that last."

"Can I guess?" he said, teasing.

"I don't think you have to," she said. "I hear you had a discussion of politics with him last night."

"Just out of morbid curiosity—where *did* you pick up Mr. Cockspur?"

"Daddy found him."

"If he's good, though—you can put up with a lot from somebody who knows what they're doing."

"Good!" Lindy laughed. " 'Good' and 'neo-Shakespearean' are mutually exclusive terms."

"What's a neo-Shakespearean?"

"Somebody who 'interprets' Shakespeare for contemporary audiences. Mr. Cockspur does his own translations."

"Is he that bad?" Jim asked.

"Wait and see," she said, ominously.

Somehow, two hours passed without Jim's being aware of them. He found Lindy incredibly easy to talk to, to listen to. He almost told her about Carol Marcus, but changed his mind without being quite sure why. His feelings tangled. He was powerfully attracted to Lindy, he thought she liked him, too, and yet he shied away.

He told her more about Sam and Winona, he told her about his father, he told her about Gary. Suddenly, he found himself telling her about Ghioghe.

"I knew everybody else had got out, but I knew I'd lost my ship. I was angry at myself for getting hurt too bad to walk. I couldn't see because of the blood in my eyes. I was yelling—I thought I was yelling, but I couldn't have been, because I could hardly breathe—at the ship, at the miserable mess outside—'Just go ahead and get it over with!' Then Gary appeared. And *he* cussed me out for getting hurt too bad to walk. What I remember is that he told me he'd come looking for my help, and I was an ill-mannered jerk to make him do all the work." Jim tried to smile; he tried to maintain his pose of grizzled veteran telling exciting stories to an innocent. But Ghioghe was still too close, too painful, and he had lost too much. Ghioghe had not been exciting. It had been a terrifying, horrible disaster. And it had been unnecessary.

"Gary dragged me out of the control room," Jim said softly. "We were the last people on board . . . the last people alive. The ship—the *Lydia Sutherland,* it was a great little cruiser—started to come apart around us. Gary dumped me into the escape pod and piled in after me and blasted us free. He got the bleeding stopped . . ." Jim absently touched the scar on his forehead. "I thought he was all right. He had a gash just below his ribs. It didn't seem like much. But then . . ." He took a deep breath, embarrassed to be shaken by memories. He wanted to stop, but he could not. "He'd been hit by a sneak. It's a terrorist weapon. It looks . . . insignificant. It breaks your skin, it burrows down, it finds your heart or your spine or your brain. And it explodes." He remembered the quiet, sedate little explosion. Gary had looked mildly surprised as he collapsed.

"He was bleeding . . . I ripped open his shirt. That was weird. The sneak hurt him so badly, but it didn't even tear his shirt." Jim remembered the warmth of Gary's blood. "Blood flows so strangely in zero g, Lindy. It doesn't pool up. It doesn't hide anything. I could see Gary's heart," Jim whispered. "Every time it beat, it pumped blood out of a tear in its side. I didn't know what to do—I just knew it shouldn't look like that. I . . . I held his heart together in my hands."

"It's over," Lindy said. She touched his arm, a quick gesture of comfort. "Jim, it's all over."

"I know." Again he brushed his fingertips across the scar

on his forehead. "Bones keeps promising this will disappear." Again he tried to smile. "Gary was lucky, you know? If the sneak had been doped with radiation, the specialists wouldn't have been able to induce regeneration. If that had happened . . ."

He wished Lindy would touch him again. He liked the way her touch felt. He liked the color of her eyes, and their depth; he liked the way her hair framed her face with iridescent strands, all black, but almost imperceptibly streaked with highlights of the deepest possible purple and gold and green. Then he realized that her eyes were filled with tears that he had put there, tears of horror and disbelief—no, not disbelief, but not-wanting-to-believe.

"I'm so sorry that happened to you," she said. "To you, to your friend . . ."

"Lindy—I never should have told you about Ghioghe. I'm sorry. You didn't need to hear about it—"

"But you needed to tell about it," she said simply.

At the other end of the corridor, the door slid open and closed again.

"Lindy, hey!" Stephen said.

"Down here." Lindy's expression lightened at the sound of Stephen's voice.

Jim felt disappointed and at the same time relieved. The strength of his attraction to Lindy surprised him, yet he did not think he could stand having the same thing happen again that had happened with Carol. Besides, it seemed to him that Lindy felt relieved at Stephen's approach.

I shouldn't have told her about Ghioghe, Jim thought. No, I shouldn't. What a fool.

Stephen strolled toward them. Ilya balanced on his right shoulder, steady despite his perilous perch.

"It looks like everything's nearly ready," Stephen said.

Lindy smiled at him and took his hand.

Jim called the bridge. Uhura reported the deck repressurized, the temperature nearly normal.

"I can let her out?" Lindy said.

"Any time."

Lindy slid off the railing into Athene's stall. The equiraptor sensed her joy and excitement. She trembled, every

179

muscle tense, her wings quivering at her sides. Lindy put one hand on her nose and one on the crest of her neck.

"Okay," she said. "Open the door."

Lindy let Athene into the dirt-carpeted shuttlecraft deck. Athene walked gingerly, placing each foot lightly, her wings spread; she walked like a tightrope artist. Her hooves crunched on the fine-ground comet debris. She snorted.

"That's better, isn't it, sweetie?" Lindy said. One hand twined in her mane, she urged Athene into a jog. Lindy led Athene back over her own path, inspecting it to be sure she did not dig all the way through to the deck.

"Now or never." She let go of Athene's mane and stepped away.

Athene stood still for a moment, head up, ears pricked forward. Her wings opened, closed, opened; Jim could hear the flutter of the big primaries. Then she flattened her wings against her sides and sprang forward.

She galloped so fast Jim feared she would crash into the far bulkhead. But at the last second she slid to a dirt-spraying, spraddle-legged stop, spreading her wings wide as if she were coming in to land. Then she squealed and spun and galloped in the other direction, straight toward Lindy.

Before Jim could move, before he could shout a warning, Athene reached her. Lindy grabbed her mane, swung up, and straddled her. She slipped her legs beneath Athene's wings and rode her across the deck, laughing, her arms spread wide.

Athene bounced to a halt, flung up her head, and snorted. Sweat covered her shoulders and flanks. The scarlet lining of her nostrils flared as she breathed.

Lindy stroked her neck, then urged her forward. Mane and tail flying, wings open, Athene trotted down the center of the deck, hesitating for a split second before she put each hoof to the ground. The pause made her float between each step, almost as if she really were flying.

Lindy looked up. Members of the *Enterprise* crew filled the observation tunnels and crowded onto the catwalk above. Athene circled the deck in her floating trot. Lindy waved at everyone as she passed. Jim saw McCoy and Sulu, Uhura and Cheung, Yeoman Rand, and even, there in the corner, Mr. Spock. The bridge must be almost entirely deserted, but for just this one brief minute, Jim could not mind.

"She's really something, isn't she?" Stephen said. Jim had not even noticed the Vulcan when he came alongside him.

"Yes," Jim said. "She really is."

# Chapter 8

LATE THAT NIGHT, Commander Spock left the bridge and returned to his cabin. Though he could work without rest for days at a stretch, to remain at his intellectual peak he needed a few hours of sleep and meditation each night. He had skipped those hours during the past several days; and meditation spent considering what, if anything, to do about Stephen hardly qualified as rest. He wanted to be alert during the passage of the *Enterprise* into the Phalanx.

Stepping over the gravity shelf, he entered his cabin.

He stopped.

Even before red light dispelled the maroon darkness, he sensed a difference. Someone had entered while he was gone.

The Siberian forest cat leaped from the bunk where Stephen lay sleeping. The cat's huge fur-tufted paws thudded on the deck in the Vulcan gravity. It plopped itself down and licked its shoulder with two quick strokes.

Stephen had wrapped himself in the bedclothes so nothing of him showed but locks of his blond hair.

Spock said Stephen's name—his true name, not the Terran name he had adopted to accentuate his perversity.

Stephen slept on.

"Wake up."

Ilya rubbed against Spock's leg. It miaowed piteously, complaining of inattention or hunger or the universe in general. Spock picked it up.

"You should choose your traveling companions more carefully," Spock said to the cat. "Especially if one is going to lead you to a life of petty burglary."

"What are you trying to do, Spock?" The bedclothes muffled Stephen's voice. "Incite my crew to mutiny?"

"If I thought I could have any effect, I might do precisely that." The forest cat rubbed its forehead against Spock's hand, kneaded his arm with its long curved claws, and stretched its neck to let him scratch beneath its chin. Its sharp fangs projected beyond the lower curve of its jaw. "I see you retain your preference for dangerous pets."

"That's an interesting comment, coming from someone who used to have a full-grown sehlat." Stephen pulled the blanket down. "Lindy said you kept a Vulcan environment. I came in to get warm. And earth gravity makes me lightheaded."

Spock had perceived the same effects that Stephen described, but he refrained from complaining about them or even acknowledging them.

"I would have thought," Spock said, "that your years on earth, your preference for human beings, would have accustomed you to earth-average conditions."

Stephen sat up and rubbed his eyes like a sleepy child. Many of his reactions resembled those of a child. But children grew and learned and increased their discipline. They did not strive to overcome it.

"You lose your tolerance after a while," Stephen said. "Good of you to leave your cabin open for me."

"It had nothing to do with you. I do not use locks."

"I thought you might not. You're the stubbornest person I ever met, when it comes to sticking with customs that don't fit the circumstances."

"How did Ms. Lukarian know I keep a Vulcan environment in my cabin?" Spock said.

"I was going to ask *you* that." Stephen put his hands behind his head and lounged against the wall.

"I have no idea," Spock said.

"A few years ago, I might have gotten a satisfying reaction out of you with that insinuation. You've been practicing." He shrugged. "It's good to know at least that you're speaking to me again."

"It would be difficult to ask you to leave if I were not speaking to you."

"Leave your cabin or leave your ship?"

"The former will suffice. The latter would be preferable."

"You're mad at me about this afternoon, aren't you? You thought I'd tell them your personal name."

"First, I do not get angry," Spock said. "Second, nothing you do could surprise me. Third, few on board this ship would understand the significance of my personal name, in the unlikely event that they could remember it and in the even more unlikely event that they could pronounce it."

Stephen chuckled. "You really are angry."

"I have better things to do," Spock said, "than listen to your ravings. If you do not leave, I will."

Stephen threw aside the blankets, grumbling. "It wouldn't hurt you to let me nap." He rose sulkily and gestured toward the meditation stone. "You won't even use your bunk. You'll prove to yourself how worthy you are by sleeping on that damned thing." He stalked toward the door. "Ilya—come on, kit."

The forest cat purred in Spock's arms, kneading his sleeve with its long, sharp claws, and made no effort to move. Spock had been stroking the creature during the entire conversation.

Spock detached Ilya from the velour. "Why do you persist in this fraud?" he said to Stephen as he handed the cat over. "It does not become you."

Stephen's expression suddenly hardened into impassivity. His blue gaze turned icy. But in an instant he flung off the Vulcan calm.

"I'm not the only fraud in this room," he said with an easy grin.

Spock let the accusation slip past him. His lack of reaction should prove Stephen's accusation false.

Stephen laughed at him and left him in peace. Spock lay on his meditation stone. For the first time in a long while, he experienced difficulty in relaxing toward deep trance.

His bunk remained as Stephen had left it, rumpled and empty.

The director of the oversight committee owned efficient spies.

One of his best operatives, a veiled Rumaiy whose namelessness the director chose to respect, dragged in a creature of complete inelegance. The Rumaiy bowed, stiffly and with minimal civility. He flung his captive to the bone tile floor and jammed his boot against the back of the captive's neck when he tried to rise.

"Salute your betters," he said, his voice no less dangerous for being muffled by three layers of iridescent gauze. The captive pressed his face to the polished floor.

"Let him up," the director said.

The Rumaiy obeyed. The director congratulated himself on holding his loyalty—or at least his service.

Trembling, the young captive raised himself to his knees. He dressed in the manner of a merchant of minor status.

"His tale gives me no pleasure to bring you," the Rumaiy said. "No pleasure for you, or for me."

"Nevertheless, I will hear the tale."

The captive's brow ridges contracted in fear, and he raised his shackled hands in supplication.

"Sir, if I tell you the true tale you will kill me, though there are many other witnesses and you cannot hope to find them all. But if I tell you a lie, you will find some of the witnesses and discover that I lied, and you will kill me. So my only choice is which tale will give me the quicker death. Perhaps I should hold my tongue altogether."

The director gestured abruptly for the spy not to use his boot on the young merchant's ribs.

"Silence is the worst of your choices, I assure you," the director said. "Tell the truth. If my operative confirms your story and I find it necessary to kill you, I promise you a painless death."

The captive's shoulders slumped as he gave up hope of gaining his life through bravado. Still, the director had to offer him grudging admiration, for physical courage was not fostered among the merchant classes.

"Tell your tale," the director said.

The story was the worst he feared: a squalid narrative of his son's debauchery.

"—and then, sir, when he knew he had lost his ship, sir, he attacked her from behind. She defended herself. And then instead of killing him, she offered him a duel. She said she wanted to take his life-disk fairly. She chose blood knives. Hers is dark. The depth of the color frightened the officer. And then instead of fighting when the signal came, he threw his knife. He reached inside his vest—he had a power sling. But she deflected his blade, and then she moved so quickly he never launched a point at her before he died. Sir, I am sorry, sir."

"What happened to this duelist afterwards?"

"She took his disk and showed it to the crew of his ship. They submitted their allegiance to her."

*"Where did she go?"*

"Sir, I don't know, sir, but . . ." He took a long unsteady breath. "Before the game, before the duel, we spoke together. She found me . . . amusing. She offered me advice. She said good pickings and little interference were to be had near the Federation Phalanx. She said Starfleet and the Empire ignore what happens there, so as not to come into conflict over disputed territory—"

"Silence," the director whispered. "An astute observer, your renegade." He considered the information for a moment. "This duel—it had witnesses?"

"Sir, yes, many, sir."

"So how is it that you are here, and not one of those others?"

"I didn't know any better," the youth said, downcast.

"Explain."

"It was my first visit to Arcturus. I hoped for a quick arrangement, a quick profit. I thought I could not afford to leave without some . . . commerce. The others fled. So now my bones will decorate your floor." He essayed an expression of resigned amusement, but failed.

"So." The director turned, paced to one wall, and stared at a dark painting for a long time. "My spies are everywhere. Your presence here proves it." The director faced the merchant again. "Do you understand this?"

The youth made a sign of abject acceptance.

"Stand up."

He obeyed, trembling violently.

The director coded open the wrist shackles. "I will make it a point," he said, "to keep a spy somewhere near you. If you ever speak of this incident, I will know it. I will be sure to give you a long time to die."

The youth stared at him, unbelieving.

"Mercy is unfashionable," the director said. "I am not a fashionable man. I will spare you."

"Sir?"

"I say, I am adding no bones to my floor today!" He waited until his reprieve penetrated the youth's fear-stunned mind. "But someday, I may come to you and demand repayment for your life. Do you understand?"

"Sir, yes. Yes." The youth's voice failed him.

"Get out. Go home. You weren't made to be a smuggler."

The youth backed from the chamber, his sandals scraping across the tiles. As soon as he disappeared beyond the doorway, he fled. His footsteps echoed and faded.

The director looked at his spy. The layered veil revealed nothing. "And why does this tale bring you so little pleasure?" the director said.

A less honorable man, a more tactful man, would have offered false condolences for the dishonor and death of the director's son.

"The renegade," the director's spy said, "is named Koronin. She shows her face to the world. She is Rumaiy."

Jim tossed in his bunk. He sat up in the darkness and squinted at the chronometer. Thirty minutes to go. He thought he should lie down again and sleep—or at least pretend to sleep—rather than fidget just because his ship was nearing the Phalanx. No official craft of the Klingon oligarchy had attacked a Starfleet vessel in the Phalanx since the completion of Starbase 13. They were unlikely to begin now. Even raiders confined themselves to sneak attacks on undefended traders. At the very worst, one of the raiders might swoop in for a look. Even if some fool did attack a constellation-class starship, Jim would have plenty of warning from the sensors, plenty of time to get up and dress at leisure and go to the bridge.

For all those reasons, Jim had decided not to change the *Enterprise*'s normal routine.

Now, though, he had second thoughts. Suppose the bandits—unlikely as the possibility sounded—formed an alliance against Phalanx traffic? Suppose—one time out of a million—the oligarchy attempted a surprise attack?

He gave up trying to sleep, threw aside the bedclothes, dressed, and headed for the bridge.

Most of the time, unless emergency conditions prevailed, the *Enterprise* worked on a regular diurnal rhythm. Jim had chosen to maintain it for the entry into the Phalanx. Most of the crew served the high watch; a skeleton staff worked middle and low watches.

Jim arrived at the dim and quiet bridge. The glow of screens provided an eerie light; the pulse of gossiping machines provided the only sound.

A single ensign stood low watch, ready to recall the full staff at any unusual occurrence. The ensign glanced back when Jim stepped from the lift.

"Captain!" The ensign vacated the captain's seat.

"Good morning, Ensign—?"

"Chekov, sir. Pavel Andrei'ich Chekov."

Jim felt as if he ought to explain his presence; on the other hand, he was the captain. He was not required to justify his actions to his subordinates. He settled into his place, while the ensign took the navigator's position.

Jim inspected the tactical display on the viewscreen. The *Enterprise* headed straight into the concentric circles that led down the perspective of the Phalanx.

"What's our ETA into the Phalanx, Ensign Chekov?"

"That depends, captain. Display is most misleading, sir. Starfleet Command, Federation Survey, Klingon Empire— all choose different borders."

"Starfleet borders will serve our purpose."

"Yes, sir. Starfleet borders overlap Imperial claim; territory is in dispute. ETA 0619. Ten minutes."

"Thank you, Mr. Chekov."

The bridge doors slid open. Commander Spock paused.

"Good morning, Mr. Spock."

"Good morning, captain."

He took his place. Screens lit up around him.

"What are you working on, Mr. Spock?"

"Nothing specific, captain."

"Are you ready to run the gauntlet?"

"We are unlikely to encounter harrying, captain; the local bandits prefer easier targets."

So Commander Spock is no more ready to admit he's nervous about going in there than I am, Jim thought. But if he thinks I ought to have called an alert, he's not about to say so—tactless he might be, and indifferent to other people's feelings. But he's neither stupid nor indifferent to his own interests. Telling your captain you think he's a fool would not be . . . logical.

"Five minutes, captain," Chekov said.

Jim busied himself at his own place. He glanced over his schedule for the day—which was fortunate, since he had forgotten his morning class. The recreation director had noted the athletic abilities of everyone on board, including the captain, and had suggested that Jim teach a judo class. Jim had agreed, and left a slightly apologetic note for Rand to work the class into his day. Somehow, she had done so.

Jim took a look at the ship's efficiency reports, opened a log entry, and closed it again, empty, when he could think of nothing more to say than that the *Enterprise* approached the Phalanx, sensors showed no other ships in range, and the captain felt bored.

If I'm so bored, he thought, why is my pulse rate so high?

"Entering the Phalanx, sir."

Even Spock turned his attention from his console.

But nothing happened.

The *Enterprise* flew on, as peacefully as if it traveled in the Federation's heart instead of on the farthest fringes.

Jim laughed at himself, amused by his own feeling of relief: the Phalanx grew more dangerous along its length, not less. If Jim were setting an ambush, he would attack at the midpoint of the line, far from any possibility of Federation reinforcements. His current nerves had more to do with the psychological aspects of leaving the main body of Federation space than with any real danger.

As he took the stairs one at a time to the upper level of the bridge, his knee twinged faintly. He was sure it would be all right if he was more careful. If he could hold McCoy off for a day or two he might avoid another course of treatment or, worse, another bout of regen.

Spock had returned to his computer. Jim leaned against the console beside him, deliberately nonchalant.

"Mr. Spock."

"Yes, captain."

"Every ship I've ever served on has gravity anomalies," he said casually. "Is this true of the *Enterprise?*"

"Certainly, sir. It is unavoidable."

"Where are they?"

Spock brought up a technical diagram that looked like five amoebas doing rude things to each other. Eukaryote pornography, Jim thought, and had to stifle a grin.

"Where the fields intersect, nodes occur." Spock touched the screen at several points.

"Yes, Mr. Spock. But exactly where are the nodes?"

"Here, here, and symmetrically—do you mean in relation to the physical layout of the ship?"

"Yes, Mr. Spock. I want to . . . make certain they're correctly posted. For safety."

Spock brought up an overlay of the *Enterprise*. "The major zero-g anomaly is congruent to the zero-g laboratory, as planned. Another node occurs at the base of the saucer section. The symmetrical pair occur on either side of the main hull, two decks below the physical joining of the struts. The port node is a cabin occupied by a being who finds gravity fields most uncomfortable."

"I see. And where's the starboard node?"

Spock consulted the chart. "In the arboretum, sir."

"The arboretum."

"Yes, sir."

"Thank you, commander."

The lift doors slid aside. Stephen sauntered in, yawning, his cat riding his shoulder. Jim wished Stephen had performed his docking maneuver less flamboyantly, less dangerously. After Spock's comments, Jim had been prepared to like the anomalous Vulcan. Stephen had made that difficult. Jim leaned idly against the console, a motion that conveniently took him farther from Ilya's claws. Rocking to the motion of Stephen's walk, the cat swiveled its head to keep Jim within its suspicious green gaze.

Stephen raised an eyebrow at Spock. "Sleep well?" he asked, a note of sarcasm in his voice.

"I had no intention of sleeping; I needed peace and privacy for meditation."

"Don't you get bored being so perfect all the time?"

Spock ignored the comment.

"Are you looking for something in particular?" Jim asked Stephen. "It's a little late to be wandering around on an unfamiliar ship."

"Is it late?" Stephen yawned again. "I hadn't noticed."

*"Pazhalsta,* sir," Chekov said. "Is he Siberian forest cat?"

"Yes." Stephen joined Chekov by the navigation console. "His name's Ilya."

Chekov gingerly extended his hand. The big cat sniffed him, approved, and deigned to be scratched.

"I have only seen Siberian forest cat in Russia," Chekov said. "My cousin Pavi has one as pet."

"Does she? They aren't common."

"No, but Pavi did student project at Vladivostok Genetics Institute where cats are bred. She is outstanding student—following in steps of Lysenko!"

Spock's eyebrow arched in disbelief. "Ensign Chekov, do you dislike your cousin?"

"Why, no, sir! She is little pest sometimes, I tease her, but she is good kid."

"Then why do you wish her to follow in the footsteps of Lysenko?"

"Are you not familiar with Lysenko, sir? Why, he invented whole study of genetics on earth."

"I was under the impression that Gregor Mendel had that distinction."

"Oh, no, sir, I beg your pardon. Lysenko discovered dominant/recessive gene inheritance, structure of deoxyribonucleic acid, and process for recombinant DNA."

Spock gazed at Chekov, then turned back to his work without replying. Jim got the impression that Spock had had similar conversations with Chekov before.

"Lysenko must have lived a long time," Stephen said.

"Why, I don't know, sir." Chekov rubbed the forest cat beneath the chin. Ilya's contented purring reverberated across the bridge.

The lights rose slowly, obeying their diurnal program.

Nearly high watch, Jim thought. It really is morning.

Because of the information brought to him by his spy, the director of the oversight committee mobilized his security fleet before the oligarchy had reason to notice that the prototype ship had been lost.

The director had not personally commanded a mission in many years. He ascended to the command deck, oblivious to space and stars, intent only on his pursuit of Koronin, the renegade who could expose his son's unworthiness to the world.

The course he ordered sent his fleet toward the Federation Phalanx.

Still half asleep, Roswind dropped her robe on the floor of the bathroom. It was great to have the cabin to herself for a while. Sharing with that wimpy little Janice Rand had been just about more than she could stand. Roswind smiled, thinking about how Janice had looked in the oversized uniform. That would teach her to get promoted over people with more seniority and more skills. Roswind wondered when the new roommate would move in. She wondered what the new roommate *was*. If she was green . . . maybe a Vulcan? That might be interesting. But, did Vulcans hibernate? They surely were not timid.

Roswind stepped into the shower and onto something warm and slippery. She shrieked and leaped back, shocked awake.

A large lumpy green creature nestled sleeping in the sonic shower. The mark of Roswind's toes marred the faint pulsating sheen of its translucent skin. Roswind could see its—her—internal organs moving and working.

"What are you doing in the shower?" Roswind said, indifferent to the possibility of scaring her new roommate into hibernation. The being—Roswind had not asked what her new roommate's name would be, or even whether she had a name—lay quiet and silent. "You're worse than Rand—she just didn't know what a sonic shower was. But you—you think it's a bed!"

Jim hurried to the recreation deck. In the locker room he changed into his *gi,* the white canvas jacket and pants that were the uniform of so many martial arts. As he tied his black belt around his hips, he greeted Mr. Sulu, who was dressing for a fencing lesson.

"How about that match?" Jim said.

"Oh . . . sure, captain." Sulu sounded doubtful. "Sometime when we're both dressed for it?"

"I can change after my class," Jim said. He wondered if Sulu was looking for a diplomatic way to back out. "Unless you'll be tired after your lesson?"

"Tired?" Sulu said quizzically. "No, sir, I won't be tired."

"Then we're on."

"All right, captain."

Jim went to the mat to meet his beginning class.

Jim first had to teach them to fall down without killing themselves. They started with forward rolls and progressed (should that be "regressed"? Jim thought with a smile) to backward rolls. A few of the students even tried leaping over a rolled-up mat and landing in a forward roll.

At the end of the hour, the students bowed to each other and to him. "That was a good first class," Jim said. "Next time we challenge the record for jumping over mats. And learn some throws."

The class dispersed.

Teaching beginners did not offer much exercise; Jim, having warmed up during class, was ready for a real workout. He changed into fencing garb and strolled across the gym, past a pheodanthis class and a calisthenics group.

Like Jim's class, Sulu's consisted of beginners too new even to be comfortable holding the epée. Sulu, on the other hand, looked like he ought to be playing d'Artagnan. Jim watched, impressed with the lieutenant's technique. Even his half-speed demonstrations were clear and clean and powerful.

The class ended. Sulu raised his mask and saluted Jim from the fencing floor.

"Ready, sir?"

"Sure," Jim said, thinking, I did ask for it.

The other people in the gym noticed something interesting about to happen. Naturally, they all gathered to watch.

Jim and Sulu saluted each other with their epées, put on their masks, and took the *en garde* position.

For half the match, Jim nearly held his own. He won one touch to Sulu's two. He was soaked with sweat and panting and exhilarated and thoroughly enjoying the competition. He would probably lose, but Sulu had not beaten him yet.

His knee twisted. Somehow he kept his feet. The cold sweat of pain overwhelmed the sweat of exertion. Trying to hide the limp, he retreated, lunged, missed Sulu by a couple of handsbreadths, and ran into Sulu's epée.

"Touché," Jim said.

"Are you all right, captain?"

"Yes. *En garde.*" Begging off with a claim of injury was a ridiculous way to avoid losing. The pain receded. It was probably just a muscle cramp anyway.

Parry—parry—lunge—retreat. Sulu powered him right off the end of the fencing floor, which counted as Sulu's fourth touch against him. The kid was terrific, Jim had to admit it. The quality of competition had risen since his own days in the Academy. Jim shook the sweat out of his eyes and stepped gingerly back onto the floor. His knee felt wrenched.

"*En garde.*"

He lunged blindly. His epée bent against Sulu's jacket as Sulu's epée squarely touched Jim's heart.

"Double touch."

Five touches for Sulu: a win. Jim had two, though the second was a fluke. He hoped Sulu had not held back, but he would never know. The lieutenant was that good.

Jim saluted Sulu and shook his hand.

"Thank you, lieutenant. I'm glad to have had the chance to fence with a real champion."

"You're, uh . . . you're welcome, sir."

"We'll have to do it again sometime," Jim said, though what he most wanted in the universe now was an ice pack.

"I need to talk to you for a few minutes, captain. The subject sort of relates to that."

"Did Yeoman Rand make an appointment for you?"

"Yes, sir, but it isn't for three weeks."

"Ask her to move it up. Tell her I said it was all right. I'm afraid I can't talk to you now—today's schedule is too tight."

"It would only take a minute—"

"I'm sorry, lieutenant. Not now."

Alone in the corridor, Jim leaned against the wall and rubbed his knee. He wiped the sweat from his face. His skin felt clammy. He made his way back to his cabin and spent the next hour icing his knee. Then he canceled the physical exam he was supposed to take that afternoon.

Back in the gymnasium, Hikaru wished he had not pushed Captain Kirk to give him a few more minutes. He had obviously gone over the line. Nevertheless, Hikaru was impressed with the captain's grace in losing. Especially after what had happened at the championship.

Hikaru had realized early in the match that he could not lose to the captain even if he wanted to. If he threw the competition, Hikaru would look like a panderer and Captain Kirk would look like a fool. So Hikaru had not held back—well, not much. He was amazed that it had turned out so well.

"Lieutenant Sulu!"

Hikaru almost groaned out loud. It was too late to flee Mr. Cockspur and his interminable stories.

"Mr. Cockspur, sir—I'm on duty this morning, I'll have to hurry or I'll be late."

"This will only take a moment, my boy. I watched your match—nice, very nice, though you might consider the difference between discretion and valor. Never mind that. Are you familiar with Shakespeare?"

"Why . . . yes, sir."

"Good! I'm thinking of changing my scene. Making it a bit more martial for this tour. What do you think? I usually do a soliloquy . . . but perhaps Hamlet's death scene, the sword duel at the end of the play, would be more appropriate."

"That sounds fine, sir," Hikaru said, wondering why in the world Cockspur was asking him.

"I hoped you'd say that. I have no understudy—no one who can take the part of Laertes. What do you say?"

"To what, sir?"

"To playing Laertes."

"Oh." Hikaru almost refused outright, but stopped and thought about it. He doubted he would be able to avoid Mr. Cockspur's company during the tour, unless he avoided the rec deck too. The actor spent his evenings in the lounge. Why not put the time to use? Hikaru would rather play Hamlet, of course—for one thing, he was the right age. But Laertes would be fun. "All right," he said. "I'd like that. Thanks for asking me."

"Excellent, my boy. Can you learn the lines in time for two o'clock rehearsal?"

"That's a problem," Hikaru said, disappointed. "I'm on duty till sixteen hundred. I'm familiar with the scene, though—I could probably learn it by showtime."

"No, that won't do at all. We must rehearse, and you must learn my translation—"

"Translation? Of *Shakespeare?*"

"—so I'll speak to the captain." He bustled away.

Feeling grumpy and badly used, Roswind went to the rec deck locker room for a shower. The place was packed with people getting ready to go on duty. Whenever a starship set out on an extended voyage, practically everyone on board signed up for some kind of exercise class: tai chi or yoga, martial arts from several worlds, beginning fencing (that was a new one), and even an obscure and esoteric practice whose name translated as "deep breathing," but which sounded to Roswind like nothing more than an excuse for people to shriek at the top of their lungs for an hour.

Within a few weeks half the people would have dropped out of classes and gone back to their usual sedentary ways, but for the moment the locker room was one big traffic jam.

Just how long am I going to have somebody sleeping in my shower? Roswind wondered. If she's going to do this all the time, can I get away with filing a complaint?

Personnel looked askance at any frivolous—or bigoted— objection to a roommate of a different species. If the roommate emitted methane or some other noxious gas, if two roommates required widely different temperatures, or if one were allergic to the other—Roswind wished she had not assured Lieutenant Uhura that she had no allergies—then Personnel would grant a transfer. But a complaint that a new recruit had mistaken the shower for a bunk would bring nothing but a reprimand and a lecture on tolerance. So Roswind grumbled, took her shower in the locker room, and snapped, short-tempered, at everyone who spoke to her all day.

At noon, Captain Kirk gave Hikaru the rest of the day off. The fledgling actor received the scene from Mr. Cockspur. He read it . . . and realized what he had let himself in for.

After the two o'clock rehearsal, feeling relatively pleased, Mr. Cockspur sent the lieutenant off to review his lines. Mr. Cockspur himself sought out Amelinda Lukarian, who was, of course, as usual, with her wretched pet.

He picked his way carefully across the shuttlecraft deck. No telling what might be concealed in the sprouting grass. "Ms. Lukarian."

Insolently, she brushed the creature's coat. Finally she acknowledged him. "Yes, Mr. Cockspur?"

"I've changed my scene."

"I saw it. Hikaru is charming in the part."

"Yes, he shows promise. And I've explained to him that the original is incomprehensible to the modern audience. He'll have the lines letter-perfect by tonight. So the only question is—where should the scene appear."

"Same as always, next to last, just before Newland."

"But my dear child, the death scene is the final scene in *Hamlet*. It should come last in the show."

"We've been through this. Billing is the manager's responsibility. Newland Rift gets to go last on any bill I put together."

"Puppies," Cockspur said before he considered the effect of his impersonation on Lukarian.

"And I won't end the show with a tragedy, either." She turned to her horse as the ill-mannered beast bit her.

"In that case, I must protest."

"Your privilege."

"If you dislike me so much, Ms. Lukarian, why don't you buy out my share in the co-op?"

"I can't afford to. Why don't you abandon it?"

"That would be financially foolish, would it not?"

"Then run for manager. If you win, you can decide who goes first and last."

"Run for manager? My dear young lady, I am an artist."

She faced him again. "Mr. Cockspur, I've tried to be civil, because you were a friend of my father. But I won't displace Newland so you can have better billing!"

"In that case, I am on strike."

"On *strike?* You can't go on strike! You're on the bill! You signed a contract!"

"I have a right to protest intolerable working conditions." Cockspur stalked away.

Ship's news announced the special performance of the Warp-Speed Classic Vaudeville Company. Soon all the places for the evening's two shows had been spoken for and the standing room was going fast.

Jim strolled to the shuttlecraft hangar, along the catwalk, to the companionway. He stared at the deck in pure astonishment.

A gauzy emerald sheen covered the gently rolling landscape; new grass grew on what had been part of a barren astronomical body the day before. Three gnarled pines twisted together in one corner, and a huge stone, jagged and broken on one side, meteor-pitted on the other, rose from among their roots. The shuttlecraft had been lined up along one bulkhead, close together, and partitioned off from the pasture so Athene would not become trapped between them. Sulu had planned well. The shuttlecraft stood atop the dirt and could be launched if they were needed. The sprouting grass shimmered against their skids.

It smelled like spring.

Lindy ran across the field. Athene sprinted after her, bucking, nipping at her heels, playing. She bounced to a stop, her wings half spread. Lindy petted her and *tsk*ed to her. Athene began trotting in a circle around her, controlled by her voice. Lindy chirruped; Athene broke into a canter and widened the circle. When she spread her wings, she looked as if any instant she could leap from the ground and fly.

Lindy saw Jim. She waved to him and he joined her.

"Hi, Jim. What do you think?"

"I'm impressed," Jim said. "I forgot we carried ADG seed—planting accelerated desert grass was a good idea."

"I never heard of it before. Hikaru said it's descended from desert plants that grow after rainstorms."

"Yes. It's invaluable in controlling erosion."

"So we threw a few kilos around, and, *voilà!* You've got a ton of it—why does a starship carry grass seed?"

"We've got about fifty metric tons, if I remember correctly. Terraformed planets sometimes use it—after a flood, say, or a volcanic eruption. You don't get much call for it, but when you need it you need a lot of it and you need it fast."

"We brought the big rock in with the dirt, and we borrowed the trees from botany." Lindy smiled. "Athene loves it. But . . . she still can't fly. Jim, will you change the gravity?"

"Isn't the ceiling too low?"

"The deck isn't perfect. Obviously I'd rather have a ninety-nine percent earth environment with one-tenth gravity. Jim, whatever we do, she probably won't get off the ground. More likely she'll just be able to float along for a few steps. But it might make her *think* she's flying. It might be enough."

"Let me check with the chief engineer." He contacted Engineering and posed the question to Mr. Scott.

"Tenth g, just on the shuttlecraft deck? I dinna ken, Captain Kirk, 'twould be complex. The structural stress—"

"Mr. Scott, the structure of the *Enterprise* ought to be capable of standing the stress—unless the ship's maintenance has been neglected. Is that what you're trying to tell me?"

"Neglected! Begging the captain's pardon!"

"Yes or no, Mr. Scott?"

"Nay, captain, the maintenance hasna been neglected. And aye, captain, 'tis possible to change the gravity."

"When?"

"A few hours, captain."

"Very well. Keep Ms. Lukarian informed so she can be here when you make the change."

"Aye, captain."

Jim cut off the connection.

"Jim, thanks," Lindy said. "I'm afraid this isn't making Mr. Scott very happy . . ."

Jim shrugged. "That isn't your problem. He just isn't used to having . . . an 'inexperienced tyro' for a captain. By the way, it's standing room only at tonight's performances."

"SRO? Already?" With a whoop of triumph, she raised her arms, her fists clenched, and spun once around.

"Ticket scalpers may start work any minute." Jim grinned. "How about heading them off by adding some more shows?"

"You need a bigger theater." She laughed. "Of course we'll add more shows, are you kidding? Like I told you, we're used to doing two a day. And there's nothing a performer likes better than being held over."

"Good. I'll put it on ship's news."

Lindy whistled and Athene trotted to her side.

"Jim, can you ride?"

"Sure. Iowa farm boy, you know."

"Would you like to ride Athene?"

Jim had not been on a horse since the last summer he spent on the farm. Winona kept a small herd of Shires as part of an endangered domestic species preservation project. Jim and Sam used to ride Earthquake and Tsunami all over the countryside, swimming in the lake, even fishing in the river. The broad back of a Shire draft horse made a comfortable resting place on a hot, lazy afternoon. The gray-dappled horses stood in sun-dappled water, chest-deep, dozing, splashing droplets up from the surface with their slowly swishing tails.

Jim flexed his hand, where the scabbed-over cat scratches stung. I haven't had much luck so far with the animals on this ship, he thought.

"Yes," he said. "I'd like to ride Athene."

"Come on, I'll give you a leg up. Just slide your knees under her wings." She laced her fingers together, cupped her hands where a stirrup would be if Athene were wearing a saddle, and tossed Jim easily onto Athene's back.

Jim felt the muscles of the equiraptor tense beneath him; he thought for a moment she might bolt, but Lindy laid one hand lightly on her neck and urged her into a walk.

Athene had a lively, rolling, bouncy gait. Earthquake, Jim's Shire, had a deliberate and powerful step. He had been about three times Athene's mass and four hands taller, over two meters tall at the withers.

Instead of getting in the way, Athene's wings acted like the kneepads of a jumping saddle. Jim was glad of something to brace against, for Athene's balance was completely different from any horse he had ever been on.

The equiraptor jogged in a circle around Lindy. Jim held on with his knees and touched his heel to her side. She leaped into a canter, nearly unseating him. He grabbed for her mane. She slid to a stop and he nearly pitched over her head.

"That's okay—try it again. Subtle, remember."

Jim squeezed his legs gently against her sides: walk, jog, canter. Growing more comfortable, he relaxed into her gait.

"You look wonderful!" Lindy said. "Born to the saddle."

His knee twinged, but he was having too much fun to quit. So, he thought, why not give the knee a rest?

Jim put one hand on either side of Athene's withers. Then he hesitated, thinking, I may be about to make the universe's biggest fool of myself . . .

"Nice and steady, Athene," he said, more for his own reassurance than in a serious hope that she understood.

He pushed himself up so he was kneeling on her back. Again he paused, accustoming his balance to the bouncy canter. He could see a rim of white around her gray eye; and her ears swiveled nervously. Jim bent forward, braced his shoulder against her neck, and pushed off with his feet.

He balanced precariously in a shoulder stand, upside down, wing feathers tickling his face, as Athene cantered in a steady circle.

Jim let himself down. Athene slowed to a trot, a walk, a halt.

"That was fantastic! How did you do it?"

Jim rubbed his shoulder. "I wasn't sure I remembered how. It's been a good long time since I did it."

"Will you teach me?"

"If you like." He plunged ahead. "Lindy, can I show you something? Something about the *Enterprise?*"

"Sure."

The turbo-lift carried them from the shuttlecraft deck to the main body of the ship. The door of the arboretum slid open. They stepped into its dense, damp warmth.

Lindy let out her breath in surprise.

Someone with a considerable aesthetic sense had arranged the area, for though the plants that grew side by side came from many worlds, in combination they harmonized. Here the familiar shape of a small apple tree accentuated the curious bulk of a Deltan stone cactus; a Vulcan ground creeper, its growth accelerated by the relatively unlimited supply of water, blossomed all over in great blue flowers. On Vulcan it flowered perhaps once every hundred years.

"This is incredible," Lindy said.

"It isn't easy, getting this many different species to grow together," Jim said. He knew some of the problems from Sam and Winona's work with alien species. "It takes a lot of juggling microenvironments. In some ways it's even harder than getting people from different cultures—different worlds—to get along."

"At least with people you can get them to talk to each other," Lindy said.

"Some of them. Some of the time."

They walked along the path, passing beneath drooping giant ferns, under a thick sprawl-branched conifer. Feathery vines covered the ground with a springy tangle. The heavy, humid air made everything damp. Jim thought about walking hand in hand with Lindy, but he was not quite ready to reach out to her, to risk rejection . . . or acceptance.

The trail narrowed and turned. Jim led Lindy in a different direction, off the path entirely. He listened hard and kept an eye out for signs that others had passed recently. He did not want to startle anyone by coming upon them unaware. He heard no voices except his and Lindy's. They were alone.

"How big is this place?"

"Smaller than it looks—smaller than the shuttlecraft deck. But you can't see its sides because of all the trees, so it looks bigger."

"Where are we going?"

"That's a surprise."

He saw the spot just ahead. In it, even terran trees looked alien, for their branches grew in strange and unexpected directions. Jim led Lindy to the edge of the clearing. Tree branches almost completely surrounded a spherical space five or six meters in diameter.

Jim launched himself into the empty space. He glided through the null-grav point, plucked a branch of dark purple lilac as he somersaulted at the far edge, and kicked off toward Lindy again. He judged it perfectly, coming to a halt an arm's length from her, still floating in zero g. He presented the lilac to her.

"Jim . . . thank you." The lilac had formed a spherical bloom in null-grav, rather than its usual tapering spray. Lindy breathed its deep fragrance.

"This is one of those gravity anomalies I told you about. Want to try it? Move slowly at first—it takes a little while to get used to the feeling." He wondered suddenly if he had made an awful mistake, for many people found their first few minutes in freefall not exhilarating but nauseating. And some people never got used to it at all.

Lindy stepped off into zero g, giving herself a push and a twist at the same time. She tucked her head and drew up her knees and spun like a diver, then stretched out her body to slow the spin. After three revolutions the friction of the air brought her to a halt.

"It's like being on the trapeze, only better!" she said. She drifted to the far side of the sphere, touched a branch, and pushed off toward Jim.

He met her, caught her hands, and spun with her around their mutual center of gravity. She ducked away, slipped around him as if they were swimming, caught a branch at the far side of the clearing, and brought herself to a halt. She laughed. Gazing at her, Jim let himself float free.

"Say, Jim?" Lindy said tentatively.

"Yes?" Jim heard the questioning tone in her voice, and his heart beat harder.

"What do you do when . . ." she hesitated. "When you feel close to somebody you work with? I mean when you want to feel close, but . . ." She blew out her breath in frustration. "You know what I mean."

He hoped he did, but he was not certain.

"That depends," he said. "I think it's generally a bad idea to get emotionally involved with subordinates—"

"But there aren't any subordinates in the company."

"—but if it were someone outside your own hierarchy . . ." He stopped when what she had said got through to him. "In the company?" he said lamely.

"Yeah." Lindy shrugged, looking sheepish. "This never happened to me before. I mean, sure, when I was a kid, I made a fool of myself with the occasional bout of puppy love, and later, if we stayed in one place long enough, once in a while I'd meet someone." She grinned. "And sometimes I have the urge to tackle Marcellin around the knees, but he's awfully elusive, he never lets anyone very close."

"Lindy," Jim said, feeling confused, "you're going to have to be a little clearer about what exactly it is that you're asking me."

"I think," she said, "that I'm falling in love with Stephen."

"Stephen!" Jim felt a quick flash of jealousy, jealousy he knew he had no right to, then a rush of envy, and finally disbelief. "Stephen! Lindy—I don't care how elusive Marcellin is. A Vulcan will make him look demonstrative."

"Not Stephen," she said. "He's different."

"Maybe, maybe not. But Mr. Spock says he seeks out emotional experiences. Maybe you're . . . just another emotional experience to him."

"That's not fair!" she said. "I said *I'm* falling in love with *him*—I don't know if he . . . I've been trying to decide whether to say anything to him."

Jim felt rejected, without even the comfort of having had a chance to be accepted. He started to say something to Lindy about his own feelings, but his pride silenced him. Trying to think of something else to say, he fell back on ethics.

"It can get difficult," he said. "You are manager, after all, with responsibility and authority the others don't have. If Stephen reciprocates your feelings, you'll have to be sure not to show favoritism. If he doesn't, you'll have to be careful not to use your position against him—"

"I wouldn't!" she said, shocked and offended.

"—and if you get together, then break up, that's the most complicated of all." He wished she would accuse him of trying out of jealousy to deflect her feelings for Stephen. At least then she would be acknowledging that he had feelings for her. At least she would have noticed.

Lindy nodded thoughtfully. "I see what you mean."

So do I, Jim thought gloomily. Now that I've given Lindy a lecture on how to behave if you're turned down, I'm going to have to see if I can follow my own advice.

Lindy looked at him and smiled. "Thanks, Jim. I'm grateful for your advice. You're so easy to talk to. I feel a lot better."

Jim felt a lot more depressed.

# Chapter 9

THE SMALL THEATER on the recreation deck was nearly full. Jim tried to accept his reserved front-row seat as a courtesy, but he felt on display.

The rustle and hum of conversation increased. Jim made out disconnected bits: expectation, laughter, curiosity.

Commander Spock entered the auditorium. The shadows accentuated the angular planes of his face.

He took the seat beside Jim's that had been reserved for him. He sat straight and stiff, his hands resting on his thighs, his expression one of studied neutrality. Jim glanced at him quizzically.

"Commander Spock."

"Captain."

"I didn't know Vulcans went in for frivolous entertainments."

Spock arched his eyebrow. "I was under the impression, captain," he said, "that you had issued an order to attend."

"What? Certainly not. Where did you get that idea?"

"From your announcement, captain."

Jim thought back over his wording. He had not ordered anyone to attend. Neither had he thought to specify that attendance was optional. He had to remember that the officers and crew needed time to become familiar with him. They might all assume, as had Janice Rand, that he was a martinet who expected them to treat his most subtle hints, his offhand whims, as unbreakable orders.

"Commander Spock, when I give a direct order, I'll make it clear that it's a direct order."

"Very well, captain."

Spock remained in his seat.

"That means you don't have to stay," Jim said.

"Is that a direct order, sir?"

"No, it is not a direct order."

"In that case, I will remain. I am most curious about Ms. Lukarian's profession. Perhaps I misjudged her character. I wish to observe her performance."

"By all means, then, observe."

"Thank you, captain." Mr. Spock glanced around the theater. "Though I would prefer to have been assigned a seat in the back. That way, I could observe both the performers and the audience."

"Why don't you relax, Mr. Spock?" Jim said. "You can observe the audience at the second show."

If Spock realized Jim had made a joke, he gave no sign of it. "An excellent suggestion," he said. "Humans have so many quaint and contradictory beliefs. It is interesting to observe them under unusual conditions. Are you aware, captain, that branches of the Flat Earth Society have sprung up on several worlds colonized by human beings?"

"No, I wasn't aware of that." Jim wondered if Spock were pulling his leg, but that seemed rather out of character. "But I don't see how you can equate a vaudeville show with believing that the earth is flat."

"Not the show itself—the magic. Magic has been used to defraud, to engender a belief in the supernatural—"

"Mr. Spock," Jim said with some asperity, "this is an entertainment, not a conspiracy. Are you expecting Lindy's company to set up a seance? To help you—for a suitable fee, of course—contact your dead great-aunt Matilda?"

The house lights flickered. The chatter faded. Spock regarded Jim with an expression very near a frown.

"How did you know, captain, that my mother's deceased aunt was named Matilda?"

"I—" Jim started to say that he and half the other adult human beings he knew had a great-aunt named Matilda; it had been a very popular name two generations before. Instead, he grinned. "Psychic, I guess."

The house lights flickered again. The audience settled.

As the house lights faded to darkness, and Jim waited for

Lindy to come onstage, he explored his feelings about her. He had lectured her on ethics; now he would have to find out if he could follow his own rules.

Since he had shown her the null-grav node, he had been busy; she had been busy. He had barely seen her: a wave at noon, across the mess hall. A pang of regret that her smile meant no more than "Hello, friend." A flash of jealousy, instantly controlled, when he saw Stephen touch her hand.

Jim wished once more that he had never told her about Ghioghe, about those few dreadful minutes in the rescue pod. He felt that somehow, if he had not told her, her feelings about him would have been different.

She doesn't need one more person to worry about, he thought. She needs someone steady, someone she knows she could lean on. Even if she never did, just knowing she *could* . . .

And even if I never did, just knowing I could . . .

But he knew that for him, there was no one to lean on.

It's just as well, Jim decided. I'm glad I didn't tell her how I feel. Even if I told her, even if she returned my feelings, it would have ended the same way things ended between me and Carol. I'm glad Lindy didn't realize what I was trying to say to her.

Or maybe she did, he thought. Maybe she understood perfectly, but she didn't want to love another person who would stay awhile, and then be gone.

A blue spotlight flashed on center stage.

Amelinda Lukarian—Lindy no longer—gazed out, silent, aloof, somber. She wore a silver suit glittering with multicolored highlights. Jim would have sworn the stage had been empty, even when the house lights dimmed. Amelinda had simply appeared—as if by magic. He wondered how she created the illusion.

You're beginning to think like a Vulcan, Jim told himself. Take your own advice: sit back and enjoy the show.

"Honorable members of the crew of the starship *Enterprise*." Onstage the magician's voice took on a low and powerful timbre that sent an extra thrill down Jim's spine. "Welcome to the first interstellar performance of the Warp-Speed Classic Vaudeville Show. I am Amelinda, and I am a magician. I will show you illusion—or I will show you a deeper reality. Only you can judge which it is."

She plucked a glittering object from the air. The audience murmured in surprise. The transparent blue disk caught the light, concentrated it, and flung it out again.

"The people of Tau Ceti II possess great mineralogical expertise. They crystallize their currency from pure sapphire," Amelinda said. "Jewels have transfixed the imagination of sentient beings since before history—but some would say that jewels have powers of their own, powers that transcend even the imagination."

She held up the sapphire coin, grasped it with her other hand—and it disappeared.

"My daddy used to tell me, a fool and her money are soon parted," Amelinda said. "But you know how aggravating children can be. I always replied—" She reached up and plucked another coin from nothingness.

Jim found himself applauding along with the rest of the audience, except, he noted, for Commander Spock.

Spock leaned forward, intent on the stage. Two narrow parallel furrows creased his brow. Then, as if he had become aware of Jim's scrutiny, his forehead smoothed and his expression regained its impassivity.

The applause stopped. The audience waited expectantly.

"It is, of course," Spock said in a normal tone of voice, "the same coin."

Jim glanced sidelong at the commander. Amelinda hesitated so briefly that Jim was not certain she had heard.

"It came in handy, my 'magic money,' as my daddy used to call it," Amelinda said, "when I was little. There was a bully in school who stole money from anyone smaller than him. Whenever he tried to steal mine, I made it disappear."

She reached for the second coin; like the first, it vanished from her hand.

"The coin is still in her hand," Spock said.

"Commander Spock!" Jim whispered.

"Yes, captain? No evidence of phaser or transporter dematerialization. Therefore, the coin must still be in her hand. Unless," Spock said in a thoughtful tone, "it was a holographic illusion."

"Shut *up*, commander. That's a direct—"

"House lights," Amelinda said.

Jim looked up. Amelinda stood at the edge of the stage, glaring down. Her heavy iridescent hair gleamed, shoulder-length around her face, falling below her hips in back.

"House lights!" she said again. The power of her voice came from her alone, without the aid of amplifiers.

The house lights brightened.

"Commander Spock," Amelinda said, with perfect composure, "would you care to repeat your comment so the rest of the audience can hear you?"

"I said that the coin was a holographic illusion, or that it was still in your hand," Spock said.

"A holographic illusion? That would be cheating." She held out her open hand. "And the coin is not in my hand."

"Your *other* hand," Spock said.

"The coin isn't in my hand—or in my hand." Amelinda extended her other hand, open and empty.

Spock raised one eyebrow.

"We're lucky—aren't we?" Amelinda said. "If my birthplace were Tau Ceti II, and I were one of its octomanual inhabitants: 'It is not in my hand, or in my hand, or in my hand . . .' Why, we'd be here all night."

The audience laughed with her.

She offered her empty hand to Mr. Spock.

"I usually ask for a volunteer later on, but since you're so eager, Commander Spock, you can help me now."

Spock rose from his seat, and sprang onto the stage.

Amelinda regarded Spock with a smile, accepting him as a worthy opponent. "You claim that I have only one coin."

"I said you plucked the same coin from the air both times," Spock said.

"I don't blame you for thinking that. Air is so barren. I wonder what we might find in more fertile fields? Hold out your hands."

Spock complied. Reaching up to his left ear, Amelinda plucked out a coin and dropped it, glittering, into Spock's outstretched hands.

The audience loved it. Jim laughed, impressed by Amelinda's audacity in inviting a Vulcan to watch her illusions at close range. Amelinda plucked a coin from Spock's right ear. One after another, she pulled coins from Spock's ears and dropped the sapphire disks into his hands till there was no question of their being holographic projections. Each crystal hit the next, ringing with high, piercing notes. Spock watched, nonplussed.

"So much more to work with than air," Amelinda said. Then she blushed. "Sorry," she said, the only break in her stage presence. "Cheap joke."

Spock tried to hold all the coins, but one slipped from the double handful. It spun on the stage and rolled into the shadows. Ignoring it, Amelinda scooped coins from Spock's hands and pitched them into the audience till Spock stood empty-handed once more.

"Now they've disappeared for good," Amelinda said, "and even I can't make them return."

The audience erupted into applause. Amelinda bowed low. Her hair fell forward, nearly touching the floor. When she stood again she flung it back, like a dark, iridescent cape.

Spock started toward his seat.

The magician stopped him with her voice. "Not so fast," she said. "I have more work for my volunteer."

Tzesnashstennaj and another felinoid pushed a great box onto the stage. Clear glass molded in an openwork filigree pattern formed all four sides. The assistants spun the box and stopped it at stage center.

Amelinda opened it and rapped her wand against its solid inside. Jim wondered where the wand had come from.

"An empty box." Amelinda waved the wand beneath it. "It stands high above the floor, it has no hidden escapes, no electronics. Mr. Scott!"

Amelinda made a sweeping gesture. The spotlights flashed onto a circular mesh plate, which had till now hung unseen in the shadows over the stage.

"If you would be so kind as to explain this device."

"Aye," Scott said. " 'Tis a transporter-beam shield. No transporter can operate near that little device."

"And it is fully functional?"

"I installed it myself," Scott said.

"Thank you. Dr. McCoy!"

McCoy joined Scott onstage.

"Do you have your tricorder, Dr. McCoy?"

"I do."

"Check the magic box—for electronics, for anything suspicious."

"My pleasure." McCoy fiddled with the tricorder, causing it to emit beeps and whines. "Nothing," he said. "It's a perfectly ordinary box."

"Do you think so? Please set your tricorder to signal the use of a transporter beam, and place the instrument in front of the box."

McCoy did as she asked, then stepped back beside Scott. Spock looked as if he wished he were somewhere else.

"And now, Mr. Spock, if you would enter the box—"

"Why would I wish to do this?"

"Because—" By her second word, Amelinda had smoothed the edge from her voice. "Because, as before, I have nothing up my sleeves."

She pushed her sleeves to her elbows. The muscles of her forearms were clear and well defined. She turned her hands over to show that they were empty.

She reached toward Spock, offering to escort him. Again, he pretended not to notice her hand, but he did climb inside the box. He wore an expression of bemusement.

Amelinda closed the box. Spock stood within transparent latticework walls. The lights shifted and changed, reflecting from the glass, obscuring all but the vague outline of Spock's body.

"Now I'll secure him."

Tzesnashstennaj loped forward with a carrier full of swords. Amelinda chose one, placed its tip against the floor, and leaned on it till it bent like a fencing foil. She released the tension and it sprang straight.

She thrust it through an opening in the filigree.

The audience gasped.

"Silence, please," Amelinda said. "You mustn't disturb my concentration. It could be . . . dangerous."

At the level of Spock's chest the sword's point protruded from the far side of the box. The changing lights sparked on the sharp metal. The magician chose a second sword and slid it through the lattice. Soon a dozen swords penetrated the box and the science officer's shadowy shape.

"By normal means, no person, nothing, could escape. Some would say no one could survive."

The assistants spun the box a third time. The changing lights washed over their fur and over the glass, dappling them like light on water.

"Stop!"

Amelinda withdrew the swords from the box and flung them clattering onto the stage. She reached for the latch, hesitating, letting the tension build.

She flung open the door. In the same instant, the lights steadied. Jim blinked, dazzled. A figure stood inside the box. Amelinda took his hand.

Leonard McCoy stepped from the magic box and into a moment of stunned silence. Jim glanced to the side of the stage, where Scott still stood watching. He never noticed how or when McCoy had moved. Cheers and applause crashed over the stage like a wave. Amelinda and McCoy both bowed.

The lights faded, and they were gone.

Stephen met Spock on his emergence from the "magic" box.

"Vulcans are a tactless bunch at best, but you're in a class by yourself," Stephen said.

"As usual, your meaning eludes me," Spock said.

"Stay here till Lindy comes and gets you."

"I would prefer to return to the audience."

"You already almost spoiled one of Lindy's tricks! You stay here. Don't worry, you won't have to put up with my presence. You'll miss my act—but I'm sure that won't bother you." Stephen hurried out, leaving Spock alone.

Spock inspected his surroundings. The secret exit from the "magic" box led into a briefing room adjacent to the theater. All manner of unusual equipment filled the room: exotic costumes, hand-built machines, musical instruments, boxes of makeup, masks, harness.

Spock would never have guessed the method of escape from the box, but having experienced it he admired its simplicity. He wondered why the captain had behaved in such a perturbed way before Spock climbed onto the stage. Spock's observations had been logical. Furthermore, they had provided him with an opportunity to observe the performance at closer range. Spock had not expected to reap such a benefit, but one must take advantage of serendipity when it occurred.

He believed his original observations and comments still to be accurate: the magician *had* plucked the same coin out of the air twice, and the coin *had* been in one hand while she induced the audience to look at the other. But what she did with it when he challenged her, Spock could not determine. Nor did he understand the mechanism by which she had produced a double handful of sapphire disks—whether from his ears or from thin air did not matter. Spock felt considerable respect for the magician and her technique. He wondered what was happening onstage. The magician might be perpetrating any sort of fraud on her credulous fellow humans. Perhaps she had planned all along to spirit Spock away so he could no longer observe.

Spock picked up a mask and stared into it. Deep furrows sculpted the face into a furious scowl. Black gauze covered the eyeholes, to obscure the eyes of the actor.

The door slid open. Amelinda strode in and stopped five paces from him, her hands on her hips.

"What do you mean by heckling my performance?" Her voice was taut with the anger she had repressed onstage.

"Heckling?" Spock said. "I merely pointed out—"

"Merely? Merely! Why didn't you get up and explain everything I did? Then everybody could say, 'Oh, but that's so *easy*—anybody can do that.' But everybody *can't* do that—not unless they're willing to spend a couple of hours every day of their lives practicing it! Mr. Spock, how could you do that to me? I thought you liked me."

"I do not like anyone," Spock said. "It is not in my nature to like, or to dislike. It was not my intention to disparage your accomplishments."

"You could have fooled me!"

"Far from disparaging your abilities, I cannot explain all of your illusions. But you implied that the coin had disappeared by supernatural means, and I felt it my duty to point out that no such thing happened."

"Supernatural means—!" She looked at him with disbelief. "You don't think I expected anybody to swallow that swill, do you?"

"I beg your pardon?"

"Did you think I meant for anyone to believe what I did was anything more than a trick? Did you think anybody *did* believe I was using"—she laughed—"supernatural means?"

"Magicians have been known to perpetrate frauds. As for making assumptions about the beliefs of any particular human at any particular moment, I would not presume to try."

"For cat's sake," Amelinda said. "Sure, there've been frauds. But for every illusionist who ever pretended to be a medium, or a prophet, or a telekineticist, or whatever, there were always a hundred who said, 'We're performing. We're creating illusions. Come and let us fool you.' You can be sure that nobody who's working a scam is going to advertise that they're a stage magician!"

"That is a telling point," Spock said. "I had not considered it."

"Everybody in that audience knew I was performing a trick. That's what they came to see. They didn't want to know how I did it—you could have spoiled it for them. Never mind for me. Didn't you understand that?"

"No," Spock said. "I did not."

"Vulcans and children," Amelinda said. "Never perform for Vulcans or children. That's what my daddy always said. And I guess he was right."

"If you did not intend people to believe you work by supernatural means, why did you claim that as your method?"

"That's the schtick."

"Please define your terms."

"The schtick. That's . . . it's kind of hard to define."

"Ah. A technical term."

She giggled, then sobered and nodded. "Right. A technical term. It's the line you use to pull the audience into your world. To persuade them to go along with you."

"Willing suspension of disbelief," Spock said.

"I guess. It's a fancy way of putting it, but you could describe it that way if you wanted."

"I am quoting an earth poet. That was how he described the art of poetry. I thought all humans studied his work."

"They probably do in school. I don't know, I never went."

Recalling her performance, Spock cocked one eyebrow. "But onstage, you said—the schoolyard bully—?"

"I made that up. It sounds good."

"Part of . . . the 'schtick'?"

"Very good, Mr. Spock. You know . . . you're very effective onstage. You have natural presence. How about a repeat performance for the second show?"

"I had planned to observe the audience."

"You can observe them from backstage. After you heckle me and I disappear you. It's the least you can do, after you nearly spoiled my act."

Spock considered the proposal. "But I did not spoil your act. My questioning your illusion allowed you to demonstrate the more impressive trick. I suspect you planned the entire sequence."

"Planned it?" Amelinda laughed again. "No, I didn't plan it. I'm good, but I'm not that good. Maybe my daddy can work an audience that slick. Maybe someday I'll be able to, but I didn't this time. Not intentionally."

"In that case, you improvise most effectively."

"You try to be prepared," Amelinda said. "How about it? Will you help me out?"

"Very well," Spock said. He would have many chances to observe audiences, but this would be a unique opportunity to observe a unique human being. "I will aid you, as long as I do not have to promote a belief in the supernatural."

"That's great," Amelinda said. "Just one other thing."

"What is that?"

"I'll have to show you how some of the illusions work. That makes you my assistant—it makes you one of us. You aren't allowed to tell anyone else the secrets."

"Please give me an example."

"Okay. For example, you can't tell anybody how you got out of the magic box. You can't tell anybody I use a codepicker in my escape illusion later on." She magically produced a miniaturized instrument that electronically broke security codes.

Spock considered. "That is a highly illegal piece of equipment, Ms. Lukarian."

216

"They're only illegal because criminals use them to break into and out of things. Magicians always have a pack full of tools they'd get arrested for if they used them anywhere but onstage. What do you say—are you going to promise, or are you going to turn me in?"

"I will promise."

"Good. Come on, let's watch the show from the wings."

He followed her to the backstage area. In the spotlight, Stephen tossed burning, twirling torches in high arcs, hardly appearing to touch them as he caught them and flung them spinning into the air again. A blue silk ribbon drew back his long blond hair.

"By the way, Mr. Spock," Amelinda said, "you don't have anything else to wear, do you? Something flashier?"

Spock thought to demur, then changed his mind.

"I believe that could be arranged, Ms. Lukarian."

Amelinda and Spock returned to the backstage area. "You can see the audience from over there, Mr. Spock," Lindy said. "Oh—Hikaru!"

Hikaru Sulu was waiting backstage, wearing tights and a doublet, a prop sword at his side. He had not yet seen Mr. Cockspur. He supposed he was in his dressing room.

"I'm all ready," he said.

"He didn't tell you?" Lindy said.

"Who didn't tell me what?"

"Mr. Cockspur is on strike."

Hikaru was surprised by the strength of his disappointment. Then he brightened. "Am I the understudy? Maybe I could go on instead."

"Could you? That would be great. Have you been onstage before? Do you know a soliloquy?"

"No, I haven't, but I do know . . . I mean . . ." Being familiar with Shakespeare and being able to walk onstage and play a scene were two very different things. "I guess I spoke too soon," he said.

"Could you learn a soliloquy by tomorrow?"

"Sure!"

"Okay. Auditions are a bitch, but if you think your ego can stand it, come to rehearsal tomorrow."

"I'll be there!"

In the audience, Jim watched Stephen's act. The spectacular culminated in twirling knives and flaming torches. It was every bit as flamboyant as the man himself. At the finish, Stephen caught the torches and knives, freed his hair from the ribbon, and bowed.

McCoy slipped into the auditorium and sat in Mr. Spock's seat.

"Bones, I think you have a future in vaudeville," Jim said softly.

"You're in trouble, boy," McCoy said. "I'm gonna borrow Lindy's magic box long enough to get you into sick bay for your physical."

"Shh!" Jim said. He could practically see McCoy's regen culture working away on a tub full of glucose solution, turning it into a tub of pulsating green slime. "Don't talk during the performance."

After Greg and Maris tap danced the house down, Marcellin glided onto the stage. By the reactions of his body to his imagination, he created an invisible world out of the air around him.

Jim became completely entranced with the show. Intermission came and went and he forgot even to wonder what had happened to the science officer.

Philomela sang, and first the audience laughed, then they cried, then they laughed and cried at the same time.

Tzesnashstennaj and the other felinoids, including two members of the crew of the *Enterprise,* danced a performance of the hunt. Jim had heard of the dance, a mythic representation of their species' history, but he had never seen it before. It was eerie, erotic, and disturbing.

The curtain closed and the lights dimmed. It must be time for Mr. Cockspur's neo-Shakespearean act. Jim felt curious, though since he knew more or less what to expect, he supposed it was a morbid curiosity.

But Mr. Cockspur never appeared. The curtain opened. Instead of the actor, a pastel cloud of fluffy poodles bounded onto the stage and scampered in a circle. Newland Rift followed, imposing in a white hakama and layers of white silk kimono. The puppies sat up in a line across the stage, their paws tucked beneath their chins, their little pink tongues lolling, their little white teeth gleaming. Jim wished he had sat farther back.

To his utter astonishment, Rift's act was every bit as entertaining as Lindy claimed. The puppies were as different onstage as Rift had assured him. They jumped through hoops, they barked in chorus and in harmony, they leaped over and under each other, they formed a six-layer pyramid, balancing delicately and precariously on each other's backs. At the end, even Jim found himself applauding. Rift swept across the stage, followed by the puppies in perfect single file.

The performers came onstage to take their curtain calls.

Commander Spock stood among them. He had changed into a brown and gold velvet tunic, and he took his bows like a trouper.

All Roswind's friends had gone to the vaudeville show, but Roswind had to wait for tomorrow's performance because she had not been able to get a seat for either of tonight's shows. It was all the fault of her new roommate; if Roswind had not had to take her shower in the locker room, she would have had plenty of time this morning to reserve herself a place in the theater.

Roswind returned to her cabin. Her new green roommate showed no sign of coming out of the shower. Roswind got angry, and then became concerned. Lieutenant Uhura had warned her not to scare the being into hibernation, so what had she done first thing? She stepped on her. Then she yelled at her. Roswind tried to convince herself that she could claim not to have bothered the strange being, but the marks of her toes remained.

The being's superior was bound to call soon to ask why she had not reported for duty. Perhaps by then the bruise would have healed.

Commander Spock wore his brown velvet shirt to the second show, too. Onstage, he stepped inside the filigree glass box. Amelinda told the audience what she wanted them to see her do. The glass muffled her voice. He heard a metallic scrape as she drew a sword. She had borrowed Mr. Sulu's antique saber, which was unmistakably real.

Spock prepared to disappear.

The box lurched into another spin, throwing him against

its side. A sharp pain pierced him, as if something had gone wrong with the illusion, as if one of Amelinda's magic swords has penetrated his body. Spock fell—

In the audience, Jim felt the shudder of the *Enterprise*. He leaped from his seat as the emergency alarms sounded and raced toward the bridge.

He slid into his seat. Sulu, incongruous in velvet doublet and silk tights, followed close behind and took his place at the helm. Stars spiraled across the viewscreen as the *Enterprise* tumbled.

"Something ripped us out of warp-speed!" Commander Cheung said. "We're back in normal space."

Scott's voice crackled through the chaos of the intraship channels. "Warp drive's out, captain. What hit us?"

"Trying to steady our course, sir!" Sulu said. "I can only get about half power from the impulse engines!"

—and after a moment of silent blankness, Spock found himself on his hands and knees in the briefing room.

"Mr. Spock!" Amelinda knelt beside him.

"That was not, I trust . . ." He had to stop to take a breath. "Not one of your more successful illusions."

The alarms pulsed. Down the corridor, Mr. Rift's puppies barked hysterically, and Rift's deep voice rumbled soothingly. Spock stumbled to his feet and put one hand on the wall to steady himself. He still felt dizzy, but he had not been wounded by the magic swords.

"I don't know what happened," Lindy said. "It felt like somebody picked up the whole ship and threw us into a hole. I was afraid you were trapped in the apparatus—"

"I am quite all right."

Lindy accompanied him into the corridor.

"Can you get where you're going by yourself?"

"Certainly," he said.

"I have to be sure everybody's okay."

"Do not be concerned about me." He entered the lift.

She nodded quickly and hurried away.

"Bridge," Spock said. The lift squealed. The acceleration, normally so smooth as to be nearly imperceptible, thrust the cage into quivering motion. Spock staggered but kept his feet.

Spock reached the bridge while the alarms were still

shrilling. He sorted information out of the reports streaming from the intercom channels. He went to his station. The gravity field fluctuated. Pathological phenomena gripped the *Enterprise*.

The ship had fallen out of warp-speed. He usually perceived the change as a perturbation in gravity and in the quality of light. This time it must have happened as he tumbled through the escape from Amelinda's illusion. What malevolent violence could tear a starship from warp space and drag it back into the Einsteinian universe?

Captain Kirk peered eagerly at the viewscreen.

"Jim, you want to steady us down a little?" Dr. McCoy's slow drawl came over the intercom. "Or I'll have space sickness to deal with, as well as abrasions and contusions."

"No gravity-wave sources in this sector, captain," Uhura said.

"Mr. Scott!" Jim said. "I need steady power!"

"I'm doin' my best."

A powerful signal appeared. "Captain," Spock said. "Anomaly, dead ahead."

The *Enterprise*'s bucking and shuddering ceased abruptly. An eerie peace possessed the ship.

Jim unclenched his fingers from the arms of his seat. "Thank you, Mr. Spock. Maximum magnification, Mr. Sulu."

Spock tried to match his readings to a planetary or stellar or interstellar or quasi-stellar object. He failed.

"Maximum magnification."

An enormous curved surface filled the viewscreen, hurtling closer. Jim pulled back in surprise.

"Shields on full!" Jim said.

"It is several hundred thousand kilometers distant, captain," Spock said.

"Lower magnification, Mr. Sulu. Drop shields."

"My god," McCoy said. "What is it?"

Jim had not even heard McCoy arrive. "Bones—any injuries?"

"Nothing serious, physically. A lot of concern about what happened." McCoy waited. No one made any attempt to explain. "What *did* happen?"

"When we figure it out, you'll be the first to know."

"Reducing magnification, sir," Sulu said.

As Sulu decreased the magnification, the iridescent curved surface resolved itself into a sphere, a mammoth pearl. It receded farther and became one pearl among many. A webbing of silvery strands connected the spheres together, forming a cluster. The magnification decreased again. The construct shimmered, as if soap bubbles had collected to create a surface. Most of the bubbles were spherical, but some extended long translucent projections, like the spines on the shells of diatoms.

Jim watched in amazed excitement. The image on the viewscreen gave him a weird feeling. Though the magnification was decreasing, the object continued to fill the screen from edge to edge. As a result, it appeared not to diminish in size, but to expand as if it had no limits.

Its enormity became clear, then startling, then frightening.

Sensors and instruments forgotten, everyone on the bridge stared in awe at the immense structure.

Finally its limits came into view. Extraordinarily beautiful, it shone with its own light. A luminescent skeleton supported the soap-bubble skin. Patches and sparks and streams of light followed its branches and formed a webbed translucent pool above its center. At this magnification, the soap-bubble surface became a smooth and translucent pearl-gray skin stretched between the glowing ribs.

"It looks . . ." McCoy said slowly. "It looks alive."

"Anybody recognize it?" Jim said, and immediately regretted the levity. This was hardly a time for jokes, especially obvious ones; besides, the only laughter was a nervous titter from an ensign behind him.

"It does not belong to any member of the Federation," Spock said.

"Thank you, Mr. Spock," Jim said. He clenched the muscles of his jaw. The last thing he needed was to start giggling like a nervous ensign.

"Its diameter is . . . nearly seven thousand kilometers," Mr. Spock said.

"That's half the size of earth!" Uhura said.

"Half the diameter," Spock said calmly. "In terms of mass, of course, it would be much less."

"Captain," Sulu said, "that structure isn't on any charts. Also, the sensors were on long-range scan. They detected nothing. It wasn't there a few minutes ago. It wasn't anywhere within range a few minutes ago."

"What are you saying, Mr. Sulu? That it *moved* here under its own power?"

"Yes, sir."

Jim gazed at the structure. No energy source of the Federation's technology could power a thing that size into warp space. If the Klingon Empire had discovered how to do it, would they keep it a secret? Maybe they would. But Jim thought they would announce it. Loudly.

"Mr. Sulu is correct, captain," Spock said. "The sensors detected nothing—no approach of an unknown craft, no planetary body in our path—until after the gravitational perturbations that altered our course."

"What did it do, Spock?" McCoy asked. "Appear out of thin air?"

"Certainly not, doctor. There is no air."

"I was using," McCoy said, "an idiomatic expression."

Spock raised an eyebrow at the word "idiomatic."

"A metaphor," McCoy said. "It doesn't really mean what it says."

As Jim was about to interrupt, to try to keep McCoy from digging himself in any deeper, Lieutenant Uhura caught her breath.

"Captain, listen—"

A cascade of high-pitched song and low wails, thunderous rumblings and electric spatters of noise filled the air, calling and pausing and answering. Jim had never heard anything like it. The eerie scale, the alien combination of sounds, thrilled and disturbed him.

"I've never heard singing like it," she said. "And it has no words I recognize. The universal translator thinks it's random noise. The safeguards are routing the transmissions into storage—the translator can't find a way to work with them. It's ambient transmissions, sir—radio frequency energy, over a broad spectrum. It isn't—it doesn't seem to be—broadcasting a message toward the *Enterprise*."

"Then we'd better introduce ourselves."

"Wait a minute, Jim," McCoy said. "They aren't even aware that we're here—are you sure you want to tell them? Or it? We don't know who they are, what their intentions are—"

"Before you decide to fear them, Dr. McCoy," Spock said, "you might wait for evidence that 'they' exist. To gather such evidence, we must attempt communication."

"What kind of evidence do you need, Mr. Spock? What does that thing look like to you? A little lost planetoid? The product of erosion? I know! The effects of magnetism on interstellar dust!"

"It is not impossible to imagine a natural process whereby such a structure might be created. It would be rather unstable, of course—"

" 'Not impossible'—only for a Vulcan! That thing was obviously created by a culture to which we might be nothing more than monkeys—or cockroaches!"

"Whatever their intentions," Spock said, "we must demonstrate our goodwill."

Bones has a point, Jim thought. The inhabitants of the construct—if they existed—might not have noticed the *Enterprise*. He could still turn, run, hide out, and repair warp drives and subspace communications. Then he could contact Starfleet, announce the possible discovery of an unknown sentient species . . .

. . . And have Starfleet send another ship, with a more "experienced" captain, to take over his job.

"Hailing frequencies, lieutenant," Jim said.

"Hailing frequencies open, sir."

The alien cacophony faded to a background whisper. Jim hesitated. He had gone too far to stop. But he had no idea what to say. He had read all the accounts of interspecies contacts, he had studied the ones that had gone right and he had committed to memory the ones that had gone wrong. But no thread linked the successful ones, just as no thread linked the disasters.

"This is James T. Kirk, captain of the starship *Enterprise*. I represent the United Federation of Planets, an interstellar alliance dedicated to peace, to knowledge, to friendship between all sentient beings. Greetings, and welcome. Please reply, if you receive my transmission."

The background noise ceased.

Uhura scanned through frequencies that a moment before had hummed with energy. "Quiet on all channels, sir."

"The silence would seem to be some evidence of intelligent intervention," Spock said.

"Jim, at least raise the shields again!" McCoy said.

Jim chuckled.

"Dr. McCoy," Spock said, "an entity with the power to move that construct would make short work of our shields. Raising them might be regarded as provocative."

"Hailing frequencies, captain."

"This is James T. Kirk, of the starship *Enterprise,* on a mission of peace. Please respond."

The speakers remained silent.

"Nothing, sir," Uhura said. "Complete silence."

"Go to visual," Jim said. "Simplest protocol. Black and white bit map, one bit per pixel. Give them the horizontal and vertical primes so they'll have a chance of deciphering the transmission before next Tuesday."

"Aye, sir. You're on visual . . . now."

"Everybody look peaceful," Jim said. Trying to appear relaxed, he gazed into the sensor. He rested his hands on his knees, palms up and open. The other people on the bridge faced the sensor and opened their hands. Aware of the irony of proving his peaceful intentions by opening his hands to beings who perhaps did not even have hands, Jim thought, You do what you can with what you've got.

"Sir, I'm getting a transmission!"

This was it; this was a first contact.

"Let's see it." Jim tried to keep his voice as matter-of-fact as Commander Spock's, but he failed. His pulse raced. He took a deep breath.

Picture elements formed lines; lines built up to form a two-dimensional surface.

Jim whistled softly.

"My mother's magnolias," McCoy whispered.

A being gazed at Jim from the slightly blurred image on the viewscreen.

He had no way to estimate its size, but it possessed a humanoid shape of delicate proportions.

Its face was less humanoid, though it had two eyes, a

mouth, a nose. At least Jim assumed the organs to be analogous. The being's jaw and nose projected forward, and its huge, luminous eyes glowed in its dark face. A structure like a mustache surrounded the nostrils and bracketed the mouth, but it was neither hair nor a longer outgrowth of the being's short, sleek pelt. The structure was flesh, dark-pigmented and glistening. The being extended its tongue and delicately brushed the tip across the structure. What color it was he could not tell, for the transmission, like the one he had sent, arrived in black and white.

Outwardly calm, Jim struggled to maintain inner control. What he wanted to do was leap up and shout with glee.

"I am James Kirk," he said, articulating each word with care. Translators functioned better for careful speakers than for mumblers. Perhaps, even though the *Enterprise* could not yet translate the new beings' language, the beings could translate Standard. "Welcome to the United Federation of Planets."

He spread his hands, offering them palms up to the being who gazed at him in silence.

The being did the same.

Then it sang.

The melody soared and dipped in unfamiliar intervals, reaching above Jim's range of hearing, gliding below. The voice created several tones at once and sang in chords.

"Remarkable," Spock said.

Jim had an idea. "Lieutenant Uhura . . . Would you consent to sing it something?"

Mesmerized by the voice, she did not react at first. Then she rose and began to sing.

Jim recognized the melody, though he could not understand the words. In the lullaby Jim heard peace and beauty, endless rivers and ageless mountains. Uhura painted a picture with her voice. With difficulty Jim turned away from her and observed the being on the viewscreen.

The image had begun to take on color and detail. The being had turned a dark red, the land behind it gray-green. It stood some distance in front of a high wall built of great pearly spheres.

It's inside, Jim thought. I'm seeing the shell from inside the . . . spacecraft? Starship? The alien world?

Uhura let the final note fade to silence.

"Thank you, lieutenant," Jim said, wanting to say more, wanting to say, That was extraordinarily beautiful.

The being's large, pointed ears rose from the sides of its head. The bristly tufts at their tips stiffened.

"A cousin of yours, Mr. Spock?" McCoy said softly.

"This is hardly the time for your feeble attempts at levity," Spock said, his voice as cold as liquid nitrogen.

For once Jim agreed with Commander Spock. "This is not a good time for the two of you to argue," he said.

The being raised and spread its hands.

A new image radiated onto the viewscreen, taking it over with intense colors and sharp detail.

Dark lines, center-streaked with light, formed the shape of the alien construct, spreading, curving up, curving in like some ghostly, skeletal ceramic pot. A tiny spot of light, a glass miniature of the *Enterprise,* hovered in the foreground. It moved toward the structure, sailing over it, into it, and among the glowing lines. It vanished.

"Can you give me a similar schematic, Mr. Spock?"

"Certainly, captain."

"Lieutenant Uhura, transmit this to our friends."

A rectangle in the corner of the viewscreen cleared. An image of the alien structure appeared, made tiny by perspective; in the foreground, the *Enterprise* hovered. The computer sketched the outlines, which remained as the rest faded.

"And a humanoid stick figure, inside the *Enterprise.*"

Spock raised one eyebrow, but complied.

"Now dissolve the stick figure, trail the bits to the alien craft, and reform them."

"Are you out of your mind, Jim?" McCoy said.

"Don't you want to come along?"

The new being returned to the viewscreen. It touched its sensory mustache with its tongue. Then, with a gesture perfectly comprehensible, it pointed at Jim and at the ground beneath it. Sharp nails tipped its long, delicate, three-fingered hand.

Jim touched his own chest, and pointed toward the being.

"Well, Bones?"

"Captain Kirk," Commander Spock said, "Dr. McCoy

has not recently updated his first-contact clearance. It has expired. Mine is current."

"Wait a minute!" McCoy said.

"Bones, dammit—!"

Jim pointed at Mr. Spock, then at the new being.

The being showed them its hands, palms up, fingers spread, empty.

"An invitation, I believe, Commander Spock."

"Indeed, captain."

"Lieutenant Uhura, take the conn. And—make an announcement about what's happened."

"Yes, sir."

He rose and took the stairs from the lower to the upper bridge in one stride. The turbo-lift doors slid aside for him. Spock followed, and McCoy came close behind.

"You can't go traipsing off—"

"I *told* you to update that clearance!" Jim was furious. "What are you doing out here, anyway, if you can't be bothered to keep up your credentials?"

McCoy started to retort, then leflated. "You're right," he said. "It was a stupid oversight.

In the transporter room, Jim attached a field-suit control to his belt and turned it on. The suit spread around his body.

"Ready, commander?"

"Yes, captain." Spock, too, stood within the nearly imperceptible shimmer of a field suit.

The suit made Jim's own voice sound louder to him, and attenuated sound from outside. But it would protect him against infection, as it would protect the beings against infection from him. It provided him with oxygen, should the atmosphere be inimical to his life, and it would even protect a fragile human body against extremes of temperature and pressure long enough for a transporter beam to sweep him back to safety.

Sensors showed a moderate environment at their destination. Jim hoped to find, as it often happened, that microorganisms adapted to the ecosystem of one world did not thrive on another, and posed no danger to the new planet's inhabitants. But he and Spock would wear the suits till they knew for certain.

McCoy grumbled as Jim stepped onto the transporter platform. Spock joined him.

"Energize."

"Energizing," Kyle said.

Jim felt a quick coldness, a moment's disorientation. The transporter locked in on the being's transmission.

Jim and Commander Spock materialized. They stood on an enormous open plain. Jim tried to take everything in at once: the new environment, the low gravity, the sounds, the sensations . . .

And the group of strange beings who watched from a few paces away. Jim picked out the one with deep scarlet fur. Its ears pricked forward; its long horizontal pupils dilated to ovals. The sensory structure above its mouth ruffled, and the being touched it again with its tongue. Jim assumed it was smelling them or taking some measure he could not conceive of. The field suit entirely cut off outside smells.

The being moved. Its muscles slid smoothly beneath its short fur. Taller than Jim—taller than Spock—it had fine, narrow bones. Its chest was deep from front to back. Its small feet possessed claws even more impressive than those on its hands. Along the sides of its sleek, streamlined body grew a narrow frill that extended to the backs of its arms and the edges of its hands, and down the sides of its legs and feet. It had three fingers and six toes.

"It will be edifying to discover in what base this species does arithmetic," Spock murmured. The tricorder blipped and blinked.

Jim stepped toward the scarlet being.

It stretched out its hands, palms up, empty.

Jim matched its gesture. It held his gaze. Jim hoped he would not do anything the beings would perceive as a threat, or as offensive. Perhaps they were thinking the same thing; perhaps each species had attained a level of civilization that would not take offense at any innocent gesture.

"The biology resembles no system with which we are familiar," Spock said. "The possibility of our infecting them with microorganisms, or vice versa, is ten to the minus nineteen."

"What does that mean in real terms, Spock?" Jim asked softly.

"It means, captain, that it is . . ." He hesitated before so unqualified a word. ". . . impossible."

"Why didn't you say so in the first place?"

"I did, captain."

The being sang a few notes. Jim's universal translator ran the sounds through its programming and produced what it believed to be a translation. Like the translating functions of the *Enterprise*'s computer, it produced gibberish.

"I can't understand you," Jim said. He and the being needed to talk to each other, even if they could not understand each other, so his translator could collect data to analyze and contexts in which to analyze them.

The being replied. The translator emitted a strangled whistle. The being's ears flicked back, forward, back. Jim stepped toward the being, his hand outstretched.

"Captain—" Spock said.

Jim's hand encountered an invisible barrier, a featherbed that yielded, then pressed him back. The suit fields and the alien barrier interacted with an electronic crackle and whine.

"I'll bet you were going to tell me they're protecting themselves like we're protecting ourselves."

"Precisely, captain. But the problem of infection is nonexistent. The air is breathable. The partial pressure of oxygen is slightly higher than in earth's atmosphere, and considerably higher than in Vulcan's. The temperature is well within the comfort zone for human beings."

"What about Vulcans?"

"For Vulcans, comfort does not enter the equation. The suits are unnecessary." He turned his off.

Jim touched the control of the field suit. The suit sighed— the sound always reminded him of a deflating balloon—and the faint pressure slid away. He swallowed hard to make his ears pop. The air smelled strange and wild, like cinnamon and fiery pippali.

Jim pressed into the alien field till it stopped him. The beings watched gravely. Jim waited.

The force faded.

The scarlet being stepped forward. The two species touched for the first time.

The being's hand felt hot and dry. Beneath the skin and fur, the being's flesh felt so hard and tense that it might have been made of tendon rather than muscle. Perhaps it was. Perhaps the words "muscle" and "tendon" had no relevance to the structure of these beings.

"Welcome to the United Federation of Planets," Jim said.

"Thank you for welcoming us to your ship."

The scarlet being had eyes of amber gold. Each being had fur of a different color, eyes of a different color.

Jim wondered if the scarlet being was "he" or "she," or something else entirely.

In the controlled environment of a starship, clothing existed for custom's sake, for decoration, for modesty. None of these beings wore clothing, though several wore bangles on fingers or toes. The beings had nothing, in human terms, about which to be modest; nothing immediately recognizable as generative organs or secondary sexual characteristics. Jim put aside his curiosity on that subject as well as many others, until he could communicate with the beings and until he knew their customs and taboos.

He kept talking in order to elicit more information for the translator to work on. Each word Jim spoke, every gesture he made, brought a new chorus of song. Though the beings sang on a scale unfamiliar to Jim—or perhaps on no scale at all—they reminded him of a chamber orchestra. Their voices floated and soared and blended. In response, the translator continued to make futile and meaningless sputters.

"Captain, if I may suggest—?"

"What, Commander Spock?"

"Disable the translator's output. The processor will then turn all its power to collection and analysis. Forcing it to translate beyond its capabilities will cause a crypto-schizoid breakdown. In addition, it could unintentionally produce an . . . offensive noise."

Jim did as Spock suggested. His translator was a good one. If it cryptoed and he had to have it blanked and reprogrammed, it would never be the same.

Spock scanned with his tricorder, his mind following several simultaneous trains of thought. First, he observed the behavior of the new beings. He could detect no single one of them that took the lead in speaking to or about James

231

Kirk, no leader in their gestures and actions. Instead, they gave every impression of discussing at every turn what to do next. Though the captain concentrated his attention on the scarlet being, which of the group spoke to Kirk or made the next gesture was random choice or moved according to some pattern that Spock had yet to perceive.

Second, Spock observed his surroundings. The environment exceeded by far the strangeness of any other he had ever encountered. In one direction, gentle dunes led to foothills, foothills to mountains, mountains to higher and higher peaks till distance obscured them. In another direction, tall stone spikes jolted from broken ground to form an eerie landscape.

The concavity of the land eliminated horizons. Distance and the atmosphere, rather than the curve of a planet, attenuated the view. Across 180 degrees, the world stretched on without end.

But in the other half of the circle of view, the world did end. The craft's enclosing wall leaped upward, vanishing into the distant heights of the sky's geometric pattern of light. The fabric that made up the wall consisted of great pearly globes of many sizes, packed densely together.

Overhead, a delicate glowing webwork cast an even light that surrounded every object with a faint circular shadow. Here and there, where strands of the asymmetric webwork diverged sufficiently, a bright star shone through.

Third, he observed the behavior of the captain. Captain Kirk attempted to elicit information in a systematic manner, touching his own chest, speaking his name, recording the beings' responses, pointing at one of them with a probably futile questioning glance, recording the replies, going from one material item to the next. The system, though simple, had been known to work.

The difficulty was that each recording Kirk made contained an enormous amount of information. Spock doubted the beings used parts of speech as simple as the noun, for the responses they offered possessed a complexity that might describe the history, evolution, fabrication, cultural relevance, and material significance of each object.

Captain Kirk turned on his translator's output. The instru-

ment replied with meaningless chirps. He turned it off again.
The beings conferred.

James Kirk possessed the severe flaw, in Spock's eyes, of
impetuosity. Certainly he was far more headstrong than
Christopher Pike. Of course he was much younger, but even
at the age of thirty, Pike had possessed a gravity unusual in
the normal run of human people. Pike's serious view of life
had persuaded Spock that working with him might be tolerable.

James Kirk's ebullient, reckless humanity gave Spock no
such reassurance.

Captain Kirk joined him. "I can't get the same answer
twice. Even when I choose the simplest object, I get a
different reply from each of the beings, and sometimes I get
different replies from the same being if I point to the same
thing twice. At least I *think* it's different. I'm not much for
music. I can't reproduce any of their speech. Have you
observed anything that might help us communicate?"

Spock had the beginnings of some ideas, but he was
unwilling to present them in their current state of flux. His
suggestion might solve their problems; or it might result in
disaster. He would offer it without doubts or second
thoughts, or he would not offer it at all.

"It is possible, captain, that your perception is accurate.
Many groups of beings possess different dialects of the same
language. In addition, this ship may hold different ethnic
groups with different languages."

"But if that were true, wouldn't they send representatives
who all spoke the same language, so they'd have at least a
chance of communicating with us?"

"That might be logical," Spock said. "Under certain
conditions, and from our point of view. But these beings do
not have our point of view. They may operate under a
different system of logic entirely. They may not be prepared
to meet other sentient beings."

"But that's the whole point of star travel!" Kirk exclaimed. "Discovering new places, new people—"

"Again, captain—it is a major point for us. Their reasons
may be entirely different."

Kirk's communicator signaled. "Kirk here."

"Lieutenant Uhura, sir. A Klingon ship is approaching the alien spacecraft."

"Civilian or military?"

"It's an armed cruiser of a design computer doesn't recognize, sir. The owner claims it's been decommissioned."

Kirk glanced at Spock.

"Within the realm of possibility, captain, if it is obsolete. But in that case, computer *should* recognize it."

"How close is it?" Kirk asked Lieutenant Uhura.

"About a million kilometers, sir. Well out of range of its weapons, or ours."

"Warn it off, lieutenant. Tell it . . . misunderstandings might occur if it remains in Federation space."

"But, sir . . ."

"Yes, lieutenant?"

"There's some disagreement about where Federation space is."

"That is true, Captain Kirk," Spock said. "Both the Federation and the Klingon Empire claim certain volumes of space along the Phalanx. Since nothing of value exists within the disputed region, neither government has pressed its claim. But neither government has seen fit to withdraw, either."

Kirk blew out his breath. "All right. Lieutenant Uhura, suggest that they might be encroaching. See what reaction you get. Use tact. If they come within weapons range, raise shields. Tell Mr. Kyle to beam us up on my signal."

"Yes, sir."

Kirk folded his communicator and indicated with hand signals and pantomime that he and Spock had to leave, but would return. The beings whistled occasionally and sang high fluting notes.

The scarlet being raised its hands. Spock's tricorder detected odd electromagnetic emanations and erupted into a cacophony of powerful signals. Spock had never seen anything like it. But, then, he reflected, he had never seen anything like this world within a ship before, either.

"Captain Kirk," Uhura said, "we're getting a visual transmission—are you sending it?" She described it: an echo of the schematic the *Enterprise* earlier had transmitted to the strange starship. The tiny stick figures traveled from the starship on a glittery beam, then disappeared inside the *Enterprise*.

"Thanks, lieutenant." Captain Kirk touched his chest, pointed out of the worldship, then pointed at the ground.

"That's right," he said. "We have to go for a while. But we'll be back. We'll be back."

The being folded its hands. The chaotic readings faded from Spock's tricorder. Then the being spread its arms, hands open, palms up.

Kirk replied with the same gesture. The human and the new being gazed at each other. The scarlet being flicked its tongue over the structure above its lips. Spock noted still another strange set of readings from the tricorder. The worldship inhabitants had no equipment—no visible, mechanical equipment—for making visible transmissions. Sensors found no recognizable alien electronic technology within range.

Kirk flipped open his tricorder. "Kirk to *Enterprise*. Beam us up, Mr. Kyle."

The cold dislocation of the beam surrounded Spock.

He reappeared beside Captain Kirk on the transporter platform of the *Enterprise*.

"We've *got* to find a better way to communicate with them," Kirk said on the way back to the bridge. "If I put my translator's data into ship's computer, what are the chances of getting any results?"

"Impossible to judge, captain. The language is sufficiently strange that I would advise caution. Forcing computer to try to make sense of it could cause difficulties."

At Kirk's arrival on the bridge, Lieutenant Uhura returned to the communication station.

"What happened out there?" McCoy demanded.

"It's incredible, Bones. Lieutenant Uhura . . . intraship channel, please."

"Channel open, sir."

Jim hesitated. How do you announce meeting an entirely unknown sentient species? he wondered. Especially one that has a technology higher than your own?

"Kirk to all personnel. The gravity field of a spacecraft has drawn the *Enterprise* from its course, but the ship has

235

incurred no structural damage. We have established peaceful contact with the spacecraft's inhabitants, a previously unknown sentient species."

He wondered if he should say something else, something about historic encounters, but doing so seemed overly dramatic and at the same time rather feeble, considering the occasion, so he gestured for Uhura to close the channel.

"Lieutenant Uhura, what about the Klingon ship?"

"The owner prefers not to change course, sir."

"Oh, really. Let's take a look at it."

Spock raised one eyebrow at the image that formed on the viewscreen. This was no elderly, battered hulk, no irreparable, decommissioned military craft, but the most advanced technology of the Empire, so new that Spock had never seen a cruiser like it.

"Captain, it is very nearly beyond the range of possibility that this ship belongs to a civilian."

"I see what you mean, Commander Spock. Lieutenant Uhura, I'll speak to the owner."

The owner's image appeared on the screen. Spock thought, Even when the chances are one to one million, or one to one billion, that one chance *does* exist. For though the ship was a military one, the owner was a civilian.

Unlike any member of the Klingon military, this citizen of the Empire dressed in flamboyant garments of bright flowing fabric and silver-filigreed leather. Her coppery hair fanned over her shoulders, loose and wild beneath her headband, and she had highlighted her brow ridges with glittery gold makeup. She carried unique weapons: an old-fashioned and overpowered blaster on one hip, an edged weapon—could it be a blood sword? Spock had heard of them, but had never seen one—on her other side. The sword and blaster depended from a belt inlaid with an intricate pattern of precious stones. A fringe of small mica disks also hung from the belt, as if to add to the decoration. But Spock recognized the crystal circles as something far more significant than tasteless excess. The disks formed a trophy fringe, a claim to all who could read it of the owner's exploits. Among the colored disks glistened an appalling number of clear ones: disks that represented lives taken in direct combat. She had acquired one quite recently, for its colors had not completely cleared.

"I am Captain James T. Kirk," the captain said to the intruder. "Your ship has strayed into Federation space. Starfleet is charged with maintaining those boundaries."

"I am Koronin, owner of *Quundar*. The Empire might disagree with you about the boundaries." She glanced to one side and snapped her fingers. "Starfleet!"

A monkey-sized pink primate dressed in miniature Starfleet uniform leaped into her arms. She twitched the leash attached to its collar, forcing its head up. It yelped and whimpered.

"You see," Koronin said, "how fond I am of Starfleet."

"I think you'd find the *Enterprise* a stronger opponent than a helpless pet," James Kirk said. Even Spock recognized tense anger in the captain's voice.

Analyzing Koronin's dress, her physical form, her accent, Spock identified her as a member of the Rumaiy group, a political and ethnic minority of the Klingon home world. The highest class of Rumaiy often veiled themselves in public, and indeed Koronin carried a veil. But she wore it unfastened, draping from her headdress like a scarf, an announcement to all who could understand it that she rejected the customs of her people. A renegade, then. Spock sensed difficulties ahead.

"Don't underestimate me, Federation captain," Koronin said. "Or my ship. You'd be making a serious mistake. Were I representing the government, I would invite you to depart our space, and I would enforce the invitation. But I represent myself. I have no interest in scarring my ship's pretty new paint in a battle."

"No one is suggesting battles," Kirk said.

"Excellent. Then neither of us will trouble the other. We may each explore the interesting construct before us. It is certainly large enough to permit two landing parties."

I do not believe, Spock thought, that this renegade will prove overinterested in advances in scientific knowledge, or in the opportunities inherent in peaceful interspecies contact.

"What is your earth phrase?" Koronin said. "You *are*

from earth, I believe, captain? A human being?" She chucked her primate pet roughly beneath the chin. "Ah, yes. I wish you 'happy hunting.' " She laughed.

Kirk rose in protest as Koronin's transmission faded. "Damn! If she goes down there, armed, looking for who knows what . . . anything could happen."

"Anything could happen when we go down there, captain," Spock said. "We know little more about the worldship people than she does."

"How did she get that ship? The Empire certainly didn't give it to her—could she be undercover?"

"No undercover operative would advertise her position by flying a state-of-the-art military vessel," Spock said.

"Unless that's what they want us to think," Kirk said.

"We cannot guess the labyrinthine plots of the most secret minds of the Klingon oligarchy," Spock said. "That way lies madness. We must wait, and observe, until we possess more information."

"Captain Kirk . . ."

"Yes, Mr. Sulu?"

"Just a possibility, sir . . . Maybe the same thing happened to *Quundar* as happened to the *Enterprise*—dragged off course, warp drive blown . . . Maybe Koronin couldn't get out of Federation space if she wanted to. Maybe she's vamping till she can fix her ship."

"Vamping?"

Sulu blushed. "Sorry, sir—it's a word the people in Lindy's company use to mean stalling till they're ready to start."

"I see." Captain Kirk leaned back in his chair.

On the viewscreen, the worldship drifted in perfect peace. Spock was all too aware that it could become a pawn, a flashpoint for war. Much would depend on the actions of the young human captain of the *Enterprise*.

The science officer created an interface between his tricorder and ship's computer and began to analyze the data. The new people possessed unusual abilities.

"Fascinating," Spock murmured.

"What is it, Spock?"

"The scarlet being transmitted the images we see on our

screen. It created the radio-frequency energy from its own body. Biological control over electromagnetic radiation. Most unusual."

"I don't know," McCoy said. "Back on earth, electric eels do the same thing."

"Dr. McCoy," Spock said, disbelieving, "your contempt for unknown beings does not become you."

"Mr. Spock—"

"Their control is precise. It is unprecedented. They create images, they transmit them, without benefit of what we would recognize as technology."

"Commander Spock—!"

"I think what Mr. Spock is trying to tell you, Bones, is that electric eels don't project home movies."

"It was a *joke,* Mr. Spock! A joke!" McCoy said. "Didn't you think it was funny?"

"Certainly not," Spock replied.

"See if I ever tell you a joke again!"

Spock regarded him dispassionately. "I will consider that a promise. I will be grateful if you keep it." He turned his back and proceeded to ignore Dr. McCoy.

Jim turned his back and ignored both of them. He gazed at the worldship. "Incredible." But staring at it would not get him any closer to understanding it, or to communicating with its inhabitants, or even to protecting his ship and crew from the intruding Klingon ship.

"Mr. Spock," Jim said, "how soon can you prepare to return to the worldship? I want to explore it—I want to see what its outer structure is made of. Lieutenant Uhura will accompany us as communications adviser, and—"

Spock interrupted. "Captain, you have made dangerous assumptions."

"Just what do you mean by that, Spock?" McCoy said.

"You speak of research strategies as if we were visiting an average planet of average preindustrial culture. But this is *not* a planet. The beings may or may not now employ mechanical and electronic technology similar to ours, but they are certainly not preindustrial. They built the world-ship. We cannot pick up our sampling devices and intrude upon their civilization. We have not been invited."

"We have, though, in a manner of speaking," Kirk said.

"You are of course free to look at the situation that way," Spock said. "But I suggest contemplating how we would react if we invited the worldship people to visit us, and they materialized on the bridge and began taking samples of our air, our blood, and the very fabric of our ship."

Kirk gazed at Spock thoughtfully. "You feel strongly about this, don't you, Commander Spock?"

"Certainly not, captain," Spock said, wondering if Kirk was insulting him deliberately or in ignorance. "But I wish to point out that while we can study a pre-electronic culture in any way—ethical or not, considerate or not—we choose, simply because the culture has no defense against us, we cannot presume to treat this culture in a cavalier fashion. On the evidence of their spacecraft, we may safely conclude that their technology is in advance of ours. I suggest that we mind our manners."

"What evidence do we have," McCoy said, "that the people you and Jim talked to—"

"Communicated with," Spock said. "Through their inherent abilities, not ours."

McCoy glared at him. "—that you and Jim talked to are the same people who built the worldship?"

Spock fell speechless. McCoy had seen the data, and still he asked this question? Spock had encountered situations in which a single pointed query had changed his perceptions completely and irrevocably.

This was *not* one of those times.

"Our brief communication convinced me that the inhabitants built the worldship," he said.

"Translation: You guess they built it."

"It is my opinion."

"And it's just slightly different from your previous opinion that the worldship could be a natural occurrence."

"It could have been," Spock said. "It is not. I altered my opinion on the strength of additional evidence."

"You referred to inherent abilities. Suppose building is inherent—instinctual for them? Suppose the beings created the worldship without conscious thought?"

"As you cannot be proposing that the worldship is a

gigantic beehive," Spock said, "I must conclude that you have broken your promise not to beleaguer me with jokes."

Captain Kirk chuckled and Lieutenant Uhura smiled. Their amusement gave Spock no pleasure.

"I'm not telling you any jokes," McCoy said petulantly. "And it *could* be an instinctive creation. It's possible."

"As is your suggestion that someone other than the world-ship people built it. What scenario do you propose? That aliens from outer space built it for them? I would be fascinated to know your conception of the aliens from outer space. I do not doubt you see them as primates."

"Now look here, Spock—!" McCoy exclaimed.

"Commander Spock, Dr. McCoy," Kirk said, "there's no reason to fight over speculation. We won't have to speculate, *if* we decipher their language."

"I believe their language originated outside the local unconscious," Spock said.

"If that's true," Uhura said, "then . . . we may never be able to translate their language at all."

"The local unconscious!" McCoy laughed. "You don't—you can't—believe such a flight of theoretical fancy!"

"I find it aesthetically satisfying," Spock said. "As you are perhaps aware, the most aesthetically satisfying theory often proves the true one."

"The local unconscious *is* an intriguing theory, Dr. McCoy," Uhura said.

"It's mush!"

"You are entitled to your opinion," Spock said coldly. "Even if it is intellectually bigoted."

McCoy sputtered.

"Would you care to let me in on this theory, Spock?" Kirk said. "What is the local unconscious?"

"It is the proposition that all beings within a local area are united in a way such that their intellectual processes are connected at a basic level. That is why—the theory proposes—languages from a different evolutionary system prove amenable to translation."

"On earth it's Jung's theory of the collective unconscious," Kirk said. "Whether you believe it or not, it's hardly controversial."

"The ideas are similar, sir. But in this case the word 'local' encompasses more than a single species, a single planet, even a group of stars."

"What he's saying," McCoy said, "is that he thinks these beings came from another *galaxy.*"

"I think it extremely likely," Spock said.

"Wonderful!" McCoy said. "Creatures from a star system outside the limits of our exploration isn't enough! You have to find a species from another galaxy! Why don't you go all the way and decide they're from another universe?"

"I have no empirical evidence of the existence of other universes," Spock said.

"Commander Spock, if this theory is true and we can't translate their language, we'll never be able to communicate with them at all."

"On the contrary, captain," Spock said. "The theory proposes that a language outside the local unconscious cannot be translated. It does not say it cannot be learned."

"I don't know about the local unconscious, Commander Spock," Kirk said, "but your points about the worldship are well taken. Perhaps we can get the inhabitants to give us permission to study their world. In the meantime, we'd all better reassess our strategies in regard to . . . minding our manners."

"Captain Kirk!"

"Yes, Mr. Sulu?"

"Sir, a ship's approaching—"

"Koronin again? Warn her to back off."

"It isn't *Quundar,* sir—it's a very small ship, a boat . . . a sort of sailboat . . . from the worldship."

The tiny ship, like a spiny pearl attached to a huge silken sail, sped toward them on the viewscreen.

Kirk glanced at Spock. "I wonder," he said, "if our new guests come bearing sampling devices?"

# Chapter 10

THE WORLDSHIP PEOPLE carried nothing: no sampling devices, no communications equipment.

Their little sailboat floated toward the *Enterprise* on a beam of power. On nearing the starship, it balanced itself delicately between the worldship's gravitational attraction and the beam. The worldship people transmitted a detailed visual message to the *Enterprise*, making clear their wish to be transported on board.

"What about your precious regulations now, Mr. Spock?" Dr. McCoy said. "If Jim lets those folks on board the *Enterprise*, we'll be busting the prime directive six ways from Sunday."

"The prime directive is meant to protect younger, developing cultures from the shock of encountering advanced technology," Spock said. "But perhaps you are correct for once, Dr. McCoy. Perhaps we require protection from the shock of meeting the worldship people, and should invoke the prime directive in our own defense."

"That's absurd!"

"Is it, doctor?"

Kirk broke in to forestall another argument. "Maybe I ought to invoke the prime directive to protect you two from each other—but I have plenty of evidence that the worldship people don't need its protection."

Aboard *Quundar*, Koronin observed the sailboat of the newly discovered aliens as it left the giant ship and floated toward the Federation starship *Enterprise*. She swore a dreadful curse. If the Federation believed she would stand by and do nothing while they tricked the new aliens into an alliance, they were worse fools than she thought. She strode from one end of the command balcony to the other, her attention on the observation ports. The work crew labored feverishly on the hyperspace engines. Starfleet scampered at her heels and whined for petting and food.

"Go!" she shouted. "Be still and be quiet, or it's back on the leash for you!" The primate slinked to her bed, huddled on its fur blanket, and watched her every motion.

"Stations!"

The crew leaped to her command.

"N-space engines!"

*Quundar* thundered into motion.

"Captain—*Quundar* is powering up engines."

Helpless, Jim watched the renegade fighter approach the *Enterprise* and hover, provocatively within range. Where, he wondered, does Koronin think she's going with that ship and her creepy primate pet? Jim could do nothing, not even raise shields, till the worldship people arrived.

"Keep an eye and all your sensors on her, Mr. Sulu," Jim said. "That's all we can do for now." He rose and, with McCoy, headed for the transporter room to wait. Lieutenant Uhura and Commander Spock followed.

The worldship people show no evidence of possessing anything like the the transporter, Spock thought. Yet they treat it as something mundane, perhaps even primitive.

Spock had no doubt that they could duplicate it if they found it to their convenience.

Spock had begun to make his own assumptions about the worldship people, assumptions he knew quite well he had formed from insufficient data. But he prepared himself to cast aside any assumptions that proved untenable, as many would in the inevitable course of things. In the meantime, he needed some base from which to work.

He interpreted the sailboat as an instrument of play. The worldship people could have transmitted a request to beam directly to the *Enterprise*. They chose instead to arrive on a small craft propelled by the reflection of photons against a sail. Though this struck Spock as a frivolous way to travel, and though he would have preferred to meet a people as single-mindedly dedicated to rationality as Vulcans, an ability to play served his argument with Dr. McCoy well: he doubted the doctor would again compare the society of the worldship people to that of bees. McCoy still might attribute their high level of technology to outside influence, but that obvious misapprehension would soon fall to the evidence.

Sleek, naked, empty-handed, the tall scarlet being began to form on the transporter platform.

Spock realized the mistake he had made.

"Wait! The gravity—" Spock leaped forward and caught the being as it materialized in a gravity field several times what it was used to. The frailty of its bones, the insubstantiality of its body, astonished him. The physical touch brought him into abrupt contact with its mind. Its power crushed his defenses utterly. Only his strength and well-schooled reflexes kept him and the being on their feet.

"Mr. Kyle!" Kirk shouted. "Beam our guests to the shuttlecraft deck. Now!"

Kyle caught his breath. The danger—! But as the other worldship people materialized, the gravity dragged at them and they cried out in a high keening song. Kyle responded.

The beam swept Spock and the beings to the tenth-g environment of the shuttlecraft deck.

Spock let the scarlet being go and collapsed to his knees, his body stunned by the power of its mind.

Three other beings re-formed near Athene and Amelinda Lukarian. One had cream-colored fur, the fur of another was patterned in narrow stripes of gold and brown, and the third's fur swirled in an intricate paisley pattern.

The music of their communication soared around him like a wind-rider, the insubstantial creature of Vulcan that never touched the ground. The equiraptor snorted in alarm. Her feathered wings cut the air as Amelinda Lukarian tried to soothe her.

The three new worldship people spread their arms wide. Long fingers that lay tight against the backs of their forearms unfolded, the frill at their sides extended, and they spread their wide wings.

They took flight into the dangerously low sky.

Spock tried to rise, but his strength had vanished. His hands trembled on his knees. He could barely lift his head. When he did, he found himself gazing into the amber-flecked gold eyes of the scarlet being, who knelt facing him. It brushed its tongue across its sensory mustache; it raised its hand to its face and touched its forehead with one sharp-clawed finger. It made a sound in a tone that Spock interpreted as questioning.

"Very well," Spock whispered, his voice hoarse almost to silence. He had known this must occur, but he had expected it to be on his initiative; he had expected more time to prepare.

Spock lifted his hands to the scarlet being's face.

He touched its mind.

Back in the transporter room, Jim bolted for the nearest lift before the beam finished dematerializing Spock and the worldship people. He could get to the shuttlecraft deck on foot faster than the beam could recharge. McCoy barely managed to squeeze between the closing doors.

"Stupid!" Jim shouted. "Stupid! I didn't stop long enough to think! Damn!" He slapped the wall in fury and disgust. The lift crawled toward the shuttlecraft deck so slowly that Jim began to wish he *had* waited for the beam. The doors slid apart. He sprinted down the corridor.

On the catwalk he stopped, astonished.

Far from being injured, three of the worldship people glided back and forth, flying in the shallow airspace of the deck. Flying! Graceful and beautiful, they reminded Jim of falcons seeking prey over summer fields.

Athene, unsure of her wings, half-trotted and half-flew after them, trying to follow, her head up, ears forward. The music of the beings reverberated against the bulkheads.

"Mr. Spock!" Lindy said. "Mr. Spock, what's wrong?"

Lindy knelt beside Commander Spock and the scarlet being. The Vulcan lay rigid on the soft new grass, his hands clenched, the left side of his face bruised and dark with a smear of pulverized stone. The fourth being, the scarlet one, pushed itself up on one elbow, dazed.

Jim leaped down the companionway, cursing himself.

Could the flying people have attacked in retaliation for Jim's mishandling the gravity?

"Lindy, what happened?" Jim knelt beside her.

Commander Spock looked terrible. His skin had paled to an unhealthy yellowish green and his scraped cheek oozed blood of a deep emerald hue.

"I'm not really sure," she said.

"Give him some air. Let me see him." McCoy felt Spock's pulse. "The beat's slow for a Vulcan," he said.

"Dangerously slow?"

"No . . . I don't think so. He stormed out of sick bay before I got much feel for his version of normal. Blast!"

"Not much point in swearing at him now, Bones."

"I was swearing at me." McCoy shook his head. "It was my fault—my mistake. I'll get a stretcher down here."

"I'll do it—you be sure our guest isn't injured."

"I am . . . I am not . . . I am not physically damaged."

Jim bolted to his feet. The words formed song, the music created the words. The scarlet flyer slid its long-fingered hands over its arms. It opened its outer three fingers, the elongated ones that supported its wings, and stretched the short-furred skin. Its wide scarlet wings rose up above it. It swept them forward and curved them in a circle, touching the tips behind Jim's back. Under the curtain of the wings, Jim wanted to shiver.

The scarlet flyer folded its wings again. The flying webs folded with a sound-shimmer like silk.

"Did you . . . speak to me?" Jim said.

"I have been speaking all along, but you did not understand me. The singing one might comprehend, in time. But this language of yours is so simple—"

"How did you learn it so fast?"

"I learned from—" The flyer spoke several words that sounded not at all like the sounds it had made before. "From Spock."

The flyer sat on its heels beside the Vulcan. The backs of its hands touched the ground at its sides, as if it hunched with drooping wings. Spock's rigid body had begun to relax, but he showed no sign of regaining consciousness.

"What happened?" Jim said.

"I thought to exchange patterns with him. He agreed to the exchange. But our communication went far beyond that."

Jim struggled to think of something to say that would make sense. "We don't often meet people with abilities like yours, with a technology as high as yours. This is a new experience for most of us . . . I'm afraid he is injured—I have to get help—"

"Stretcher's coming, Jim," McCoy said. He returned from the intercom at the bottom of the companionway.

The other flyers landed and joined them, curious.

"Your flying area is very low," the scarlet flyer said. "How does your colleague exercise her wings? Where does she hunt?"

It was talking about Athene. "She's only just learning to fly. It's a long story. You're all right, aren't you, you and your friends? The gravity in the transporter room didn't harm you?"

"It would have, had Spock not stopped me, had you not moved us to this place."

"I'm sorry—I made an inexcusable mistake."

The flyers whistled and sang at each other.

"That is of the past," the scarlet flyer said.

"But what did you do to him?" Uhura said.

"I thought to give him joy and song," the scarlet flyer said. "But my patterns cause him distress."

A couple of stretcher operators arrived, and McCoy took Spock away. Several security officers appeared on the catwalk, but Jim gestured for them to stay where they were.

The scarlet flyer blinked. "You, the singing one, you are Uhura, and you are Captainkirk."

"My name is James Kirk. My title is captain—I'm in charge of the ship. Are you the captain of the worldship—of your vessel?"

The scarlet flyer touched its tongue to the sensory mustache. Jim had begun to think of the gesture as thoughtful.

"I am still assimilating the information Spock gave me. A name is applied to you at birth, and a title is given you at adulthood. Is this true?"

"That will do for the moment."

"I am not, then, 'captain' of our—" The flyer hummed,

somehow producing two simultaneous notes. " 'Worldship' must suffice, though it is a misapprehension. But you have no suitable word, and I fear your vocal apparatus may not duplicate its true pattern. As for 'captain'—I have no such concept."

"Who gives the orders? How do you run the worldship? Who makes sure it doesn't break down?"

"I neither give orders nor accept them. The worldship cannot break down. It . . . renews itself."

"Do you mean it's a natural astronomical body? It evolved? You didn't build it?"

The scarlet flyer conferred in music with its companions. Uhura edged nearer to them, entranced.

"The worldship is a natural body," the scarlet flyer said. "How could it be otherwise? What would an 'unnatural' object be? Of course it evolved, and still evolves. All things evolve. And, no, I did not build it. I am but young, while the worldship is old."

That will disappoint Commander Spock, Jim thought, and please McCoy. Bones never can resist saying "I told you so."

"Since you know who we are," Jim said, "perhaps you'll consent to introduce yourselves." He waited expectantly.

The scarlet flyer blinked, touched its sensory mustache, blinked again. "I have no name," it said. It whistled to the three other flying people, who replied. They gathered closer, head and shoulders taller than the humans, looming.

"Oh." Jim felt foolish.

"But your language would adapt to our patterns with difficulty. Perhaps I should do as Spock does, and adopt a name your speech can reproduce."

"That might make things easier," Jim said.

"How are names chosen in your civilization?"

"By family descent or personal preference. Patterns of stars in the sky or historical figures . . ."

Again it transmitted the information to the other flyers, but the conversation continued for several minutes, and Jim got the impression that the scarlet flyer had done something to displease the others.

"I have none of these things: no family names, no historical figures. The patterns of my sky are inconstant."

"You could use nicknames," Uhura said. "They come from physical characteristics, vocations—whatever you choose."

"For example," Jim said, "I think of you as 'Scarlet.' "

" 'Scarlet.' Scarlet will do for the moment. More talk must be of the future."

"But—"

"The companionship must confer."

"We have so many questions to ask you—"

"May I listen?" Uhura said. "I'd like to try to . . . to learn your patterns."

Scarlet remained silent.

"Lieutenant!" Jim said. "After what happened to Spock—"

"Did Mr. Spock mind-meld with you?" Uhura asked Scarlet. "I can't do what he did—I have to learn more slowly. I'll be all right, just let me listen. Captain, I think this is important!"

Jim could hardly bear the possibility of her lying unconscious, her elegant face scraped in a convulsive fall. But her training had prepared her for an encounter such as this; if he ordered her to avoid it, he would be giving her notice that he distrusted her judgment and competence. That was the last message he wanted to give Uhura.

"All right, lieutenant, if Scarlet doesn't object. But . . . be careful."

Without assenting to or refusing Uhura's request, Scarlet joined the companionship and gathered Uhura into their circle. Their voices soared and blended and enraptured her with their music.

Keeping an eye on the circle, Jim backed away and contacted the bridge.

"*Quundar* isn't doing anything, captain," Sulu said. "Nothing at all. But it's still here."

"Just sitting there?"

"Just sitting there."

"Then we'll do the same," Jim said. "For the moment. Yeoman Rand, announce change of environment. Ten-minute delay for critical objections."

The customary delay between announcing change of environment and making the change existed primarily to warn researchers doing experiments that a variable soon would change, but since the *Enterprise* still lacked its research staff, Jim received no critical objections.

He opened a channel to Engineering.

"Mr. Scott," Jim said, "please cut the gravity to one-tenth g on the whole ship."

"D'ye think that's wise, captain? D'ye—"

"We have guests, Mr. Scott. I'd like them to feel welcome."

"But captain, ye'll be giving these people free run of the *Enterprise!* We dinna know—"

Jim cut the connection. He glanced at the companionship, not wanting to leave. But Scott had argued with him once too often.

"Lindy—I'll be back in a minute. Don't get too close to them, all right?"

He leaped up the companionway, ordered the security officers to call him if anything changed, and headed for Engineering.

Halfway to the lift, he tripped over the one-g gravity ledge that he knew, but had forgotten, was right there. He pitched in a header toward the deck. Almost by reflex, he ducked and managed to roll out of the fall. Tumbling, he ended up flat on his back, more surprised than injured.

Jim climbed to his feet, gingerly testing his knee. It hurt no worse than before he fell. Now the whole rest of his body felt bruised.

That's just great, Jim thought. They'll put this in my official biography: On his first first contact, he lets his science officer rush off and get killed, he can't get his chief engineer to follow a direct order . . . but he can fall down almost without killing himself.

He felt carefully, calmly infuriated: angry at himself, angrier at Scott, and furious at Spock. The science officer had made an unconscionable decision when he communicated with the flyers without considering the risk. The Vulcan deserved to be brought up on disciplinary charges for the mess he had gotten himself into—assuming he survived. And as for the chief engineer—

Jim reached the engine room, which looked as if someone had taken it apart without reading the instructions. Jim

251

stopped where several pairs of feet protruded from beneath a complicated piece of equipment.

"Mr. Scott." None of the feet moved. "Mr. Scott!"

"Aye, captain?"

Jim started. Behind him, Scott stood peering at him curiously, holding a set of plans.

"I want to talk to you about the gravity," Jim said.

"Verra good, captain. I'm to leave the fields alone, after all?"

"You are not. The warning announcement is out. I don't intend to rescind it. Are you going to make the change—now—or shall I do it for you?"

Scott gave him a wounded glance, but took himself off to a complex instrument panel. The change-of-environment alarm flashed a moment later. In thirty seconds the gravity faded to one-tenth g.

"There, captain. Ye've got the environment ye want. But—" At Jim's expression, he fell into an uncertain silence.

"Mr. Scott," Jim said, too softly for anyone but the engineer to hear. "You've disputed every order or request I've given you since I took command. I've put up with that till now, because you're a good engineer. But I can't put up with it any longer. I choose to believe that this is a problem of lack of rapport, rather than deliberate insubordination. So I won't bring you up on charges. But one of us has got to go, and it isn't going to be me. I think it's best that you request a transfer. With any luck, Starfleet will find you a more congenial environment soon."

He waited for a reply.

Scott stared at him.

"Is that understood?"

"Transfer, captain?" Scott said, stricken. "Off the *Enterprise*?"

"Transfer. Off the *Enterprise*."

Scott said nothing. Jim turned and stalked out, aggravated, knowing he should have been able to solve this problem in a more satisfactory way, but having no idea at all what the way might be.

On the shuttlecraft deck, Lindy stroked Athene's iridescent sweat-soaked shoulder. She twined one hand in her mane and urged her forward. Her wings half-spread, the equiraptor walked as if she could not bear to touch the ground. Her ears swiveled nervously, and a white rim showed around her eyes.

"It's okay, sweetie," Lindy whispered. "Easy, sweetie, it's going to be okay." But the flying people both fascinated and terrified the equiraptor. Though Lindy urged her away, she edged closer to them as she walked, and she resisted turning away. Whenever the pitch of the companionship's conversation changed, Athene snorted and pranced, tossing her head and jerking Lindy off her feet. Nothing Lindy did made any difference.

Lindy saw Jim on the catwalk. He climbed down the companionway and joined her. He was as keyed up as Athene.

"What happened while I was gone?"

"Nothing. They just kept singing to each other."

"Are you all right? Is Athene?"

"She doesn't understand why they can fly and she can't." Lindy's fingers hurt from holding Athene's mane, and her arm ached with the fatigue of trying to guide the tremendously strong equiraptor, of trying to stay with her even when she reared.

"Do you want me to get a rope?"

"No. The harder you fight her, the spookier she gets. She just needs to get used to the flying people."

The song of the flyers crescendoed. Athene snorted and pranced sideways, jolting Lindy and knocking the wind out of her. Jim backed off fast.

"At least put her in the repair bay."

"No! I can't keep her quiet in there. Not now. She'd hurt herself."

"Lindy, I have to think of everybody's safety—"

"I won't do it, dammit! Besides, she's too hot, she's got to keep walking or she'll get sick. Just leave us alone and she'll be all right. Jim, I can't talk to you and calm her down at the same time."

Jim walked away from Lindy without another word, his shoulders stiff. He felt like he needed to do something, but he did not know what, so he called the bridge. Koronin's *Quundar* still showed no sign of aggression. Jim wrestled down his wish that Koronin would take some action, knowing it to be a reflection of his own frustration. He patched a channel through to sick bay.

"Bones, how long before Commander Spock can be back on duty?"

"Back on duty!" McCoy said. "Don't count on him soon, Jim. He's still unconscious."

"Damn." Jim tried, without much success, to keep the aggravation out of his voice. *The one time I could use a science officer,* he thought, *and he goes and gets himself put out of commission.*

"Jim—" McCoy said.

"What?"

"What's going on down there?"

The song soared, but the flying people had hardly moved; Uhura stood among them, silent and attentive.

"Bones," Jim said, "it beats the hell out of me."

He remembered soaring above the land, gathering the wind to him, his bones thin and hollow, his fingers enormously elongated, his narrow muscles powerful and tireless. He perceived sensory stimuli he had never before imagined. His preternaturally acute eyesight distinguished every blade of grass, every movement, every shadow. A small furred creature, oblivious to his presence, rose on its haunches in a tuft of grass and sniffed the air.

He felt an acute surge of hunger. He swooped.

McCoy puzzled over the readings on the medical sensors. Commander Spock's pulse beat rapidly enough to sustain him. Treatment for shock pushed his temperature back toward its normal blast-furnace intensity. McCoy could find no permanent physical damage. Yet the Vulcan remained in a state of deep unconsciousness, the patterns of his brain depressed and erratic.

"Maybe he's just asleep," McCoy muttered, annoyed at himself for their first conversation, for getting into the argument that had driven Spock from sick bay. Spock's medical record contained practically nothing. Apparently half-Vulcans never got sick. The previous doctor had made a note: Vulcans cure Vulcans more often than doctors cure Vulcans. It is generally unwise to rouse a Vulcan from a healing trance.

So, impatient with his inability to do anything useful, troubled and mystified, McCoy kept watch on Spock and let him rest. Every so often the electrical patterns of the Vulcan's mind pushed themselves toward normal, but they always retreated again.

Jim sat on the bottom step of the companionway, watching the flyers and Uhura. The intense communication continued. He wondered if he should make Lieutenant Uhura come out of the circle, but she showed no sign of the stunned shock that had affected the science officer, no distress or even fatigue.

He thought about what she had said to Scarlet: "Did Mr. Spock mind-meld with you?" He had never heard the term, and he wondered if it meant what it seemed to.

A footstep scraped the deck above him and Stephen climbed down the companionway. He sat on the step above Jim and rested his elbows on his knees.

"I hope you won't expect me to entertain your friends," he said, "because juggling in one-tenth gravity is about as boring an activity to watch as I can think of."

"I asked for *critical* objections," Jim said.

"Oh, I'm not objecting, just making an observation. Vulcans do that. What are *they* doing?" He nodded toward the flyers.

"I think they're talking to each other." Jim started to tell him—to ask him, since he was more or less a guest—to go back to the vaudeville company's quarters. Then he abruptly changed his mind. "Stephen, do Vulcans have some sort of extrasensory perception?"

For the first time since Jim had met him, Stephen expressed himself in a way entirely Vulcan. He raised one quizzical dark-blond eyebrow.

"What makes you think that?"

"The term 'mind-melding.' "

"What do you know about mind-melding?"

"Nothing," Jim said. "That's why I'm asking you."

"Where did you hear about it?"

"Lieutenant Uhura seemed to think that was how Spock communicated with the flying people."

"A Vulcan mind can link with the mind of another sentient being," Stephen admitted. He said the same short phrase Scarlet had used; it must be in the Vulcan language.

"Can any Vulcan form the link? Can you?"

"Most Vulcans will go out of their way to avoid the experience. It's . . . emotional. As for me—much as my family wishes I weren't, I *am* still a Vulcan."

The long symphonic conversation ended with a complex fluting exchange between Scarlet and a flyer person with fur patterned in paisley swirls of tan and brown. The music faded. The circle disbanded.

Uhura drew herself from their spell. All her life she had sought out music that enraptured her as the flyers did. She wanted time by herself to feel it and think about it and understand it. She hummed a phrase. Not quite right. She tried once more. Not perfect, but closer.

Uhura feared she would never understand this music.

Captain Kirk joined her. "Everything all right?"

Uhura nodded.

"Has Spock returned to us?" Scarlet said.

"No," the captain said. "He's still in shock."

The paisley flyer hunched its shoulders and stretched, gradually unfolding its wings until they shivered above its head. Nearby, Athene snorted in alarm and spread her wings, holding them open as if for balance, for defense.

The paisley flyer gazed at Uhura, blinking its brilliant purple eyes.

"Your language," it said, forming the words with care, "is monotonous. And its pattern is trivially simple."

The density of the flyers' language awed Uhura: it had described another tongue and taught it in a few minutes.

The flyer meant its criticism literally. Standard contained neither tone nor melody. Feeling as if she had lost her bearings in her own world, she grasped at the flyer's statement gratefully. At least she could reply to it.

"There are Federation languages that are sung," she said. "There are even human languages with tone." She spoke a few words of Chinese. "But a large number of different kinds of sentient beings can speak Standard—I mean they can physically produce it. It's useful to have a common language."

"How do you learn so fast?" the captain asked. "Can you mind-meld?"

"Spock's abilities are unique in my experience," Scarlet said. "We have other ways of exchanging information quickly. That is why I had to stop speaking to you—to convey your language to the companionship. They objected to my speaking for them, and I felt unhappy, taking a place beyond the rest."

"What do you mean?" Kirk said.

"It is as if . . . as if I made myself a captain. I told you, James, we do not have such things."

"And now—you can all speak Standard?"

"This small companionship has the ability. In a few of your days, the information will make its way around the edge of the worldship."

Athene and Lindy approached. Athene watched the flyers nervously, her wings still half-opened and quivering at her sides. The flyers regarded her gravely and curiously.

"She's frightened," Lindy said. "She wants to follow you when you fly."

"This is Athene, and you are Amelinda the magician?" Scarlet said.

"Yes. I'm called Lindy."

"A nickname?"

Lindy nodded.

Scarlet extended one long sharp-clawed hand to Athene. "Athene is not fully evolved to her environment. She cannot fly. She has no talons, and cannot hunt. She is unhappy."

"I'm afraid that's true," Lindy said.

The equiraptor touched her nose to Scarlet's hand. Uhura caught her breath. Since Athene was essentially an herbivorous animal changed into an omnivore, the equiraptor might perceive Scarlet as a competitor or as a dangerous predator. Uhura did not see how either interaction could turn out well. But Athene showed neither fright nor aggression. Now that she had gotten used to seeing them, she seemed to accept the flying people. Perhaps she perceived them as some odd kind of human being.

"Poor thing," Scarlet said. At the flyer's comment of pity and dismissal, Lindy looked stricken.

"This creature is very interesting, but I would like to see your craft." Gold and brown stripes followed the curves of the third flyer's body in a subtle shaded pattern.

"The gravity is suitable for you now. You can visit the *Enterprise* without risk."

A few paces away, Stephen watched with fascination. He shook his head in amazement. "I don't believe it."

"What?" the captain asked.

He laughed. Seeing a Vulcan laugh freely discomforted Uhura; and Stephen's was not an entirely joyful laugh.

"Spock has them all talking just like he does."

Uhura could not help but smile, for Stephen was right.

"Do different people have different ways of speaking?" Scarlet asked.

"Yes," Uhura said. "Mr. Spock belongs to a group of people who stress rationality and precision over emotion—"

"Who crush in themselves and in others the factors that make life worthwhile," Stephen said. "Joy, and love . . ."

"You are Stephen?" Scarlet said.

Stephen hesitated. Uhura knew what he was thinking: when Scarlet called her by name, she had wondered what Spock told the flyer about her during the mind-meld.

"Yes," Stephen said.

"I will find great interest in meeting all the different beings here and in your companionship." Scarlet touched its sensory mustache with the tip of its tongue. "I have never met another sentient species."

"And I have still never seen a Federation starship," the gold and brown flyer said.

"Please come with me," the captain said.

Scarlet and the paisley flyer climbed the companionway with Uhura and Captain Kirk, their claws scraping the treads, but the gold-striped flyer and the cream-colored green-eyed being who had not yet spoken in Standard leaped from the deck and soared the ten meters to the catwalk.

Athene snorted and whickered when the flying people left. Lindy knew it was silly to attribute feelings to the equiraptor, who was no smarter than the average horse. Still, to Lindy, Athene sounded lonely and confused.

"Maybe they'll come back," she said. But she wondered if they would. Scarlet disapproved of Athene, Lindy believed, because she was not properly adapted. When she saw the beings fly, Lindy had imagined Athene flying with them inside the worldship. Now she wondered if that could happen, if Scarlet would allow it. She let go of Athene's mane and patted her neck.

Over by the viewport, Stephen glanced toward the worldship. "You can't *say* anything about it. It's too incredible to say anything about."

Athene trotted across the deck, reared and leaped in a half-turn, and sprinted to the other side. Her hooves cut into the fragile new turf. She skidded to a stop like a cowpony, spun, and galloped toward the catwalk to which the flyers had flown. She spread her wings. They beat the air. Her hooves left the ground.

"Athene!" Lindy cried.

Lindy knew the equiraptor would keep going. Athene leaped into a shallow glide. Somewhere in her small horse brain she believed that if she could just follow the flying people, she, too, would be able to fly. But she had neither practice enough nor room enough to clear the companionway. At the last instant she tried to turn. Her shoulder crashed against the railing. She tumbled to the deck, flapping her wings wildly, tumbling.

Lindy ran to her. The equiraptor lay in a heap, her legs splayed around her, one wing beneath her and the other beating at her side. She flung up her head and screamed. In terror, she snapped at Lindy with her sharp teeth. Lindy hardly noticed. She grabbed Athene's forelock in one hand and put her other hand just above Athene's nostrils, desperate to keep her from moving. If she had broken a leg or a wing and she got to her feet, she would hurt herself even worse.

"Whoa, Athene, easy, sweetie—"

Lindy's weight, especially in one-tenth gravity, was nothing to Athene, but her voice slipped through the terror and calmed the animal so she did not try to bolt. Lindy whispered to her, nonsense words that soothed her. Keeping one hand on the equiraptor's nose, she carefully ran the other hand down one foreleg, then the other. She found no sign of injury or break. The cannon bones felt smooth and strong beneath her fingers. Reassured about Athene's forelegs, Lindy touched the free wing, stroking till its frantic beating slowed and ceased. She tried to reach Athene's hind leg, but could not do so and keep one hand on her head at the same time. If she let go, Athene would lurch to her feet and try to run.

Stephen touched Lindy. He put one hand on Athene's crest, the other over Lindy's hand on Athene's nose. His skin felt hot, as if he had a fever.

"It's all right," he said, half to Lindy, half to Athene. "She'll stay still for me, Lindy."

Lindy slid her hand from beneath his, grateful for the help. If Stephen could even approach Athene when she was in this state, he could probably persuade her to remain motionless as well. He spoke to her in soft strange words. Her ragged breathing eased. Lindy stroked her hand along Athene's side, over her near hip and stifle, down her gaskin and hock and shannon bone and fetlock.

"Stephen, let her up now, please. Stephen—?"

He looked at her blankly. Then he shook his head, and the blank expression vanished. He urged Athene to her feet. She struggled up, clumsy not through injury but because horses always look clumsy getting to their feet. Lindy checked her off hind leg and her off wing and found no serious injuries.

"Let her walk—just a few steps."

Her head down, Athene let Stephen guide her forward. She ruffled her wings and folded them. As far as Lindy could tell she was sound. Now that the terror and the fear had faded from her, Athene looked as if she had run a long, hard race and broken her heart by losing.

Lindy's vision blurred. She fought to regain her composure. Failing completely, she burst into sobs.

"Lindy, hey." Stephen touched her shoulder. "She's okay—nothing broken."

"She isn't okay!" Lindy scrubbed her sleeve across her eyes and dashed away the tears. She faced Stephen angrily—not angry at him, but angry at herself, angry at the world, just angry. "I've done everything I can. But she *almost* has room, she can *almost* fly. That's the worst thing I ever could have done to her!"

He raised one eyebrow. Only in the moments when he slipped into grim thoughtfulness did he really look like a Vulcan.

"Logic reveals," he said, "that since she cannot fly here, we must take her where she can fly."

"The worldship—"

He shook off the serious expression. "Are you game?"

"Of course! But Jim—"

"Jim? What does Jim have to do with anything? The question is, do you want to risk going to an alien place in an unarmed yacht with a Klingon bandit hanging around?"

That slowed Lindy. "But . . . she wouldn't have any reason to bother us."

"She might not need one."

"I don't care about her," Lindy said. "But what about the flying people? What if they don't want us in their world?"

"They invited Jim Kirk. They even invited Spock. We're much more fun. Come on."

Lindy urged Athene forward. The equiraptor nuzzled her halfheartedly. Stephen parted the wide double doors of the docking hatch.

The obsolete decommissioned admiral's yacht was worn with use and age. Its main cabin had been stripped to the interior wood inlays. Only the pilot's and copilot's seats remained.

"Come on, sweetie," Lindy whispered. Athene hesitated at the threshold, her ears swiveling back and forth. She stepped delicately on board. Her hooves thudded hollowly on the wooden parquet decking.

"How much trouble are you going to get into for doing this?" Lindy asked.

"I'm going to the worldship," Stephen said. "I'm going with or without you and Athene, and I don't need Captain James T. Kirk's permission. Are you coming?"

"Yes."

The engines filled the craft with smooth subsonics. Stephen freed his ship from the docking module and eased *Dionysus* away from the flank of the *Enterprise*.

On the command platform of *Quundar*, Koronin pretended ignorance of the consternation traveling through the work pit. Her crew could not understand why she had done nothing, why she simply waited and watched.

They have insufficient patience, she said to herself. If they had practiced waiting for fifteen years, as I did, they would comprehend its uses. If they survived.

At the moment, though, they wondered why she had let the sailboat pass, instead of capturing it; they wondered why she did not incapacitate the *Enterprise*. They believed the Imperial propaganda, that *Quundar* could conquer any ship of the Federation. Koronin had sufficient experience and sufficient knowledge to understand that while *Quundar* might destroy a constellation-class starship, the starship would destroy *Quundar* as well. Mutual destruction offered no profit.

She observed a small ship detach itself from the docking module of the *Enterprise*. But it was a shabby little Federation ship, not the sailboat. A quick scan produced some unusual data, but nothing to indicate that the alien creatures were trying to slip past her in secret. The sailboat continued to drift off the flank of the starship, between *Quundar* and the *Enterprise*.

So, for the moment, amused by the distress of her subordinates, Koronin waited, and she watched.

The flying people all adopted names: the paisley one was Cloud Touching; the cream-colored, green-eyed, silent one was Green; and the striped one took the name Sun-and-Shadows. Jim took them to the bridge.

"Captain Kirk!" Sulu said. "*Dionysus* has undocked from the *Enterprise!*"

"What—? *Enterprise* to *Dionysus*. Stephen, this is Jim Kirk. What the hell do you think you're doing?"

Stephen's image appeared on the viewscreen. "I'm going to the worldship," he said.

"But you can't!"

"Certainly I can."

"Stephen, this is a first contact—" He stopped, all too aware of the flyers behind him, watching curiously.

"And only certified members of Starfleet could possibly talk to these people without starting an intergalactic war?" Stephen asked. "I appreciate the vote of confidence."

"I can't allow you to go."

"How do you propose to stop me? Shoot my ship out of the sky? Declare martial law?"

Jim hesitated. Under certain circumstances, Federation first-contact laws and Starfleet brass would back him up if he were to shoot down an unauthorized ship. But Jim had no intention of firing on *Dionysus,* and Stephen knew it. He probably knew that *Dionysus* was out of range of tractor beams, too. Jim could chase him, but *Dionysus* had far more speed and agility over short distances than the *Enterprise; Dionysus* would vanish into the worldship, where the *Enterprise* could not go at all, before Jim's ship could reach pursuit velocity. As for martial law: Jim had the authority to declare it, but Stephen was hardly any more likely to obey Jim's orders then than he was now.

"Do you know how close the border is? Not to mention our local bandit out there?" Jim glanced at Sulu. If *Quundar* attacked *Dionysus,* Jim would have to respond in some way; he would have to balance his responsibility to protect a civilian against his responsibility to the rest of the Federation.

"What's life without a little risk?" Stephen said.

"No activity on *Quundar,* captain," Sulu said.

"Stephen, you can't visit the worldship on your own!" Jim said.

Scarlet broke in. "But whyever not? Stephen, you are welcome to visit, as is anyone from your companionship."

"Scarlet, please—" Jim faced the viewscreen again. "Stephen, don't do this. The Federation comes down hard on people who meddle in first contacts without a clearance. Besides, it could be dangerous!"

"The interior can be dangerous," Scarlet said. "It is . . . wild. But no one will harm you at the perimeter. James, why do you wish Stephen not to go to the worldship?"

"We have rules—laws—that govern how we contact people we've never encountered before."

"How very odd," Scarlet said.

"You'd better check your contact list before you send the fleet out after me," Stephen said.

"Stephen!"

The Vulcan's image faded. *Dionysus* stopped responding to signals from the *Enterprise*.

Serves me right for trying to talk to him rationally, Jim thought. He got the feeling Stephen had enjoyed the argument. Scowling, he rose and joined Sulu at the helm. Sulu gestured at his sensors.

"Nothing, captain. Koronin's just watching."

"Waiting," Jim said.

"What are all these . . . things?" Scarlet said.

"What things?" Jim said to Scarlet, distracted. And Uhura's remote expression troubled him. "Lieutenant, are you sure you're all right?"

"Yes, captain." She returned to her station, humming.

"All these artifacts," the striped flyer said.

Sun-and-Shadows wandered across the upper level of the bridge, looking at the instruments, touching the controls.

"Please don't do that!" Jim said.

"Don't do what? Walk? Touch? Look?"

"Touch, mostly."

"Why not?"

"Those 'artifacts' are the ship's controls. It's dangerous for untrained people to change their settings." They're like curious children, Jim thought. Always wanting to investigate one more bright light or one last switch or control button.

Cloud Touching said something in the flyers' language, Green replied, and all four flyers spoke simultaneously.

"I don't understand," Sun-and-Shadows said. "What are controls?"

"Devices for directing the *Enterprise*—for choosing its course. The worldship must have something similar."

"No."

"Then how do you guide it? How do you stop and start it? How do you monitor the environment?"

The flyers conversed again.

"None of those words applies to the worldship," Cloud Touching said.

"Now *I* don't understand," Jim said.

"The worldship does not move," Scarlet said. "It does not start, it does not stop—so no one guides it."

"But it did move—it moved from wherever you come from, and it came here."

"No, it stays in one place. It . . . this is difficult to say in your language. It *defines* one place. The universe moves around it."

"But . . ." Jim stopped. He wished the science officer had not been so inconsiderate as to put himself out of commission. Perhaps a Vulcan could argue physics with the flyers, or at least choose a set of terms so everyone knew what physics was being talked about. If it was physics at all. This sounded more like religion.

Sun-and-Shadows, by the science station, poked at the sensor controls with unrestrained curiosity.

"Sun-and-Shadows, please don't change the settings on the sensors," Jim said, keeping his patience with considerable difficulty.

Sun-and-Shadows stopped playing with the controls but continued to hover near the station.

"Captain," Sulu said. "If the worldship drifts on its current course, within the hour we'll pass into a region over which even Starfleet claims no jurisdiction."

Jim needed to study the schematic; but the flyers also had to be kept amused.

"Yeoman Rand," Jim said, "please give our guests the grand tour."

Rand timorously joined the four flyers and tried to keep them from playing with the controls while they pelted her with an interminable series of questions.

Jim began to think of Scarlet as a guest who had brought along three uninvited children and overstayed the welcome.

So much for the first contact between two highly developed cultures, Jim thought in disgust.

Sulu put the schematic up on the viewscreen. Three concentric circles represented the boundaries: Federation Survey had marked the inner one, the Klingon Empire claimed the middle one, and Starfleet considered the outer one to enclose Federation territory. The worldship's appearance had dragged the *Enterprise* outside the middle ring. Once they crossed the outer ring, the *Enterprise* would be an outlaw ship, invading foreign territory.

"Thank you, Mr. Sulu," Jim said.

After a moment, Sulu realized Jim had no intention of giving him any instructions for a course change. With a grin, the helm officer turned back to his place.

"Scarlet," he said, "I must talk to you about something very serious. Your worldship is moving—"

"But I explained before, it does not move."

"All right! I won't argue semantics. The universe is moving a dangerous part of itself toward the worldship. My ship isn't allowed inside that part of the universe. I'll have to move out of it. If the worldship stays where it is, you may find yourself surrounded by hostile beings."

"I have no reason to be hostile to other beings, nor they to me."

"I know that. But the Klingon Empire has been known to attack first and ask questions afterwards."

"They will not want to attack the worldship, but they are welcome to visit, as you are."

"Please don't discount what I'm saying," Jim said. "You, all your people, and your world will be in danger, unless you can persuade the universe to keep you in a safer place."

"I would be sorry to move the universe right now," Scarlet said. "I have more to learn about you and your people, and about the beings who oppose you."

"Do you understand 'war'?"

"It is a word Spock gave me."

"War is terrible, Scarlet. If the Klingons do behave in a hostile way, don't wait around to experience it. Move—the universe, if you have to."

"I will remember what you have told me, James."

"Captain Kirk!" Uhura said. "Dr. McCoy is calling Security—it's Mr. Spock!"

Jim scowled and decided he had better find out what was going on. Scarlet followed him into the lift.

"Please go back to the bridge, Scarlet," Jim said. "I don't know what's wrong. It might be dangerous."

"You fear so many things, James," Scarlet said.

"I'm only worried you might get hurt in a strange environment!" Jim said, offended.

"James," Scarlet said gently, "I fly with lightning."

In the confined space of the lift, the flyer opened one wide wing. A black scar slashed across delicate furred skin. Scarlet folded the wing again.

The lift opened. Shouts echoed down the corridor. Jim headed for sick bay, skating along in the low gravity.

Two security officers tried to restrain Spock. One of them tumbled past and fetched up against the far wall. He slid to the floor, stunned. He was over two meters tall, massive, heavily muscled. Spock had flung him across the room with the sweep of one arm.

"Commander Spock!"

The Vulcan struggled, freeing himself from the grasp of the second officer. He spread his arms and flattened his hands against the walls that formed a corner behind him.

"Hold him still!" McCoy carried a hypo-sprayer.

The two security officers looked at McCoy, looked at each other, and warily approached Spock.

"Commander Spock!" Jim hoped his voice might get through to a part of the science officer that still responded to orders. Not that I've had much luck ordering Vulcans so far, Jim thought.

Spock's shoulders tensed. Jim braced himself for impact. Wild-eyed, oblivious to Jim, the Vulcan saw something beyond him. Instead of plunging past or through him, the Vulcan flung both arms up and out. He clutched the air. He shrieked, his back arched, and he collapsed.

McCoy knelt, touched the corner of his jaw, and felt for his pulse. Scarlet came farther into the room.

"Did he speak to you?" Jim asked.

"No," Scarlet said. "But he told me . . . he told us all, didn't you hear him? His pain is great. He believed I would touch him again."

Spock spread his hands on the deck. "Not the ground," he whispered. "The sky . . . This place has no sky . . ."

He tried to rise. The hypo-sprayer hissed as McCoy injected a sedative. Spock struggled against it briefly, then sagged, unconscious.

"I've been trying not to drug him, but I'm afraid he'll hurt himself," McCoy said. "He doesn't know where he is. He raves about the worldship. About flying."

Scarlet regarded Spock sadly. "I never meant to hurt him. I would return his knowledge if I could exchange it for the pain I gave him."

"Bones, what's wrong with him?"

"I don't know!" McCoy threw the hypo-sprayer onto a lab table. It clattered and bounced in the low gravity.

"Did that make you feel better?" Jim asked dryly.

"Yes," McCoy said. "It did. If I knew what was wrong with him, I could probably do something." He picked Spock up and laid him on one of the exam tables. The weight of a full-grown person was negligible in one-tenth g.

"What exactly happened when you exchanged information?" Jim asked Scarlet. "If you can describe the process . . ."

"My people communicate in many ways," Scarlet said. "I can speak with another's mind, by a simple electromagnetic transmission and reception. Spock can . . . absorb information and offer it by influencing the patterns of the brain."

"He must have absorbed too much," McCoy said. He frowned thoughtfully. "There's very little in the medical literature about mind-melding . . ." His voice trailed off.

"He understood—long before I did—that we could never begin to communicate without his ability," Scarlet said. "*His* ability, not mine."

"*His* ability," Jim said. "Mind-melding?"

"Yes," Scarlet said. "That's what I said." He repeated the unusual word. "That is Spock's term."

"I don't speak Vulcan," Jim said.

"Oh," Scarlet said. "What a shame. You should learn. It's a fascinating intellectual construction—"

"Excuse me," Jim said. "If I could learn a language in fifteen minutes, like you, Vulcan would be one of the first I tried. But—I don't mean to be rude—I have other things to worry about than linguistics."

McCoy studied the readings on the medical sensors. "I'm worried, Jim. His life signs are getting weaker. The note in his medical records says to let him sleep if he's injured—it *doesn't* say let him slip into a coma. I have no way to pull him out."

"He took this risk of his own free will," Jim said. "He may have to suffer the consequences."

"But he's withdrawing—he's weakening!"

"I understand that, Bones. What I don't understand is what you expect me to do about it."

"I'm going to talk to Stephen. Maybe he can draw Commander Spock out of this fugue. *If* he has the ability—I have a hard time thinking of him as a Vulcan."

"You have something in common with Commander Spock, after all," Jim said. "But Stephen isn't going to be much help. He's left for the worldship, and he's turned off all his communications."

"Jim, we've got to get him—bring him back!"

Jim weighed the suggestion. "No," he said. "The danger to the *Enterprise* is too great."

"But Spock may *die!*"

"I'm sorry for that, of course. But I have my ship and my crew and Federation boundaries to consider."

Newland Rift entered sick bay hesitantly. "Dr. McCoy?"

Jim winced, expecting a chorus of barks and whines and snarls. But Rift had left his puppies behind. He seemed uncomfortable in the low gravity, and he looked worried.

"Yes, Mr. Rift?" McCoy said. "I'm very busy—"

"Have you seen Lindy?"

"Not for some time."

"I've been looking all over for her. Captain, have you seen her? You have spent so much time together . . ."

"I'm sorry, I don't know where she is." Jim wondered if the massive former wrestler had assigned himself the position of Lindy's stand-in father, and had come to demand if Jim had honorable intentions. The thought was fairly intimidating. Rift ought to ask Stephen the same question, Jim thought gloomily.

"Lindy must be with Athene," Rift said. "Where might they have gone?"

"Gone? What do you mean, gone? Only the shuttlecraft deck and the repair bay are big enough for Athene."

"But Athene isn't in either place."

Jim had a horrible suspicion. Lindy spends a lot of time with Stephen, he thought. And Stephen is on his way to the worldship.

On the worldship, Athene could fly.

# Chapter 11

ONE DID NOT have to be an expert tracker to figure out what had happened on the shuttlecraft deck. Athene's hoofprints and Lindy's and Stephen's footprints led through the grass to the module at which *Dionysus* had been docked.

Jim swore softly.

"Why are you so troubled, James?" Scarlet asked. "They are in no danger—they'll be welcomed."

"Lindy's in danger from the other people I told you about." Jim called the bridge. "Lieutenant Uhura, it's essential that I contact *Dionysus.*"

"I'm sorry, sir, I've tried, but Stephen won't answer."

"Captain, she has no experience in space," Rift said, deeply distressed. "She's fearless, and she believes the company might someday help make friends with the Empire. She . . ."

Jim felt sorry for the powerful man, whose strength and skill and affection for Lindy could not help her. Jim, too, worried. What was more, he was responsible for her safety. As Rift said, she had no experience out here, no way of knowing what Stephen might be taking her into.

"Don't worry," Jim said to Rift. "I'll find her."

Jim had no trouble getting volunteers to go on the rescue mission. While a machinery crew came to the hangar to move the partitions, Mr. Sulu and Lieutenant Uhura prepared the shuttlecraft *Copernicus* to depart. Then Jim was faced with the problem of whom to leave in charge.

I'm running out of senior officers, Jim thought. Gary is

light-years away in the hospital, Commander Spock is in a coma, and McCoy has to take care of Commander Spock. And then there's Mr. Scott . . .

Jim went to Scott's cabin and stopped outside the door. He had no idea what he was going to say to the engineer.

He knocked.

"Come."

Scott glanced up from the crumpled, scribbled-on piece of paper on his desk.

"Captain Kirk!" He rose.

"As you were."

Scott sat down again.

"We have a problem," Jim said.

"Aye, captain, that we do."

"We're going to have to put aside our conflict. This is an emergency, and I need your cooperation."

"I canna call back my actions," Scott said. "Nor my words. I thought ye were imprudent to open the ship to beings we know nothin' about. 'Tis what I still believe. Captain Pike would never ha' done such a thing. His style was . . ." Scott's voice trailed off.

"More cautious?" Jim said.

"More prudent, captain."

"You're going to have to overcome your problems with my style for the time being," Jim said. "I need you to take the conn."

"What!"

"I'm going to the worldship."

"But, captain—!"

"Don't argue with me anymore, Mr. Scott! The *Enterprise* is drifting toward Empire territory. If I don't return before we reach the boundary, you're to keep the ship inside Starfleet jurisdiction. If the Empire sends scouts, you may raise your shields, but you are not under *any* circumstances—even faced with a hostile force—to use weapons. To do so within disputed territory is an act of war. Do you understand?"

"I understand, captain, but . . ." He sounded doubtful.

"Can you carry out those orders?"

"I'm no' to use weapons, captain? Even in self-defense?"

"No weapons under any circumstances. If you're at-

271

tacked, raise your shields. If you're in danger of losing the shields, retreat."

"And if you're no' back, captain?"

"That has no bearing on your actions. Will you do as I ask?"

Scott considered. "I canna swear, captain. I ha' my own judgment, my own conscience, to answer to."

Jim had no more time to spend in discussion. His mood was grim. "I hope your conscience isn't so prudent that it starts a war."

Stephen brought *Dionysus* down inside the worldship, where a wide, parched plain met weathered rock convolutions. The engines sighed to silence. Athene shifted nervously.

Lindy looked through the port. "It's beautiful!"

Strata-striped columns of eroded sedimentary rock thrust from the land; in the far distance, low foothills rose toward unending mountains.

Stephen's methodical mind began analyzing the scene, speculating on different ways in which the landscape could have been produced. He had to shake himself out of a train of thought that compared building the landscape like a great model against setting up conditions within the worldship that would, after geologic eons, produce it.

He tried to feel anger at himself for slipping into the Vulcan way of thinking, which counted beauty and joy beneath analysis and information. The anger flickered, then failed, but he pressed himself beyond the analysis. Only then could he see how Lindy perceived the worldship.

"It *is* beautiful." He equalized the pressure between inside and outside. "I'm going to open the hatch."

"Okay. I'll try to keep her from bolting."

The double doors slid apart. The wind of the alien world smelled dry and dusty and sweet. Despite the brightness of the worldship's light, the air felt cool because of its low density. The high partial pressure of oxygen made Stephen dizzy and slightly drunk.

Lindy led Athene to the open hatch. The equiraptor quivered with excitement and fear. Lindy put one hand on her withers and jumped easily, gently, onto her back. She slid her legs beneath Athene's wings and urged Athene forward with her knees. Athene hesitated, spraddle-legged, her ears pricked, her nostrils distended. She drank in the alien air.

Suddenly she sprang into a gallop. Her wings lifted from her sides. The feathers whispered. The thin air attenuated the pounding of her hooves. Athene's wings rose and fell and began a steady, rhythmic beat. Her hooves touched the ground more and more lightly. She leaped.

And she flew.

The wind fluttered Lindy's hair behind her. She hunched close against Athene's neck, feeling fear and wonder and joy. The cool thin wind cut through her shirt. But her heart beat furiously till she was too excited to feel the cold. Athene spread her wings and soared. She kept her legs pulled up under her as if she were leaping a high fence, the widest steeplechase jump in the universe.

Athene dipped one wing, banked, and turned. Lindy gasped. The ground tilted toward her. Far below, Stephen gazed up at them. Athene swooped over him. He turned to follow, laughing, running, waving his arms, shouting in triumph. Behind him, Ilya scampered like a kitten.

Sweat streamed down Athene's shoulders and flanks and frothed to white foam where the leading edge of her wings touched her sides on the downstrokes. Her breath began to labor. Her wingbeat slowed, and she dropped toward the ground, but at the last second she lifted her head and struggled back into the sky. Lindy had no idea what signal to give her to get her to land. She sat up straighter, deeper, giving Athene the dressage signal to slow and to collect herself. Athene responded. She increased the angle at which she carried her wings. Their ground speed slowed; they descended. Athene's wings beat in powerful downstrokes, cupping the wind. She reached for the land with her hooves like an eagle for its prey, touching into a gallop, half-running, half-gliding. Lindy collected her, easing her into a canter, guiding her in a wide circle around Stephen's ship.

The canter slowed to a trot. Athene ruffled her wings and folded them against her sides, covering Lindy's legs with the warmth of the blue-black feathers. Lindy was breathing harder than Athene. The wind had brought tears to her eyes. Athene jogged to Stephen. She stopped.

Lindy slid from Athene's back. Her knees shook and she shivered. She hugged Athene's neck, burying her face in her thick mane. She was laughing and crying at the same time. Athene nuzzled her side.

"You liked that, didn't you, sweetie?" Lindy said. "I did, too. Oh, I did, too."

Stephen put his hand on Lindy's shoulder. His warmth cut through the chill of the wind.

"At first I wasn't sure you were going to take off." He, too, sounded breathless. "Then I wasn't sure you were going to land."

Lindy wiped her eyes on her sleeve. "All those dressage lessons," she said, "and I never learned the signal for 'come down out of the sky.' "

Stephen smiled.

"I have to walk her," Lindy said. "Do you have an old blanket—?"

He disappeared into *Dionysus*. Lindy started Athene walking to keep her from getting stiff and sore. When Stephen returned, he offered her a light blanket that looked like white silk.

"It'll get awfully dirty," she said.

"That's all right. It won't mind."

She thought he was joking. But the blanket clasped itself to Athene, caressing her sides. Lindy touched it, curious. It had a warmth of its own.

"What is it?"

"A silken."

"Is it alive?"

"Sort of. It's right on the borderline. It 'knows' to wrap you up and keep you warm. That seems to make it happy, if you can use that word on something this far from sentient, and unhappy, too—if you don't use it, it dies."

Lindy slid her hand beneath it. Athene felt dry and warm, not sweaty and overheated, where the silken touched her.

Lindy let her walk free. Athene must have expended an enormous amount of energy in her flight, but now she showed no sign of being tired. Relaxed and energetic, she strode with long, low-gravity strides. Every so often she raised her head and gazed at the strange, light-patterned sky. Her wings lifted and rustled beneath the silken.

Lindy turned and hugged Stephen hard.

Stephen put his arms around her and held her gently, gingerly, all too aware of his own tremendous strength. Lindy touched his cheek and brushed her fingertip along the upswept stroke of his eyebrow.

He perceived her intelligence, her determination, and, yes, her beauty. Even Vulcans did not train all aesthetic sense out of their children. Yet Stephen felt nothing.

He put his hand over hers, where she touched his cheek. He drew her hands away from him.

"Lindy, don't, please."

"What's wrong?"

He turned away. "I can't . . ."

"Why not?"

"Because that's the way Vulcans are!"

No human being could have moved him by force. Lindy touched his elbow and turned him to face her again.

"But you're different," she said.

He sat on the skid of *Dionysus*. His shoulders slumped.

"I've tried to be," he said. "But I was raised a Vulcan, trained . . ." He cupped his hands together, forming a sphere of air between them. "They teach you to wall off your feelings. To put them inside a shell and cover the shell, layer after layer till it's so thick it can't be broken. If you rebel, if you question, they take more patience with you. More time . . ."

"That's what they did to you."

He nodded. "I keep chipping away at that shell, trying to break through it, hoping to—but I'm afraid if I ever do, I'll find . . . nothing." He opened his hands and flung the space between them at the sky, like a magician producing a dove. But no dove appeared. There was nothing.

"I've never loved anyone, Lindy. Someone loved me once, and I wanted . . . I pretended . . . But she knew. Finally she knew. I don't want to hurt anyone ever again the way I hurt her. I don't want to hurt you."

Instead of drawing away, she put her arms around him and held him, offering comfort, perhaps looking for it. Stephen stroked her hair, knowing his gesture to be empty and wishing, desperately, that he had some true response to give.

He opened his eyes. His sight strangely vague, his hearing dim, he inspected his unfamiliar surroundings as best he could. The dense air smelled artificial. He longed for mountains and plains and cold wind buoying his body.

He tried to sit up. Heavy straps bound him at chest and hips and thighs. In a fury he flung himself upright. The restraints ripped away. He knew no one of his own people so cruel and mad as to imprison another person. He had traveled to the newcomers' ship, trusting their gestures of peace, and they had responded by trying to cripple him.

He prowled the angular room. He felt as if he were looking at two images, one well known and one completely strange. The part of his mind that identified the image as alien drove him to escape; the part that recognized it helped him find a way out.

A creature sat near the entrance, studying some strange object. It was personlike in form, but it wore protective garments as if it planned to go into space outside a sailboat. If it saw him he might have to injure it to pass, and no matter what its people had done to him, he would never stoop to their barbarian ways.

He moved stealthily toward the creature. But his body seemed alien to him. He stumbled. The creature saw him and leaped up.

"Spock!" it said.

It never felt him touch it at the junction of neck and shoulder, it never felt unconsciousness overcome it. It never felt itself fall. He caught it and laid it down.

Careful to avoid detection, he walked through the low-ceilinged corridors. He found the familiar yet alien mechanism he sought. As he changed the settings, he mused upon the device. It was ingenious, but primitive and poorly executed, with all these mechanical parts and electronic circuits. He would have designed it to reply to the touch of the mind.

He climbed onto the platform and waited out the delay until the beam dissolved him.

He re-formed within the sailboat. Beyond the translucent walls of the spherical chamber, the bulk of the *Enterprise* hovered nearby, and the gently curved bowl of the worldship glowed and shimmered at a great distance. The boat's sail rippled in concentric circles that trembled from its outer border to its center and back to its edge again, forming interference patterns where they crossed.

The flexible glassy spines that formed the shrouds of the sail grew from the exterior surface of the chamber. On the interior, the bases of the spines formed eight-pointed stars, translucent at the points, pearly within, a brilliant point at the very center, where the spine collected light and concentrated it.

The spines flexed and changed, altering the set of the sail. For a moment the sail trembled and twisted uselessly and the sailboat fell toward the worldship, caught by its gravity. He stroked the bases of the spines; the spines contorted again. The sail caught the power beam, straightened, filled. The sail acted as a brake, a parachute catching photons instead of air, changing the boat's headlong fall into a steady, slow descent.

He was going home.

The shuttlecraft *Copernicus* had traveled half the distance to the worldship. Sulu flew; Uhura took the copilot's seat and continued trying to get some response from Stephen. Jim paced in the cramped space and fumed at the Vulcan's impulsive stubbornness.

Cloud Touching, pleading hunger, had transported back to the worldship, but the other three flyers came along for the ride, poking around and asking questions about the instruments, the layout, the uses of the craft. They acted as if the trip were a picnic. Perhaps, for them, it was.

Jim was glad both Sulu and Uhura had volunteered to come along, because he was fully occupied keeping the flyers from dissecting the shuttlecraft out of curiosity.

"Which of your companionship has taken up sailing, James?" Scarlet said without any hint of anger.

The flyers' sailboat sped past *Copernicus*, falling toward the worldship and vanishing into the distance of complex visual and electromagnetic background noise.

"I don't know," Jim said.

ENTERPRISE

"*Enterprise* signaling, captain."

"Scott here, captain. 'Tis Mr. Spock—he's escaped from sick bay! He used the transporter—"

"—and stole the sailboat," Jim said. "So I see. Is Dr. McCoy—?"

"He isna hurt, captain, but Mr. Spock left him wi' a monster headache. 'Twas the nerve-pinch . . ."

Jim had no idea what Scott was talking about, not that it mattered.

"Commander Spock is on his own just as he was before. If we see him, we'll bring him back. If we don't—I'm sorry for him."

"But, captain—"

Jim nodded to Uhura to close the channel. Unbelieving, she obeyed.

Feeling stunned, she tried again to reach Stephen.

"*Copernicus* calling *Dionysus*, come in please. This is an emergency—please respond." Again, the only reply was the static of the worldship's magnetic field, and silence.

Scarlet flexed wing-fingers and closed them. "James, is it important that your contact with Stephen be conducted through your machines?"

"That's the only way we—can *you* contact him? Is that what you mean?"

"I have already requested that the companionship watch for Spock. If you wish, I will ask them to look for *Dionysus* and Stephen as well."

"Scarlet, I would be grateful—if anyone sees Lindy, please tell them to tell her how important it is that she come back."

"That is more difficult. Cloud Touching will convey your language to those who want it, when he finishes hunting, and Green and Sun-and-Shadows and I will convey it to others when we return. But until then, no one else on the worldship speaks Standard."

"Can't you transmit it mind to mind?"

Scarlet regarded Jim curiously. "Could you teach someone to listen by giving them things to smell? Could you teach someone to feel by demonstrating colors?"

"Of course not."

"In the same way, I cannot pass on a new method of speech without speaking."

"But that's how Spock taught it to you!"

"But I am different," Scarlet said patiently. "James, you saw me, you heard me, give your language to Green and Cloud Touching and Sun-and-Shadows. I cannot do it as Spock did it, because Spock and I are *different.*"

"I do understand that, it's only—" Jim stopped, wrestling with frustration. "Couldn't Cloud Touching look for *Dionysus?*"

"He is hungry. When he has hunted, he may choose to search. Or perhaps he will sleep."

"If we don't find Lindy and get back soon—our lives are at stake. The ship is at stake!"

Scarlet regarded him calmly. "Yes. People live, and they die."

Jim felt as if he had run head-on into a wall of incomprehension. "How soon before we might hear something?"

Scarlet touched his sensory mustache. "I do not know. I cannot even promise that anyone will tell me who sees the ship. They will if it pleases them."

"Is there anyone who *can* promise?"

"Are you seeking someone in the worldship who holds a position analogous to yours?"

"Please don't be hurt, Scarlet, but, yes, I would like to talk to someone with responsibility for the worldship. I can understand why your leaders might want to observe us before revealing themselves. But surely you've seen enough to know we're peaceful."

"I believe that your intentions are peaceful because of what I learned from Spock," Scarlet said. "But what I have observed is that your ship carries engines of destruction." Scarlet waved off Jim's objection. "That is all beside the point. There *is* no person who leads. The worldship has neither leaders nor followers."

"What do you have? Anarchy?"

"I have myself. I live my life as I choose."

"I don't understand how your system works—I don't understand your organization. Who directs the worldship? Who designed it, and why, and where are they? Who decides what will happen to it? Who put you on it? Is there another species of people?"

"Too many of your concepts have no analogy on the worldship. I am different from you. The group of all flying people is different from the group of all *Enterprise* people. The people who created the worldship are dead, many generations, a few generations. I hope that the people who must decide the worldship's fate have not yet been born."

Jim blew out his breath in frustration. The more questions he asked Scarlet, the less he knew. His instinct urged trust, but his judgment made him question the truth, at least the completeness, of what Scarlet said. No leaders, no builders, no direction for a construct the size and complexity of the worldship: he found this all very difficult to accept or even grasp.

Philosophical problems like truth would have to wait.

"If you'd ask the other people in the worldship to look for *Dionysus*," Jim said to Scarlet, "and to let you know if they see it, I'd be very grateful."


The diaphanous appearance of the worldship's outer skin resolved itself into the pebbled surface of close-packed spheres. The sailboat touched a landing extension. The shroud-spines contracted, furling the sail. The free spines curled around the extension. The boat slid downward, slowing, coming to rest against the surface of the worldship.

He drew the boat's operculum from the ventral opening. The boat had matched its opening to a similar circular opening, closed by a similar pearly disk, in a larger, more thickly walled sphere that formed a part of the worldship's wall. The silky webbing that held the spheres together also sealed the connection between sailboat and worldship, keeping the air inside.

He pushed the second operculum away and entered the worldship wall.

The familiar gray illumination welcomed him. Yet he found himself, confused and unhappy, seeking a darker, redder light.

The sphere against which he had landed contained nothing but a large builder, creeping along the ceiling, leaving a slow trail of hardening pearl as it searched for a new sphere in which to take up residence. He hoped it would not move into the sailboat. If it did, it would ooze in through the ventral opening and make the interior its home. While it lived there it would add two or three coats of pearl to the inside, thickening the wall till it squeezed itself from its habitation and must seek a larger one.

Once a sphere accumulated enough coats to turn opaque, it no longer made a good sailboat. It was possible, but pointless, to sail without being able to see. The joy of sailing lay in the search for the delicate photon winds of space and in admiring the stars.

He had replaced the sailboat's operculum. The builder might believe another of its kind still lived within. It might crawl on till it found a more welcoming spot to house its large sluggish form.

Making his way through layers of interconnecting spheres, he headed always inward. As usual, the routes through the wall had changed. A large, fully adult builder would slowly press its way between spheres and secrete a new, thin-shelled sphere, changing some paths and closing others completely. A younger, medium-sized builder would move into an unoccupied sphere and temporarily obstruct the way; or a smaller builder would leave interior layers that reduced the size of the chamber till a person could no longer pass. Eventually every sphere closed up completely but for the smallest passage from major dorsal to major ventral opening, and even the most juvenile builder could no longer live within. Then the weavers would eject the solid sphere from the wall, and, when the universe moved around the world-ship, it would carry away the enormous unstrung pearls, like a river swirling soap bubbles to the sea.

The light grew stronger, penetrating even thick-walled opalescent spheres. He reached the edge of the wall, the interior of the worldship.

Koronin watched the exquisitely detailed transmissions that appeared in her communications area. They fascinated her, for the longer she refrained from replying, the more complex the transmissions became. At first the image of an alien being had appeared, spreading its hands in a gesture she perceived as supplication. Later it had flown for her.

Other flyers joined it, performing an eerie aerial dance. The transmission transmuted itself into patterns and three-dimensional graphics that could only have been produced by a powerful artificial intelligence. The transmissions continuously increased their control of her communications capabilities. She recorded everything. When she played back the segment in which the flyers changed to abstract patterns, she began to wonder if every scene she had watched had been computer generated, and none taken from life. It was possible that the worldship inhabitants showed her only what they thought she wanted to see.

At the same time, she reserved a portion of her communications area and used it to keep track of goings-on around the *Enterprise*. When the sailboat returned to the worldship, she thought of capturing it, but changed her mind and let it land.

Her serjeant, immensely flattered to be permitted on the command balcony, stared at the image. "*Quundar* can follow—the limpet hatch will seal us to the sphere, that one, there, sensors show it is hollow and thin-walled. We blast through, follow—"

"Silence."

The serjeant obeyed.

"Shall we attack, in full view of a Federation ship?" Koronin said. "Fool. We have no reason to enter as invaders. We can arrive as guests. Do they teach you nothing but force in the armada? Do they beat your sense out of you?"

"Forgive me, Koronin."

"I will respond to the aliens' transmission; I will accept the invitation they offered me. We will not put aside our sense—will we? Our continued existence may be evidence of the aliens' goodwill. But it may not. Keep alert."

"Yes, Koronin."

"Return to your post. Prepare for acceleration."

She considered taking *Quundar* completely out of sight of the Federation starship and entering the worldship in secret, but her pride intervened. If she concealed her plans, she as much as admitted the Federation possessed rights to the worldship that she did not.

Suppose, she thought, just suppose this marvel is the product of a degenerated civilization. I have seen no weapons, no defense. Suppose the inhabitants can be conquered. If I claim this place, it will bring me power. Power can be the means to revenge. Power can be better than revenge.

Sun-and-Shadows loomed behind Sulu, watching the helm officer manipulate the controls.

Just like a kid, Jim thought, with a new Christmas toy.

"Scarlet, I feel responsible for the theft of your sailboat—"

"James, I own nothing. Nothing can be stolen from me."

"I'm glad you can regard the incident with such equanimity. But I still feel responsible."

"That is your choice. I cannot take it from you."

"May I sail this boat?" Sun-and Shadows asked Sulu.

"No, sir, I'm sorry—it takes quite a lot of training, it isn't as easy as it looks."

"Of course it is." He reached his long arms over Sulu's shoulders and spun the shuttle on all three axes.

Jim shouted and gulped.

The spiraling, tumbling spin ceased and the shuttlecraft continued on its path as if it had never deviated.

Sulu flung himself at the controls. But nothing needed fixing. Sulu looked distinctly green. Sun-and-Shadows blinked at him calmly, touched the edge of his sensory mustache with his tongue, and said nothing.

"Scarlet!" Jim said. "Please ask your friends to stop endangering my people with their little games!"

After a long hesitation, Scarlet replied. "James, why do you shout at me for something that happened over there, when I am over here?"

"Why do you speak only to Scarlet?" Green spoke in Standard for the first time. "You act as if Cloud Touching and Sun-and-Shadows and I never existed, and only she does. We learned your language, too," he said petulantly.

Jim looked from one flyer to the next, feeling confused. "She?" he said. "Who is she?"

"I am, in your language, she," Scarlet said. "What does that have to do with Green's question?"

"I hadn't realized . . ." Jim said.

"Why should you?" Scarlet said. "I see no reason for you to care one way or the other."

"You still have not answered my question," Green said.

"I don't have a good answer. I began by speaking to you, Scarlet. I got the feeling you were in charge."

"That was your perception, not reality," Scarlet said. "I told you we do not have leaders."

"Green, I apologize," Jim said. "I didn't mean to offend you."

Green flicked his tongue against the edge of his mustache. "You are but young," he said. He blinked.

*I'm* young? Jim thought. What about everybody else on this shuttlecraft?

"Captain! *Quundar* is going inside the worldship."

Jim joined Sulu, glad of an excuse to escape his own discomfort. *Quundar* arced up and over and inside the wall. "Increase velocity."

"Yes, sir." Sulu refrained from mentioning that *Quundar* was heavily armed and *Copernicus* carried no weapons at all. James Kirk knew that.

This was proving to be an interesting trip.

He paused at a ventral opening of an interior sphere, gazing into the beauty of the worldship, drinking the wind, spreading his arms to the light. The land lay many times his height below him, a moment's flight to reach.

But he could no longer fly. His voyage had changed him, the starship beings had changed him. They had taken his wings, half his sight and hearing, most of his ability to communicate. He cried out again into the silence of his mind. He received no reply, not even echoes.

He had spent time in silence, by his own choice, a response to grief and loss. Now he was forced into it. He could see only one course for his existence.

He began the long climb to the ground.

Koronin had wondered if the interior of the worldship would contain riches similar to the giant pearls outside. But when *Quundar* penetrated the light web that covered the sky, she found a landscape of plains and mountains, sparse forests, streams.

The transmission she followed emanated from a place high above the ground. A flock of the aliens played in the updrafts and eddies that whispered along the worldship's wall. The aliens circled her ship, diving, counting coup by brushing their wingtips against the outthrust control chamber. They impressed her with their disregard of danger, if not with their intelligence. One balanced on the bubble above her, azure flying webs folded. It leaped into the air, revealing the flame-yellow undersides of its blue wings. It soared off to join its fellows.

Three of the aliens landed on the ground. *Quundar* touched down near them at the base of the wall.

The aliens watched and waited, perhaps a hundred paces away. Koronin maintained an unhurried pose. Instead of rushing outside like a supplicant, she took her time. She secured the work crew within their stations. She collected portable sensors, translator, recorder. She put on a purple silk shirt, and the boots with the gold tracings. She fastened Starfleet's collar around his throat, ignoring his pitiful attempts to thrust his tiny hands between buckle and strap. She snapped his leash to the collar. Instead of following obediently, he held back. She tweaked the leash; when he could resist its pull no longer, he scampered past her and crouched till she passed him and jerked the leash again. It was most unsatisfactory. He needed more training.

"Come along," she said to the serjeant.

"Koronin, wouldn't it be better to break out more weapons? Shouldn't I stay here and guard you from inside?"

She laughed at him. "You need no weapons when you're with me. Come along. Now. Or I'll leash you, too."

He followed, unleashed but more docile than Starfleet.

The three worldship inhabitants watched in silence. Koronin approached, alternately dragging Starfleet behind her and jerking his collar when he fled too far ahead. The delicate breeze ruffled dust around her boots.

"I am Koronin," she said.

The three aliens sang together for an inordinately long

time. Both sensors and translator gibbered and babbled till she grew bored with them and shut them off. She had little use for scientific data, anyway. If things worked as she hoped, she would not have to understand the inhabitants. They would have to understand her.

The aliens' song soared beyond her range of hearing. She could tell they were still singing only by the movements in their throats and mouths. Finally they stopped.

"I am Koronin," she said again.

"I don't understand you," the golden-winged blue alien said. "Yours is a language Cloud Touching didn't give me. Do you have the means of conveying it?"

The creature spoke Federation Standard.

"What makes you think," Koronin said coldly, "that I speak the Federation's degenerate tongue?"

It began to speak another Federation language, one she did not understand but recognized as Vulcan.

"Stop!" Koronin said. If the Federation thought they could invade Empire space, claim the worldship, and subvert its inhabitants without a fight, they thought quite wrong. "I understand you. I will give you the means to learn my language soon, but Standard will suffice for the moment."

An alien, so purple it appeared black at certain angles, moved around her till it could see Starfleet. The primate fled. Koronin switched the leash from hand to hand to keep her pet from wrapping her legs in the strap. This was not properly dignified. She jerked hard on Starfleet's collar. He crouched, whimpered, peeked up, then hid his face.

"What is this?" the purple alien said. "Food?"

"No. I have resources. I feed pets, I don't eat them."

"Captive food is tasteless." The purple alien turned toward Koronin's serjeant. "This is a pet, too?"

The serjeant, having too little knowledge of Standard to be offended, stared agape at the alien.

"That is my serjeant. My subordinate."

"I heard you had such things. Pets. Things like pets."

"Who among you is the leader?" Koronin said.

The aliens spoke in their own language, rudely. Koronin had the impression they found her amusing. She put one hand on the haft of her dueling blade. It gave her comfort, though under these circumstances she would find her blaster more useful. Quicker. Though the aliens carried no mechanical weapons, their teeth and claws would be dangerous in hand-to-hand combat. She wondered where they kept their computer and transmitter. Perhaps in the bangles they wore. Perhaps some other entity kept the computer, and the flying creatures as well.

"It is contrary of you guests to ask for leaders," the third alien said. It had black fur dappled in gray on back and flanks and legs. "The more often the companionship tells you no leaders exist, the more often you ask for one."

"I have never—" She reined in her temper. The aliens implied she had asked the same question as the Federation invaders, so she would ask a question no member of the Federation ever asked. "I claim this land in the name of the empress. Do you dispute my authority?"

Ignoring her, the purple alien stroked Starfleet.

"I told you that isn't food!" Koronin shouted.

"I know," the alien said. "But it is unhappy." It unbuckled the collar from her pet's neck.

Koronin strode to the wall. Her blade sang like crystal when she drew it. The aliens could not know that when she acquired it, it had been transparent and colorless. It had grown dark with spilled blood. But the aliens could hardly fail to be impressed by the way the light of their strange world flared from the blade's edge. They could not fail to be impressed by what she was about to do.

She stopped beside the curved flank of a pearly sphere. She swept the blade above her head and sliced it down against the wall.

The blade cut deep into the iridescent surface, gouging a deep, dramatic mark into the fabric of the worldship.

Koronin heard a keening wail, a combination of the song of the aliens and a high, agonized vibration. The silky webbing around the sphere trembled and contracted. Koronin wrenched her blade free, spun, and ran.

The sphere exploded against her back.

He saw the flying machine descend, and saw it land below; he heard the explosion, but needed his attention for the climb. The vibration nearly cost him his balance. Flinging himself into the webbing that linked the spheres, he hung on tight. When the wall's shuddering ceased, he continued his dogged descent.

Where the land met the wall, the flying machine rested on singed vegetation. Nearby, one wingless being crouched over another who lay motionless. The second being must have tried to damage a wall-sphere, and the wall-sphere had reacted. How foolish: people knew better than to behave like that before they ever left the aerie, if they were smart enough to live.

He smelled the scent of people, but none remained. High and distant, they parted from each other to return to a solitary way. He wondered if the wingless ones had bored the companionship, or simply disgusted them.

"You!"

The wingless being waved a bit of machinery. "Come over here! Carry my lady Koronin into the ship!"

He understood it poorly, but its meaning came across.

Sulu swooped *Copernicus* over the iridescent wall of the worldship, between the rays of the light web, and through the clouds to hover above the easy curves of the land.

*Dionysus* continued to ignore all transmissions.

"I will leave now," Green said.

"Green, I know I offended you," Jim said with consternation. "But it wasn't intentional. Please accept my apology. Please stay with us."

"You are but young," Green said again, his tone gentle. "You cannot offend me. I will leave because I am hungry, and because this enclosure cramps my wings."

"I wish you'd said something before—I'm sure we could have programmed the *Enterprise*'s synthesizer to produce something safe for you to eat."

"I saw your food," Green said. "It was dead."

"Many people find it quite palatable," Jim said.

"But it was *dead*." He made a sound of disgust.

"That's true . . . but most of us prefer it to be dead before we eat it." He chuckled. He stopped. "But you don't like it that way . . . do you?"

"Dead food makes one ill."

"I see." Jim thought he now understood Spock's reaction to watching other people eat animal protein. "Very well . . .

We'll land and let you out. I wouldn't keep you against your will."

"No need to land," Green said. He opened the hatch. The wind wailed in with cutting cold. Green leaped into the air. Jim lunged for the hatch. Ten meters below, Green fell as if in slow motion. He gradually extended his wing-fingers, putting himself first into a glide, then a turn, finally a high, fast soar.

"Will you come?" Sun-and-Shadows said. "Hunt with us."

"No," Scarlet said. "I'm not hungry yet."

"Good-bye."

Sun-and-Shadows leaped after Green. They soared into a duet of aerial acrobatics. They approached so closely that Jim caught his breath for fear they would collide, but they stroked each other with their wingtips and chased each other higher.

Lieutenant Uhura appeared beside Jim, watching the flyers and humming an eerie tune. She leaned toward the open hatchway. For an awful instant Jim thought she was going to plunge out into the sky. He grabbed her arm.

"Lieutenant Uhura!" She said nothing. Drawing her back, Jim closed the hatch. "What's wrong?"

She raised her head to look at him. Her face glowed with joy and wonder.

"Nothing, captain. Why do you ask?" She hummed again, a refrain Jim did not recognize.

Scarlet laid one long delicate arm across Uhura's shoulders. He—*she,* Jim reminded himself—let her wing-fingers open so her wing draped across Uhura's back like a scarlet cloak. She drew Uhura deeper into the shuttlecraft. She hummed a simple musical phrase. Uhura copied it. Scarlet hummed the phrase again; Uhura copied it with more assurance.

Jim left them humming to each other and rejoined Sulu at the controls.

"Any sign of *Dionysus?* Or of Athene?"

"Not yet, captain. They could be anywhere by now. *Quundar* has got to be around here someplace, though."

Jim gazed out the viewport, hoping for some sign of *Dionysus,* wondering if he preferred to have Koronin close enough to keep track of, or a long long way away. He searched the clouds, wondering if Lindy had finally found a place where Athene could fly.

That would be some sight, he thought. It would.

Koronin woke slowly and painfully. So, she thought, the oligarchy caught up to me faster than I believed it would . . . She opened her eyes.

She expected a prison cell or the interrogation chamber of a dreadnought. Instead, she found herself in her own bed. She sat up. Her body ached all over and her inner ears pained her. But she was alive, unwounded.

The serjeant dozed on the floor nearby. A poor job of guarding: she wondered why he had not simply locked her away.

Then she saw her dueling blade and her blaster, laid side by side at the foot of her bed. She picked up the blade. The edge was not so much chipped as melted away. She cursed.

"Koronin!" The serjeant clambered sleepily to his feet.

"Why did you bring me back?" Koronin said. "Why didn't you kill me and take the ship?"

"I offered you my loyalty," he said in a hurt voice.

She stared at him till he dropped his gaze. "Now," she said. "The truth."

"The empress's mercy is said to be expended. If I return, who would forgive me? I'm safer staying here. But I know my weaknesses, Koronin. I know your strengths. If you command *Quundar*, I may remain a free renegade. If I command it, I soon become an imprisoned renegade. Or a dead one."

"Did those aliens have a weapon? What happened?" Koronin slid her blaster beneath her belt. She would accept the serjeant's story, until the moment he overstepped his position and demanded her gratitude.

"I don't know, Koronin. It appeared to me that the surface of the sphere exploded."

"It defends itself." The unfamiliar voice spoke in Standard.

A Vulcan in black trousers, boots, a sleeveless black singlet—the remains of a Starfleet uniform—sat on the deck on the far side of the command balcony. A restraining forcefield shimmered around him.

"Can't anyone in this benighted place speak a civilized language?" Koronin shouted. "Who are you? What are you talking about?"

"I took him hostage," the serjeant said proudly.

"The worldship," the Vulcan said. "It defends itself."

"Captain, here's an odd reading."

The gray-green plain stretched beneath them, endless, featureless—except where Sulu had found the strange ground marking.

"Let's take a look."

Sulu guided the shuttlecraft to a landing.

The patch of scorched succulents and the crushed places in the vegetation traced out the lines of Koronin's fighter. The shattered sphere in the worldship wall added to the story.

"She must have fired at something," Jim said. His imagination set to work on the reasons Koronin might have used her blaster. He did not like any of the possible conclusions.

"You say 'fired,' James," Scarlet said. "This is a term associated with weapons?"

"Yes. She probably had a blaster. Look, the beam exploded the whole side of the wall-sphere."

"If she directed either energy or a projectile at the worldship wall, her ship would be spread in pieces on the field. So would she."

"What? How? I thought you didn't have any weapons."

"She forced the wall to react, and it reacted in a way commensurate with her actions. That is its design." Scarlet's tongue flicked over her sensory mustache.

"But if she didn't fire, what *did* she do? What did the wall react to? A fight? Could Spock . . ."

"I do not know, James."

Sulu picked up one of the iridescent fragments. Light streaked through the pearly surface. The dust of mother-of-pearl covered the ground. Sulu looked warily through the blasted hole. The wall-sphere was as beautiful inside as out, faintly luminescent, cool and mysterious. An opening in the lower curve of the sphere led deeper into the wall. Curious, Sulu entered the sphere and peered down.

A pale shiny *thing* reached out of the opening. Sulu yelped with surprise. He jumped back, by reflex grabbing his phaser. A synapse of caution kept him from drawing and firing. His boot slipped on the edge of the broken wall. He tumbled backward and bounced to the ground. In one-tenth g, he did not even fall hard enough for the broken shards to scratch him.

"Sulu! What is it?"

"I don't know, captain—there's something alive in there!" He climbed to his feet and brushed himself off. "It didn't do anything—it just startled me." He felt embarrassed. He returned to the opening. His boots crunched the shards. He touched his phaser again, then thought, If I'd fired it, it'd be me who was in pieces on the ground.

"What is that thing?"

Sulu peered into the sphere. The creature resembled the giant slugs he had seen on hikes across the northwest coast island where he had taken his vacation. But the earthly variety would barely span his hand. This one had oozed several meters of its length into the sphere as if it had every intention of filling the interior. Captain Kirk made an exclamation of surprise.

"It's only a builder," Scarlet said.

"A builder?" Jim said.

"They help maintain the structure of the wall. This one will secrete several layers onto the interior of the sphere till it makes the wall whole. It is quite harmless."

Jim glanced at the slimy and thoroughly repulsive-looking creature, and wondered . . .

Scarlet spread her wings with a snap of the webs, leaped, and flew nearly straight up the worldship wall.

"Wait!"

But the flyer's soaring climb never slackened.

Behind him, Uhura began to hum.

"Lieutenant Uhura?"

She remained where she was, gazing after Scarlet.

"Lieutenant Uhura! What about *Dionysus?*"

She acted as if she heard him from a great distance.

"Stephen doesn't answer," she said. "He's there. I know he's there. But he's silent."

Jim left her alone and sat on his heels beside the wall's jagged opening. "Can you hear me?"

"Yes, captain," Sulu replied.

Jim held up his hand in a quick "be silent" gesture.

"Can you hear me? Can you understand?" Jim spread his hands in the gesture of peace he had used with the flyers. He tried to imagine how a creature like the builder might indicate friendship, but he could come up with nothing better for the moment.

"No response," Sulu whispered. His tricorder warbled: background noise. "Nothing outside our range of sight and hearing, no chemical reaction, nothing resembling pheromones."

Jim stepped over the shelf of broken pearl. The creature continued to ooze into the sphere, creeping over the curved floor. Jim touched it, thinking, We come in peace.

He had to repress his gag reaction, for the touch of the creature was every bit as cold and slimy as its appearance hinted. He heard nothing and felt no response, except that the creature continued to expand. It pressed against him till it pushed him completely out of the worldship wall.

"James," Scarlet said, "what are you doing?"

Slime covered Jim's hands and his arm and his side, everywhere the giant slug had touched.

"I was trying to communicate with the builders of the worldship," he said.

"Why?"

"Why? Because you said you didn't create the worldship."

"I didn't. How could I, or anyone else alive?"

"You said that was a builder." Jim pointed to the giant slug. Its slimy brown flank filled the broken segment of the sphere. "I don't care if I talk to exactly the people who built the worldship. But I want to talk to their descendants, to people who have the ability to build it." The slime hardened, taking on its pearly sheen. Jim rubbed his hands together. Dusty iridescent flakes drifted away.

"People did not build the worldship. Builders built it. But

people created the worldship in their minds, and they created the builders to make it real. People created everything you see. I am among the descendants of the people who created the worldship. You have talked to me."

"But you said—" Jim stopped. The discussion had consisted of one misapprehension after another. "What I meant by my question was, did people like you create the worldship?"

"Oh," Scarlet said. "Yes. Of course they did. But that isn't what you asked me."

"I understand that now. Do *you* know how it was made?"

"Of course."

"Could you make another?"

"Not while this one exists. Two entities cannot occupy the center of the universe at the same time." Scarlet sang a trill that made Jim shiver. Lieutenant Uhura responded.

Jim wondered what other misunderstandings lay hidden among his assumptions about Scarlet. He tried to think of a way to rephrase the question, but Uhura's and Scarlet's singing distracted him. He felt like he was trying to solve a difficult mathematical equation in his head while standing between the tenor and the soprano during a passionate duet in a grand opera. He clapped his hands over his ears. "Could you two stop for just a minute? I can't hear myself think!"

They stopped. Jim could not read Scarlet's expression, but Uhura's was shocked and hurt.

"I found this in the passage above." Scarlet held something out to him. "But I saw no sign of Spock, there or on the land around us."

Uhura hummed again, the sound like a whisper.

Jim took Commander Spock's blue uniform shirt from Scarlet's hand.

# Chapter 12

THE DIRECTOR OF the oversight committee, pacing the command balcony of his fleet's flagship, tossed aside the reports from his myriad of spy probes. In the past, he might have found their information intriguing. In the future, he might review it and use it to eliminate or co-opt the petty thieves and smugglers and the minor traitors it had exposed. So far, though, the information gave him nothing that he wanted.

"Sir—!" His adjutant hurriedly saluted. "The captain begs your attendance."

"More reports?"

"We've reached the Phalanx, sir."

The flagship captain hovered over the sensor stations, astounded by their findings but not quite ready to believe them.

"The Federation has broken all agreements, tacit and stated, signed and unsigned. This is no natural phenomenon! It can have no purpose but as a staging area for war!" He turned in awe to the director. "Sir . . . our intelligence had no hint of this. How did you *know?*"

The director had spent his career taking credit for whatever would benefit him, even when it meant disguising luck, or lies, or uncertain information as preternatural knowledge.

"I may not speak of state secrets," he said.

"Of course, director, I understand—please pardon me."

"What of the captured prototype?" the director said, trying to sound indifferent.

"What?" The captain's expression slowly gained comprehension. "The new fighting ship? Oh, it's there, director. This is its sensor signature." He pointed out a small set of speckles among an enormous pattern. His brow ridges darkened with excitement. "We'll soon punish the Federation for its arrogance."

The director regarded the image, wondering if the fleet captain really believed the Federation responsible for what they had found, or if he were being ingenuous. The director knew the Federation had nothing to match this.

The display extended across the width of the command balcony. Its insubstantial edges flowed around the director, the captain, and the adjutant like a flood around small islands, and still it could barely contain the image of the incredible alien starship.

On the bridge of the *Enterprise*, Chief Engineer Scott uneasily occupied the command position. He had only a little time left before he would have to make the decision about pulling back. His orders left him no leeway. He worried about the shuttlecraft. He had no faith in Mr. Sulu's piloting ability after his performance back at Spacedock.

Dr. McCoy came out of the lift.

"Dr. McCoy," Scott said, "should ye no' stay in bed? Ye look terrible."

"Thanks," McCoy said. "I'm glad to know I look better than I feel." His smile was sickly. "It hurts just as bad lying down as standing up, so I might as well know what's going on." He rubbed his eyes, his temples. "Mr. Spock has a lot to answer for, when Jim brings him back."

"If Captain Kirk brings him back."

At the helm, Pavel Chekov tried to convince himself he did not want to yawn. He usually stood low watch, during quiet late-night hours. Today he had been called out of sound sleep to take Mr. Sulu's post at the *Enterprise*'s helm. He was not yet quite awake.

He detected signals headed straight toward *Enterprise*, and adrenaline wiped away every wish for slumber.

"Mr. Scott—unidentified ship—no, ships—at scanner limits! Heading toward us, toward worldship, at high warp factor. From Klingon Empire!"

"Thank ye, Mr. Chekov," Commander Scott said. He waited.

"Scotty, you've got to warn Jim!"

"Nay, doctor—'twould alert the fleet that *Copernicus* is within their realm. If we're silent . . . perhaps they'll no' detect the shuttlecraft."

The Klingon fleet dropped from warp-speed to normal space and swept toward the worldship.

Scott held the *Enterprise* steady at the farthest edge of Federation space. The worldship drifted deeper into the Empire's realm.

Scott knew he would be challenged, and he knew James Kirk was right. He could not respond with force.

"Starfleet invaders, retreat to your own territory."

"There are those who'd say we're in our own territory," Scott replied. It was only ninety-nine percent bluff. The boundaries out here really were carelessly surveyed. The *Enterprise* drifted along the indeterminate border.

"Then they are fools." The person who appeared on the viewscreen wore elaborate civilian attire. Scott wondered what that meant, for this was a military fleet.

"I dinna catch your name," Scott said. "Who do I ha' the honor o' addressing? My name is—"

"Of no interest to me whatever. My name," he said, "is a state secret. You may address me as 'director,' or 'your honor.' "

"We canna leave!" Scott said, winging it. "We're on a mission o' mercy."

"Ah. You have traveled to this interesting construct between us, with the intent of rescuing it?" He spread sarcasm heavily on his words.

"I dinna know o' the worldship when I responded to the distress call. Did ye no' hear it? Did ye no' come to help?"

"The only one in need of help is you—because you're caught making preparations for the Federation's war."

"We came on a mission o' mercy," Scott said again.

Scott sweated through an interminable silence from the director.

"Your fantasies bore me," the director said when he deigned to speak again.

A powerful jamming field settled around them, cutting off the *Enterprise* from the shuttlecraft and from its captain.

"Mr. Scott, one of the fleet ships is changing course," Chekov said.

"I can see that, lad." One of the director's battle cruisers dropped toward the worldship.

"Scott, we've got to stop it!" McCoy said. "The shuttlecraft hasn't got a chance against a cruiser!"

"I canna stop it, Dr. McCoy," Scott said. "If 'twere offerin' a direct threat . . ." *And* if it were to leave its own realm . . . Then he might justify a fight. But as things stood, Scott had no legitimate excuse even to object to the fleet's presence. "I canna stop it. We can only hope it believes in mercy missions . . . or canna take the trouble to notice *Copernicus.*"

As *Quundar* thundered slowly over the land, as the land rose into abrupt crags, Koronin considered what the Vulcan hostage had told her. Good luck had saved her life when she struck the wall-sphere, for the worldship protected itself from impact by interstellar dust clouds, asteroids, stellar flares—or sword strikes—by turning the force back the way it had come. It possessed no intentional aggressive ability; in fact, its most extreme reaction was complete, irrevocable, annihilating retreat. It could be made to carry out a terrible revenge, once before it vanished. But that was for a last resort.

If Koronin wished to rule the worldship, she must begin by asserting her authority upon individual inhabitants. Soon they would give up concealing their leaders, denying the existence of leaders. She hoped she did not have to kill too many of the flying people before they surrendered. They intrigued her. Besides, she despised waste.

The Vulcan hostage slumped on the deck, his hands drooping at his sides, his knees pulled to his chest. He had not even tested the limits of the forcefield around him. He appeared uninjured, but he also appeared unwell.

She scanned again, searching for a flock of the aliens. She planned to demonstrate her power by shooting one down in view of the others.

"They've gone to ground, the cowards," she muttered. "But *where* . . .?"

"In the center."

She swung toward the Vulcan. He stared at her, strain and intensity in his gaunt face.

"What did you say?"

"They are in the center. Of the worldship."

"Who?"

"The silent ones."

"Make sense, Vulcan, or I'll rip the words out of you!"

She fancied that his solemn expression hinted at a smile. The mockery angered her. She already knew better than to threaten a Vulcan with pain.

"The silent ones are in the center of the worldship," he said. "And they are waiting."

That was as direct a threat as the fate she had offered him. Koronin laughed. A threat was a challenge, and a challenge, if taken up, could be won.

"They won't have to wait much longer," she said.

The worldship was thinly populated, its people solitary. By the time someone paid attention to Scarlet's request for help in locating *Dionysus,* Sulu had found the ship on scanners. *Copernicus* sped toward the location.

"Captain, look!" Sulu pointed.

High above them, soaring on ebony wings, Athene cavorted with one of the flying people. It skimmed beneath her, flicking a wingtip upward. She snapped at it playfully. It dodged and reversed to sail over her. She tried to follow it, turning so quickly she nearly stalled. The flyer noted her inexperience, stopped its aerobatics, and flew in a swift straight race.

Below, Lindy and Stephen sat on the yacht's skids, watching Athene fly. They waved as the shuttlecraft approached. Lindy met Jim when he opened the hatch.

Scarlet sailed after Athene and the other flyer.

"Can you believe her, Jim?" Lindy said. "She flies like she's been doing it all her life!" She grabbed his hands and swung around with him. "Isn't she beautiful?"

"She is," Jim said. "But can you get her to come down?"

"She'll come back eventually, Jim. I hate to call her, she's having so much fun—"

"We've got to get back to the *Enterprise*."

"Why?"

"Why? What do you mean, why? Lindy, you shouldn't have come here to begin with! You don't know anything about this place, it's about to move into hostile territory, a Klingon renegade has abducted Commander Spock, or arrested him as a spy—and she could have done the same with you!" He found himself shouting.

"Mr. Spock! Is he—? I'll bring Athene down."

She cupped her hands and whistled. Athene sailed higher and farther, a strangely shaped bird. Scarlet spiraled above her.

Jim strode over to Stephen, who lounged arrogantly against the landing skid of his yacht.

"It's one thing for you to put yourself in danger, Stephen," Jim said. "But Lindy? She's got no off-earth experience—she has no way of knowing what you might get her into!"

"I got her into keeping her horse from going insane," Stephen said. "If I'd kept in communication with the *Enterprise*, I just would have had to listen to you rant at me. Aren't you a little young—"

"I'm a little tired of hearing that I'm a little young, is what I am!" Jim said.

"—a little young to be so stodgy?" Stephen said.

Jim began a retort, but took hold of his temper instead.

"I've probably deserved that," he said. "But not this time. Stephen, I need your help. The *Enterprise* can't follow the worldship into Empire territory. Lindy's got to get out of here."

"What Lindy does is her own affair. But I'm staying. I have a lot to learn from the worldship people."

"What do you mean? Stephen, what are you planning? After what happened to Spock—?"

"I'm . . . different. It's none of your business. Maybe you can persuade Lindy to go back with you."

"I can't go back yet."

"After all your lecturing—!"

"Commander Spock has let himself be captured—kid-

300

napped—I don't know what to call it. I will *not* have one of my officers paraded as a spy." Far away on the plain, Athene touched down long enough for Lindy to swing up. The equiraptor cantered, galloped, glided. "Maybe I can persuade Lindy to transport back . . ."

"Forget it, unless you can transport Athene at the same time."

Jim knew Stephen was right. "Then it's got to be up to you. Please, get her to safety. We don't have the right to endanger her—"

"We don't have the right to dictate her life!" Stephen said.

"We don't have time to argue! The *Enterprise* will back off soon. If Lindy's stranded here . . . Look, if you want to come back afterwards, I can't stop you. I give you my word not to try."

"And in the meantime, you're taking a shuttlecraft after an armed fighter—to do what? Talk Spock free?"

"I don't know," Jim admitted.

"Sometimes," Stephen said, "I think Vulcans are right after all, and human beings *are* crazy." He hesitated. "All right. Let's get going."

Jim stuck out his hand, forgetting Stephen was a Vulcan, but before he could draw back, Stephen met his hand and clasped it.

Jim waved his arms, shouted for Scarlet, and sprinted for the shuttlecraft. Scarlet swooped down and followed him on board. As soon as the hatch closed, *Copernicus* lifted off.

Athene slowed to a canter, her hooves barely touching the ground. With a touch of Lindy's heels she would follow *Copernicus* into the sky. Instead, Lindy signaled for a halt with a shift of her weight. Athene spread her wings and slid to a standstill in front of Stephen.

"Where's Jim going?" Lindy slid from Athene's back. "What about Mr. Spock?"

"Jim went after him."

"Why didn't he wait for us?"

"Because you're supposed to go back to the *Enterprise.*"

"The hell I am!" Lindy said angrily. "Mr. Spock is lost out here somewhere. Let's go help find him."

Athene clattered on board, Stephen powered up his ship, and *Dionysus* roared after *Copernicus*.

For a moment of calm in the midst of chaos, Lindy had nothing to do. She stroked Athene's neck, but the equiraptor took the flight well and had no need of soothing. Lindy glanced at Stephen. He was completely involved in his ship, in navigating through this unfamiliar environment. His thin shiny shirt draped close around his shoulders; wisps of his fair soft hair curled over his collar.

Her thoughts kept returning to what Jim had said in the null-grav node of the *Enterprise*'s arboretum, when she told him she hoped Stephen reciprocated her feelings: "If he doesn't, you'll have to be careful not to use your position against him." Now she had to test the truth and strength of her own resolve not to let her disappointment make any difference. She would have to pretend that she had never offered and he had never refused, that she did not long to touch him, to feel his touch in return.

It would not be easy, pretending not to hurt. But she had a lot of practice at it. She knew she could do it.

But it would not be easy.

Scarlet watched the trace of *Quundar*'s drive. "Spock has persuaded Koronin to take him to the center."

"But why?" Jim asked. "How does Spock know anything about the worldship's center? You said it was wild . . ."

"Spock knows the same way he knew how to sail, and how to pass through the worldship's wall: he has some of my knowledge, as I have some of his."

"What's out there?"

"I fear for him, James. He is seeking the silent ones." Scarlet gazed unseeing at the trajectory formulae flickering across the screen.

"I don't know what you mean!"

"When you choose the life of a silent one, you heal yourself . . . or you die."

Jim scowled. "I doubt Koronin will let him do either."

On board *Quundar*, the pitiful animal cowered. He petted it. It feared him, yet desired his comfort. It clutched him, but trembled in terror of him. He whistled softly, trying to soothe it. How strange that it wore garments so similar to

302

his, though the upper garment he had dropped had been blue, while the animal's was gold.

A bit of knowledge crept into his consciousness: it was odd for an animal to wear clothing. But it was also unusual for people to wear garments when they did not need to be protected from space. So again he had the odd feeling of watching two incompatible images at the same time. He tried to make sense of them, but finally retreated in confusion and exhaustion.

He continued to pet the animal. Knowing the pain of his own confusion, he helped it forget its own.

"Vulcan—why are you crying?"

He raised his head. He tried to think of a reply to the strange, bare-faced, copper-haired being who approached him. But he was not even certain the being meant to address him. He felt the tears on his face, he tasted their salt warmth on his lips. He knew that people could cry, but did not feel grief—but he knew also that people could not cry, though they felt grief deeply. With a groan of despair, he pressed his hands to his temples and tried to understand what had happened to him. The small animal plucked at his arm with its tiny hand and made a soft, singing sound. But he felt no comfort. He knew only that he had to reach the center.

"They are waiting," he said.

Koronin cursed. If the Vulcan had lied about finding the rulers here, she would make him regret it. Other ways than pain could be found to distress him. Sensory deprivation might be a good place to start.

She wanted to play with Starfleet—or perhaps she disliked seeing the primate so content with its new friend—but it was too much trouble to get Starfleet out of the forcefield imprisoning the Vulcan. She shrugged and turned her attention to her ship.

*Quundar* reached the center of the worldship. The land below lay in jumbled destruction. If the worldship were made up of crustal plates like a real planet, then the plates jammed together here in the center. They crushed each other into abrupt mountain ranges, then crushed the ranges, working with such violence and geologic speed that erosion never softened the edges of broken stone.

"Where now, Vulcan?" Koronin said, suspicious. "What kind of rulers would choose a wasteland for their palaces?"

"Koronin!" The serjeant drew her attention to the image in the scanner. A flyer spiraled in an updraft. "You asked that one be captured . . ."

"Let it go," Koronin said. "No need to give the rulers warning of our power."

"To the ground," the Vulcan said. "They are waiting."

She landed on a tilted stone slab that in normal gravity would have been too steep to use. Her ship sighed between the crags to land at the top of a precipitous cliff.

Koronin permitted the Vulcan to walk out onto the warm stone.

She scanned the broken land. "There's nothing here, Vulcan. You've lied to me."

"I must . . . call them," he said. He breathed the thin air. In the mountains, the sky was very close. He searched the ravaged landscape with his gaze. He pointed to a solitary pinnacle, a broken corner of the slab on which they stood. It lay with its face almost perpendicular to the ground, at the edge of a cliff so high that the river at its base resembled a silver string. "There."

The wind scattered tiny stones at Koronin's feet. Her unclasped veil fluttered at her throat. She did not trust the Vulcan, and she wondered if he had the strength to climb that pinnacle. He looked none too steady on his feet.

"I've nothing to lose if you climb rocks to call to phantoms," she said. "Go."

He crossed the gray stone and began to climb. The serjeant peered after him.

"Koronin, these Vulcans, they're clever—he's planning some escape—"

"What will he do, sprout wings? Even Vulcans aren't that clever."

Bounding on all fours, Starfleet sped past her. She snatched at him, but her fingers only brushed the sleeve of his shirt. She took an angry step after him, but stopped. Like the Vulcan, her pet had nowhere to go.

*Copernicus* followed the trace of *Quundar* across the worldship's plain and over its central mountains.

"Lieutenant Uhura—see if you can raise the *Enterprise*."

Without replying, she bent over the console. She hummed an eerie phrase in an endless series of sequential variations. Every so often, Scarlet joined the melody with harmony or counterpoint or some accompaniment with no name.

Jim wished they would stop.

"No response, captain."

Scott's backed off, Jim thought. That's good. At least the ship is safe.

"We're making up distance, captain," Sulu said. *"Quun-dar* isn't designed to travel in the atmosphere—it has to move carefully." Then the aft sensors showed Sulu something he had not expected. "Captain Kirk—"

"One second," the captain said to Sulu. "Uhura—contact *Dionysus*. Ask Stephen to relay us the position of the *Enterprise* as soon as he gets out of the worldship."

"Yes, sir." She hummed as she complied.

"Captain . . ."

"What is it, Mr. Sulu?"

*"Dionysus* is right behind us."

"What!"


Wrapped in her fur cloak, Koronin sat on her heels and sharpened the slagged blade of her dueling sword. The Vulcan toiled up the nearly vertical pillar of stone. Starfleet clambered ahead of him, then scampered back to his side, a bright patch of gold against gray.

"Koronin, I could follow . . ." her serjeant said.

"When I want you to do something, I will tell you."

He subsided into a worried silence.

Koronin, too, felt uneasy, but not because she feared the Vulcan could escape. At first she could not identify the reason for her unease. Then the subsonic throbbing increased to a perceptible level. She felt as if she were inside an enormous drum. Its beat crushed against her.

She rose and looked into the sky.

The pulsation intensified. Only the thinness of the atmosphere prevented the pressure waves from evolving into a violent windstorm.

From beyond the peaks of distant mountains, a battle cruiser appeared. Above it, the light web sparked and dissolved, painting the starship in luminous colors that lasted an instant, then bled away in rainbow discharges.

The shock waves of the cruiser's antigrav field pressed her cloak against her. The vibrations changed as the cruiser rotated, nosing toward her with its bulbous prow.

Koronin strode toward *Quundar*. The serjeant stared at the cruiser, mesmerized.

"Come! Hurry!" she said.

"It might . . . it might not find us if we stay—"

"It will find us, you fool, if it hasn't already!" Koronin spun the serjeant around and shoved him toward *Quundar*. "Do you want to be caught helpless on the ground?"

He started toward the ship, then, irrational, he stopped. "The Vulcan—!"

"Forget the Vulcan!" She sprang into *Quundar* and started the launch sequence. The hatch rose. She heard the serjeant scrabbling on the stairs. The idiot! What good did he think a Vulcan hostage would do her? She could imagine saying to the captain of the fleet, "You cannot fire on me because I hold hostage a member of the Federation of Planets." The blast of a torpedo would reach her before she ever heard the laughter.

The hatch sealed itself. Koronin noted with complete indifference that the serjeant had made it inside.

"Station!" she shouted.

She heard no activity on the transmission frequencies, no coordination of an attack formation, only the crackling patina of a jamming field. Perhaps a single ship had followed; perhaps it had not yet found *Quundar* against the chaos of the worldship's center.

The jamming field faded briefly on a single channel.

"Koronin, surrender the ship and I'll allow you to survive!"

She hurried the preparations for liftoff. She did not believe the smooth promise. Survive? Yes, certainly—for as long as the oligarchs could contrive to make her life last. They would drag it from her atom by atom. She preferred a blast of flame and vacuum.

"Shoot me down, if you can," she replied. "Or are you as cowardly as the miserable captain who gave me this ship?"

*Quundar* lifted off and accelerated at a dangerous rate. The bow ports glowed with the heat of friction and the structure groaned with the strain of a full-power launch through the atmosphere. It plunged between the strands of the light web and gained the freedom of space.

Beyond the light web, the sight of the rest of the fleet blasted her illusions of escape.

In the flagship, the director dragged the captain away from the command console. In a fury, the captain tried to free himself and complete the attack sequence.

"You'll have her soon, captain. She's trapped." The director raised his open hand and slowly squeezed his fingers into a fist. "And your orders were *not* to fire!"

"She insulted me—!"

The director heard in the fleet captain's tone the accusation of cowardice.

"The empress gives no commendations for destroying our own prototypes."

"The renegade deserves to die!" the captain growled, trying to excuse his rashness.

"And she will," the director said, savoring the words. "She will beg for her death. She is not yet ready to beg."

Slowly, ponderously, the enormous dreadnought rose from the worldship. Koronin was trapped.

Almost directly below, Sulu struggled to hold *Copernicus* steady against the turbulent antigravity pulses. The shuttlecraft plunged and bucked like a maddened animal, like one of Dr. McCoy's rafts in a twisted four-dimensional waterfall.

The pummeling ceased.

The shuttlecraft sailed onward. The waterfall transformed itself into a limpid stream.

Above *Copernicus*, the light webs re-formed. The dreadnought had passed over *Copernicus* and vanished as abruptly and as astonishingly as one of Lindy's illusions.

It had in sight more important quarry than *Copernicus*: Koronin's ship, fleeing into space just ahead of the dreadnought. With Commander Spock aboard.

Jim cursed. The Empire would get incredible propaganda out of a captured Vulcan Starfleet officer. First they would wring a confession from him. Jim doubted even a Vulcan could hold out against their methods of persuasion. As difficult as Jim found Commander Spock to deal with, he did not wish this fate on any being.

"James . . ." Scarlet said. "Spock must have convinced Koronin she would serve her own interests by bringing him here. He is seeking the sky. Perhaps he persuaded her to let him out . . ."

"—and maybe she took off without him—?"

"It is possible."

Koronin had ascended from beyond a high, jagged peak. *Copernicus* circled the mountain and came upon fields of tumbled, broken rock, canyons, cliffs, a vast landscape of rubble in which Commander Spock might be lost. They followed *Quundar*'s trace as far as they could, but the backwash of its abrupt departure muddled the trail to its landing spot.

Scarlet opened the shuttle hatch and dove out to fly, so their search area would be increased.

"Mr. Sulu," Jim said, "touch down long enough for me to get out. Lieutenant Uhura, do you feel up to a ground search?"

"Certainly, Captain Kirk . . . why shouldn't I?"

He was troubled by the distant look in her eyes, by her obsession with the language of the flyers. But she did not seem to have anything physically wrong with her.

"Come with me. There are a million places Commander Spock could be hidden from the air."

"You can't search a million places on foot, captain."

"I'm aware of that, Mr. Sulu." He was also aware that he could turn back now. Koronin would soon be in the hands of the dreadnought. If Commander Spock was with her, then he was lost, and nothing Jim could do would save the Federation from an ugly public trial. If the Vulcan had escaped into the wasteland below, he might never be found. "I *am* aware of that," Jim said again to Sulu. "Dammit! I didn't come this far just to quit! We'll stretch our resources to the limit for one hour. After that, we'll have no choice but to return to the *Enterprise*."

*Quundar* sped out of the worldship. The fleet hemmed the fighter in. An escape into hyperspace would be useless, for the larger craft could outdistance *Quundar*. Koronin's ship had been designed for attack conditions: speed and agility and powerful acceleration in normal space.

She feinted toward one of the cruisers, teasing it, daring it to fire on her, accelerating at the last instant to try to slip by. It and a second craft laced together a threatening forcefield net. Their actions told Koronin for certain that the fleet had no intention of destroying her. They would hunt her down and capture her; she had only one other choice.

*Copernicus* touched down, *Dionysus* close behind. Jim and Uhura left the shuttlecraft. Sulu took off again to continue the air search.

Lindy led Athene out of *Dionysus*.

"Lindy—don't, dammit, I asked you to go back to the *Enterprise*—"

"I'm going to look for Mr. Spock. I'll take Athene up as soon as I can. The gravity storm spooked her." Her voice was taut with worry, both for Spock and for the equiraptor. Blood flowed from a gash across Athene's near foreleg. Lindy knelt to bandage it.

*Dionysus* lifted off again before Jim could tell Stephen what he thought of him. Angry, Jim strode past Lindy and Athene and stared at the endless landscape of sheer drops and abrupt outcroppings—

The granite surface of the pinnacle's sheer face felt rough and cold against his bruised cheek. Above him, Starfleet clung to the pinnacle's tip. Sighing with the wind, the primate reached out, as if its minuscule strength could help him climb the last few lengths of stone.

He looked down. The height revived him. The cold wind dried his sweat and soothed the scrapes and bruises on his hands and arms and face. He tried to make sense of the changes he felt. This was the way people had dealt with grief and pain since they *were* people, by coming to the wilderness and healing themselves in solitude and freedom. Other vague memories troubled him, intimations of different ways, but he could neither recall them completely nor escape them.

He stood up, balancing precariously on the soaring spear of stone.

—and at Commander Spock's tall, gaunt figure, high on a granite spire, spreading his arms to the wind as if he had wings.

Jim had no time to consider, no time to explain, no time even to think.

"Lindy! Look out!" He ran toward Athene. He stepped just wrong on his right leg, hearing the twist and snap of the joint but barely feeling it, anyway it did not matter, one more step and he lunged over Athene's hindquarters and onto her back and propelled her forward with his heels and his voice. Lindy jumped away with a shout of surprise. Athene plunged into a rough gallop. She, too, favored one knee. Jim clutched her mane. Her wings spread and rose and beat. She lurched into the air. Her feathers brushed against him from ankle to shoulder. He wished he had flown on Athene, not just ridden her. He wished Athene liked him better. He wished she had a bridle.

He leaned into a turn. Athene responded, flying toward Spock. The Vulcan looked exhausted and confused and at the limits of his strength. He wavered.

Athene swooped past him. As Spock's legs buckled, Jim grabbed him by one arm. Spock fell against Athene's side. The extra weight and the abrupt, awkward change made her falter. Her wings hesitated, then pounded harder as she struggled to remain in the air.

Jim barely kept his seat. Though Spock weighed little, the low gravity did not diminish his mass, his inertia. Jim had no leverage. Leaning sideways with his arm extended against Athene's flank, he dragged Spock along. He clamped his legs to Athene's sides. Pain stabbed through his knee.

"Commander Spock! Dammit, give me some help!"

Athene's wing joints squeezed against his knees with every downbeat. The stiff primaries scraped against his face and neck with each upswing. His sweating hand slid on Spock's wrist. Athene labored to turn, struggling across a canyon so deep that its river flowed among wall-spheres, the bedrock of the worldship.

Jim heard the beating of a second pair of wings. But if

Scarlet could have helped another flyer carry a disabled person, she could not help Athene.

Slowly, painfully, the Vulcan's fingers clasped Jim's wrist. He reached up with his other hand and grabbed Jim's arm.

Jim pulled him upward. The Vulcan clambered onto Athene's back.

Starfleet scrambled up from where it had been desperately clutching Spock's ankle.

Athene touched down, stumbled, recovered, stretched her wings wide, and came to a trembling halt. As she limped toward Lindy, Jim sagged over her withers. He could hardly believe he was on the ground again. It seemed as if he had been aloft for an hour, but it could not have been more than a couple of minutes.

Lindy ran to him and eased Spock down. Jim dismounted, landing on his good leg, leaning against Athene's side to try to catch his breath.

"Jim, are you all right? Mr. Spock—?"

"I think so. Lindy, I'm sorry, I couldn't see any other way—I hope I didn't hurt her . . ."

Blood soaked the rough bandage on Athene's knee. The sight of it made Jim's knee feel as if someone were tickling the inside of the joint with one of Athene's wing feathers. He wished it would just hurt. He gritted his teeth and tightened all the muscles of his right leg.

His knee responded by folding away under him and pitching him unceremoniously to the ground.

Jim stood gingerly, his knee supported by a temporary splint from *Copernicus*'s first aid kit. Nearby, Athene nibbled Scarlet's shoulder as the flyer soothed her and Lindy rebandaged the cut across the equiraptor's foreleg. Starfleet climbed up Sulu and clung to his shoulder and his hair, screeching down at Ilya, who arched his back and fluffed his fur and spat and snarled while Sulu tried to untangle himself from the primate. Inside *Copernicus*, Uhura tried to contact the *Enterprise* through the jamming field, and whispered to herself in Scarlet's language.

Spock lay unconscious on the ground. Stephen, kneeling next to him, looked around and managed to smile. "We're quite a crew, aren't we?"

"Let's get out of here," Jim said. *"Dionysus* is faster than *Copernicus*——you take Lindy and Athene and Spock back to the *Enterprise.* I'll be right behind you."

Stephen calculated instantly that the proposal would not work. "We don't have time," he said. "Even if the *Enterprise* is still out there, Spock doesn't have time."

"I'm not going to risk the life of everybody here—!"

Stephen launched himself at Jim, to grab him by the shirt and shake him in fury. But in the low gravity, the motion flung them both tumbling into the air. They came down in a tangle, bouncing. Athene shied sideways, snorting.

"What's the matter with you guys?" Lindy shouted.

"If I'm willing to risk my life you can at least cooperate!" Stephen shouted at Jim. He picked himself up. He felt angry, truly angry, but the feeling snapped itself out of reach, and vanished.

Jim rose. "What do you mean, risk *your* life?"

"If I mind-meld with Spock when he's in this state, I might be able to bring him out of it—or we might both end up in a coma."

"I can't permit—"

"You don't have anything to say about it!" Stephen picked Spock up and carried him into *Copernicus.*

Fuming, Jim watched him go. They could not just sit here in the open as the worldship drifted farther and farther from Federation space. They could not just sit and wait for the Klingon battle cruiser to take care of Koronin and come back after them. If the Empire could wring propaganda value from one Starfleet officer, imagine what it could do with four, one of them a captain of recent notoriety.

"Mr. Sulu—"

*"What?"* Sulu said, distracted by the fact that Starfleet had clamped its hands and feet in his hair and ear and the collar of his shirt. "I mean, yes, sir?"

"Can you fly *Dionysus?"*

Starfleet plastered one hand across Sulu's mouth, muffling whatever the lieutenant might have said, which Jim suspected had nothing to do with Stephen's ship. Sulu persuaded Starfleet to stay wrapped around his upper arm.

Jim was glad Starfleet had adopted the lieutenant. The primate gave him the creeps.

"I can fly an admiral's yacht, captain," Sulu said.

"Good."

In the aft cabin of *Copernicus*, Stephen laid Spock on a bunk formed from unfolded seats.

Spock's face, in unconsciousness, relaxed into a truer, more vulnerable image. Stephen smoothed Spock's hair into its usual patent-leather impeccability.

The composed Starfleet officer had vanished. Spock's bruised cheek and developing black eye and his neatened hair gave him the appearance of a small boy who had disobeyed his parents' orders to stay clean because company was coming, who had instead played with the other children and got hit with a baseball, but was bluffing it out. Stephen tried to smile at the image, but the necessity of focusing his attention drew him inexorably into an emotionless Vulcan state of mind.

"Stephen?"

Stephen looked up blankly.

"Can you help him?" Jim Kirk asked.

"I will try," he said, his voice cold.

The captain frowned. "Are you all right?"

"It has been a very long time since I attempted deep trance." Stephen changed. He abandoned his desperate determination to feel as well as think; he grew impassive, cool, and disinterested. He felt no apprehension about the risk.

Mind-melding with an injured intelligence is dangerous. Only a dangerous process can save Spock's life. Only a Vulcan can conduct the process. I am—still—a Vulcan. Therefore, I must make the attempt. Q.E.D.

The logical, rational progression could result in two deaths.

"Stephen—" Jim said.

Stephen turned away. He knew, intellectually, that a word of reassurance would ease the captain's worries. But a word of reassurance would be a lie. A direct lie was inconceivable, reassurance meaningless.

For Stephen, James Kirk ceased to exist.

Spock grew weaker. He depleted his mental and physical resources in an attempt to reconcile Scarlet's memories and knowledge with his own lifetime of study. Stephen could sense the tendrils of confusion interweaving and contorting, dragging Spock into darkness like a weighted net.

Stephen placed his fingertips at Spock's temples, accepted pain, grief, and confusion, and took a slow breath.

He let his intellect sink through the layers of Spock's mind. Stephen believed the mind-melding ability descended to his people from the time before they had put aside any reliance on emotion, from the time when close emotional connections helped ensure survival in a difficult land. His experience with mind-melding had helped him understand, and regret, what Vulcans had given up.

Stephen encountered the memories that Spock had perceived, Scarlet's memories. Their power astonished him. No wonder Spock had been left stunned and confused. Stephen wondered if he himself would have survived the direct connection.

The flying people existed for intensity of experience. They had designed and constructed the worldship on the basis of a technology far beyond the Federation's electronic and mechanical abilities. To a superficial inspection, their work looked mysteriously like no technology at all.

They understood it so well that they thought about it as often as they thought about breathing. They did not need to think about it. And so they had freed themselves to concentrate on a life of the mind. Stephen hesitated, awed by even a shadowy third-hand reflection of Scarlet's reality. Philosophy and imagination, reminiscences and fantasies, generations of stories from her ancestors, from the worldship's poets, physics and mathematics so esoteric that they became indistinguishable from philosophy and poetry: all expressed in the language of the flyers, a language of which not a single word could be translated (it did not use words), but which Stephen felt he understood all the way to the atoms of his substance.

Stephen experienced the exhilaration of Scarlet's flights through thunderstorms, the pain of a lightning strike across one wing, the terror of a thousand-meter freefall before she struggled back into exhilarated flight.

And finally, deepest and most powerful, Stephen felt the love and grief that had overpowered Spock and drawn him inexorably to the wild center of the worldship, where flyers came to be silent and to heal themselves, or to die.

Spock had come very close to dying.

When two flying people chose to love each other, their love crossed the whole spectrum of the word's meanings. Scarlet and her mate loved each other in that way, and fiercely. When he died, her love transmuted to grief.

Scarlet overcame the pain and the loneliness during her long sojourn in silence. But she had not forgotten it. It would never occur to her to try to forget it.

Poor Spock, Stephen thought. Vulcans claim they control all their emotions in order to eliminate anger and violence, as if anger were the hardest thing to conquer. But it's ridiculously simple compared to grief, compared to love. And Spock ran head-on into both.

Stephen let himself drift deeper.

Something had gone wrong with Stephen's training. He had learned his lessons well: he had completely conquered his own emotional responses. And yet, once he hid his emotions away where he could no longer find them, his wish to experience them remained. But Spock, who wished to achieve the perfect ideal of control, who almost always succeeded in outwardly maintaining it, was not nearly so unfeeling as the image he presented to the world.

Stephen envied him bitterly.

Stephen felt a silent presence observing him.

Spock? he said in his mind.

I did not recognize you in your Vulcan avatar, Spock said to Stephen, more clearly than if they were speaking face to face.

Stephen felt a quick flicker of his own true joy. Like a shivering child he grasped it and tried to fan it into a flame.

The spark faded, and Stephen knew that he lacked the ability to make it return.

Do you know where you are, Spock? he said. Do you remember what happened?

Yes, Spock replied.

Come with me. Come back. Your body weakens.

I cannot, Spock said.

You have no choice!

I have a choice. I choose to send you back to the world alone.

But why?

Spock hesitated.

What I experienced . . . he replied. But the thought faded, incomplete.

Stephen realized how much Scarlet's exhilarating emotions had distressed Spock. They had driven him to this featureless place, and now they blocked his return.

If he had been talking to Spock face to face, he would have put on an act of extreme emotion, shouted at him, taunted him . . . But here, everything he said had to be true. The connection between them permitted no deception.

You survived once, Stephen said. Surely you can survive again.

You do not understand, Spock said. You . . . cannot.

No, Stephen admitted. I cannot. I wish I could.

You are a fool, Spock said, with exhausted anger. You have always been a fool. You were the best of us, the most promising of a generation. When we were children I admired you above all others, though I knew the emotion to be unseemly, unworthy of a Vulcan. At times I even envied you. Self-discipline and self-control came so easily to you. But you threw them away.

I fled them, Stephen said. They pursue me, and I cannot escape them. Spock, when we were children I did not envy you—

Of course not. You felt nothing.

—but I do now. I have progressed that far.

Stephen, Spock said, if you succeed in this quest, it will only give you pain.

Even pain would be preferable to nothingness. Spock—we could have helped each other when we were children. We never did. Now we must. Come with me. We can go back together.

The silence stretched on so long that Stephen thought Spock had slipped away forever.

Spock—?

Very well, Spock said quietly.

The labyrinthine pattern of Scarlet's experiences closed in around Stephen as he sought to return. Fascinated, mesmerized, he moved deeper into it. He knew that if he lost himself in the maze, if he let the maze permeate his spirit, its power would permit him to reach his own center, which had been locked away so long.

Then he felt Spock drifting from him. He realized how close to his limits Spock had pressed himself.

Unwillingly, Stephen retreated from the perceptions he found so tempting. He abandoned the complex path and returned to one of simplicity.

Come with me, Spock, he said.

The shadowy presence responded, reaching out for him, gratefully accepting the strength Stephen offered.

The memories and perceptions weakened, faded, vanished. Spock shut them away, freeing himself from them, taking them forever beyond Stephen's grasp.

Regaining consciousness, Spock raised himself from the bunk in the aft cabin of *Copernicus*. He watched dispassionately as Stephen sagged onto one of the passenger benches, hunched around himself as if he were cold, and fell into an exhausted sleep. His long gold hair, damp with sweat, curled against his forehead and his neck.

Spock, too, felt drained. He remembered everything that had happened since he communicated with Scarlet in the grassy shuttlecraft bay.

He remembered everything.

He remembered the blast of hot wind as *Quundar* accelerated toward the worldship's sky; he remembered the pulsing gravity waves of the Klingon dreadnought ploughing away in pursuit.

And he remembered what would happen if the dreadnought opened fire and a stray volley hit the worldship.

He hurried forward.

"Captain Kirk—"

"Spock—! What happened? Is Stephen—"

"Are you in communication with the *Enterprise?*"

"No, it's out of range, or jammed—I don't even want to consider the possibility that Mr. Scott took the ship into battle—"

"We may already be too late. If Koronin has provoked an attack from the dreadnought, if Mr. Scott has engaged the Empire forces . . . Captain, a dreadnought torpedo, an

*Enterprise* phaser volley—either would deliver enough energy to cross the worldship's reaction threshold."

"Anybody who starts flinging torpedoes at an unknown starship deserves to have their ship blown away," Kirk said in a clipped impatient tone. "It just better not be Scott who does the flinging."

Spock regarded James Kirk with a grudging admiration. He knew human beings were more emotional than Vulcans; he had never before realized that they could also be much colder.

"Your equanimity is . . . impressive, captain. Even a Vulcan would have difficulty contemplating this magnitude of destruction with dispassion."

"The loss of a ship and its crew is tragic, of course," Kirk said quickly. "But—"

Spock realized that Captain Kirk did not yet comprehend the enormous destructive potential of the worldship.

"Captain, we are not speaking of the loss of a single ship. If violent attack causes the worldship to reach threshold, the universe will displace itself by approximately one hundred thousand light-years. An uncontrolled change of state of the universe would result in the destruction, by nova or collapse, of every star that passed the worldship for approximately one hundred light-years."

Captain Kirk and Lieutenant Uhura stared at Spock, uncomprehending.

"Captain . . . if the forces outside have engaged in battle, it is likely that the worldship is—that we are—unimaginably distant from our homes. It is likely that the worldship left devastation—"

Jim flung *Copernicus* into full forward acceleration. He rammed it through the light web, through the energy currents. He plunged into space, seeking a familiar sky, or the constellations of a universe a hundred thousand light-years away.

The shuttlecraft emerged from the worldship. The worldship remained where it had been, drifting through the territory disputed by Federation and Empire. But instead of a single dreadnought, a whole fleet surrounded the worldship. As the ships closed in, *Quundar* dodged and feinted, taunted and teased. *Copernicus* lay right in the path of the chase.

The sensors picked up the *Enterprise,* poised at the edge of Federation space as if ready to plunge forward.

"Good work, Scott!" Jim exclaimed. "Keep it up, don't lose your nerve, *stay* there." But Scott could not hear him. "Uhura, put every bit of transmission power on one hailing channel. We've got to try to break the jamming!"

She sang a few words under her breath; in a moment he had the channel he requested.

"James Kirk of the starship *Enterprise* calling fleet captain. *Do not fire!* I repeat, do not fire. The worldship meets attack with attack. The consequences are inconceivable!"

The fleet was so close that Jim felt his transmission *must* get through. It was so close he felt as if he ought to be able to shout at them, violate the laws of physics, and have the sound penetrate the vacuum. They had not fired yet, but Koronin continued to taunt and evade them. If one weapons-master decided he no longer cared if they took her alive—

The fleet pulled its net tight, contracting around *Quundar* and *Copernicus* as well. Jim knew how it must look to Scott aboard the *Enterprise.*

Would I have the nerve to stand still under these conditions? Jim wondered. He could not answer.

Koronin abruptly decelerated.

*Quundar* hung dead in space, waiting for the net to haul it in.

Jim stopped shouting his warning and sagged back in the pilot's seat. He was drenched with sweat.

The danger was over.

At Koronin's command, *Quundar* decelerated and drifted, dead in space. She looked at her star map, considering. If the Vulcan had told her the truth, she could power *Quundar* to the extremes of acceleration and aim it into the worldship wall. If the Vulcan had told her the truth, the worldship would drag the universe across a transverse vector and rip a swath of destruction through space-time. She could choose the direction: plunging into one side would cause it to react toward the Federation; the opposite would wreak destruction through the center of the Klingon Empire, a path a hundred light-years long of novaed stars and cindered planets.

ENTERPRISE

She began to understand the satisfaction of an unobserved revenge.

She caressed the controls of *Quundar.*

On board *Copernicus,* Jim saw the flicker of rocket ignition. "My gods," he said. "Does she prefer suicide to capture?"

"Quite possibly, captain," Spock said.

*Quundar* slowly spun toward the worldship.

"She knows," Spock said suddenly.

*"What?"*

"She *knows,* captain! She knows of the worldship's ultimate reaction. She intends suicide—and when she rams *Quundar* into the worldship, she will take half the Klingon Empire with her!"

*Quundar* hurtled toward the worldship.

Jim had not an instant's doubt of the truth of Spock's statement. *Quundar* would pass the shuttlecraft, slam into the worldship wall, and force a reaction from the flyers' home. Jim, and the *Enterprise,* and the Klingon fleet would have nothing left to do but watch the beginning of absolute destruction.

Jim's hand hesitated above a control. He had one choice left to make. If he did nothing, he must watch from safety as the worldship's reaction destroyed the suns and worlds of a hundred different star systems, systems inhabited by people who thought of him as the enemy. If he acted, he gambled death for Uhura and Stephen and Spock and himself against the minuscule chance of stopping *Quundar.*

The image of blood, ruby and emerald, swept over his sight.

Jim's hand shook. He cursed himself and slammed his palm against the control.

"Secure for impact!"

He rammed on every bit of power the shuttlecraft possessed.

The gravity died under the strain. It was just like Ghioghe again, the zero g, the punishing acceleration of the engines, and the sense of time coming to a halt.

Piloting Stephen's ship, Sulu saw *Copernicus's* change of course. He cut acceleration and turned *Dionysus* toward the worldship, keeping his touch light. For all its battered appearance, it responded instantly and with an on-edge tremble of power in reserve. It was no ordinary decommissioned admiral's yacht.

Sulu groaned a curse. Koronin planned suicide, and Captain Kirk was going to try to stop her. The shuttlecraft did not have a chance against the Klingon fighter. Sulu lunged for an unobtrusive set of controls: *Dionysus* was not as toothless as Stephen had claimed.

But then Sulu hesitated. He *could* shoot *Quundar* out of the sky. But James Kirk's first and strongest order had been to forbid the use of weapons. Sulu believed himself strong enough to disobey an order if he thought the cause right. But here and now, James Kirk was right. Firing on an Empire ship—even a renegade Empire ship—in Empire territory could too easily be misinterpreted as an act of war. Captain Kirk's order had been in the service of peace.

Sulu did not know why the captain turned *Copernicus* toward *Quundar,* why he chose to try to save Koronin's life at the risk of everyone on board his ship. But he did know that in only a few days' acquaintance, James Kirk had inspired in him a deep, strong trust. Sulu had only a few seconds in which to make his decision, a decision that could mean the deaths of four people he had already begun to admire, respect, and care for.

He withdrew his hands from *Dionysus*'s firing controls.

As *Quundar* sped toward *Copernicus* and the end of their violent, silent dance, Sulu cried out and turned away.

*Quundar* swept in from behind *Copernicus* with terrifying speed. Jim engaged the ventral steering rockets and wrenched his ship toward Koronin's.

The two spacecraft touched. The contact, for an instant, felt quite gentle. Then the hull transmitted the roar of *Quundar*'s engines and *Quundar* dragged itself across *Copernicus*'s dorsal surface with a shriek of rending metal. A glowing shower of molten alloy shards flew over their bow. Jim groaned, hearing and feeling the damage to his little ship, fearing that his desperation move had not perceptibly altered *Quundar*'s course. The aft section of *Quundar* rammed into *Copernicus*'s stern, catching the shuttlecraft and dragging it on toward the worldship. Jim shunted the shuttlecraft's drive force into the steering rockets. The lights flickered and failed. Reflected light from the web of the worldship provided the only illumination.

The wall of the worldship plunged toward him.

With a shout of rage and grief, his hands clenched on the controls, Jim willed the locked ships to turn.

The skid of *Copernicus* smashed against one wall-sphere. A tremendous explosion sent shuttlecraft and fighter tumbling. The impact flung Jim against a bulkhead.

The wail and scream of *Quundar*'s engines and the whisper of the steering rockets ceased, leaving *Copernicus* silent and dark.

# Chapter 13

RELEASED FROM STRESS, tortured metal creaked. The air reeked of ozone. Friction and overstrained engines penetrated the shielding with oppressive heat. The disorienting spin of a ship tumbling out of control gave a sense of erratic gravity, first strong, then almost nonexistent. Jim felt his body being pressed to the bulkhead, released to drift, then pulled down again, as if a tide, the memory of Ghioghe, had come to wash him away.

He tried not to open his eyes. He thought, If I never wake up, that means it's all a dream, it never happened, it never will happen, it isn't happening again. He let himself sink into the warmth and the oblivion.

A frightful cry of pain echoed through his darkness. Uncertain of what he had heard, whom he had heard, he dragged himself back to awareness.

A flash of light blinded him. He blinked, trying to get his bearings, trying to clear his sight. As the ship tumbled and the sensation of gravity pulsed, a single source poured light through the port for a few degrees of every spin. In the strobe-light illumination, Jim crawled toward the sound of crying.

Someone grasped his arm. His whole body chilled with the visceral memory, repeating: one of his crew members, dying, had reached out for help and found him, and died.

"Are you hurt? Gary—? Someone's hurt—"

"It's only Ilya, he's just miaowing."

The voice dissolved his visions. It was a voice from some other time, some other place, a beautiful voice. He could not

323

quite recognize it. He knew it meant he was not still at Ghioghe. But he knew it meant he was part of an even worse disaster.

"The worldship . . ." he whispered.

"It's all right," Uhura said. "You stopped Koronin, the worldship's still here."

Jim gasped, his breath nearly a sob. He shuddered with relief and abruptly released strain. Uhura reached toward him in a gesture of understanding, of comfort. At that moment the only thing Jim wanted was to collapse into her arms and let her soothe away the nightmares.

But James Kirk caught his breath and flung himself around, turning his back to her, embarrassed by his impulse. If he broke down now, how could he ever trust himself again, how could he ever call himself a captain? He grabbed the back of the pilot's chair and clenched his fingers around it. The ridge cut into his palms. The gravity rose and fell and the light of the worldship flashed each time the port faced it. He must try the engines, slow the spin, and get the tumbling shuttlecraft and himself back under control. But he could not make himself stop shaking. His vision blurred.

Behind him, Uhura sang a few wordless notes, slipping back into the flyers' language.

The high-frequency hum of a tractor beam filled the cabin. Another tractor beam cut in. The frequencies beat together, heterodyning, but the dizzying tumble slowed and finally stopped. The power systems of *Copernicus* began to recover. The emergency lights glowed faintly and gravity returned at a few percent of normal.

Jim wiped his forearm across his eyes, as if dashing the tears quickly away would make them never have existed. He straightened up and faced Uhura again.

"Lieutenant Uhura, I—"

She knew she should have pretended never to have seen the brief moment of pain in his eyes. She knew she had embarrassed him by witnessing his despair. She could not comfort him, she could not help him. She could do nothing more than pretend the last thirty seconds had never happened.

"Yes, captain. I'll—I'll contact the *Enterprise* immediately."

Spock heard the voices of Captain Kirk and Lieutenant Uhura and knew they had survived. James Kirk's impulsive act had turned *Quundar*'s suicide crash into a glancing blow.

Spock climbed through the erratic gravity to the aft cabin of the shuttlecraft. The forest cat had retreated to a corner. He howled piteously, but the strength of his cries indicated that he was unhurt. Spock was not so certain of Stephen. The crash had flung him from the bench. He lay on the floor, still huddled around himself, shivering.

The tractor beams slowed and stopped the spin of *Copernicus*. Spock carried Stephen to the fold-out bunk and found a blanket in a storage bay.

When he returned, Ilya had left his hiding place. He curled in the crook of Stephen's elbow, purring as if to call the attention of enemies to the threat he posed. Ilya blinked at Spock, slowly, grandly, and deigned to permit him to approach.

As Spock spread the blanket over Stephen, he contemplated the other Vulcan. The tenuous family connections between Stephen and Spock could hardly explain why Stephen had chosen to endanger himself. Helping Spock escape the powerful enchantment of the flyer's mind could have pulled Stephen into the same complex fugue. Stephen had chosen to risk death in return for an emotional experience.

But perhaps Stephen had known all along that he would only be tantalized by the experience that had overwhelmed Spock. As he had when they were children, Spock envied the underlying equanimity that Stephen tried so hard to break.

Spock wondered if he would ever understand Stephen on even the most superficial level. He doubted it.

Spock admitted to himself a reaction of embarrassment at having permitted Scarlet's experiences to overwhelm him. He should have been stronger. Given time, he would have brought the alien feelings and knowledge under control without Stephen's help. He felt sure of it. Nearly sure . . . fairly sure.

Spock realized he had nothing on from the waist up but the shredded remains of his black singlet. This, too, embarrassed him. His uniform shirt had been tossed onto one of the seats. It was dusty from being dropped in the tunnel of the worldship wall, but otherwise undamaged. He pulled off the ruined singlet and put on his uniform shirt.

"Commander Spock."

Spock turned. "Yes, captain."

"Is Stephen injured?"

"No, captain. He is asleep."

"Asleep? He wasn't injured by the . . . ordeal?"

"As I explained to you, Captain Kirk, he is a pursuer of sensation, emotional or physical. Whatever he experienced, he sought out."

"You speak very coldly of a man who saved your life."

"You asked me a question. I answered it."

"You appear to have come out of this unscathed."

"I am physically and intellectually undamaged. I was in control of my faculties when I set out upon this course of action. Therefore, on my return to the *Enterprise,* I will submit myself to Security, preparatory to a court-martial."

Kirk frowned. "A court-martial!"

"Certainly, captain." Spock wondered if Kirk truly had not thought beyond this moment, if his mind worked on such an intense focus that he had to be told the consequences of what Spock had done. "You have no choice but to court-martial me."

"There are *always* choices, Spock," Captain Kirk said gently.

"I disagree. Sometimes circumstances demand a single course of action. I believe that if you consider the problem logically, you will come to the same conclusion. Though I confess," Spock said, curiosity in his tone, "that I do not understand how any conceivable logical progression of thought caused you to behave as you did."

"What particular behavior are you questioning, commander?" Kirk said sharply.

Spock wondered what had caused the captain's tone of voice to change so suddenly. "Your decision to come to the worldship. Your pursuit of *Quundar.* Your flight to the rock pinnacle."

"I came to the worldship to get Lindy. It had nothing to do with you. But—you allowed yourself to be captured. The Empire would have submitted you to coercion, and then

326

they would have tried you for espionage! Didn't you realize you were compromising yourself—and Starfleet, and the whole Federation—with your irrational acts?"

"I performed no irrational act," Spock said.

"You don't call mind-melding with a completely unknown alien species an irrational, impulsive act?"

"Certainly not, captain. It was obvious that we could never begin to communicate with the flying people until someone took drastic action. Once a decision is made, it is pointless to delay implementing it."

"You endangered yourself, and you endangered my ship." He paused, and his expression hardened. "Perhaps you're right—perhaps you'd *better* prepare yourself to accept the consequences of those actions."

"As I have already stated, I am prepared. But you, too, endangered yourself by what you did. Some might judge that you also risked the ship. Captain, you have not explained why you prevented me from falling from the pinnacle."

Kirk gave him a strange look. "Maybe I'm just a thrill-seeker, like Stephen."

Jim returned to the main cabin of *Copernicus* and tried to get some reaction from the control panel of the shuttlecraft, while Uhura attempted to resuscitate communications. He could hear her humming under her breath as she worked.

Irrational acts, Jim thought. My decision to keep Commander Spock from falling was different—different in kind—from his decision to mind-meld with Scarlet. Wasn't it?

The shining sparkle of a transporter beam cast its illumination over *Copernicus*'s instrument panel. A Klingon noble materialized in the shuttlecraft main cabin and loomed over Jim and Uhura.

Jim, having chosen to visit the worldship unarmed, was all too aware of the blaster fastened to the noble's sapphire belt.

"Who are you?" Jim said.

"Why did you stop her?" the noble said.

"What do you mean?"

In a fury, the noble strode forward and grabbed Jim and lifted him from the deck.

"Koronin curses you for stopping her! Could the worldship do what she claims? Could it destroy the Klingon Empire?"

"Yes," Jim said. "Or the Federation of Planets."

"She would have destroyed your enemies!"

"You aren't my enemy," Jim said.

"Our governments are opponents—"

"We aren't at war! Even if we were—do you think I could stand by and watch the deaths of millions of innocent people?" Jim grabbed the noble's wrist. "Let me go."

Spock, in shadows behind the noble, approached stealthily.

The noble released Jim, muttering something incomprehensible but unpleasant in a grudging tone.

"Is everything in order, captain?" Spock said.

The director spun, startled.

"Yes, Mr. Spock." Jim straightened his shirt. He addressed the noble again. "Did you have anything else to ask me?"

The director reached for his belt. Jim tensed, but the director pulled out a communicating device. He spoke into it, then folded it and put it away.

"I have ordered a truce, captain," he said. "I have given your starship—and the unknown craft—permission to remain in the realm of our revered empress."

"That's . . . very civil of you," Jim said.

The noble dematerialized.

On board the disabled *Quundar,* Koronin waited, relaxed and ready, her blaster in one hand and her blood sword in the other. She had considered overloading *Quundar*'s engines and letting them go critical, but had decided that if she had to die, she would die striking with her dueling blade. If she saw any chance to survive, she might find the blaster useful, but she suspected the next, and last, weapon she ever used would be the blade.

She only wished for the chance to face the Federation captain who had frustrated her plans. She could always hope that the fleet would capture the *Enterprise* and its crew, and that some high-ranking fleet officer had a taste for blood sports.

She could always hope.

*Quundar* shrieked like a trapped animal as the tractor

beams ripped it from the shuttlecraft. Metals had fused with the heat and force of the collision.

A transporter beam penetrated her ship. She smiled: she could destroy any number of invaders before they got their bearings after transporting.

A silvery metal sphere appeared on the deck. Koronin scowled at it, suspicious. It looked like no bomb she knew of—

It burst with a soft gray puff, filling the command balcony with fog. Koronin backed away, but too late.

She collapsed, not knowing if she would ever open her eyes again.

As the *Enterprise*'s tractor beams pulled *Copernicus* home, Jim looked out at the worldship, drifting placidly in space.

"It looks so peaceful—yet it's the biggest, most destructive weapon ever built," he said.

"On the contrary, captain," Commander Spock said. "It is not a weapon at all."

Jim looked askance at the science officer. "You're the one who realized what it would do if anyone attacked it!"

"But the—" Spock pronounced a trilling, soaring musical sound—"the flying people have never conceived of war or of weapons. Under normal circumstances they would cause the universe to exist around the worldship in one safe configuration, then—when they wished to explore a different portion of space—to change to another safe configuration. It is only under conditions of unnatural stress—such as attack, which the flying people could not have imagined, since they have never imagined war—that the worldship forces the universe to move along unsafe vectors, distorting the fabric of space."

"They even have you talking as if they moved the universe instead of the worldship!"

"They do, captain, in their frame of reference and in the terms of their physics."

"That makes no sense at all! It's ridiculous to say that one arbitrary point stays still, and the flyers make the universe move."

"And yet," Spock said, "it moves."

"But that's impossible!"

"You overlook one fact, captain."

"What's that?"

"The system works."

Jim thought about what Commander Spock had said. Suddenly all his assumptions about the flying people came together, then exploded into shards like the wall-sphere. When they settled, they possessed a different shape entirely. He remembered the flyers' fascination with the *Enterprise*'s instruments; he remembered Sun-and-Shadows's perfect aerobatic stunt with *Copernicus*. He remembered Green, blinking at him and saying, "You are but young."

He had not been dealing with a group of children, or tribal people controlled by some shadowy master. He was talking to people so highly sophisticated that they barely bothered to think about their technology anymore. They were not amazed by the *Enterprise*, they were amused, like adults encountering a clever children's toy.

The fleet flagship pulled *Quundar* inside itself, and the *Enterprise* tractored *Copernicus* into the shuttlecraft deck. Jim waited impatiently while the deck repressurized.

Uhura hummed a musical phrase. Spock repeated it, maybe with a slightly different inflection, but Jim could not be sure. Uhura started to hum the phrase again, but stopped halfway through.

"I won't ever learn it, will I, Mr. Spock? Not all of it, not *really*."

Spock hesitated, as if the Vulcan, who claimed such complete disinterest in anyone's feelings, were searching for a gentle way to answer.

"No," Spock said finally. "None of us will."

She hardly reacted, but a moment later when she started to hum again, she cut off the sound sharply.

The all-clear signal sounded. Jim opened the shuttlecraft's hatch and climbed stiffly down. The tender new grass had shrivelled and died from vacuum exposure.

McCoy and Commander Scott hurried down the companionway. Scarlet and Lindy followed a moment later, as soon as Lindy had let Athene free in the repressurized shuttlecraft dock. Sulu, too, stood nearby. Starfleet had moved from Sulu's arm to his leg, but he was still plastered against him like a limpet.

"Jim!" McCoy clasped Jim's hand, then abandoned restraint and gave him a bear hug.

As soon as Jim extricated himself from McCoy's hug, Lindy hugged him, too. "That was quite a performance," she said. "If you ever decide to run away to show business, I'll put an aerial act on the bill."

Jim smiled and returned her embrace.

"Captain Kirk," Scott said sincerely, "ye nearly gave me a heart attack—and ye led us on a merry chase, ye can be verra sure of that. 'Tis no simple matter to counteract angular momentum with naught but a tractor beam!"

"I know it isn't, Mr. Scott." He offered his hand to the engineer. "But you did it. And you kept the *Enterprise* out of combat at a time when all your instincts must have called for fighting. At the very least you prevented a war. You should be proud of yourself for both accomplishments."

"I willna say which action was hardest," Scott said, but he wrung Jim's hand.

"The difficulty was worth it. I'm . . . very grateful to you."

"Why . . . thank ye, Captain Kirk."

"Spock." Scarlet swept her wings in a circle around the Vulcan, in the flyers' gesture of greeting. "You have returned from your silence. I thank you for the gifts you have given me, and I regret the pain I caused you with my ignorance."

"Vulcans are not susceptible to pain," Spock said.

Stephen heard Spock's comment and choked off a laugh. Spock ignored him.

"My only regret," Spock said, "is that I cannot incorporate your language as you can mine."

Scarlet nodded, understanding. "If our people meet again someday, you will be older, it may be possible." She brushed her wingtip against Uhura's cheek. "It may be possible," she said again. "You are but young."

Her wings whispered like silk. She leaped into the air and glided across the deck. Athene tossed her head and trotted after her.

"Scarlet!" Lindy cried. "Please don't tease her!"

"She has practiced flying, now, Lindy-magician," Scarlet said, hovering a few meters above Lindy's head. "The worldship cannot sustain her, so she must learn to fly in a smaller place." The flyer glided to the other side of the deck, very, very slowly. Athene reared back, leaped into the air, and flew.

Jim watched Athene practice touch-and-go takeoffs near Lindy, till Lindy leaped on her back and they glided in a slow game of tag with Scarlet.

"Mr. Scott," Jim said, "just how far outside Federation territory is the *Enterprise?*"

" 'Tis hard to say, captain. 'Twas still inside when *Quundar* came barrellin' out of the worldship, and then, er, I disobeyed your orders a wee bit in case it came to a rescue mission, as it did. Since then, dispatches have been buzzin' about like gnats, and seems the *Enterprise* has been granted embassy status. Anyplace it is, is Federation territory. The director is verra grateful to you."

Spock raised one eyebrow. "Fascinating."

"I should hope he would be grateful," McCoy said. "And grateful to you, too, Mr. Spock, considering what's happened. If you hadn't known enough about the worldship, we'd be in the middle of some pretty heavy fireworks right now."

"I believed my actions to be necessary," Spock said.

"And you were right," Jim said suddenly.

"Of course," Spock said.

"I mean it, commander. I said some ill-considered things to you a little while ago. And I agreed with you on the subject of a court-martial. But I was wrong. And so were you."

"I beg your pardon," Mr. Spock said, sounding—was it possible?—highly affronted.

"No, Commander Spock, listen to me. There will be no court-martial. If you hadn't had the guts to mind-meld with Scarlet . . ."

"Would you claim bravery for yourself, in stopping Koronin?" Spock said. "I think not. There is no bravery involved when there is no choice."

Jim could think of no reply.

"I, for one, disagree," McCoy said. "But I hope I can disagree in a civilized manner."

"Your manner appears quite civilized to me, doctor," Spock said.

"Why, thank you, Mr. Spock. By the way, if you come by sick bay, I can do something about that black eye."

Spock headed for the bridge, taking the stairs of the companionway three at a time. McCoy climbed after him. Jim followed more slowly, hampered by the temporary splint that supported his knee. Scott headed for the shuttlecraft and opened its engine bay.

"Now that we've all got done complimenting each other . . ." Stephen yawned elaborately.

Sulu passed him, on his way to *Copernicus* to check on the damage to its navigational systems.

On Stephen's shoulder, Ilya bristled at Starfleet, who cowered and hid his face against Sulu's knee. "Looks like you've acquired a friend, Mr. Sulu," Stephen said.

"Oh, I hope not," Sulu said with intense sincerity.

Stephen grinned. "How'd you get along with *Dionysus?*"

"Just fine, sir," Sulu said. "I noticed it has a few added attractions."

"I'm glad somebody noticed something around here," Stephen said.

Hazarstennaj, arriving from Engineering to work on *Copernicus,* glided down the companionway. She stopped when she saw Stephen and Ilya. Her whiskers bristled in disapproval, but she restrained herself from making a comment. She joined Mr. Scott. She heard a strange noise, a sort of cheerful chirp, that she could not identify as a mechanical sound.

"Is anything left of the engines?" she said.

"No' verra much," Scott said.

Hazarstennaj heard the chirping again. "Mr. Scott, what is that sound?"

"What? Oh, 'tis Mr. Sulu's new pet. Revoltin' thing."

Curiosity overcame Hazard.

She looked into the main cabin of *Copernicus.* Sulu was trying to work, but a clever little animal kept getting in his way. It saw Hazard and scampered to her, chirping in a friendly fashion.

"What a dear creature," she said.

Sulu glanced up. "You've got to be kidding."

"You do not like it?"

"It's kind of a pest," he said.

"I think it charming," she said. It nuzzled up against her, twining its fingers in the longer fur at her throat. "It must be very uncomfortable. Furred beings should not be forced to wear clothes."

"It wasn't my idea," Sulu said.

Hazard helped the creature out of the shirt and trousers. It was completely covered in pink fur that shaded to mauve on its back and legs. It scratched its side contentedly and let Hazard smooth the soft fur back into place.

"That's better, little one, isn't it?" Hazard said.

"I think it's orphaned," Sulu said. "It just grabbed onto me because it was scared of Stephen's cat. Say, Hazard, it seems to like you a lot better."

"That is true," Hazard said. "It will come with me, if it pleases."

To her pleasure, and Sulu's relief, Starfleet followed when Hazard returned to the shuttlecraft engines.

Crossing the shuttlecraft deck to return to *Dionysus*, Stephen glanced up at Lindy and Athene. Lindy caught his gaze. She hesitated, then raised her hand in a brief wave. But she did not turn Athene toward him; she did not say anything to him. He could hardly blame her.

Inside his ship, Stephen checked over the systems. Sulu had left it properly shut down and undamaged. Stephen felt proprietary about *Dionysus;* the helm officer was the only other person to fly it since he had acquired it.

Stephen let himself collapse in the pilot's seat. He felt bone-weary and drained, too tired even to go aft to his bunk. Ilya jumped into his lap and settled down, kneading Stephen's thigh with his big front paws. Stephen stroked him.

"It's all gone," he said softly to the forest cat. "I can almost remember, but it's all shadows and dreams. They're all slipping away, and I can't feel them anymore." He felt empty and disconnected. In order to free Spock from the power of Scarlet's experiences, Stephen had given up what

334

little contact he had made with his own emotions. He rested his hand on Ilya's broad head. The forest cat blinked. "There's always time to start over again, isn't there?"

The proper reaction, Stephen thought, is a cynical laugh. But I am too tired.

"Stephen—?"

He dragged open his eyes. Uhura stood in the hatchway.

"Are you all right?" she asked.

"I don't know," he said.

"Stephen . . ." She stopped, as if uncertain what to say. "Captain Kirk hasn't been on the *Enterprise* long. He doesn't know Mr. Spock, and he doesn't know much about mind-melding. He doesn't understand what you did—how difficult it was, and how dangerous. I don't think Dr. McCoy realizes it, either."

"Most human beings wouldn't," Stephen said.

"But I do," Uhura said. "Thank you. Mr. Spock didn't thank you, or he couldn't . . ."

"He can't entirely help the way he is," Stephen said. "I ought to be used to it by now."

She touched him. Her hand was cool and strong. He sought some reaction within himself, but found nothing. Not even grief.

"Uhura . . . would you stay here for a few minutes? Would you just sit with me?"

"Of course I will."

He lay back in the pilot's chair. Uhura sat beside him in the copilot's seat, still holding his hand. She could see the exhaustion in his face, and she felt glad when it eased and he drifted into a deep sleep.

Uhura rose, kissed Stephen gently on the cheek, and left *Dionysus* to return to the bridge.

Jim wondered why it surprised him that the bridge looked so normal. He felt as if he had been gone for months, as if things should have changed. But the warp engines registered full capability; communications had returned with the cessation of the jamming field. Spock took his place at the science officer's station. Yeoman Rand worked at environmental systems, and Commander Cheung at navigation. Mr. Sulu returned, freed, Jim noticed, from Starfleet's clinging presence, and a few minutes thereafter, Lieutenant Uhura took her place at communications.

Only the schematic in the corner of the viewscreen troubled Jim. It showed the *Enterprise* well outside the Federation, drifting farther every minute as it followed the worldship. But the viewscreen showed Federation space in blue, Empire space in green. A fuzzy ring of blue surrounded the *Enterprise*.

"Captain Kirk—Admiral Noguchi on subspace."

"Thank you," Jim said, since he could hardly refuse the call. Surrender gracefully, he reminded himself. He had no idea what to say to the admiral, and he suspected he would be just as happy if he never found out what the admiral had to say to him.

"Well, Jim," the admiral said. "You were due at Starbase 13 yesterday."

"I know, sir. But we encountered . . ." He hesitated, trying to think how to explain the worldship. "A first contact, sir."

Admiral Noguchi chuckled. "You always have had a talent for understatement. A first contact, indeed. Yes, I've seen the transmissions."

"Transmissions, admiral? We haven't had time to send any—or the capability."

"The transmissions from the fleet."

"Oh."

"I would have bet," the admiral said, "that any single Federation ship encountering the oversight committee's fleet would have been wiped out of space—or captured, and its commander paraded as a spy. Do you know what they want to do to you?"

"Er, no, sir." Jim had not thought of what would happen beyond a trial. He felt a very strong desire never to need to find out the Empire's penalty for espionage.

"They want to give you a medal."

"A medal? That's absurd!"

"Perhaps. But—"

"I can't accept a medal from the Klingon Empire!"

"—you'll accept it, and with good grace. Jim! Who knows how long this will last? Maybe only ten microseconds! But somehow, you've got the governments talking to each other instead of trading insults. And beyond that, if it's true the people in the worldship won't move it back to the Federation, someone's got to represent us to them. Our scientists and diplomats won't arrive for at least a week. So you are ad hoc ambassador to the Klingon frontier and to the worldship. I'm counting on you, my boy."

"I'll . . . do my best, admiral."

"I know you will. Now, and in the future. We'll have a good long talk about the future, and about your next mission, as soon as you return." He smiled as Jim struggled to think of something to say. "By the way, Jim—tell Lindy that the director of the oversight committee has expressed interest in seeing the company perform. If she agrees, please arrange it. Oh—here's somebody who wants to talk to you."

Another image flickered into being.

"Gary!"

"You're in deep trouble, kid," Gary Mitchell said. "I warned you not to leave Federation space without me."

"You sure did," Jim said. "I won't do it again, I promise." He felt like laughing with joy to see his friend back on his feet, to *know* he would be ready when the admiral presented Jim with his next mission. Gary still looked thin and drawn, and he supported himself with a cane, but a cane inlaid with ebony and topped with a flamboyant gold head had to be at least partly for show, for attention.

Does it matter? Jim thought. Not a bit. "I missed you, Gary. We needed you." He did not even feel his usual irritation at Gary's calling him "kid."

"Damn right. Look at you—no sooner out of the hospital than you put yourself back in a cast."

Jim glanced at his knee with resignation. "Bones has already got the green slime mixed for me."

"I wouldn't doubt it. I always knew he was a sadist at heart." Gary laughed.

He thinks I'm joking, Jim thought. I wish.

"How soon can you get out here?" Jim said.

"Not for a while, kid. You'll have to muddle on without a first officer till they let me out of the torture chamber."

The reminder that Gary could not be first officer attenuated Jim's happiness. "I have to talk to you. Later . . ." He wanted to talk to Gary about Noguchi's orders; he wanted to ease the broken promise both for himself and for his friend. But in private. He was painfully aware of Commander Spock just behind him. He trusted Gary to pick up on the hint.

"Soon," Jim said.

"Yeah, all right." Gary tossed his head to fling his heavy dark hair back from his forehead. "Later." His hair immediately slipped down again. "Soon."

Gary fell silent. Even the short conversation had tired him.

"I have to go," Jim said quickly. "Just one thing—"

"What?"

"Get a haircut."

"Aye aye, cap'n kid sir," Gary said, smiling.

"And get better," Jim said softly.

Gary let the transmission fade.

Spock could not help overhearing. He knew what the future conversation would be about. Captain Kirk would be forced to explain that Commander Mitchell could not, after all, occupy the position of first officer. Spock had taken little note of Kirk and Noguchi's argument on the subject, and until now he had seen no reason to involve himself in any part of it. But now only he could have any influence, and he felt he should take action. He asked the computer for a file, the transfer request he had drafted and which he had thought to withdraw.

As he waited for it, he became aware of Dr. McCoy standing nearby, arms folded, tapping his fingers impatiently.

"You have that look of medical fervor in your eye, Bones," Captain Kirk said.

"That's right. I want you and Spock to get down to sick bay—right now."

Spock raised his eyebrow in disbelief. "Do you think it wise, doctor," he said, "for both senior officers to leave the bridge at the same time?"

McCoy looked at him with a very strange expression.

Spock gazed back with utter seriousness.

"You're absolutely right, Spock," McCoy said, after a

lengthy pause. "It would be a mistake. Jim, didn't you once say something about never asking anyone under your command to do anything you wouldn't do?"

"I never said that," Jim said. But, resigned, he pushed himself to his feet and limped after McCoy.

Wondering why McCoy had behaved so oddly in response to his comment, Spock completed his request to transfer off the *Enterprise*.

In sick bay, McCoy gave Jim a quick once-over, but devoted most of his attention to his knee. It looked even worse than Jim expected. Freed of the temporary splint, it started to hurt. A deep bruise circled his kneecap.

"I know you've already got the green slime growing," Jim said.

"What? No, not at all."

"But I saw the requisition—!"

"Oh, you did, did you? Is that why you've been avoiding this exam?"

"Pretty good reason, wouldn't you say?"

"I did mix up a batch of regen culture. But it doesn't have anything to do with you. Not everything does, you know. And I do perform the occasional bit of research down here."

"Sorry, Bones."

"Damn right. If it will ease your mind: No. You aren't going back into regen. Regen's for serious stuff. You've got a bad muscle pull and some bruising." McCoy grinned. "Just think of all the years of med school behind that diagnosis. Lay off the cowboy acrobatics for a while—"

"No argument there."

"—and postpone any more fencing tournaments."

"You heard about that, did you?"

"My spies are everywhere." He enclosed Jim's knee in an electro-stimulant brace. "Everything else looks just fine. A biofeedback refresher wouldn't hurt, just for safety's sake. Regen changes you, even if you can't consciously tell. And you've obviously been neglecting your knee exercises."

"I've been so busy . . ."

"I'm too busy to nag you. Grow up, Jim. You can either do them, or you *will* end up back in regen. Understood, captain?"

"Understood, doctor."

"Good. Now go be the senior officer on the bridge and send Spock down here."

As Spock routed his transfer request to Captain Kirk's comm unit, the captain returned from sick bay.

"Your turn, Mr. Spock."

"I have already completed my required physical—"

"Don't argue, Commander Spock!"

"Very well, sir."

Spock knew Dr. McCoy would find nothing amiss.

"You're a lucky man," McCoy said.

"I do not believe in luck, Dr. McCoy."

"You ought to. If Stephen hadn't been around—"

"His presence disproves your theory that I am lucky."

"There's something awfully personal in your dislike for him, Mr. Spock. What is he—the family nonconformist?"

"We are . . . distantly related."

"Somehow," McCoy said, "it's comforting to know that even Vulcan families have relatives they don't talk about. So Stephen's your weird cousin, eh?"

"That explanation will suffice. Vulcan kinship ties are complex."

"I think I can follow the explanation," McCoy said. "Use short words."

"My father's father's sister's daughter is Stephen's mother. Therefore we are related through a three-level direct transgender line, in the second degree."

McCoy frowned over the explanation. "Then you are cousins."

"If Vulcans counted kinship as your culture does, our relationship would fall into that category."

"Why didn't you say so in the first place?"

"I did, doctor," Spock said, wondering why human beings persisted in their contrariness.

But a few minutes later, on the way back to the bridge, he could not help but recall what McCoy had said about Stephen. Much as he preferred not to admit it, he and Stephen had one factor in common.

They both were exiles.

\* \* \*

The next twenty-four hours passed in a blaze of activity. Scarlet, hearing of the planned performance, expressed a wish to see it, and hinted at interest from other of the worldship's people. The audience would be so large that neither the *Enterprise* nor any of the ships of the director's fleet could hold it. Scarlet found a natural amphitheater within the worldship. Lindy agreed that the site would work, since the company brought all its own scenery and props. Besides, on the worldship and outdoors, Athene could be part of the show. The only thing that worried Lindy was the possibility of rain.

"It will not rain, Lindy-magician," Scarlet said.

"That's easy to say—but hard to be sure of."

"No, I am sure."

"Okay, we'll do it."

And, to Jim's surprise, it was just that easy.

Hikaru Sulu arrived at the worldship's amphitheater, wearing black tights and vermilion doublet, with his sword belt buckled around his hips. It was a great costume. Maybe he would even get to wear it onstage.

He worried about his lines. He knew them—but he was not certain he could stand to say them. He wondered if he could get away with speaking the unrevised lines and pretending he had been too nervous to remember Mr. Cockspur's version. He almost wished he were playing Horatio instead of Laertes. Horatio had several speeches after Hamlet died. If Hikaru ignored the revisions while playing Laertes, he would have to recite them to Hamlet's face, and Hamlet would be facing him with a sword. The duel might turn out to be more real than anyone expected.

In either event, Cockspur would be furious, but then, he was furious about something most of the time anyway.

"Er . . . Mr. Sulu." Mr. Cockspur joined him. The actor wore black velvet. Until this minute, Hikaru had not known whether Cockspur would deign to end his strike and perform.

"I'm all ready, Mr. Cockspur."

"I see you are. But there's been a change in plans."

"Oh . . . Are you on strike again?" *Maybe Lindy will let*

me give Hamlet's soliloquy, Hikaru thought. I did learn it, after all, just in case.

"No, no—Admiral Noguchi persuaded me that I should participate, for the good of the Federation."

"A different scene, then?" Hikaru asked, not at all sure he could stand to learn another set of Mr. Cockspur's lines.

"Yes. Exactly. The dueling scene has been canceled. Too arousing, I feel, given the, er, martial proclivities of our guests."

"I don't think it would be arousing," Hikaru said. "What about catharsis? 'Incidents arousing pity and fear, wherewith to accomplish its catharsis of such emotions.' "

"What are you babbling about?"

"I'm quoting Aristotle."

"But we're doing Shakespeare. Perhaps it's just as well that I'll be doing one of Hamlet's soliloquies. Alone."

"Oh," Hikaru said. His visions of understudy-saves-show dissolved.

"It's for the good of the performance," Cockspur said. "The show must go on, and that sort of thing."

He walked away.

"Whatever happened to 'all for one and one for all'?" Hikaru said plaintively.

Nearby, Stephen checked the balance on some new juggling equipment. He had discovered that if he juggled very large and very heavy objects, or used more objects and threw them higher, he could put on a decent show despite the low gravity. In the high partial pressure of oxygen, torches worked spectacularly well. The first time he lit one, he almost singed his eyebrows.

Just as well, he thought. You need something to keep you on your toes.

Tzesnashstennaj, Hazard, and Snarl came by, sliding past and over and under each other as if they had already begun the powerful and erotic hunt performance. Ilya bristled. The hunters stopped. Stephen caught his juggling clubs and put them down, wondering if he was going to have to break up a cat fight. He did not understand why the hunters disliked Ilya so much.

With a chirp, Starfleet peeked from behind Tzesnashsten-naj's shoulders.

"Stephen," Tzesnashstennaj said, "have you met my new pet?"

"Here and there," Stephen said.

"Is he not charming?" Tzesnashstennaj scratched it gently on the chin. Sighing with pleasure, Starfleet flopped on its back with its arms and legs splayed in the air. "Hazarstennaj gave him to me . . . as a love-token."

Hazard made a snarly, purring sound. "As Tzesnashsten-naj will not let me kidnap him into Starfleet, I am compelled to give Starfleet to him."

"I think he does not like the name Starfleet," Tzesnash-stennaj said. "I may change his name. His ears are a little pointy . . . what do you think of the name Vulcan?"

"I think Starfleet would be the only mauve Vulcan in the history of the universe," Stephen said.

Tzesnashstennaj nodded. "That is true. He would be even more unusual than a Vulcan who was blond. I will have to wait for him to find his own name. But I will teach him to juggle! Perhaps Lindy will put him onstage, and we will become rich and famous. What do you think of that, Stephen?"

"I think there's only room for one juggler in a vaudeville company," Stephen said, and realized he was clenching his teeth with irritation.

Snarl chuckled. "I told you all—did I not?—there is not a Vulcan in the universe with a sense of humor."

Laughing and yowling they bounded off, a sleek and gleaming flow of muscle and arrogance. Starfleet perched on Tzesnashstennaj's shoulders like a jockey.

Ilya unbristled and sat down to wash.

"Do you think we deserved that?" Stephen asked Ilya. "I don't think we deserved that."

Roswind hurried to her cabin to get changed. Like most of the rest of the crew of the *Enterprise*, she had permission to transport to the worldship and see the vaudeville perform-ance. It was about time she got her turn.

She opened the door.

She shrieked.

Green slime covered the floor, and the nauseating odor of decomposing regeneration gel permeated her cabin.

She spent the next several hours cleaning up the remains of the green "roommate," while all her friends enjoyed themselves at the show.

Roswind knew she had been had.


In a makeshift dressing room in the amphitheater, Jim straightened his formal tunic for about the ninety-third time, gave up trying to feel comfortable in it, and wandered outside. He found Lindy, who looked perfectly comfortable in her silver suit.

"This is ridiculous," Jim said to her. "I don't belong on that stage."

"Sure you do." She straightened one of the triangular ribbons on his chest. "Did you leave a place for the new one? Come on, it's a tradition to have heroes talk about their exploits on the vaudeville stage."

Jim groaned.

She laughed. "You'll do fine. I've got to hurry—wait till you see my entrance!"

She disappeared in the visual cacophony of performers doing their warmup routines between the curtained dressing rooms. Jim walked around, trying to look calm. Nearby, Spock observed the backstage activity. He appeared perfectly serene, and he wore his brown velvet tunic.

"Commander Spock."

Solemn, emotionless, Spock watched James Kirk approach. "Yes, captain?"

"What's the meaning of the transfer request I found on my desk this morning?"

Spock raised one eyebrow. "I assumed it would be self-evident," he said.

"You assumed wrong. Commander, I thought we'd made our peace."

Spock looked into the sky, where Scarlet soared free in the exhilaration of flight. Spock recalled the resonances of Scarlet's grief; he recalled his own desperate climb toward silence or death. He would have plunged slowly to oblivion, except for James Kirk's dangerous and impulsive rescue. For all his imperturbability, Spock valued his life, his experiences past and the experiences to come.

"Indeed, captain, we did."

"Then why the transfer?"

"I believed, when I first observed you, that I could not work with you. You are very different from Christopher Pike. You are emotional, headstrong, and stubborn. But I have come to understand that these differences should be valued, not despised. I realized that working with you would be a valuable, if difficult, experience."

"Thanks for the compliment," Kirk said dryly.

"One must face difficulty if one wishes to learn," Spock said.

"None of this explains why you've requested a transfer."

"I thought only of myself and whether I wished to remain on the *Enterprise* with you as captain. I never considered whether you wished to work with me. If I resign the post of first officer, you may promote Commander Mitchell."

"Why exactly did you decide to make this sacrifice?"

"It is a sacrifice only of my personal wishes. That is little enough to offer in return for the risk you took in the center of the worldship. Vulcans do not collect debts. We prefer not to owe them, either."

"You don't owe me anything, Spock. Dammit—"

"Captain—"

"It's your turn to listen. A few days ago, I probably would have let you go ahead with your noble gesture. I probably would have appreciated it. But even if I thought Admiral Noguchi would let me finagle Gary in as first officer over his objections, which I don't, I wouldn't try. I've learned a couple of lessons, too, over the last few days. Lesson one: Admiral Noguchi is right."

"I do not understand."

"A starship needs differences. It needs good officers—and Gary is one of the best—but it needs checks and balances, too. Gary and I are very much alike . . ." He paused, staring into a distance of recent memories. "I owe him . . . my life. But I have to do what's best for the *Enterprise*. And that is to persuade you to stay on as first officer."

"But what of Commander Mitchell—your friend?"

"Balancing friendship and responsibility won't be easy—and telling all this to Gary is going to be harder. I'll hear the end of it in, oh, twenty years or so. Which will be at least fifteen years after he gets his own command. Forcing you off the *Enterprise* in his favor would do him—and me—more harm than good. If you turn down your first senior position, you won't win any prizes with Starfleet, either."

Spock rubbed his chin, deliberating. The captain made telling arguments; they could even be said to possess an element of logic.

"Mr. Spock, I'm going to rip up the transfer applications I found on my desk today. I hope I won't find more tomorrow."

"Very well, captain. I will consider what you have said. But—you received more than one application?"

"I received two, but one was from Mr. Scott. A misunderstanding. It's cleared up."

"I see." Spock also saw Mr. Sulu, sitting on an equipment trunk a few meters away. Though he looked rather disconsolate, he must have decided that staying on the *Enterprise* was not, after all, the disaster he first thought.

"Commander Spock," James Kirk said, "aren't you supposed to be out in the audience, waiting to volunteer?"

"Yes, captain. But I wished to observe backstage preparations."

Captain Kirk was right, though; it was time he took his seat. Kirk walked with him toward a path that led into the amphitheater.

"Good lord," Jim said. "I have to speak in front of them all."

"A challenging audience," Spock said.

Federation, Klingon, and worldship people sat together on the natural stone terraces, a restless group of at least a thousand. But the restlessness appeared to be good-natured. Jim hoped it stayed that way.

The Empire fleet's transporter area shimmered. The director of the oversight committee transported into being, accompanied by his entourage. Jim and the director had agreed to prohibit weapons on the worldship. The director had kept the bargain. He brought bodyguards who could protect him without weapons. Each was nearly the size of Newland Rift. A mysterious veiled figure also accompanied him, and a second figure wearing an unfastened veil draped across her shoulder.

"Captain—" Spock said.

The director's bodyguards prodded Koronin forward. Her hands were shackled. She resisted, moving only when continuing to resist would rob her of the last of her dignity. Jim winced. No matter what Koronin had done or attempted, Jim hated seeing a sentient individual displayed like a captured wild animal.

The director strolled toward Jim.

"I hope you have prepared yourself for this honor, captain," he said. He showed him a tooled leather box.

"Your excellency, I protest this barbarism!"

"Captain, what are you talking about? This creature, do you mean? Don't let her concern you. You will display your prize, I will display mine."

"What you're displaying is—"

Spock's hand gripped Jim's arm, gently restraining him.

"—uncivilized—"

Spock's fingers tightened around his biceps.

"Captain!" the director exclaimed, with mock distress. "We had agreed to forbid fighting and name-calling among our subordinates. I took it on faith that the prohibition extended to you and me."

Jim subsided. There was nothing he could do, not without jeopardizing the fragile peace he had helped create, and not without endangering his entire crew.

"Besides," the director said, "this is Koronin's last glimpse of freedom. I could have left her in her cell. It has no windows, no light at all. In fact it has nothing. My magnanimity in bringing her with me will do my reputation no good whatever."

Seething, Jim glanced at Koronin. She must have seen pity in his eyes.

"I challenge you, Federation brigand!" Koronin shouted at Jim. "And if you decline, you're a coward!"

"Quiet, traitor! No name-calling today." The director chuckled and strode toward his seat. His bodyguards followed, pushing Koronin along.

"You can let go now," Jim said.

Spock released him. Jim rubbed the bruised place on his arm.

"I understand your objections, captain," Spock said. "Perhaps better than you think. I cannot excuse Koronin's actions . . . but they were not entirely gratuitous. She has reasons for her hatred, both of her own people and of us. She acted out of a deep desire for revenge."

"What does a Vulcan know about revenge, Commander Spock?"

"You know little of Vulcan history," Spock said gravely. "Our capacity for vengeance is a primary reason we chose to eliminate our emotions."

In the audience, surrounded by the director's graceless thugs, Koronin sat rigid on the natural stone bench. I claimed this world, she thought. I own it. But I will never be permitted to present it to the empress, and for that, somehow, I will take my revenge.

The great low voice of Newland Rift rumbled over the crowd.

"Guests, old friends, new friends, welcome! May I present—the Warp-Speed Classic Vaudeville Company!"

The audience waited, silent and expectant. One of the fleet members glanced up, saw the flyers swooping toward them, and shouted in alarm.

Koronin saw the director tense. He suspected an attack, a trap. For herself, she welcomed it. She was watching for a chance; chaos might work to her advantage.

High overhead, flyers soared and dipped and stroked each other with their wingtips. The light web silhouetted them from above and illuminated them from the sides.

The audience gasped as the flyers dived toward the stage. But one of the flock was not a flyer. It was a four-legged being with feathered wings. It beat its wings, hovering, and touched down. A human sat upon its back.

The human leaped to the stage. The Federation people applauded wildly. The director's personnel waited in silence. As soon as something pleased them, they would cry out their wild, eerie howl of approval. They felt confused, for they did not know if they were supposed to appreciate the human's ability to balance on the four-legged person's back, or the human's ability to train the flying creatures, or what. They certainly did not feel like applauding after having been frightened.

The flyers departed the stage and sat or perched on various spots around the amphitheater. The four-legged person took off and flew. Its threatening shadow passed back and forth.

"Honorable people," the silver-clad human said. "Welcome."

She introduced the director. Koronin wished the human would make some humiliating gaffe and plunge the audience into a brawl. But the human could not reveal the director's name, since she did not know it, and as far as Koronin could tell she used all his titles properly.

The director joined her on the stage.

"As representative of our revered empress," he said, "I come to honor a member of the Federation who risked his life to thwart the miserable traitor Koronin—"

He went on for some while. Koronin took pleasure in smiling at him the entire time he railed against her.

Jim Kirk just wished the whole thing were over. The director finally finished his verbal abuse of Koronin.

"I honor the captain of the starship *Enterprise*."

Nervously waiting for his name to be called, Jim did not realize for a moment that it was his turn to get up.

McCoy nudged him in the ribs. "C'mon, Jim, don't rain on the parade."

Jim stood too fast for the low gravity. He leaped halfway to the stage in one step. Blushing, he recovered and proceeded in a more dignified way.

The director opened the leather box, drew out a necklace, and lowered it over Jim's head. A chain of heavy gold-colored links supported a garish pendant made of blue and red stones. It looked like costume jewelry.

"I name you a Guard of the Empress."

The director stepped back.

Jim faced the audience.

An unearthly howl filled the amphitheater, overwhelming the applause of the *Enterprise* crew members. Jim tensed, thinking that the fleet personnel were about to attack despite the truce. But they only shrieked. He had not thought to ask how people applauded in the Empire. Now he knew.

"Thank you." Can I stop there? he wondered. I guess not. "I am most honored and humbled by the director's gesture, and gratified that this occasion brings us together in friendship and peace. May the friendship between the Empire, the Federation, and the people of the worldship continue and grow stronger."

Somehow he got off the stage and back to his seat. His hands were slick with sweat. He was glad that shaking hands was not, apparently, a custom of the Empire.

McCoy leaned over to inspect the medal.

"Quite a bauble," he said.

"Looks like a brooch my great-aunt Matilda used to wear to church," Jim muttered under his breath.

Scarlet leaned forward from where she sat cross-legged on the next tier of seats.

"It is bright," she said, "but if you flew, it would weigh you down."

The applause and the shrieks faded. Amelinda returned to the stage.

"And now," she said, "entertainment for our heroes."

Relieved to be done with his part in the evening's proceedings, Jim sat back to enjoy Lindy's show.

The director watched the magic, his irritation increasing with each act of witchcraft. He wondered if the Federation people had planned this to offend him, or if they expected him to leap onto the stage and attempt to cleanse away the diabolical presence, or if they actually thought he would enjoy such a display. He decided to thwart all their plans. He would do nothing in protest, for now; neither would he pretend to approve or, worse, enjoy.

Since he did not react, neither did anyone else from his fleet.

Koronin, though, watched the magic act in fascination. Unlike the director, whose discomfort amused her, she knew it was all show, all tricks. Rumaiy were not superstitious, at least not about diabolical presences. Besides, she had encountered sleight of hand at Arcturus, where a roving Federation outlaw used it to entertain acquaintances and defraud strangers.

But Koronin had never seen anything to match Amelinda Lukarian's escape act. Her assistant wrapped her up in restraints and locked the electronic locks and fastened her inside a trunk and covered the trunk with a cloth and let twenty-three flying people grab robes attached to it and lift it off the ground. When they lowered it again it was empty, and Amelinda Lukarian stepped out from behind the stage curtains with a flourish. Koronin howled in approval and would have applauded in the Federation manner, too, if her hands had not been chained.

The puzzle of how Amelinda Lukarian escaped so intrigued Koronin that she hardly noticed the rest of the performance.

And it gave her ideas.

At the end of Lindy's act, the applause of the people from the *Enterprise* sounded feeble in the huge amphitheater, for they were outnumbered by fleet personnel three to one. Lindy left the stage, stunned by the reaction of the crowd. She never got nervous onstage, but after fighting this audience she was dripping with sweat. Tzesnashstennaj and the rest of the hunt troupe glided past.

"Break a leg," she said.

"Don't you mean, be sure the audience doesn't break *my* leg?" Tzesnashstennaj bounded onto the stage.

Mr. Spock returned from the end point of the disappearing trick.

"I died out there," Lindy said. "Mr. Spock—do you understand what's going on? I couldn't have been *that* bad—the *Enterprise* people liked it. Or were they just being polite?"

"I can offer only a hypothesis," Spock said. "The director did not appear to be pleased by what he saw."

"But *nobody* applauded!"

"He did not applaud; therefore his subordinates did not applaud."

"You didn't applaud at first—that didn't stop anybody on the *Enterprise*."

"Lindy," Spock said, "unlike the director, I do not have the power of life or death over anyone on my ship."

"Oh."

"I believe we are involved in a cultural misunderstanding.

It is a shame, but there is nothing to be done about it except continue."

"Yeah. The show must go on," Lindy said.

It went on, all right: straight downhill, if that was possible. Either the director hated Lindy's act so much that his dislike carried over, or he hated everything.

Backstage morale was not good.

Out front, Jim leaned toward the director.

"Aren't you enjoying the show?" he whispered.

The director glared at him. "Your civilization, if one may dignify it with the term, is in extreme decline."

With that, he gave Jim the cold shoulder.

At intermission, Jim went backstage. Lindy was trying not to look downcast, but she was not succeeding very well.

"I just came back to—" Jim stopped. Saying he wanted to offer sympathy seemed undiplomatic.

"To offer moral support? Thanks, Jim . . . I need it."

"I'm afraid I offended the director with my speech," Jim said. The truth was he had no idea what had offended the director, but it *might* have been the speech. Since Jim did not make his living giving speeches the way Lindy and her company made their living by performing, he was perfectly happy to take the blame.

"Do you think so? Honest?" She suddenly blushed. "Jim, I didn't mean that the way it sounded—"

He grinned. "I know. It's all right."

"This is going to be one of those shows you remember forever, and tell your grandchildren about, and afterwards it seems funny." She smiled ruefully. "About a hundred years afterwards."

Out front at the temporary bar, McCoy offered the director a frosted silver cup.

"Try this," he said. "It's one of the high achievements of human civilization."

The director vetted it out with an instrument like a tricorder.

"No poison," McCoy said cheerfully. "I'm a doctor, and doctors are forbidden to prescribe poison."

"How odd," the director said. "What's this called?"

"It's a mint julep. Look, I'm having one myself." He sipped from another frosted cup.

The director sipped. The director considered. "Drinkable," he said.

"It'll put hair on your chest," McCoy said.

In horror, the director flung the cup at McCoy's feet. Crushed ice and sprigs of mint splashed over McCoy's boots. The director stamped back to his seat.

"Good grief," McCoy said.

Jim saw Scarlet strolling around backstage. He joined her.

"Scarlet," he said. "Are *you* enjoying the show?"

Scarlet brushed her tongue across her sensory mustache. "It is charming. I will tell my grandchildren about it."

Jim grinned. "That's what Lindy was saying. But maybe your grandchildren will get to see it, or something like it, themselves."

"I do not think so, James."

"Why? Scarlet—"

The signal sounded and they were separated as the crowd returned to their seats.

In the amphitheater, Hikaru Sulu slouched despondently on the stone bench. He knew he ought to take off his costume, but he thought he would wait till after the show just in case.

Captain Kirk paused beside him and smiled. "Mr. Sulu, you're either out of uniform, or you're on the wrong side of the stage."

"I got canceled," Hikaru said.

"That's too bad," the captain said. "Or maybe not, considering."

In the wings, Lindy screwed up her courage and entered, stage left, to announce Stephen.

Lindy thought he did a fantastic job of accommodating his act to the low gravity. Nevertheless, the director and his people watched in stoic silence. Only when Stephen brought out the torches did they loosen up a bit.

They're probably hoping he'll singe his eyebrows, Lindy thought uncharitably.

If they were, Stephen disappointed them. He juggled nine torches, flung them up one by one till they were all spinning above him at the same time, then caught them as they fell and arrayed them in a flaming fan in front of him. He extinguished them, put them down, slipped off the blue ribbon to let his hair fall free, and bowed. Though the

*Enterprise* people clapped long and hard, only a few howls of approval trickled out of the director's people.

"And I thought Vulcans were tough to please," Stephen said to Lindy after his exit.

Lindy hesitated. She realized she had been avoiding him, which was hardly fair to Stephen. She wanted to hug him, but she did not want to make him uncomfortable.

"Your act was terrific," she said.

"I know it," he said. "But aren't you glad we're more than halfway done?"

Lindy could not help but laugh.

Philomela barely made it through. Marcellin strolled onstage, carrying his invisibly visible universe with him. But as far as the director was concerned, it was just plain invisible.

Now it was only Mr. Cockspur—Lindy winced; if they hated the other acts, they would eat Cockspur alive—and Newland Rift. They've got to like Newland, Lindy thought. How can they not? If Cockspur can just get through without having tomatoes thrown at him . . .

Where was Cockspur, anyway? He always came out at the last possible moment. He might not even know what a disaster they had on their hands tonight.

Lindy looked around. Cockspur stood just outside his dressing room. He looked pale.

"Mr. Cockspur, what's wrong? You're on!"

His eyelids flickered and he winced.

"I do not think I can perform."

"But you have to!" She could hardly believe he would chicken out because of a hostile audience. He was pompous and arrogant, but he was not chicken. "We're counting on you!" Did I really say that? she thought. Yes, I did, and I meant it, too—I won't have anybody saying that we didn't give an audience the whole show, even if they don't understand what we're doing. Even if they do understand, and hate it anyway.

"It is impossible. The pain . . . It grieves me to let you down, Amelinda. Perhaps . . . if I rest . . ."

"But you're *on!*"

He swayed as if he were going to faint. Newland, inside a neat little circle of his poodles, reached out with one massive hand and steadied him.

"I'll go on," he said. "That will give you ten minutes."

Newland strolled onstage. Leaping more than a meter off the ground in the low gravity, the poodles followed like balls of fur on pogo sticks.

Lindy helped Mr. Cockspur sit down, then grabbed the first person she saw.

"Marcellin, can you see if Hikaru's still in costume? Mr. Cockspur . . ." She looked at Cockspur, who had staggered to a bench. "Mr. Cockspur is swooning."

As soon as he noticed the change in the order of the acts, Sulu left his seat and headed backstage. Halfway there he met Marcellin, still in makeup, coming after him. They grinned at each other. Marcellin swept low in a courtier's bow as Sulu passed.

"Hikaru!" Lindy said. "Can you go on? Do you know the soliloquy? I know the audience is awful, but—"

"Yes I can go on, yes I know the soliloquy—the original, I mean—and I don't care about the audience," Hikaru said. "It's a challenge, right?"

He suddenly became aware of Mr. Cockspur standing behind him.

"I have recovered," Cockspur said. He strolled past Lindy and Hikaru and took his place in the wings.

Speechless, Hikaru watched him go.

"Why, that—!" Lindy made a wordless sound of outrage. "I don't believe it! He wanted to go on last, and he . . . he . . . I'll kill him! Hikaru, I'm sorry."

Hikaru sighed. "Look at it this way. The audience will probably kill him for you. As for me—I'm going to find out if the flying people grow tomatoes."

Mr. Cockspur composed himself in the wings. He permitted himself only a moment's glee that Newland Rift did not seem to be having his usual success. Cockspur could not help but admire the audience. They were the enemy, to be sure, but a worthy enemy; and clearly they understood the difference between art and mere escapism.

Rift swept offstage, balancing two pyramids of French poodles across his outstretched arms. Out of sight of the audience, he let the dogs down.

"Oy," he said. The puppies huddled at his feet.

After his introduction, Mr. Cockspur waited a dramatic

few seconds before making his entrance. Onstage, he gazed into the distance above the audience and let the tension build.

And then he began Shakespeare's most famous soliloquy.

"Shall I kill myself, or not? That's what I keep asking. I can't decide if it's better to be miserable, or to end it all. If I sleep, that is to say die, all my exquisitely painful sensitivity will end. That would be wonderful! I'd like to die, I'd like to sleep. But what if I dream? Now there's a real problem. That would keep anyone from saying 'so long' to life. Who wants to get old, who wants to put up with uppity troublemakers, who wants to listen to the ignorant bellyaching of illiterate critics, when he can end it all by stabbing himself with a dagger in his bare bodkin? Who would fardel a bear, and put up with all that grunting and sweating, if he wasn't scared of going straight to hell? What if hell means having to live it all over again, or maybe even something worse, like traveling through the undiscovered universe without insurance? We all have guilty consciences, so even if we do get sick and pale, and even if we cast and pitch and heave, we keep on sailing down the current of life, because eventually we're going to lose anyway."

Backstage, Hikaru covered his eyes with one hand. He had not heard Mr. Cockspur's version of the soliloquy before. "I don't *believe* it," he moaned, embarrassed, despite himself, for Mr. Cockspur.

The whole audience sat in exquisitely painful silence.

Jim applauded politely, hoping his crew would follow his lead.

Suddenly the director leaped to his feet and shrieked, full-voiced and frenzied. Forgetting his dignity, he twirled around and howled.

The fleet personnel followed his example. The amphitheater reverberated with the howls and shrieks and foot-stampings of the director's crew. The applause continued at its peak volume for several minutes. At first even Mr. Cockspur looked stunned; then he took it as his due. He made a stiff slight bow to his new followers.

McCoy said something, but the screaming drowned him out.

"What?" Jim shouted.

"Never underestimate a mint julep!" McCoy shouted back.

Mr. Cockspur left the stage, head high, still coolly in character. He came back onstage, swaggering. The audience made him come back a dozen times before their voices began to give out.

The director fell to one knee before Jim Kirk.

"Will you forgive me, captain?"

"Of course," Jim said. "Er . . . what for?"

"I impugned your civilization. I was most unfair! It's clear to me that I misunderstood your culture profoundly—I cannot quite reconcile the witchcraft, but later you may do me the honor of explaining why you permit it. For now, I could not comprehend an intellectual discussion. My mind is overwhelmed by the sensitivity, the depth of feeling, the exquisite artistry! Captain, do you think—might it be possible—could you arrange an introduction?" Overcome by emotion, the director leaped and howled and screamed, till Mr. Cockspur returned once more and took another bow.

During the curtain calls, every performer got a wild round of applause from *Enterprise* personnel and fleet crew alike. The director led the cheering. It was as if he had seen the light, and now hoped to make up for his indifference of the past two hours.

When the director and his people let the company off, Lindy felt elated but confused. Her ears rang.

I guess I have a lot to learn about offworld audiences, she thought.

A few minutes later, Jim came backstage with the director, his entourage, and the captive Koronin. The director headed straight for Mr. Cockspur. He knelt before the actor—on both knees, Jim noted.

"Sir! I am dumbstruck with awe! Never has a performance affected me so deeply!"

The dumbstruck director went on like this for some minutes. Cockspur made modest noises at first, but finally succumbed to the temptation to point out the subtleties in his performance, the particularly clever and appropriate word choices.

"Tell me if I'm wrong," Lindy said softly to Jim, watching

the interchange between the actor and the director. "They hated the rest of us and they liked Mr. Cockspur?"

"As far as I can tell, that's about the size of it."

"Sir," the director said, "would you condescend to be presented at the court of our empress? She is renowned as a patron of the arts. Her greatest pleasure is rewarding artists who please her."

Lindy tried to keep a straight face.

"I believe I could arrange the time," Mr. Cockspur said.

"Director," Jim said, "I'd like to introduce Amelinda Lukarian, manager and magician of the company."

Lindy managed to control her laughter. She offered the director her hand.

He drew back and made a sweeping gesture between them.

"Don't touch me, witch!"

"What? *Witch?*" Lindy started to laugh again, then became quite sober when she realized how serious he was. "I'm not a witch! I'm an illusionist! I *told* you that at the beginning of my act."

"How clever, to conceal your diabolical powers under a pretense of fraud!"

"I'm an *illusionist!*"

"I don't believe you. No one could do what you did without arcane powers. No one could escape from chains, and a locked trunk high above the ground—"

"It was a trick."

"You lie!"

"Now just a minute—!"

Jim feared the incident would get out of hand. He broke into the conversation before the two of them could exchange any more insults. "Lindy, why don't you show the director how you did one of your illusions? How about the trunk escape?"

"It took me months to perfect that! I'm not giving away the secret. Besides, it isn't allowed."

"An obvious witch's ploy," the director said.

"You can't honestly believe in witches! It takes a real bumpkin—"

Jim winced. "Lindy!—er, director, pardon us for a moment."

Koronin, surrounded by the director's bodyguards, watched the proceedings with glee. A brawl among the commanding officers was even better than a brawl in the audience.

Jim took Lindy aside and spoke to her intently for several minutes. She returned, glowering.

"I'll show you how I do one escape," she said to the director. "But you have to swear you'll never tell anybody."

"If it involves no witchcraft, I will swear. Otherwise, I will denounce you."

Lindy muttered something. "Come with me."

The director turned back to Mr. Cockspur. "Honored sir, please pardon me a moment. When I return, I will write you a visa for our realm, and we may complete arrangements for your visit."

Lindy headed toward her equipment cubicle. The bodyguards and Koronin followed the director.

Lindy stopped. "This isn't a public demonstration. I said I'd show *you*."

"My bodyguards must accompany me," the director said in a perfectly reasonable tone, "and we cannot leave the traitor unguarded." He considered. "If you prefer, I will blindfold her." He twisted her veil and pulled it over her eyes. Koronin tried to draw back, but the bodyguards prevented her.

Lindy blew out her breath in frustration and flung aside the curtain. When Jim tried to come in, she stopped him.

"Uh-uh, Jim, you stay here."

"You can't go in there alone with them—suppose the director loses his temper again? Suppose he decides you really are a witch!"

"That's ridiculous. And you're not coming in. This is four too many people already."

"I can't let you go alone."

This time she glowered at him. "All right, if that's the way you feel about it." She looked around. "Mr. Spock!"

He joined them. "Yes, Lindy?"

"Would you come with me? Jim thinks I need a bodyguard."

"Wait a minute," Jim said. "How come you'll show him, but you won't show me?"

"Because he already knows how to do it."

She disappeared into the equipment room, Spock right behind her, and dropped the curtain in Jim's face.

Outside, Jim steamed. The demonstration seemed to take a good deal longer than the onstage illusion itself. He had just about decided to barge in and be sure nothing had gone wrong when the curtain opened and everyone came out. Koronin raised her bound hands and pulled the blindfold from her eyes.

"Are you convinced?" Jim said to the director.

"She's no witch," the director said. "The trick she showed me is child's play. I would have seen it immediately, but I came expecting entertainment, not trickery. Why, anyone could do it."

Jim saw that Lindy was about to blow her stack, and even Spock raised his eyebrow at the director.

"Now that that's settled," Jim said before anyone else could get a word in, "hadn't you better finish your arrangements with Mr. Cockspur?"

"An excellent suggestion." He looked at Lindy. "Child's play," he said again. He swept away, his entourage swirling in his wake.

"I knew he'd say that!" she said. "Mr. Spock, didn't I tell you they always say that?" She hid her face in her hands. Her hair swung down like a curtain. Her shoulders shook.

"Lindy," Jim said gently, "hey, Lindy, it's all right. He had to save face—"

She fled into the equipment room.

Jim looked at Commander Spock. "Do you think she's all right?"

"I have no idea, captain. I have only limited experience with emotional outbursts."

And then Jim heard shrieks of laughter coming from the equipment room. He started to chuckle. He followed Lindy inside. As Commander Spock watched, a puzzled expression on his face, Jim and Lindy laughed till tears ran down their cheeks.

Spock considered differences and similarities; and, having considered, he went looking for his cousin. He found Stephen alone amidst chaos as the company packed up.

"Stephen," Spock said, using his cousin's own chosen name.

Stephen glanced up from his equipment. "Quite an experience, Spock, wasn't it?" he said. "Survive today's performance at the beginning of your career, and no audience you ever encounter will bother you for a minute."

"It is not my intention to make the stage my life's work," Spock said.

"I didn't mean you, I meant me," Stephen said.

"I was under the impression that you were a seasoned performer. And so, I believe, was Lindy."

"I said I could juggle. I never said I had stage experience," Stephen said easily. "Now I have stage experience."

Stephen tossed Spock a lead-weighted club. Spock plucked it spinning from the air and passed it back. By the time it reached Stephen, the blond Vulcan had grabbed another club and tossed it to Spock. Spock caught it, too. Stephen continued to add items to the pattern: six clubs, a long, thick-bladed knife, an unlit torch. Spock noted, as the handle of the knife snapped solidly into his palm, that the weapon appeared unwieldy, but that it was balanced perfectly.

The clubs and the knife and the torch flew and tumbled between the two Vulcans. The pattern challenged Spock, unaccustomed as he was to juggling with a partner. He met the challenge and increased it by flinging one of the clubs in an arc high above the steady back-and-forth path of the other implements. Stephen caught the club, returned it to the pattern, and spun the torch up into the reverse of the same arc. Spock had no time for calculations. He reached up, trusting that his hand would be where he knew—where he felt—the torch would come down. It snapped firmly against his hand.

Stephen laughed. Spock wondered if anyone else could hear the faint hollowness, the artificial cheer, of his cousin's laughter. He doubted it. Human beings generally accepted as truth whatever they saw on the surface. They could not experience, as Spock had, the resonances of Stephen's quest, the moment of joy that Stephen had felt turning to despair, the moment that he finally had lost forever.

"We make a great team," Stephen said. "Maybe you

*should* consider the stage. Didn't you ever think about running away to join the circus?"

"Never," Spock said. The clubs spun and flew between them; the solid slap of wood against palm created a satisfying rhythm. "Stephen," Spock said again, trying to return to the original purpose of his conversation.

"If you didn't want to be a juggler, you could start a mentalist act."

Spock nearly flinched at the idea of opening his mind to a different random group of beings, not just a single time, but once or twice each night forever. "I think not," he said. "Stephen, I wish to speak to you seriously."

Stephen sighed.

"I have acted harshly toward you in the past," Spock said. "Perhaps I will do so again in the future, for, truly, I do not comprehend the choices you have made for your life. But . . . I am grateful for the risk you took for me. I am in your debt."

Stephen regarded him across the tumbling clubs, his gaze ice-blue and steady. "I didn't do it to put you in my debt," he said.

"Nevertheless, you may someday need more help than your ingenuity can provide. I am not entirely without resources . . ." Spock let his voice trail off as he realized that several members of the company and the crew had begun drifting nearer, attracted by the juggling. Spock had intended this to be a private talk. "Whatever your motives, I am grateful for your actions." He spoke quickly, hoping to end the conversation before it was overheard.

"You know my motives, Spock," Stephen said, pronouncing Spock's name with Vulcan intonation. "I'm a thrill-seeker." As the torch slapped into his hand, he touched the ignition switch. He flung the torch high, and it incandesced into flame.

Spock caught the blazing torch as easily now as before, but as he passed it back, he realized that though he knew how to keep all the juggling implements in the air indefinitely, he had no idea how to stop so many at once, how to end the pattern. He glanced at Stephen. The flare of Stephen's pale eyebrow, the glint of mischief in his blue eyes, hinted that he understood Spock's difficulty and found an instant of very real humor in it. This time, Spock did not begrudge it to him.

Uhura sat in the darkness of her cabin, touching the strings of her old harp in a tuneless sequence. But her fingers kept searching out the flying people's musical patterns. She put the harp aside and sank down into the silence.

A song spun itself through Uhura's mind. She wished she could make the patterns comprehensible, or she wished they would go away entirely. She knew she would never get either wish.

At first she did not reply to the knock on her door. But it sounded again, and then a third time. The harsh noise broke into the quiet Uhura sought.

She activated the lights. How could she explain sitting alone in the dark to any of her shipmates? They would think her ridiculous.

"Uhura?" Janice Rand said.

Uhura had been about to open the door, but now she hesitated. She could face almost anyone else, but she had very little emotional resiliency left right now, certainly not enough to offer Janice the encouragement and support she needed so badly. The citizen of Saweoure under whose "protection" Janice had lived had kept her powerless by telling her over and over and over again that she was stupid and worthless, until finally she began to believe it. Janice discounted her own strength, and so could only call on it in desperation. Eventually, with time, with help, she would learn to trust herself again.

"Uhura, please let me in. I'm worried about you. Are you all right? Are . . . are you mad at me?"

"Come," Uhura said. The door slid open. "Of course I'm not mad at you, Janice."

Janice remained in the corridor, watching her.

"Come in, please," Uhura said. "I was thinking about something, I didn't hear you knocking at first."

Janice stepped gingerly across the threshold. "I didn't see you at Lindy's show."

"I didn't go."

"*Are* you all right?"

"Yes," she said, wishing Janice would stop asking. If she

asked again Uhura would probably tell her the truth. The last thing Janice needed was to have to listen to anyone else's troubles.

Besides, Uhura thought, I can hardly expect her to sympathize with my disappointment. It's trivial compared to what she's survived.

"Why were you looking for me?" Uhura asked gently. Maybe listening to someone else is exactly what *I* need, she thought. It will help me get things in perspective.

"I wanted to tell you," Janice said. "I've been thinking about what you said. I've been thinking about it a lot. And I've decided you're right."

"Right about what?"

"About the commission. About testifying."

"That's wonderful, Janice," Uhura said sincerely. "You should be very proud of yourself for making that decision. It took bravery."

Janice blushed. "I don't think I'm very brave."

"Why did you change your mind?"

"Because of you. No, that's not quite right," Janice said quickly when she saw Uhura's expression. "I don't mean I'm going to testify because you think I should. I mean I'm going to testify because it's the right thing to do. You stuck up for me, even though you could have gotten in trouble. Nobody ever, ever stuck up for me before. Nobody ever stuck up on Saweoure for people like me, either, but now I can. And I'm going to. I want to be as strong as you are. Someday. I'll start by telling Captain Kirk what I told you. Every other place I've ever been, people used their power to make things easier for themselves. Even if it hurt someone else. But Captain Kirk is different. He's like you. He does things because he thinks they're right, even if they might hurt him."

"You're much stronger than you think, Janice," Uhura said.

"It's funny. I'm scared—but I'm happy, too. I feel like I can do anything!" She spread her arms as if to take in the whole universe. "Know what else?" she said in a conspiratorial voice.

"What else?"

"I'm going to let my hair grow. And then I'm going to do

something fancy with it. I was never allowed to, on Saweoure. But now I will."

Despite herself, Uhura smiled.

On the worldship, the audience departed, the *Enterprise* beamed the props and equipment back on board, and cleaning servos and volunteers finished picking up the amphitheater. As the last robot, the last *Enterprise* crew member, the last stack of trash disappeared in the transporter beam, Spock reflected that the only sign left of the show was the sound of applause, still ringing in his ears.

He strolled through the backstage area, keeping an eye out for Lindy's codepicker. Losing the piece of equipment had very much upset her. But Spock found nothing. He climbed the terraced stone platforms of the amphitheater.

At the top, James Kirk joined him.

"Hard to believe anything happened here at all," the captain said.

A few flyers soared high above. Spock felt a moment's regret that he could not join them.

"Commander Spock, I've been thinking about Lindy's codepicker . . . do you think Mr. Scott would . . . er . . . overlook regulations long enough to build her a new one?"

"The instrument is highly illegal, captain," Spock said.

"I know that, commander."

Spock realized Captain Kirk had asked him a question of fact, not posed him an ethical problem. "I believe, captain," he said truthfully, "that under the current circumstances, Mr. Scott would carry out any task you set him."

Scarlet swooped down and landed nearby. She greeted Spock with a translation of his personal name into her own language. Knowing his command of the flyers' language to be pitiable, Spock did not attempt a suitable reply.

"I am glad to see you both one last time," Scarlet said in Standard.

"One last time—? Scarlet, you mustn't leave. Everything's changed," Captain Kirk said. "The *Enterprise* can stay near the worldship. We have so much to learn—"

"No. It is impossible. We've done you no service by coming here. We've incited you to violence, we've damaged you out of ignorance—"

"Violence! You helped initiate peace!"

"It will not last, James. You know it." She blinked. "You see—do you not?—the pattern is already changing."

Captain Kirk flinched as if she had struck him. "It will last for a while . . ." he said.

"If the universe remains as it is, your peace will last a shorter time than it might. The worldship will become a point of contention between your people. Its abilities are too tempting for those who solve their disputes with violence."

"Koronin—"

"Koronin is not unique."

Jim hesitated. "I know," he said in a soft and regretful voice.

"Where is Uhura?" Scarlet said.

"She's . . . back on the *Enterprise*," Jim said, surprised by what seemed to him an abrupt change of subject. Since Uhura herself could not explain why she chose not to see the flyers again, Jim could hardly explain for her. "Your language intrigued her, but the difficulties . . ."

"I caused her great pain," Scarlet said. "I nearly caused both of you to lose your lives. Someday your people may be ready to meet us. Someday worldship people may be wise enough to meet you without causing pain. But . . . that is of the future."

"What do you mean by someday? Will I meet you again? Will Spock?"

"No," Scarlet said. "I will be gone, you will be gone. People live, and people die. Perhaps our children's children's children will greet each other."

"I have no children," Jim said bitterly.

Scarlet let her wings open; she reached out and enfolded Jim. The silky webbing slipped around his shoulders. "You are but young," she said. Her other wing curved over Spock without touching him. "Good-bye, Spock."

"Good-bye."

"You're going to move the worldship," Jim said, not wanting to believe it.

She shook her head, and Jim felt a brief flash of hope that he had misunderstood her.

"I do not control the worldship, James," Scarlet said. "I control the universe."

# Epilogue

THE WORLDSHIP GLOWED, a distant jewel. The *Enterprise* and the director's fleet lay on opposite sides of it and a good distance from it, safely outside its vortex. From the bridge of the *Enterprise*, Jim watched it and regretted its imminent departure. Lindy and Dr. McCoy waited with him, and even Spock paused in his work to gaze at the viewscreen. Uhura was absent, and Jim worried about her.

Scarlet's image shimmered into being on the viewscreen.

"I wanted to say good-bye," she said. "To all of you. You won't be forgotten."

"You won't change your mind?" Jim said.

"No. It is impossible."

"I envy you the sights you'll see, the distances that will pass."

Scarlet blinked and touched her tongue to her sensory mustache. "You, too, will see many wonderful sights and pass great distances. Who knows? Perhaps the next time our people meet, you will seek us out."

"Maybe we will," Jim said.

"Lindy-magician . . . I hope you find a sky for Athene."

"So do I," Lindy said. "Thanks, Scarlet—for everything."

"May you fly with lightning."

The turbo-lift doors swished open. Janice Rand came onto the bridge; to Jim's surprise, Lieutenant Uhura followed. Rand took her place at the environmental systems station, but Uhura hesitated, watching the worldship.

"Uhura, singing one!" Scarlet said.

"I couldn't let you leave without seeing you again," Uhura said. "It wouldn't . . . it wouldn't be right. Scarlet, I'll remember what you sang to me all my life."

"I am glad. I feared—"

"I know. So did I. But a glimpse of something beautiful is better than knowing nothing of it at all." Her voice was steady.

"May the wind buoy you, and sing you to sleep."

Uhura's eyes glistened, but she never cried.

Last, Scarlet gazed at Spock.

From his reaction no one would ever suspect it, but he longed for the flying people to remain. Despite the danger of his communion with Scarlet, her experiences and her knowledge exhilarated him. If mind-melding were always such a challenge, he would seek out the experience as assiduously as Stephen did.

Scarlet sang his name, then spoke to him in Vulcan.

"Spock, you are the fixed point of the stories we will tell. The stories could not move, without you."

"This part of the universe will never again pass the worldship," Spock said. "I know that. Time is too short, the universe is too large, and there are too many other places to see. But I am glad we met, and I am glad you will not forget us. Nor will my people forget you."

"Good-bye, Spock."

Her image faded. The worldship glowed like a swarm of fireflies, like Stephen's spinning torches, like a small hot nova.

The worldship vanished.

After a moment, Jim let out his breath. He had *known* that the worldship could move safely, but he had not *believed* it till now. It had gone, leaving nothing behind but a slowly spinning mass of wall-spheres, cast off and abandoned because they had solidified.

Inside *Dionysus*, Stephen watched through his ship's wide viewports as the worldship vanished. He tried to recapture the brilliance of Scarlet's thoughts and emotions. He tried to recreate the experience of the flyer's world. But it had all faded. A powerful current dragged him farther and farther from a center he had been seeking. For a moment he had found it. He had felt it. He wondered if he would ever find it again. He wondered if Lindy still felt willing to help him try.

On the bridge of the *Enterprise,* Uhura tried to make sense out of a translated cacophony of signals.

"Captain! Some kind of disturbance in the fleet—"

A tiny ship, an escape boat or a courier, sped away from the fleet and headed straight toward the *Enterprise.* It traveled quite a distance before the battle cruisers reacted and opened fire on it.

"Shields up! Hailing frequencies, Uhura! Director, what's the meaning of this?"

The battle cruisers accelerated.

The director appeared on the viewscreen. His brow ridges had contracted and darkened, and he was enraged.

"Koronin!" he cried. "The traitor has escaped!"

"That's no reason to blast *my* ship!" Jim said.

"Forgive me, captain. I must recapture—" The director's image faded before he finished speaking.

The little ship evaded the photon torpedoes, veered toward the path the worldship had taken, dived straight between the dangerous pearls, and blasted one of the wall-spheres with its aft phaser. The explosion set off a chain reaction, an enormous burst of energy and light and luminous dust. With the spectral flash of a ship entering warp-speed, the courier vanished into warp space.

"Wow!" Lindy exclaimed.

The fleet ploughed forward. The roiling dust-cloud occasionally flashed with brilliant light as the remaining intact wall-spheres exploded. At the last moment the ships of the fleet veered aside. They twisted into their transition to warp space, producing a wild clash of interacting spectra, a pattern of darkness and brilliant multicolored light.

The *Enterprise* floated alone in silent space.

Jim heard laughter. He turned, looked up, looked around, and finally found Lindy doubled up on the deck behind his seat.

"Lindy, what are you doing?"

"Is he gone?"

"Who? The director? Yes."

She rose, still chuckling. "I didn't want to laugh in his face."

"What are you laughing *about*?"

369

"Koronin. I can't help it, Jim, I know I ought to be glad she got caught and sorry she escaped—that was an escape worthy of Houdini!—but I feel exactly the opposite. And I know how she got free."

"How?"

"She's the one who stole my codepicker."

"What? How? She was blindfolded!"

Lindy made a sound of amused contempt. "With a piece of cloth wrapped around her eyes? That's no way to blindfold anybody." She put her hands over Jim's eyes. "Now look down the sides of your nose."

"I see what you mean," Jim said. "No pun intended. But if you didn't want her to know how you did your escape, why didn't you warn the director about the blindfold?"

"Because I was already showing him one trick—I didn't want to show him two! Koronin must have palmed the codepicker when I put it down, and used it when they took her back to the flagship . . ." Lindy whistled softly in appreciation. "Pretty good for a novice."

"I suppose . . ." Jim said. "I suppose the director will just catch her again." Like Lindy, he felt a sneaky tendril of admiration for the renegade who had outsmarted the director and all his minions.

"I think her immediate recapture is unlikely," Spock said. "She stole a courier, a craft designed for travel at high warp-speeds. In addition, the wall-spheres and their destruction formed a barrier to the larger ships. They could not follow her directly into warp space. By the time they discover her trail, she will have made her escape."

McCoy looked quizzically at the science officer.

"Mr. Spock," he said, "you sound like you're happy that she got away."

"I have no feelings in the matter at all," Spock said. "I merely stated my analysis of the events."

"I suppose you wouldn't have any feelings about it if she'd taken you back into the Klingon Empire and sold you to the oversight committee as a spy."

"I would have no more feelings of hatred toward her than I do of happiness or gratitude now. I would hope that under the alternate circumstances you propose, I might be as adept at escape as Koronin."

"You would be," Lindy said. "You've got the makings of a great illusionist."

"I'm sure Lindy's right, Mr. Spock," Jim said. "You do a very convincing disappearing act onstage."

"Thank you, captain," Spock said.

"Hey, what about me?" McCoy said in a wounded tone. "I'm in the act, too, remember. Spock only has to vanish. *I* have to appear."

Jim, who had indeed forgotten that McCoy was in the magic box illusion, maintained a discreet silence.

"It's just that Mr. Spock has so much natural presence," Lindy said, "that it's a powerful effect when he vanishes." At McCoy's hurt expression she added quickly, "Not that you aren't terrific in the illusion, too . . ." Her voice trailed off as she realized she was getting herself in deeper.

"I believe that what Ms. Lukarian is trying to tell you," Spock said to McCoy with his usual bluntness, "is that you are a doctor, not a magician."

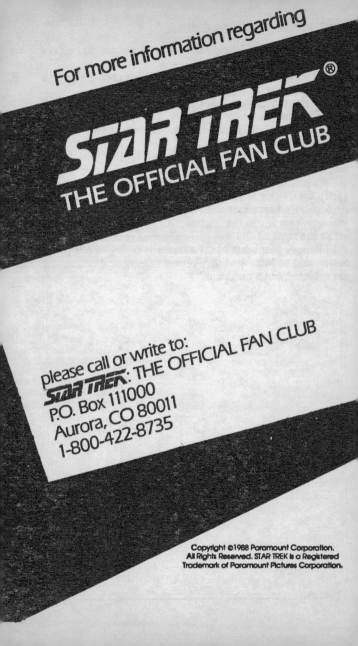

For more information regarding

# STAR TREK ®
## THE OFFICIAL FAN CLUB

please call or write to:
**STAR TREK**: THE OFFICIAL FAN CLUB
P.O. Box 111000
Aurora, CO 80011
1-800-422-8735

# THE
## STAR TREK
### PHENOMENON

# THE

## ☆STAR TREK☆

### PHENOMENON

_____ **STAR TREK— THE MOTION PICTURE**
67795/$3.95

_____ **STAR TREK II— THE WRATH OF KHAN**
67426/$3.95

_____ **STAR TREK III—THE SEARCH FOR SPOCK**
67198/$3.95

_____ **STAR TREK IV— THE VOYAGE HOME**
63266/$3.95

_____ **STAR TREK: THE NEXT GENERATION:
ENCOUNTER AT FARPOIINT**
65241/$3.95

_____ **STAR TREK: THE KLINGON DICTIONARY**
66648/$4.95

_____ **STAR TREK COMPENDIUM REVISED**
62726/$9.95

_____ **MR. SCOTT'S GUIDE TO
THE ENTERPRISE**
63576/$10.95

_____ **THE STAR TREK INTERVIEW BOOK**
61794/$7.95

_____ **STAR TREK:
THE NEXT GENERATION:
GHOST SHIP 66579/$3.95**

_____ **STAR TREK: THE NEXT GENERATION:
THE PEACEKEEPERS**
66929/$3.95

_____ **STAR TREK: THE NEXT GENERATION:
THE CHILDREN OF HAMLIN**
67319/$3.95

**POCKET
B O O K S**

**Simon & Schuster Mail Order Dept. STP
200 Old Tappan Rd., Old Tappan, N.J. 07675**

Please send me the books I have checked above. I am enclosing $_____ (please add 75¢ to cover
postage and handling for each order. N.Y.S. and N.Y.C. residents please add appropriate sales tax). Send
check or money order—no cash or C.O.D.'s please. Allow up to six weeks for delivery. For purchases over
$10.00 you may use VISA: card number, expiration date and customer signature must be included.

Name_____

Address_____

City_____ State/Zip_____

VISA Card No._____ Exp. Date_____

Signature _____ 118-09